ANGELS OF DÉSIRER
2
LIE
WITH
ME
I0770076
D.L. DARBY

Identifiers: Print - 979-8-9869973-5-3

Edited by Virginia Carey

Cover created by Aster with Asteriellydesigns

✻ Formatted with Vellum

Help is Available

If you or anyone you know is in trouble and suffering
from abuse, the National Domestic Violence Hotline
is open 24/7
800-799-7233
https://www.thehotline.org/

CONTENT WARNING

Your mental health matters. This book deals with very heavy themes. For a list of warnings, please visit my site.

Please read responsibly.

For the "Good Girls," the "Good Boys," and the "Good Pets"

Playlist

"No Mercy" – Austin Giorgio

"Man! I Feel Like A Woman!" – Shania Twain

"Another Hit Of You" – Lynnea M

"Foolish" – Meghan Trainor

"Lose Control" – Teddy Swims

"Before You" – Benson Boone

"Kiss" – Prince

"What A Man Gotta Do" – Jonas Brothers

"Six Feet Under" – Sara Phillips

"Let It Go" – PYPR, Jordan Critz

"Forgive" – Unions

"It Must Have Been Love" – Nicola Høie

"Paper Rings" – Taylor Swift

Have you ever had a desire so dark you wouldn't dare speak it out loud? You've buried it so deep in the depths of your soul, but it's always there.

Wanting.

Waiting for the moment you set it free.

Our Temptangels will awaken your deepest hunger.

Here, you can feast until you're satiated.

Here, you can be whoever you want and do whatever you wish—with consent, of course.

Whether a woman or a man, or both if you prefer, your pleasure is their delight. Take a mask, pick your angel, and let your dreams take flight.

Welcome to Désirer

A fated accident. Coy smiles and fabricated names. Your lips bled perjury until the moon disappeared from your skin, and the sun kissed your flesh with its warm glow. You trapped me in your silken strands of white lies, where we created interlaced threads of tragedy. The web we spun was beautiful. And when we released the honeyed bundles of untruth, they revealed pure reality. That I love you. I've loved you since the first time the sweet poison dripped from your lips—a nectar I will savor until the end of my days.

D.L. DARBY

Prologue

LENNI

<u>Age 10</u>

Most girls my age would be happy about hitting puberty early.

For me, it's a nightmare.

"It's okay. It's perfectly natural. You can stop back by before you go home if you need any more sanitary products," Nurse Jackie tells me.

Because, of course, my period would start in the middle of a school day. When I sat down on the toilet and saw the blood, I freaked out. My lower stomach feels like it's being torn to shreds by a velociraptor. I feel like I'm going to die.

Nurse Jackie reassures me I won't.

It seems like just last week, I was a little twig, more than happy to stay in the background of life and not be noticed by anyone. Puberty will change everything, though.

Fourth grade is hard enough as it is.

Girls are mean to you, boys pick on you, and the teachers just don't care enough to do anything about it.

My mother trades her body for drugs—the thought of what will happen to me now that I'm a *woman* haunts me.

"My little valentine. You're so beautiful. One day, you'll use those looks to help your momma out, won't you?"

When I was younger, she'd tell me how pretty I was all the time. The men who would come over to see her would always comment on my beauty. Back then, it made me feel good.

Wanted.

Seen.

But I was young and naive and didn't understand what was happening. I didn't know what the men were there for. All I knew was that Momma took them into her room, and when they left, it was with a smile on their face, and she was in a good mood.

Now, I know exactly what is happening. And I'm terrified it will start happening to me, too.

"Momma?"

"In the kitchen, Valentina!"

She sounds like she's in a good mood. I know her stash is running low, so maybe one of her men has already come by. Kicking off my shoes, the floor is cold beneath my holey socks as I dump my backpack by the front door and head into the small kitchen of our trailer.

Momma is at the stove, stirring something that smells expired in a pan. Her hair is up in rollers, and her face is painted. She's in her robe. It's pink and see-through and trimmed with fluffy fake fur.

"Are you going out tonight?" I ask, climbing onto the lone stool in front of a table tray that serves as our dining table.

"Yes! But first, we must celebrate!" she exclaims as she transfers whatever is in the pan to a plate.

Momma whirls around with a flourish. Her black eyes are rimmed with red, and they crinkle at the corners when she smiles a mouth full of half-rotted teeth at me. "Nurse Jackie called. My little girl isn't so little anymore, is she?"

My heart drops into my stomach like it's a cannonball.

"Don't worry, my little valentine. I'll stop at the QuickMart and get you some tampons." She sets the plate in front of me while taking a long drag from the Black and Mild between her fingers. "Cramps are a bitch, aren't they? I'll get you some Midol for those, too."

I've heard girls at school talk about tampons. I've heard them say how it hurts to use them the first few times. Tears line my eyes as I stare at the slop on the cracked plate. They look like scrambled eggs, but there's a weird brown color to them, and they smell even worse up close.

"Don't cry, Valentina. I know this time of the month is emotional, but I can't deal with your tears right now. Momma's got enough going on. I can't take your shit, too."

"Can you get me pads instead, please? I don't want to use tampons," I whisper to the egg slop.

"You'll use the tampons. Gonna need to get that goldmine between your legs ready." She takes another drag and blows the sweet-smelling smoke into my horrified face.

"For some reason, God blessed you with good looks. Since I feed and clothe you, you'll pay me back by using your assets to get me what I want. Momma's getting tired. It's time for you to start pulling your weight."

I know now that there is no escaping it.

My worst nightmare is about to come true.

<u>Age 14</u>

Slap…slap…slap

A shiver rolls through my body as the cold winter air licks my naked skin.

Momma hasn't paid the electric bill, and our trailer is as cold inside as it is outside.

The man in front of me grunts, and I squeeze my eyes shut as his warm, sticky substance coats my chest. It smells like dirty socks and chlorine.

My knees are sore from kneeling on the ground. These days, they have permanent bruises from holding this position on the floor for so long so many times a week.

"I'm getting tired of this shit, Lucille. When are you gonna let me fuck her?" the man complains to Momma as he tucks himself away in his pants.

As soon as I hear his zipper, I open my eyes and wait for him to turn away before I grab my robe and wrap it around me, using the collar to wipe my chest. Momma tried to get me a robe just like hers, but I picked out an oversized purple one from the Salvation Army instead.

It hides me better until I'm allowed to get up off the floor and put my clothes back on.

"As soon as she turns fifteen. Can't have her all used up before she's in her prime. Trust me, she'll be worth the wait," Momma tells him while she jabs her arm with a needle.

Her eyes turn glassy as the man turns and drags his eyes down my body. "Soon, you'll be mine, little girl. Don't worry, I'll make it good for you." He sneers before leaving our trailer without another word to Momma.

She opens her arms and beckons me to her. And like the obedient daughter I am, I crawl into them in search of some sort of comfort.

"You're such a good girl, taking care of your momma," she says before kissing the top of my head. Her words slur as her body slumps over. Slipping off the couch, I go to the bathroom to clean off.

The water is ice cold because Momma also forgot to pay the gas bill.

I've learned to disassociate when Momma's men stop by.

They don't seem to care when I lay there, silent and unmoving—like a corpse.

At least she makes them wear condoms.

I don't know what angel is looking out for me, but it's a damn miracle I haven't gotten pregnant or had a STI.

Now that the men are allowed to have sex with me, Momma makes enough money to keep the utilities on. But I'm still going to school in rags, and lunch is the only time I get a proper meal. If anyone notices, they don't care and don't say anything. High school is even worse than elementary.

The system is fucked.

We live in a bad neighborhood where the cops look the other way, and the teachers don't question if you show up with bruises shaped like fingerprints on your skin. Most of the women are dealing with abusive husbands at home, and the men are alcoholics or leer at the female students as if they are imagining what it'd be like to keep them for detention and force them on their knees to keep a strike off their record.

No one cares what happens to kids like me at home.

Which is why I plan on running away.

"Look at me, Valentine," the man above me says as he plows into me.

My eyes drift from my ratty old teddy bear on the chair next to my bed to his face. "It's Valentina."

Instantly, he grins and snaps his hips harder to the point where it hurts. He notices it when I wince. "Mouthy little thing, aren't you? That's okay. I like feisty."

His thrusts grow harder, and for some reason, I don't look away from him. Instead, I reach around his back to scratch my nails down his skin hard enough to leave welts—wanting to inflict some sort of pain back on him.

"Oh yeah, baby. You wanna hurt Daddy? Come on, make me bleed, little one," he moans.

He likes it.

The pain.

I rake my nails over his back again, and he drops his head to suck at my neck, drawing the tender flesh into his mouth and biting down on it before dragging his tongue along the bite mark.

"Fuck, you're better than I imagined. Why don't you say we make our own deal? Hmm? I'll still give your momma her drugs, but I'll give you cold, hard cash if you make it this good for me every time. What do you say?"

My nails tighten on his arms, and he mistakes my shock for a silent agreement. He fucks me quicker before coming with a string of curses flying from his mouth.

When he draws back, he fixes me with a smile and runs his eyes down my naked body. "Good girl."

"I didn't say yes." I don't know what possesses

me, but as he stares at my bare pussy, I widen my legs to give him a better view.

He lets out a short laugh as he pulls the condom off and discards it in the trash next to my bed. "You didn't say no, either. I'll be in touch."

More than an hour passes before I move from my bed to shower off his stench and sweat.

An hour where I convince myself that *this* is my way out.

I've been primed all my life to use my body to get what my mother wants. Now, I'm going to use it to get what *I* want. She wants drugs. I want money.

Enough money to get out of this low-life Pennsylvania town and set me up in New York. I've always wanted to see the bright lights of the City That Never Sleeps.

All I need to do is start pretending like I actually *enjoy* what these men do to me.

After all, men are stupid. They'll believe anything if you're a good enough liar.

<u>Age 17</u>

Blood. There's so much blood.

A dull throbbing pain blooms across my face as my vision grows hazy.

Someone is screaming. A little girl crying out for a mother who never cared enough to protect her.

Is that me?

Hazy red and blue lights fill my room, coming from outside my window.

Men dressed in navy.

Why do they care *now*?

Everything grows cold. Suddenly, there's pressure on my face while a man shouts, "Call ahead and have them prep an OR! Hang in there, sweetheart, you're going to be okay."

"Where are you taking her?" Someone is struggling, and a metal jingle fills the room, joining my mother's cries.

My head drifts to the side, meeting the lifeless, dead eyes of the man she killed. There's a kitchen knife sticking out of his back. His mouth is still open in shock, dripping blood from blue lips.

"He tried to kill my baby!" she screams.

Someone tried to kill me?

I struggle to remember the last few minutes.

The man liked pain. Liked *inflicting* pain. But it was different than what I've experienced before.

There was an empty bottle of beer. He broke it.

He said he wanted to carve me up while he used me.

I told him no and shouted for Momma.

"She's losing a lot of blood," a female says. She sounds far away, and then there's a shooting pain in my abdomen, causing stars to burst behind my eyelids as I squeeze them tight.

I swear to whatever God is listening that if I make it out of this alive, I'll never allow someone else to have control over my body ever again.

Then…there's nothing but silence and darkness.

Tripp

"You do realize you're my only son, right, Tripp? I don't want to hear any crap when I name someone else as my successor." My pops berates me over the phone as I leave the St. Regis and head up 5th toward Central Park.

It's getting dark out. The early winter chill seeps straight through my jacket and into my bones like it's trying to freeze me where I stand. Even though I just had drinks with a potential client, and the alcohol still warms my insides, an unpleasant shiver courses through my body, so I pick up my pace to get my blood pumping. The office is only a few blocks away, and I'll get back faster on foot than catching a cab in traffic.

"Pops, you know I love you, but real estate development just isn't my calling. Besides, with Jackson running Tailor Industries now, I'm on my way to becoming CFO. I love what I do. Plus, I get to bullshit with my friends all day. I hate the guys that work for you, no offense."

It's always the same argument.

He wants me to take over Kennedy Contracting, but I'd rather keep my job at my best friend's conglomerate. His uncle hired me straight out of Harvard, and I've worked my ass off for him ever since.

Sure, it's sort of nepotism since Scott Tailor was like family before his unfortunate death just half a year ago. But it doesn't mean I don't work just as hard as anyone else at Tailor Industries.

"You're spoiled, Tripp." There's no bite to his tone, as if he's amused by my decision to keep working hard instead of having a company wholly handed to me.

Which, by the way, is the opposite of spoiled.

"Says the man who wants to give me a multi-million dollar company. Listen, I just finished up a meeting at the King Cole Bar. I'm headed back to work, but I'll see you this weekend?"

The streets are crowded, everyone doing their last-minute Christmas shopping before the holiday next week. Glittering decorations adorn the buildings as I walk past, their garland swaying in the winter breeze. There's no one standing in line at a random food cart, so I grab a coffee, even though it's nearly five. Thursday nights are always late at the office, with most of the bigwigs taking off early on Fridays to jet-set wherever they spend their weekends.

Are there better coffee options at the office? Yes. But nothing beats the strong, bitter, black sludge from the food carts on the street. It's like injecting caffeine straight into your bloodstream.

"Yeah, your mother is looking forward to seeing you. She keeps complaining that you're ignoring her calls." There's a shuffle of papers in the background, and I hear his secretary tell him someone is there to see him.

"Maybe if she stopped asking about what happened with Emily, I wouldn't feel the need to ignore her. It's almost been a year. She needs to let it go. God knows I have."

Or am at least still trying.

"Well, you can't ignore her at family dinner, so figure out whatever it is she needs to hear to make her stop asking 'cause I'm just as tired of hearing about it as you are. I have a client walking in. I'll talk to you later. Love you."

"Love you too, Pops."

As soon as I end the call, a message comes through, pulling my attention back to my phone instead of the sidewalk.

JACKSON

> I finally got Carmela to agree to give you a membership. You're free to go to Désirer whenever you want.

My best friend and boss, Jackson, also took part ownership of a highly exclusive sex club when his uncle passed. The first day Jackson went to the club, he recognized his now fiancée and pretended to be someone else while pursuing her because she hated his guts in real life. I have no grand illusions of finding *my* happily ever after there, but having somewhere to let loose where no one knows who you are?

Yes, please.

In order to do anything at the club, you have to wear a mask to conceal your identity, and I've been chomping at the bit to go as soon as I found out about it.

It's about time! I didn't think a background check would take six freaking months. I don't think she likes me very much.

It's just her way. She's got a frosty exterior. Even Ginny said it took over a year before Carmela warmed up to her.

"Watch it!" a man shouts in my ear as he passes, shoulder-checking me lightly.

My arms fly up so I don't spill my coffee, my eyes rising to the people I'm walking past. The streets are always crowded. No one really pays attention to where they're going because we're all on autopilot and know precisely how to get to our destination. The only people who pay attention to the city sidewalks are tourists.

I look over my shoulder to glare at the man, who's now stuck on the corner with a no-walk signal.

Dick.

As I turn back around, I crash straight into something, my hot coffee sloshing over the sides of the white paper cup down the front of it. I realize it's a woman when she lets loose a string of curses and pulls her dress away from her body.

"Oh, god. I am so sorry!" I toss the empty cup in a nearby trash can and, without thinking, attempt to help her pull the dress off her skin.

She slaps at my hands and glares up at me. "This is a *vintage* Chanel!"

She has long, glossy, chestnut hair and sultry eyes that look like a combination of milk chocolate and honey. Her mauve-painted lips are open in astonishment, and for a fleeting moment I wonder what they taste like. The cream dress she's wearing hugs her hourglass figure beneath an open navy peacoat as she desperately tries to squeeze out the dark brown liquid staining the front.

"Again, I am *so* sorry. Let me buy you another dress. There's a Chanel just up the street–"

"They aren't going to have anything like this! This dress is a timeless classic. Everything these days is way over the top. Besides, do you *know* how much these things cost?" She looks back up at me incredulously before appraising my dark gray Brunello Cucinelli suit.

Her eyes narrow as she takes me in before landing on my face with a raised brow. "Well, with a suit like that, maybe you *do* know."

A laugh escapes my throat, short and sharp.

"Trust me, it's not a big deal. Bergdorf's is around the corner if you'd like something more *classic*."

Her hands find her hips as she asks dubiously, "You're *really* going to buy me a new dress?"

"It only seems fair since I pretty much ruined that one." I begin to walk in the direction I'd been going before we ran into each other, and even though she'd been headed the opposite way, she falls into step beside me.

"I'm Ken, by the way," I tell her. Clearly, she has no idea who I am, and that's exactly why I like staying out of the gossip rags.

People treat you differently when they know you have money.

For all she knows, this could be the only nice suit I own, and I could be charging her dress on a credit card that's nearly at its limit.

"Bianca," she replies after a moment.

"Well, Bianca, it's nice to meet you. I'm sorry it's under these circumstances. I promise I don't go around the city throwing coffee at every pretty woman on the street."

I glance over just in time to see her roll her eyes as a smile pulls at the corner of her full lips. "Well, aren't I lucky?"

We walk for a few minutes in silence before she asks, "So, what do you do that affords you the ability to buy thousand-dollar dresses for random women you meet on the sidewalk?"

Leaning over, I whisper, "If I tell you, I'll have to

tie you up so you can't let the other women know I'm an easy target for a new dress."

Her eyes light up as her smile turns feline. "Be careful making threats like that, Ken. I might just be into that sort of thing."

Pausing, I watch as she flips her hair over her shoulder and keeps walking, her hips swinging in a rhythmic way that seems to catch the eye of every male, and a few females, she passes.

Bianca walks with a confidence you rarely see in a woman these days.

It's attractive as fuck.

It's been months since I've been with anyone. Since my ex left me almost a year ago, I've been careful about what females I spend time with. Where most men in my position cover their asses with NDAs and payouts, the trouble isn't worth it to me.

Women are cold, cruel creatures. Ruthless and conniving and most of them only want the autonomy my last name and bank account can provide.

Which is another reason I'm so interested in the club Jackson owns now.

A man has needs. What more perfect place to get them taken care of than a discreet sex club?

Bianca doesn't even wait for me to catch up before she's inside the store and looking through the racks, eyes as big as a kid in a candy store. The associate takes one look at her coffee-stained dress with a disapproving sneer. When her gaze swings to me, the sneer drops, and her face lights up in recognition.

Shaking my head as the woman approaches, I slip her a crisp hundred and motion back to Bianca, whispering, "I'd like it if you didn't use my name while we're here, please. Whatever the lady wants to try on, take care of her."

The woman instantly goes into business mode with a curt nod. "Of course, sir. Will you be waiting in the bar while she shops?"

Looking back at Bianca, who already has three dress hangers dangling from her fingers, I decide I'd rather watch this beautiful stranger pick out clothes. "No, I'll stay with her. Have someone get me a bourbon, though, would you please? And bring her a glass of champagne."

"Of course, right away, sir." She nods again and leaves, whispering to another associate before nodding toward me and then Bianca, who's adding two more dresses to her collection.

When I reach her side, I notice some of them look more like they're for a cocktail party than everyday wear. She doesn't even pause when she sees me eyeing them. "What? I'm here. I might as well try them on."

"Knock yourself out."

When the associate returns to take her dresses, I make my way to a sitting area and pull my phone out.

I'm not gonna make it back to the office tonight. I'll talk to you tomorrow about the meeting.

A blonde with a tight, no-nonsense bun shows up with my drink and brings a glass of bubbly pink rosé to Bianca. I watch the stunning brunette sip gingerly while fingering multiple pieces of clothing. She browses wistfully, a deep sigh leaving her body more than once as she shops.

My phone vibrates, and I tear my eyes away from her to read the message that came through.

JACKSON

> You don't have to check in with me about when you'll be at the office. You're a big boy.

"Do you mind if I leave my coat and purse with you while I try these on?" Bianca's voice rings out.

She's already removing her jacket and has placed her purse next to me, so I flash her a smile and nod. "Only if I get a fashion show."

That feline smirk finds its way across her face again as her hands contort behind her back, reaching for her zipper. "You wanna come help me if I get stuck, too?" she teases.

"Ooh. Don't make promises you don't intend to keep," I flirt back, waggling my eyebrows as she laughs and disappears into the dressing room.

I've never been so forward with a woman before —let alone a woman I just met. I was raised to be respectful. If I treated women the way Jackson did before he met Ginny, his soon-to-be wife, my parents would have murdered me.

Bianca is playful, though. I'm extremely attracted

to our easy banter and the way she shakes her hips when she walks away from me. She seems like the type of woman who would give my mother a heart attack if I brought her home.

I don't know why the thought of that appeals to me—I love my mother.

It only takes a few minutes before Bianca comes out in a calf-length red dress with a ruffled, off-the-shoulder neckline. Her eyes are humorously wide as she scrunches her nose at me through the full-length mirror.

"Definitely looked better on the hanger," she says before swiftly retreating to the dressing room.

Personally, I think she looks amazing, but I have a feeling that will be the case for everything she tries on. She's the kind of woman who could be draped in a paper bag, and men would still drool at the sight of her.

One after one, she comes out in various dresses from Valentino, Dolce & Gabbana, and multiple other designers. Another man might be annoyed at how many options she picked, but I enjoy relaxing against the plush couch as she shows off what she found.

Definitely beats going back to the office.

A particular black Balmain with nude detailing makes her face light up. She looks positively edible in it. I sip my drink and imagine peeling it off her body. "You look incredible. I think that's the one."

She lets out a dreamy sigh. "It really is beautiful."

That's all she says before she goes to try the last dress on. Pushing to my feet, I look around for the associate so I can have her ring up the dress. As I'm scanning the store, however, my eyes catch the icy blue orbs of the last person in the world I want to see.

Emily.

My ex-fiancée.

"Tripp, what are you doing here?" she asks with a breathy laugh as she walks over to me.

As if we're old friends who haven't seen each other in years.

As if she didn't rip my heart out of my chest and crush it in her perfectly manicured hand.

Vaguely, I register that Bianca might have heard her call me by my real name. But as Emily stands there staring at me, waiting for an answer to her question, I find I can't focus enough to string together a coherent sentence.

We haven't seen each other since I found out she'd lied about seeing someone else while we were still engaged. What do you say to someone who did that to you?

Other than *fuck you, you lying bitch.*

Seeming to realize I'm uncomfortable, Emily looks around before asking, "How are you? How is everything? I've been meaning to call you–"

"Why? There's nothing we need to say to each other." Her face falls at my words, and she looks genuinely sorry, which only pisses me off more.

Don't you dare fucking pity me.

"Darling? Who do we have here?" Bianca asks behind me, clearing the rage that's brewing a storm in my brain. Her voice makes me think of soft rain, candlelight, and velvety rose petals. Entirely transformed from the playful lilt it was just a few minutes ago to something dark and possessive.

Emily's eyes dart over my shoulder, widening in surprise as she drags her gaze up and down Bianca's body. Turning, my mouth goes dry as I do the same. She's wearing a red satin dress resembling a cross between lingerie and formal wear. It molds to her body as she floats our way, eyes sparkling with mischief as she looks at Emily.

She looks like sin personified.

When she reaches us, she wraps her arm around my waist, pushing up on her toes to kiss my cheek. "Aren't you going to introduce me, babe?"

This beautiful stranger reads the room faster than a gunshot and, for whatever reason, is helping me save face even though she has no idea what the history is here.

Now that she's so close I breathe in her scent. She smells like smoky vanilla and rich coffee, and something tells me it isn't from the drink I spilled on her earlier. My arm winds around her waist, tucking her into my side where she fits perfectly. "Bianca, this is Emily. Emily, Bianca."

"Hmm, you've never mentioned an Emily before. Do you two know each other from work?" Bianca asks brightly before resting her head on my shoulder.

I could kiss this woman for the way Emily bristles as she stares at her. My ex clears her throat, lifting a hand to tuck her hair behind her ear.

My blood runs cold at the sight of the large diamond on her ring finger. "You're engaged?"

Emily's eyes slowly drift to mine as a saccharine smile crosses her face. "Yes, Neil proposed just a few weeks ago."

The news is like a sucker punch to my gut. She lied to me about seeing him while we were together, so to hear that they're now engaged enrages me.

Bianca's fingers spread over my side where her hand rests, gently squeezing before she unwraps herself from me and reaches for Emily's hand. "Wow, it's so big."

Emily looks smug as she wiggles her fingers in Bianca's grip. As she's about to respond, Bianca lets go of her hand and steps back into my side. "See, baby. I told you that size was way too gaudy. I really think something more delicate is the way to go. My hands are so petite. You'd need such large fingers to support the weight of that."

A snort leaves me, and I hurry to disguise it behind a cough. Bianca reaches up to smooth my tie before looking back at Emily with fake horror. "Oh, my goodness, I'm so sorry. I hope that wasn't offensive. He's been trying to buy me something that tells the whole world he's locked me down, but I keep telling him I just can't pull the big rocks off."

Her charade is Oscar-worthy. My chest swells with gratitude that this woman I've only met an hour ago has picked up on the tension and is running with her crazy story. There might be repercussions later, but at the moment, I don't give a damn about the consequences of her sugar-spun white lies.

"You two are engaged?" Emily asks in a stupor, looking between us both like we just said her grandma died.

"Yes! We haven't officially announced it yet, but we have been for a while now. I knew from the moment I saw him that he was the guy I'd marry. I mean, how could you *not* want to snatch him up?"

"Babe, *you're* the catch in this relationship. I'm just the mere mortal who was struck by Cupid's arrow." I look down at her, pretending I'm utterly besotted instead of laughing on the inside at how well we're improvising.

Though, at this point, I have to admit I really am as smitten as a kitten.

"Darling, don't sell yourself short. I love everything about you. Even your mere mortalness." She pushes on her toes again, but instead of kissing my cheek, she cups my neck and presses her full, rosy lips against mine.

They taste like sugared cream and strawberries. My cock twitches in my pants, and suddenly I'm wondering how much it would cost to keep the associates quiet about me taking her into the dressing room and having my wicked way with her.

She pulls back, smiling sweetly up at me and looking every bit a woman entirely in love. Without breaking our gaze, she says, "It was so nice to meet you, Emily. Now, if you'll excuse me, I should change. We have that dinner to get to, my love."

"Nice to meet you, too," Emily says as she attempts to clear her throat.

As Bianca disappears behind the curtain, I turn to see Emily backing away from me. "It was…good to see you. Congratulations…by the way," she stammers.

"Yeah, you too," I tell her confidently before spinning around and sitting to wait.

When Bianca emerges from the small room, she peeks around the corner to make sure Emily is gone. "Coast clear?"

"Yeah, she left the store. Thank you, by the way. Actress of the year goes to you." I clap slowly, applauding her performance as she comes around the corner entirely.

She's wearing the cheapest dress out of the ones she tried on—the red number she was the least thrilled about. "What happened to the Balmain?"

"It's almost four thousand dollars. I can't let you spend that kind of money on a *dress*," she stresses quietly, looking around to make sure no one hears her.

Her change in demeanor from sultry to shy is endearing. Most women would have chosen the most expensive one.

"I'm replacing a vintage Chanel. I know what that cost. It's okay. Go put the dress you want back on." Gently, I push her back toward the dressing room. Aware there are more eyes on us after the encounter with Emily.

Bianca's cheeks flush a beautiful shade of rose as

she looks over her shoulder. "I got the Chanel at a thrift store for a few hundred dollars. I'd never be able to afford it otherwise."

She says the last part softly, almost as if she's embarrassed. She also looks like she's surprised herself by admitting it to me.

Leaning closer, my words are a whisper against her bare shoulder, drawing her chocolate-honeyed eyes to my lips. "You have no idea how much I've wanted to stick it to that woman for the last year. What you did back there? That was amazing. And I appreciate it. So go back in that room, put on the dress you really want, and don't argue with me anymore. Got it?"

A shudder goes through her body. It's slight, but I'm close enough to notice. Her breath catches, eyes darting to mine before returning to my lips. "Yes, sir."

Her words hit me straight in the groin. I work hard to suppress the groan that wants to leave my throat as I watch her walk away, hips swaying as she glances back over her shoulder before drawing the curtain closed once more.

By the time she comes out in the dress she really wants, I've paid for it and am standing there with her purse in my hands and her jacket curled over my arm. "Ready for that dinner?"

The corner of her lips tilt up as she reaches for her peacoat. "I suppose I do need to show off my new dress."

I help her into her coat, discreetly inhaling her

scent as she pulls her hair from the collar and flings it behind her, hitting me in the face with her luxurious waves. I nearly grab ahold of the strands and twist them around my fingers, but then I remember we're in public and that it wouldn't do me any good to be photographed in such a precarious position in the middle of a public store.

However, I do boldly grab her around the waist and pull her back to my chest to speak into her ear. "And I suppose I need to show off my new *fiancée*."

Lenni

When I woke up this morning, I thought it would be just another dreary Thursday.

Wake up, drink coffee, maybe pick up a shift at Decadence—I decided against going to the restaurant I sometimes work at when I saw the weather—and go to the club early to maybe squeeze in a few Confessional clients before my scheduled ones in the Desires wing.

Never in a million years did I think I would be enjoying a six-course dinner tasting at Jean-Georges with a random curly-haired Adonis who spilled coffee on me on the sidewalk and bought me a Balmain dress worth nearly four thousand dollars as an apology.

The man who sits on the other side of the small table looks like sex on a nearly six-foot stick. His curls are swept back in a way that manages to look like an actual style you'd see on the cover of GQ.

And his short, groomed beard is the same espresso color as his hair. Not to mention his chiseled jaw would make an excellent saddle for me to ride.

He clears his throat with a smile, and I realize I'm staring.

"So, what's the story with the blonde?" Shaking my head, I take a sip of my glass of Sancerre. The acidic wine makes me purse my lips, and while I wait for him to answer, I take a bite of caviar.

Truthfully, I would have been okay if Ken had bought me a hot dog from a street vendor. At this point, I'm going to be late for my shifts, but my boss loves me, so when I messaged her that I'd be coming in much later than usual, she simply responded with *no problem.*

Who am I to turn down a dinner that cost over three hundred dollars a person?

"Do you want the short, polite version? Or the long-winded version that will make you run for the hills because I brought up my ex on a date?"

Raising an eyebrow at him, the corner of my mouth pulls up in a smirk. "Is this a date?"

"Well, we are engaged now, aren't we?" he teases, his open-mouth smile showcasing two perfectly lined rows of teeth so white he looks like he belongs in a Colgate commercial.

"I suppose, as your *fiancée*, I should know the long-winded version."

When we were under the bright lights of Bergdorf's, his hazel eyes looked more green, like moss in the forest after it rains. Now, with the candle-light reflecting on them, they look like two pools of jade with glittering gold flecks.

He's beautiful.

"She's my ex-fiancée," he responds dryly. "We were together for four years. We met through our parents when I was in college, and I knew I wanted to marry her within the first hour I knew her."

He gets a nostalgic look as he stares at a random spot on the table. "We had a long engagement. Almost two years. She kept putting things off, and I was busy working, so I didn't really think anything of it. Our parents were being pushy, and we both liked rebelling against them, so I thought we were just partners in crime, sticking it to our families. Little did I know, she was seeing someone else."

What a fucking idiot. Why the hell would anyone cheat on this man?

"She broke things off on New Year's. Lied to me about seeing the other guy for weeks before she finally caved and told me the truth."

"What a fucking bitch."

His eyes snap to mine, and I feel my cheeks warm as I realize I just said that out loud. "Sorry."

"No, you're absolutely right. She is."

We fall silent while the server sets down the next course and takes our empty dishes away, but as soon as the man turns his back, I lean into the table. "If you don't mind me asking, what was her reason for breaking it off?"

Ken freezes like he's been caught with his hand in the proverbial cookie jar. I wait patiently for him to figure out how to answer my question, doing my best to shove my sashimi into my mouth in one bite without looking like a starved dog who hasn't eaten in a week.

"Let's just say we didn't see eye to eye on certain things," he finally answers cryptically.

He doesn't want to tell me the real reason his ex broke things off. Rich men guard their secrets the same way they guard their money.

"So, Bianca, I feel like we've been talking about me for too long. Tell me, what do you do?" he changes the subject.

That's okay, because I have my secrets, too. No way in hell am I going to tell him I work at a sex-positive club where I get paid to make people's dreams come to life.

Some might call it prostitution.

I call it art.

And I'm a regular fucking Van Gogh.

Not just *anyone* can wear lingerie, stilettos, and a pair of angel wings and get men—and women—to spend thousands in a one-hour block.

It's why my boss and I get along so well.

There are three tiers at Désirer—the club where I work: gold Angels do the Confessional, black Angels are the Dreamers, and platinum Angels are the Desires.

Confessional Angels only talk to the clients, maybe put on a show if they want. It all depends on the mood, and the workers get to call all the shots. We're never forced to do anything we don't want to, or work in a wing we're uncomfortable with.

Dreamers can touch the clients, and they can touch you, but you're not allowed to have sex.

And Desires is where anything goes, as long as everything is consensual.

"I'm in the entertainment industry. Just a low-level assistant. Nothing special."

There. It's only a *half*-lie.

"I thought your answer was going to be an aspiring actress. The performance you gave was quite award-worthy."

He orders us both a glass of fifty-dollar Chardonnay with a French name I barely catch as they bring out a crab dish. I've never had a tasting dinner before.

It's not enough food and seems like it's going to be too much wine.

Ken must be used to mousey eaters. Meanwhile, I'm ready to tackle the passing server that's bringing someone a steak.

"You seemed really uncomfortable when I came out of the dressing room. I couldn't see your face, but your body language said enough. I just did the first thing that I could think of."

Gratitude shines through his gaze. "What would you have done if she'd known that I wasn't really engaged?"

With a slight shrug, I sample the new wine and stare down at my plate as I savor the tingle of peach on the tip of my tongue. "Probably would have high-tailed it outta there in embarrassment. Saved you a couple grand."

It could be my imagination, but I swear his foot keeps nudging mine under the table. Boldly, I cross my legs, dragging the tip of my thrifted Jimmy Choo stiletto up his leg. They're worn and tattered, with the fabric ripping on the toe and along the side. The only way they look halfway decent is because I use a black Sharpie on them. I hope that the marker, paired with the slush outside, doesn't leave ink stains on his pants.

With a devilish grin, his hand disappears beneath the table and wraps around my ankle. Just the simple touch of his fingers on my flesh ignites a burst of tingles in my spine that shoot straight to my core. Warmth floods my body as he settles my foot in his lap and begins to stroke my skin with his thumb.

"Well, I can confidently say I'm glad that isn't the case." His hand moves higher, and my eyes dart around the room to see if anyone is watching. All it would take is for someone to glance over and realize where exactly my foot is.

My nipples harden as the toe of my shoe nudges his erection—or rather, his erection springs to life, nudging the toe of my shoe.

"Something tells me you're more than worth it, Bianca." He lifts my leg and gently lowers it back under the table as our next course is placed in front of us.

His voice is rich and sensual, and I almost open

my mouth to tell him my real name, if only to hear him say it. He could be talking about potato chips, and I'd still find it sexy.

By the time I finish my fourth glass of wine, and a pumpkin dessert that literally tastes like heaven, my mind is made up, and I text my boss that I won't be making it to work.

Ken helps me into my peacoat, and before I can pull my hair out of the collar, he's doing it for me. Whether he's trying to be discreet or not, I have no idea, but it doesn't escape me that he breathes in deep as he does it, like he's trying to burn my scent into his memory.

Every nerve ending in my body is on fire. The cool, slow lick of heat that starts at the tips of your toes and curls around the most intimate places. I don't remember a time when I've ever been so turned on by a man simply *existing*.

When we reach the sidewalk, I go to hail a cab with the intention of asking if he wants to take me home. But before I can so much as lift my hand, his is around my waist, guiding me to a black town car that's idling on the curb.

"What's this?" I ask as he opens the back door.

"My driver can take you wherever you need to go. A dress like that doesn't belong in a cab," he says with a smooth smile and a tone that suggests he'd rather we spend the night together. His body is tight with a tension so thick I can feel it radiating off him.

He doesn't want the night to end, even if he's giving me his car service.

If there is one thing I'm good at, it's reading men. And this one wants me flat on my back.

Surprisingly, I want the same thing—even though I usually don't sleep with men outside the club.

"What's your address?" he asks softly, almost regretfully, like he's trying to decide whether or not he should just invite me home. The hand that's still on my waist feels heavy, like he doesn't want to let me go.

He searches my eyes, looking for a sign, meaning he's respectful enough not to force himself on me, letting me make the decision.

Giving me the green light.

Closing the distance between us, I move into him, pressing my chest against his and lifting my hand to the back of his neck. Heat fills his eyes, and he immediately pulls me closer as I lean up to kiss him.

Ken meets my lips with a passion I haven't experienced...*ever*. Our kiss is intense right from the start. Open-mouthed, tongues tasting each other as he pulls me impossibly closer, as if he's trying to absorb my body into his. It's the kind of kiss you do in the privacy of a bedroom—or a bar if you're really, *really*, shit-faced.

Not the sidewalk where random people are subjected to your mouth porn.

When we finally pull back to breathe, I ask suggestively, "What's *your* address?"

Shaking his head, he lets out a breathy chuckle. "Where have you been all my life?"

Living on the wrong side of the tracks.

"Why don't you show me what it's like to be Mrs. Ken for the rest of the night?" I don't give him the chance to answer as I slip into the back of his town car and tell the driver, "We're going to his place."

Ken is a gentleman in the car on the way to his house. Never mind that I want to straddle him like a high schooler in the back of a limo on the way to prom. He stays on his side of the backseat and asks me idle questions.

Where do I work? *I forget the name of the building. I just started at a new place.*

Am I from New York? *No.*

Where was I headed when we ran into each other? *A friend's.*

The budding anticipation is almost too much to bear. He angles toward me, elbow resting on the head of the seat, hand tangled in his curls. His smile is suggestive, eyes sinfully playful.

It's foreplay for him. Watching me grow hotter with each block we pass. Maybe it's all the wine, but the pressure between my legs is begging to be released, and I'm worried I might come the second he touches me.

When the car pulls up to his building, my hunch that Ken does more than just *finance*—like he told me at dinner—becomes a reality. It may be tucked away in a quiet cul-de-sac near the river, but this is still the Upper East Side.

Ken reaches for my hand to help me out of the car, not letting it go as we walk into the red brick building. The floors shine like they've just been freshly polished, and the concierge nods politely as she types away at something on her computer.

I'm half expecting him to hit the giant PH for the penthouse level when we get into the elevator, but the call button lights up a few floors down.

"I should warn you, her shit is still splashed all over the place. I haven't cared enough to redecorate." He sounds reproachful, like he fears his admission will change my mind.

It's been a year and he hasn't gotten rid of her stuff? Either he's majorly still hung up on her, or she tried fighting him for the place.

"Are you not over her?" I'm blunt. Straightforward and to the point. His answer may or may not affect my decision to stay, because the last thing I want is for him to fuck me while he's thinking of her.

Even if it's a one-night stand.

I'm a leading lady—not an extra.

My eyes remain forward, but I can see him turn to look at me through my peripheral. "I'm over it," he says softly. "I'm just too nice of a guy to throw her things out. And even though it's almost been a year, she hasn't bothered to send for them."

The inside of his place is ten times the size of my little apartment in Chelsea. It's all classic creamy walls with oatmeal accents and rich walnut floors.

Dusky blue accents kiss the surfaces everywhere, from decorative pillows and throw rugs to paintings and random vases filled with vibrant green plants.

There's even a custom blue Steinway with the lid lowered in the living room.

"Home sweet home," Ken says as he helps me out of my jacket before taking my purse.

I slip out of my shoes, shrinking three inches to my normal five-eight. "As much as I don't want to admit this, it's a beautiful home."

He laughs, and after hanging our coats in the closet in the foyer, takes my hand again and leads me through the open-concept layout to a chef's kitchen. "Would you like a drink? Another glass of wine?"

As he grabs glasses and surveys his built-in wine cooler, I feel the overwhelming need to scrub Emily's existence from his home. Eyeing the Steinway, an idea pops into my head, and I reach behind my shoulder to grab the zipper of my dress.

Slowly, I pull it down, the unmistakable sound causing Ken to freeze mid-pour even though I never answered whether I wanted a drink or not. By the time he turns around, his restraint looks like it's about to break.

I'm not glass. You won't break me.

We lock eyes as I step out of my dress, revealing the lacy black set of lingerie I'm wearing. Gold-flecked green slowly inches down my body as I take slow steps backward to the piano. "Do you play?"

His Adam's apple bobs hard as he swallows. He responds with a slow shake of his head as he begins to stalk toward me. He reminds me of a panther. Sleek and graceful. Ready to pounce.

The outline of his cock against his pants is impressive as he shrugs out of his suit jacket and asks, "Do you?"

With a shake of my head, I step onto the bench and sit on top of the piano, the keys letting out a shrill cry beneath my feet. I rest my weight on my hands behind me, and my pussy clenches as Ken looks between my spread legs, nudging the bench out of the way with his leg as he unbuttons and removes his shirt. My sex on a stick has a six-pack and a V-line that cuts so deep I want to crawl inside it and stay there forever.

"*Pretty Woman* is my favorite movie. I've always wanted to reenact the piano scene," I whisper into the space between us as he closes the distance.

His hands find my thighs as he steps between them and jerks me forward so that my butt is nearly hanging off the edge. "Never seen it. But I think I have a pretty good idea of how that scene goes."

The words are husky and thick with need as he lowers his mouth to mine, kissing me with as much passion as he did earlier on the sidewalk.

Ken kisses with precision and tastes like perfection. Most men drown you in saliva or lick your whole face when they kiss the way he does. But as he devours me, I can't help but think about how perfectly his tongue fits against mine.

Sliding my hands up his arms to tangle them in his hair, I gently pull him back and offer my neck.

Obediently, his lips rain kisses down my flesh, stopping now and then to suck my skin into his mouth, leaving light love bites.

His lips are soft as they trail between my breasts. He pulls the cup of my bra down to release my nipple. We lock eyes as he licks the hardened bud before drawing it between his perfect teeth and biting down.

Warmth floods my flimsy thong, smearing along my inner thighs as my legs spread wider to accommodate him as he continues his journey. Reaching for the sides of my underwear, he drags them down my legs slowly, pausing as he reveals the jagged scar that mars my tan skin just below my abdomen.

"What happened?" he asks gently. As if he knows the question might bring up bad memories.

"I was attacked when I was a kid. I know it's ugly." I laugh lightly, trying not to let the memory resurface and ruin the moment.

Ken's eyes snap from my scar to my face, blatant reverence shining through. "You're perfect," he whispers as he lowers his head and kisses my flesh directly over the ugly, bumpy tissue.

"So fucking perfect," he reiterates before his tongue swipes up my slit.

I'm almost embarrassed at how wet I am. The distinct sound of him lapping up my essence, swallowing it down while I moan and writhe on top of the piano that undoubtedly belongs to his ex, fills the room.

The tip of his tongue flicks against my swollen clit

as he leans into me, lifting my legs over his shoulders. He cages my hips, reaching up to palm my naked breast and pull the other out of my bra as well.

"Ride my face," he commands, pulling a moan from my throat at his authoritative tone.

I usually like to be in control. I've always liked to be in control during sex since I was a teenager. But here, in this room, on top of this piano, with *him*…he could tie me up and fuck me all night however he wanted, and I'd be happy to let him do it.

My nails scrape against his scalp as he continues worshiping me with his mouth. The piano keys sing their piercing notes as he leans against them while I undulate my hips against his face, creating the sweetest music. His tongue drags against my silken flesh as he swallows wave after wave of release that spills from between my thighs as I come with a cry.

When he gently pulls my legs from his shoulders, he leans forward and draws me close before capturing my lips. He tastes like the biggest mistake I'm about to make, because I already don't want to let him go.

"Do you have a condom?" I ask between kisses.

"I'm clean." He wraps my legs around his waist and drags his lips down my neck as he walks us down the hall to what I assume is his bedroom.

I nip his earlobe. "So am I, or I certainly wouldn't have let you go down on me. But no glove, no love, sweetheart."

I've been incredibly lucky not to have caught anything when I was younger. Momma always made the men wear condoms, and whatever higher power that exists always looked out for me.

We get tested weekly at the club: the workers and the clients. Safety is a top priority.

I've never fucked a man bareback.

Ken chuckles against my collarbone and tightens his fingers around my thighs as he lowers me to his bed. "Yes, I have condoms. Plural. I plan on fucking you until the sun comes up."

He walks backward as he undoes his pants, then turns into his en suite to—I assume—grab the condoms. Ridding myself of my bra that's half hanging on, I fling it to the floor and lay back, stretching out over the feathery soft duvet. The entire bed feels like a cloud, and I close my eyes while I wait for him, imagining what it would be like to sleep in this level of comfort every night.

"You're not already tired, are you?" he asks as he returns. When I open my eyes, he's naked, cock pointing proudly in my direction and sheathed in a translucent condom.

Licking my lips while I stare at his length, I shake my head. "Definitely not."

It, like the rest of him, is perfection. He looks about eight inches long and thick enough to make me feel full without hurting.

Most men assume that women in my profession are loose and have large labia from being *pounded out too many times*. It always pisses me off to hear men— and women—talk shit about a female that way. Lady bits come in all shapes and sizes. It doesn't mean we're loose because we like sex.

Ken kneels on the bed and braces his weight on his fists, crawling until he's caged me against the fluffy blanket. "Good." He nudges my nose with his. "Because I plan on staying up very, *very* late."

My legs wrap around his waist as he positions himself at my entrance and thrusts in all the way to his base. The earlier orgasm he gave me makes it easy, and my eyes roll back in my head as I feel my walls grip every inch of him.

"Oh my god." I run my hands up his arms, leaving light red marks with my nails.

Biting his lip, he lets out a shuddered breath and says, "Fuck, you feel incredible."

As he pulls his hips back slowly, he reaches beneath mine to lift them before thrusting back in at a deeper angle. My back arches as he adjusts his weight on his knees, still deep inside me, and drags me into his lap like I weigh nothing. My body bends as my hands fall to grip the bed beneath me.

"I could watch my cock disappear into this beautiful pussy all day long. Look at how well you stretch around me."

"Fuck, keep talking like that," I tell him as his warm hands skim up my body to my breasts, flicking my nipples with his thumbs.

"Yeah? Come here, baby. Watch how good your pussy swallows my cock." Again, he lifts me, balancing me on his hips as he widens his legs to support our position.

Coiling a hand in his hair, I lean back as he continues to thrust up into me, looking down at where we're joined. "Such a good fucking girl, aren't you?"

Why the fuck did that woman leave this man?

I could come just from hearing him talk like this. He's in total control of my body, and I'm willingly letting it happen. Sex has been a job for so long that I forgot how much I enjoyed letting a man completely ravish me.

"Yes, I'm your good girl," I whisper, reaching up to grab his other shoulder as I ride him. Rolling my hips, I can feel him deeper, stroking that sweet spot inside.

"Yeah? Does my girl want to come again?" His thrusts pick up, and with the way I'm riding him back, he's barely pulling out, hitting that spot repeatedly.

His hand wraps around the back of my neck, forcing me to look down at him as I nod, pushing our sweaty foreheads together before he kisses me. The arm that's braced around my lower back tenses as his tongue licks the length of mine. My walls start to flutter, that delicious shiver starting in my spine and creeping down into my toes as my orgasm crests.

He swallows my cry as I come so hard I bite down on his lower lip. But instead of pulling back, he lets out a loud, satisfied groan and grips me tighter as he snaps his hips a few more times before he comes, too.

We continue to kiss. My fingers tightening in his

hair as I lick his lower lip. It's already beginning to swell, and I'm surprised I didn't break the skin.

"I could stay buried in you until I get hard again, but we need another condom," he murmurs against my lips.

Pathetically, I whimper as he pulls out of me and lowers me back to the bed.

"Don't worry." He kisses the tip of my nose. "After a glass of wine, I plan to make you come on my tongue again before round two."

Ken gets off the bed, removing the condom while he watches me stretch out on my side and prop my head up on my hand. "How are you still single? It's like I won the sex lottery. How did I get so lucky tonight?"

He chuckles and leans down to press a simple kiss to my lips. "You've been a very good girl."

Heading out to the kitchen, still naked, he pauses at the threshold and throws a wink over his shoulder. "And good girls get rewarded."

I awaken to the heavy smell of sex and Ken's minty citrus scent—my body deliciously sore in all the right places.

True to his word, Ken rewarded me over and over and over again throughout the night and into the early hours of the morning. Between rounds, we sipped wine naked and even took a shower together, where he fucked me against the marble-tiled wall.

It was both the best and worst night of my life.

This is exactly why I don't sleep with men outside of my job. It's too easy to get attached, and what man wants to date someone who has sex for money?

But what woman would walk away from this?

The clock on the nightstand reads seven in the morning. Tangerine rays filter through the large windows, casting a glow over Ken's serene face. He's lying on his back, the sheet barely covering his lower body, head turned in my direction as he sleeps.

I'm on my stomach, arms wrapped around the most comfortable pillow I've ever laid my head on. Thankfully, we didn't wrap around each other in our sleep. It makes it much easier to sneak out this way.

Ken doesn't budge as I slip out of the bed, grab my bra, and tiptoe to the living room for the rest of my clothes. Once I'm dressed, I think about leaving him a note, thanking him for a wonderful evening.

But it won't matter. So I don't.

As much as I'd love to see him again, the truth about what I do for a living would eventually come out, dooming the relationship. And that's *if* he even feels the same way as I do about our connection.

I spend entirely too much time watching him sleep from the doorway before I finally go, leaving the only reminder of our night together on his wallet in the foyer.

My phone shows a missed call from my best

friend, Ginny, and a text message from a number I know all too well but never respond to.

> I don't want to be here anymore.
> Please let me leave.

Yet another reason why I do what I do.

A relationship would ruin everything.

Hastily wiping a lone tear as it falls from my eye, I slip out of Ken's building, and into the bustling morning traffic of the city.

Tripp

Consciousness filters through me before I open my eyes. The giddiest grin takes over my face as memories from last night resurface, and I reach out for my bona fide sex goddess.

Only to turn into a frown when my hand meets the empty spot where she fell asleep next to me just a few hours ago.

Opening my eyes, I lift my head to look around my bedroom. "Bianca?"

Silence.

My heart skips a beat as I swing my legs off the side of my bed and grab the pair of boxer briefs I threw on after our shower last night. Heading out to the living room, I call out her name again.

Her clothes are gone, and the glasses we used for wine and left on the kitchen island are drying on the dish rack next to the sink. I search every surface I can think of for a note or anything she might have left behind that would give me a clue as to how to reach her.

But there's nothing. She's gone.

The bitter sting of disappointment laces through my veins as I head back to my room to get ready for work. It's already eight thirty, and I'm supposed to be at the office by eight. I don't bother showering again, even though we had sex two more times after the one we took last night, before finally falling asleep around three.

If the only reminder of our night together is her scent on my skin and linens, I'll savor it all day and never rewash the sheets.

It was the best night's sleep I've had in almost a year.

I replay our night in my mind as I dress in a navy Prada suit and run my hand through my curls, attempting to tame them. It's time for a haircut, but Bianca told me no less than three times last night how much she loved my hair, twisting it between her fingers while I went down on her.

In my opinion, the night was mind-blowing.

I can't think of one reason *why* she would have left without saying something.

I had every intention of sleeping in and waking her up with another round before we exchanged numbers and went our separate ways—only to meet up again tonight and tomorrow and *fuck*...

She's the most intoxicating woman I've ever laid eyes on.

I promised myself I'd never let another woman ensnare me as quickly as Emily had.

But Bianca is *nothing* like Emily.

Stepping into the foyer, I freeze when I notice something on my wallet. For a split second, I wonder if Bianca took anything from it. She was, after all, a complete stranger that I invited into my home.

Did she steal anything?

As I get closer, I notice it's a piece of paper, a corner torn from a larger sheet, which would explain why the takeout menu for my favorite Chinese place on the fridge is missing a chunk out of it.

There's no name. No phone number.

All that's on it is a kiss mark in red lipstick.

Other than that, my wallet is undisturbed.

As I push open the door to Jackson's office, he looks up from his computer. "What happened to you last night? I know you said you weren't coming back to the office—not that I care—but now you're showing up late? You're never late."

He doesn't stop typing as I fall into the chair on the other side of his desk. "I met the most incredible woman last night. Like, seriously, fucking incredible. I spilled coffee on her and offered to replace her dress. We ran into Emily, and she basically gave her a big fuck you right to her face. Then I took her to Jean-Georges and was planning on being the gentleman you know I am and sending her home in my car, but this woman kisses me and tells me to take her home to my place. So, I do, and we have this amazing night. She's *so* sexy. I mean, I ate more pussy last night than I have in my entire life and would have again this morning if it weren't for the fact that she left before I woke up, didn't say goodbye, and didn't leave her number. Just a kiss mark in lipstick on a scrap of paper on my wallet."

"Breathe, Tripp. And maybe you aren't that good at it if she left and didn't leave her number." Jackson laughs without looking away from his screen.

"Fuck you, she complimented my skills multiple times, thank you very much."

Jackson stops typing and sits back in his chair, eyeing me curiously. "I don't think I've heard you talk about a woman since Emily."

"When I tell you this woman is my dream girl, I mean that in every sense. I came six times last night. Six! I didn't even know that was possible, and she didn't even suck my dick."

He lifts an eyebrow and smirks. "Only six? Ginny and I fuck that many times in an hour."

"Yes, Jackson. We all know how good you are at sex. Want a gold star?" I deadpan.

"She knows where you live. Maybe she'll show up again. Did you get her name? Pull the security footage from your building and have her face scanned. Your mom is good at that background shit. You have a plethora of options at your fingertips."

"Uh, yeah, I'm not going to ask my *mother* to do

that. Also, did I mention that the giant fuck you to Emily was making fun of her engagement ring while also telling her that *we* are engaged?" Bianca's scent saturates my senses as I scrub at my face, and I inhale deeply like a man starved.

"Funny, I don't remember you giving me a diamond."

"Funny, I don't remember you being this much of a jackass. You've been spending way too much time with Tyler. In fact, I'm beginning to get jealous that you're gonna ask him to replace me as your best man."

That wipes the smile off my best friend's face.

Tyler is his aunt's husband. He's also younger than us, putting him twenty years younger than her. And he annoys the shit out of Jackson.

"Dick." He pauses. "So, Emily is engaged, huh? How are you feeling about that?"

"To be honest, I haven't really thought of it much." My brows draw together as I realize that while the initial news stung, Bianca pushed it out of my mind just as fast as Emily had announced it.

I let out a short laugh at this discovery. This girl really was amazing. "I gotta find her, Jackson."

"You need to get to work." He goes back to typing on his computer but follows up with, "Ask your building for the security footage, and I'll get someone on it."

While my name carries a lot of weight, Jackson's carries more. And the guys in our technical department like him better than they like me, probably because he's the one signing their paychecks.

"You're the best, man. Does this mean I'm still *your* best man? Or am I gonna have to fight Tyler?"

He chucks a paperclip at me. "Get out and get to work, slacker."

Lenni

"You *never* hook up with guys outside of the club," Ginny exclaims as we slide into the corner of a crimson velvet bench at Cafe Bilboquet with our coffee and quiche.

"I don't know how to explain it, Gin. There was just this instant magnetic attraction. From the time we ran into each other throughout the entire night, we just *vibed*. And the sex…god, don't even get me started on the sex." With a throaty groan, I let my head fall back, shutting my eyes and remembering all the ways Ken made me come last night and into the early hours of this morning.

"So, why'd you leave then? He sounds like Mr. Perfect, if you ask me."

"I had to," I tell her quietly, picking up my fork to take a bite of my food. "If I'd stayed, and by some miracle he wanted to continue seeing me, I would have had to keep lying about my name. And my job."

"You say *my job* like you're ashamed of it. Once upon a time, you told me there was no shame in making money doing something you loved." She fixes me with a concerned look while she sips her iced Americano like a psychopath.

Seriously, who orders iced coffee when we have to walk four blocks back to her job in the windy thirty-eight-degree weather?

Her fiancé, Jackson, is filthy rich.

Like multi-billion dollar rich.

He likes to keep Ginny wrapped in the finest silks and draped in the most expensive jewels. He even gave up his driver for her to use whenever she wants to.

But my best friend still has trouble acclimating to the wealth she's about to marry into. She still likes to go thrift store shopping with me and walks everywhere, even in the freezing cold. She still lets me pick up the tab, taking turns like we always did before Jackson Tailor came along and gave her a Black Card and lined her wallet with hundred-dollar bills.

While I'm super happy the money hasn't changed who she is as a person, it's times like today I wish she'd at least take advantage of that personal driver.

"I'm *good* at sex."

A cheeky grin turns up her lips as she raises an eyebrow.

"Okay, I'm *great* at sex. Because it's my *job*. I don't even remember the last time I had sex just to enjoy it!" I say a little too loudly for the small space we're in.

The older ladies at the next table over turn to look at me, and I shake my head at them. "What? Don't tell me sex with your husband is enjoyable. It's a job! Am I right, ladies?"

After a pause, one of them shrugs her shoulder and nods. "You're not wrong."

They return to their lunch while Ginny tries holding in her laughter. Lowering my head, I whisper, "Seriously, though. Désirer is about making client's fantasies come true, not ours. Last night, I didn't have to worry about asking how he liked it or what he wanted to do to me. It was just natural. Our sexual chemistry was off the charts."

"You know where he lives. Just show up and say, 'Hey, I know I bailed this morning, but I regret that decision, and I want to jump your bones again,'" she whispers back.

"No! Talk about being a stalker! Besides, everything about him was dreamy. What if he ends up being Prince Charming, and then I have to come clean that I fuck people for money. Instant turn-off. No one wants to date a prostitute."

"Valentina! What is wrong with you? I've never heard you refer to it that way. Sex-positive, remember? That's what sets Désirer apart from all the other clubs. It's cleaner, it's safer, and you don't have to do anything you don't want to. What if he ends up being your Edward Lewis?" she argues.

Pretty Woman may be my favorite movie, but I realized long ago that I would never be Vivian Ward. I'm more like Kit. With a never-ending list of problems. Only difference is, I don't tell my friends about them.

Ginny is a women's counselor, and I still haven't fully admitted my life story to her. Only my boss and other friend, Carmela, knows the extent of what I went through as a child.

Shrugging, I sip my double macchiato and lean against the plush booth. "Changing the subject. How is wedding planning?"

Beaming, she pulls her phone out of her purse and shuffles closer to me. "Oh my god, you're going to die. I found your dress. I want everything to be simple. White roses and eucalyptus everywhere, no color…except you."

"What do you mean, except me?"

She holds her phone up to show me a picture of the most jaw-dropping, stunningly gorgeous dress I've ever seen for a maid of honor. It's a strapless satin mermaid silhouette with a sweetheart neckline and light ruching through the bodice.

In crimson red.

"Holy shit, that is beautiful! You want me to wear *that*?" A tear stings my eye at my best friend's consideration.

Most brides don't want their bridesmaids or maid of honor shining on their big day.

Mine *wants* me to stand out like a sore thumb in the best way possible.

"Ginny, thank you." My chest floods with warmth as she reaches over and pulls me in for a hug.

"Duh! Of course, I want my girl to look nothing

short of amazing. Besides, it's Valentine's Day weekend. Red kinda works for the holiday. Are you sure you're okay with us picking your birthday weekend for the wedding?"

"You know I hate my birthday. Seriously, who names their daughter Valentina when she's born on Valentine's Day? However, this birthday, you'll be giving me the most perfect gift of all."

"The most beautiful dress ever?"

"No! Your happiness, silly! I really am so happy that you found your happily ever after, Gin. You deserve it."

After the year she's had, she really does. Ginny used to live with her foster brother, Chris, and he turned out to be an abusive psycho who was obsessed with her. He came to the restaurant we both worked at to pick her up one day, and the next thing I knew, she was in the hospital, and Jackson's uncle, Scott, was dead because Chris pulled a gun on them and ended up firing it during a scuffle with Jackson.

Ginny deserves nothing but the best that life has to give her, and she's finally found that.

"So do you. So, I still say just show up at Mr. Perfect's house tonight. If you really don't want to though, you'll finally meet Tripp at the engagement party next weekend. He's a fun time," she says suggestively.

"How is it that you guys have been together for, like, technically, eight months, and your best friends haven't met? I swear it's bizarre that we don't all just hang out."

My phone lights up with a text message.

Valentina, please. I need you.

With a deep sigh, I pull my phone off the table and bury it in my purse.

Ginny laughs nervously. "Well, you know how Jackson is. I mean, the three of us haven't hung out either. He's been busy with taking over Tailor Industries, and during our free time, we just–"

"I know. I know. Have an ungodly amount of sex on every surface you can possibly think of. Ugh, how *do* you put up with it?" I jest before shoving the rest of my quiche in my mouth.

She shrugs and jokes. "I know, it's *such* a burden."

We both laugh as we get up and put on our matching navy peacoats, getting ready for our trek back to Chillard, where she's working until Jackson finds space for the new women's center she's opening up.

It makes me wish I'd done some type of schooling so that perhaps I could also help women in need one day. Be useful for a change.

But my demons seek to destroy everything I've worked so hard for.

Including a chance at a better life.

Tripp

I'm late for dinner at my parents' house on Sunday.

By the time I roll up, my mother is standing on the doorstep with a disapproving look, arms crossed and ready to scold me the second I step out of my car. "I can't believe you bought that death trap."

Chuckling, I look over my shoulder at the blacked-out Jaguar convertible I bought a few months ago. "Drives like a dream. I don't know why you hate it so much."

She continues to look annoyed as I kiss her cheek and head inside. "You couldn't have at least gone with an SUV? Something that won't get obliterated and kill you in an accident?"

"Why do you have to put that out into the universe, Mom? Something smells good. Did you make my favorite?" My childhood home smells like Christmas—cinnamon and pine, with the gentle sweetness of cranberry—and mother's famous pot roast.

Every inch of the colonial-style home is decked out in garland and obnoxious Christmas decorations. As always, there's a different tree in every room—including the bedrooms—even though no one lives here except my parents.

"Of course I did. Your father is already in the dining room. Sounds like you have a lot to share with us, Son." Her tone is leading, causing me to frown down at her as she steps in front of me and heads into the kitchen.

"Nothing that I can think of…"

Pops is poring over paperwork from his place at the head of the table, the bald spot that started appearing a few years ago gleaming from the light of the overhead chandelier. "You're late."

"Sorry, traffic was terrible. I don't know why people wait until the last minute for Christmas shopping. Getting out of the city was a nightmare." I kiss the top of his shiny, bare head and thank my lucky stars that my hair comes from my mom's side of the family.

"Uh-huh, and your mother has been a nightmare complaining about you being late. You better be on time for Christmas dinner on Thursday." He stacks his papers together and tosses his pen on them, throwing me a wink.

"About that…"

She enters, holding a serving tray filled with aromatic meat, golden potatoes, and honey-roasted carrots. "I don't like the sound of that. Don't tell me you're not coming for Christmas."

"I'm sorry. I'm going to stay in the city and work. We're about to close a huge deal. And Jackson is preoccupied with the engagement party next weekend, so I said I'd step up and take more responsibility."

It's only half a lie. Jackson had nothing to do with the planning of his engagement party. He told Ginny to do whatever she wanted because he wanted her to be happy. So, as far as I know, she and her best friend planned the entire thing.

We are about to close a deal, though. And I'd rather work and keep myself busy than be reminded of the second worst night of my life when everything blew up between Emily and me.

"Yes, speaking of engagements. We ran into Emily's parents yesterday," Mom states, dropping the Christmas conversation as she serves Pops.

Rolling my eyes, I reach for a slice of freshly baked bread and slather it in butter. "Yep. I ran into her, too. I know she's engaged."

Both of them stare at me as if I'm not finished talking.

Taking a bite out of my bread, I shrug. "What? I'm fine."

"Anything you need to tell us, Son?" Pops asks, waving his fork around impatiently.

"Oh, for heaven's sake. Emily told them that *you're* engaged, Tripp! Said she ran into you at Bergdorf's with your *fiancée*. We told them she must be mistaken because we weren't even aware you were seeing anyone!" Mom cries as she sets the serving dish down a little too forcefully. A carrot bounces off the side and lands on the lacquer finish of the Italian imported dining table.

Fuck.

Why the fuck *didn't I think of that?*

Of course, Emily went and told her parents. Because why the fuck *wouldn't* she want to continue destroying my life.

God fucking dammit.

Biding my time by taking a long drink of water, I internally freak out over how to respond. I have no clue who Bianca is or how to get ahold of her. It's Christmas week. Even if I get the security footage from my building, no one will be able to track her down that quickly.

Mom looks like she's about to have an aneurysm due to my silence. "Tripp, did you get someone pregnant? Is this why you didn't tell us? Is this the reason for the mid-life crisis car and not wanting to take over your father's company?"

Tears fill her eyes as she dramatically slumps into her chair. Pops reaches over and rubs her back while she drops her head to her hands and sobs. "Tripp, what's going on? Are you in trouble?"

"No! And by the way, Mom, I'd hardly call thirty-one mid-life. Geez, you guys, I didn't knock anyone up." My parents and I have a good relationship. There's no reason why I can't just come clean and explain what happened.

But I recognize this would be a great reason to move forward with trying to find Bianca.

I weigh my options quickly while my parents look at me expectantly. Telling the truth will just make me look like a jealous asshat. Not telling the truth will be hard to pull off if I can't find the woman who started this little white lie.

Mom looks like she's about to say something when I blurt out, "It's true."

Pops looks ashamed as Mom breaks down with a fresh batch of tears, "Oh, Son–"

"What? No! No one is pregnant! I'm engaged."

Mom sniffs. "Engaged? To *who*? We didn't even know you were seeing anyone. How could you be engaged if we've never even met her?"

"Well, Mom, when you know, you know. We haven't been dating that long, but I popped the question last weekend. You'll love her. You'll meet her at Jackson's engagement party." Picking up my fork, I begin eating, ignoring the confused looks they share and inwardly panicking as my lie continues to spread like wildfire.

"We're not going to be able to make the engagement party. I had a prior business meeting set up in D.C. I've already spoken to Jackson and given him our congratulations. Makes me feel like a jackass, especially now that Scott's gone and Sadie isn't coming up either," Pops says. Whether he's trying to help diffuse Mom's melodrama is unclear.

"Don't feel bad. Jackson isn't the sentimental type. The only reason Sadie won't be there is because she and Tyler already planned to be in Chicago for the holidays. Ginny tried pushing everything out so everyone could make events, but we have some big things coming up for work, so it's what worked best for Jackson's schedule. Not exactly the best time to be getting married, but he refused to push that back, too. Pretty sure he's already on a mission to plant his seed."

Pops laughs while Mom huffs and flings her napkin out to settle it in her lap—her tears magically dry. "Tripp Weylan Kennedy, you don't need to speak like that at the dinner table!"

"So, why don't you ask this girl of yours if we can do breakfast next Tuesday? I'm sure it would make your mother very happy," Pops suggests, looking at me with wide eyes before dropping his gaze back to his roast before Mom sees.

Next Tuesday?

That only gives me a week and two days to find her.

"Are you spending Christmas with *her* family? Is that why you're not coming?" Mom asks in a tone that I know all too well. She's already anti-Bianca, and she's only known about her for less than five minutes.

"No, Mom. I'm working. I promise," I tell her, around a mouthful of carrots.

"Margo, give him a break. Just because they got engaged right away doesn't mean they need to get married right away, right, Son?"

"Exactly what I was thinking, Pops." I point at

him with a forkful of potatoes. "Now, can we please talk about something else?"

Mom launches into some gossip she heard about Emily's fiancé. Glad the heat is no longer on me, I tune her out but contribute to the conversation once she stops talking about anything Emily-related.

As soon as I get home, I ask the concierge to gather the security footage from Thursday night. Hopefully, there's a good enough shot of Bianca's face for whoever Jackson has in mind to scan and find her.

I'm willing to drop a pretty penny if someone can figure out how to get ahold of her by the end of the week.

Christmas Eve

Tailor Industries is dark tonight, the only light illuminating my floor is from my office. Everyone else went home hours ago, but I stayed to finish up contracts that need to be sent out Friday morning.

Though, work is the last thing on my mind.

Staring out my floor-to-ceiling windows at the blanket of snow that covers the city, I sip my coffee and think about how much shit I'm going to be in if Teddy from technical doesn't find Bianca soon.

She's all I've been able to think about. Consuming every waking thought that isn't reserved for work.

The way she so boldly got on top of the piano.

Every breathy moan she made when she came on my tongue.

How she cursed and whimpered when she came on my cock.

When I find her, I'm going to enjoy tying her up so she can't leave me like that again.

She helped me create the mess I'm in. She's going to help me figure out how to get out of it.

If that means we have to play pretend for a little while, then so be it. We fooled Emily. We can fool my parents.

Whether or not she's agreeable is yet to be determined, but there was *something* between us that night. She can't deny the passion we shared.

And if she's hesitant, I'll *pay* her if I have to.

Bianca said *Pretty Woman* is her favorite movie. I've watched it no less than three times in the past week.

Minus the prostitute part, she's about to become the Vivian Ward to my Edward Lewis.

$$\mathscr{L}enni$$

CHRISTMAS EVE

Pretty Woman plays on my small flatscreen while I heat up dinner—leftover chicken parmesan from my favorite Italian place down the street.

Outside, the streets are filled with fluffy snow and glittering Christmas decorations. The only festive thing inside my tiny, one-bedroom rental is a small tabletop tree with blinking lights and a glowing star at the top.

It's the first year since I moved to New York that I'm spending Christmas truly alone.

For the millionth time this week, I think about Ken as I pull my pasta out of the microwave.

When I arrived at work Friday night, something about working the Desires wing had put a bad taste in my mouth. When Ken and I slept together, I'd enjoyed myself. I'd forgotten what it was like to be on the receiving end of pleasure you didn't have to fake.

Granted, I don't always fake it at work. But I haven't had it in me to have sex with anyone outside of a few specific clients who don't ever actually penetrate me.

I *want* to see Ken again.

The number of times I've almost just shown up at his door is more than I can count on my hands and feet.

Speaking of my hands and feet, as I sit on my little red loveseat Ginny and I found at a flea market, I realize I need to get my paws and claws done before her engagement party on Saturday.

Chewing my chicken, I watch as Edward snaps the necklace box on Vivian's fingers, sighing wistfully at how happy they look. "If life were a movie…"

My phone lights up on my coffee table, and I observe it warily as I swallow my bite and decide whether to pick it up or not.

After two more bites, I check it.

Merry Christmas, my little valentine.

Any other time, I wouldn't answer. Opening up a line of communication isn't good. Momma always thinks she's finally worn me down, and I'll finally go to her rescue.

She doesn't realize that she's where she's at for her safety.

And for mine.

But it *is* Christmas. And I do always eventually cave. So I reply.

My fingers tap the screen slowly, hovering over the send button before finally pressing down and immediately tossing my phone on the cushion next to me.

"I think I have a future in event planning," I tell Ginny as we sip rosé while walking through the gathering of people.

My best friend is stunning in a white lace Oscar de la Renta dress, looking like she was born into the crowd that's gathered for the engagement party.

"It came together so beautifully. Thank you for everything, Lenni," she says as she side-hugs me.

The room is draped in white roses and eucalyptus, just like their wedding will be. Touches of cream and soft green decorate everything from the tables to the bar area. Lights drape through the rafters, casting a romantic glow over the space, while the Christmas lights from the city are viewable through the large windows that offer a panoramic view of the skyline.

"Hey, all I did was make a few calls. It does make it easy when you don't have a budget, though. I still think you should have gone with the ice sculpture," I joke.

"You just like spending my money," Jackson mutters teasingly as he comes up behind us.

"You're not wrong, bossman. It's so much more fun when someone else is paying for it." Flipping my curled hair over my shoulder, I look around the room while they kiss.

Jackson and Ginny could make even the most sexually comfortable person uncomfortable with their PDA.

"I'm gonna steal her for a moment," he says, pulling Ginny toward the stage set up at one end of the room.

Leisurely, I make my way behind them, grabbing another glass of champagne as I pass a server with a tray. Jackson's best friend, Tripp, still isn't here. With the way Jackson has been whisking Ginny off whenever he can, I doubt they will stay much longer, and I can't believe the best man would be this late to his friend's engagement party.

A hush falls over the crowd as Jackson gets their attention. Ginny beams at me as I take my place next to the stage, ready for anything like a good friend should be. Maybe this is why they haven't introduced me to Tripp yet. Maybe he's just not a very good friend.

"When I asked Ginny to marry me, I knew it took her by surprise when the first thing she said was, '*Are you insane? We've only been dating for a few months,*' but I think most of you understand that when it comes to this woman, I'm completely enraptured," Jackson says.

Everyone laughs as people clink their champagne glasses. It's no secret how in love these two are. It's the type of love you find in fairytales. The type that sweeps you off your feet and slays all your dragons.

"Love is a labor, and I will work endlessly every day for the rest of our lives to prove my utter devotion to you, Ginny. Thank you for making me the happiest man alive, and for agreeing to become my prison warden until the end of our days."

"I love you," she tells him as she leans up to kiss him.

"I love you, too." He turns back to the crowd and holds up his glass. "Alright, now enjoy the party that my fiancée worked so hard to put together."

And her best friend, jackass.

Jackson and I have a love-sorta-hate relationship. I love everything he's done for my friend, and he loves how happy Ginny is when we hang out. But I hate that he constantly demeans me, even though I'm pretty sure he does it just to get a rise out of me.

I don't think Jackson has many friends.

Holding out my hand, I help Ginny get down as something else catches Jackson's attention. "He *does* know he's stuck with me for the rest of his life, right?"

She laughs and is about to answer when she abruptly whirls around at the sound of a man's voice saying something about cheese. She leans in to air kiss the guy's cheek, and I finally catch a glimpse at Jackson's best man.

Time slows.

My stomach does a somersault.

Ginny is talking, but I barely register her words. "Better late than never! I'm so excited to *finally* introduce you guys! Tripp, this is my best friend–"

"You!" I cry out.

"It's you!" he exclaims in surprise at the same time.

Ken stands before me, mouth hanging open, looking devastatingly handsome in a black Brunello Cucinelli suit.

"You said your name was Bianca!" He looks confused, but it's edged with annoyance.

"*You* said yours was Ken!" I parry. Sorry, buddy, you don't get to be the only one upset here.

Jackson and Ginny's eyes bounce back and forth between us as *Tripp* declares, "I've been looking for you for the last week! Do you know how much trouble I'm in because of you?"

"Me? What did I do besides give you the best night of your life?" I ask smugly.

His eyes sweep down the length of me with a look that tells me he can't argue with that statement, but before he can answer me, Jackson interrupts, "Wait, *she's* the girl you hooked up with?"

Ginny begins to laugh. "Oh, this is too good."

He gets heated by our friends' comments and looks like he's about to explode when Jackson grabs his arm and pulls him away, muttering something about not ruining his engagement party. Tripp and I hold each other's gazes while they head to the bar.

My heart pounds erratically behind my rib cage.

How is it, that out of the millions of people in Manhattan, it's *him* that ends up being Jackson's best friend?

My Prince Charming for one earth-shattering evening.

The man who made me come more times in one night than I thought humanly possible.

Why the fuck did I never think to Google Tripp Kennedy?

Ginny continues to giggle, and even though it's her big night, I snap, "Stop laughing!" before tossing back the rest of my champagne. "This is why I don't sleep with men outside the club."

All the illusion of anything happening between us shatters as I realize we will always be in each other's lives now.

Our two best friends are getting married. It's inevitable.

I'll be forced to watch as he eventually settles down, always wondering *what-if.*

Wondering if I'd just shown back up at his house last Friday night if *maybe, somehow,* this could have worked out differently.

"I love you, but this is hilarious. Do you know Jackson has *actively* tried to keep you two from meeting because he thinks that if you guys met, you'd be the most annoying pair in the world?"

The bitter sting of betrayal rushes through my veins as I watch Tripp unload on Jackson at the bar. "Gee, thanks, bossman."

It would have been better if they'd just introduced us. None of this would have happened. It would have been better that way.

"You know he means it affectionately when he calls you annoying," Ginny says soothingly.

Grabbing another glass from a passing server, I muse, "Wonder what he's so worked up over?"

He looks pissed, and I can't imagine what I possibly could have done to warrant this level of anger.

"You told his ex that you two are engaged. I would assume that's probably it." She shrugs.

My gaze snaps to her. "How do *you* know that?"

"Because unlike you, who only told me you had a random hook-up outside the club, *he* has been recounting every detail of your encounter to Jackson daily. Except for your name, Jackson would have known it was you immediately, *Bianca*. Good luck with that—you got yourself in a pickle."

Her attention slides to the guys, and a smile lights up her face. Sensing I've lost her attention, I poke her arm. "What pickle? Why is there a pickle? Ginny, look at me and tell me about the pickle!"

"Go talk to Tripp. I'll find you in a little bit." She walks away before I can respond, following Jackson, who has also abandoned Tripp at the bar.

Sucking up my pride, I walk over to him slowly, smoothing the pleated detailing of my black dress as I pull my hair over one shoulder. When I'm right behind him, I clear my throat. "So, Tripp, is it? Kinda crazy that our best friends are getting married."

He turns and leans against the bar, dragging his eyes down my body again and saying flatly, "Did you already forget, *babe*? So are we."

At my puzzled expression, he continues, "Emily told her parents, who told *my* parents that we are engaged. I've been trying to figure out who you are all week so that you can help me continue our little charade, *Lenni*."

Hold the phone.

What?

"It's Valentina. Only my friends call me Lenni. And what do you mean, carry on the charade?"

Tripp is looking at me like he's torn between wanting to strangle me or rip my dress off and fuck me on the top of the bar. Discreetly, I cross my legs as I lean next to him, his intense gaze making my lower body clench with want.

"Well, I *was* planning on asking you nicely to do me a solid and pretend like we are actually engaged for a little while. But seeing as how we're going to be spending a lot of time in each other's company, I don't really think you have much of a choice. Jackson loves being in the tabloids. We're bound to be photographed together with the wedding coming up. So, name your price. What will it take to get you to pretend to be engaged to me for a little while?" He takes a step closer, crowding me against the bar.

Trying to look affronted at the notion of being bought, I scoff, "What if I'm already seeing someone?"

His answering grin melts my fortitude as his hand finds my waist. Lowering his head to my ear, he whispers, "If you were seeing someone, you wouldn't have ridden my cock last week like your life depended on it."

Tripp skims his lips against the column of my neck, causing me to suck in a sharp breath and look around to make sure no one is paying us any attention. When his other hand finds the small of my back, he jerks me into him, causing me to grab his arms to balance myself in my stilettos.

"And if you *are* seeing someone, and still went home with me, then I don't want to be friends with you, even if our best friends are getting married. I don't like cheaters, and I don't like liars. And yes, I'm well aware of how ironic that is, given that I'm asking you to lie to a bunch of people about the status of our relationship."

He pulls back until our lips are mere inches apart. "So, I'll ask again, what's your price, Viv?"

My chest burns, brushing against his as I take short breaths, the air between us thick with tension. Staring at his lips, I whisper, "It's *Valentina.*"

"I know what your name is...*now.* But isn't that the main character's name in *Pretty Woman?* Vivian?"

My cheeks grow warm as my eyes widen slightly. "Yeah."

Tripp's lips move to my ear again. "Well, we've crossed clothes shopping and getting your pussy licked on top of a piano off the list. I can arrange payments to start tomorrow. Unless you want to go another round tonight?"

Memories of last Thursday flash through my mind, and I unwittingly tighten my hold on him. He makes an amused sound as he pulls back again to look at me before dropping his eyes to my lips. "Smile for the camera, baby."

Suddenly, his lips are on mine, warm and inviting, and his minty orange scent invades my senses. Tripp doesn't kiss me chastely as a few camera flashes go off. He kisses me with the same passion as he did on the sidewalk in front of Jean-Georges.

Someone whistles, and a few people laugh while others begin to murmur their distaste at our antics. When Tripp pulls back, he has a smile on his face.

I hate that I can't tell if it's for me or just for the people watching.

"So, what do you say?" he asks lowly.

A million different thoughts run through my head, yet at the same time, my mind draws a blank. It's like turning off a TV after watching the black and white *ants* war with each other after a program has ended and broadcasting has gone off the air.

"I have to go to work."

Dazed, I let go of him, turning to head toward the exit. There's no sign of Ginny and Jackson anywhere, and I don't think she'll mind me leaving without saying goodbye, given the circumstances.

Prince Charming wants to buy me.

He seems more interested in carrying on our lie than he does in *me*.

It's better that way, but it makes me feel cheap all the same.

When I imagined seeing *Ken* again, he was always ready to welcome me with open arms—and an open bed.

Now, I don't know what to think.

Tripp follows me, touching my lower back as he walks with me. "Ah, yes," his voice is low, "Jackson got me a membership at Désirer. I haven't been yet. Maybe I'll join you."

He knows.

Abruptly, I stop near the coat check, pulling him by his jacket over to the corner and punching the button for the elevator. "What do you mean he got you a membership at Désirer?"

"Relax, he's been trying to get Carmela to let me in for months. Obviously, we're not going to be able to tell anyone that's your job." He doesn't say it offensively, but I still flinch.

"I didn't say yes."

The elevator comes, and we get into it, waiting until the doors close before resuming the conversation.

"I'm sorry. I didn't mean for that to sound so rude. I don't judge you for working there. Honestly, it makes sense, given our night together."

"Don't worry, I'm not offended. And what is *that* supposed to mean?" I snap.

Chuckling, he shrugs. "Tell me that wasn't an incredible night, Viv."

I let the nickname slide this time. "Yeah, well. It

can't happen again, especially if I agree to do this. It'll just make things more complicated. So will you going to the club."

"I don't really know how I feel about my fiancée fucking other men."

Even if his proposal isn't genuine, I understand why his voice is so bitter. Glancing at him, I shrug. "It's my job, Tripp. I don't know what to tell you. It's not like anyone besides Ginny and Jackson will know. We wear masks to help hide our identities."

I don't tell him that I haven't actually *slept* with anyone since him.

"What will it take for you to *only* fuck me?" he asks, like it's only a matter of time before we fall into bed together again.

A shiver of excitement dances down my spine at his question.

"That's *really* not a good idea. It's not like I can just quit or put my job on pause. People go there specifically *for* me."

When we reach the ground floor, I exit and head for the doors, but he grabs my arm and pulls me into the corner of the empty lobby, pushing me against the wall to kiss me again. His fingers grip my naked flesh beneath the short hem of my dress while he cradles my jaw with the other hand to tilt my head back.

I'm half tempted to unzip his pants and beg him to fuck me against the wall, but I settle for wrapping my arms around his neck to pull him closer.

"How much, *Valentina*?" he questions again when he pulls back.

"What makes you think I even want to sleep with you again?" I ask breathlessly.

"Tell me you haven't thought about our night together. That it hasn't consumed your thoughts every waking moment of the day for the past week. You're all I've been able to think about, not just because I need you to pretend to be engaged to me. You cast a fucking spell on me, Viv. And I'm not sure I even want you to lift it."

Tripp's words would be beautiful under any other circumstance. But the facts remain the same.

He's a millionaire, and I sell my body for money.

My past would be a stain on his future.

Jackson once told me I couldn't go to a party that Tripp's parents were hosting because Mrs. Kennedy wouldn't have enough time to do a background check on me.

She'll never find anything on Valentina *Parks*. So I'll bet that she'll continue to dig, and will eventually uncover the truth.

Tripp will end up being embarrassed anyway.

It's too dangerous.

"You're about to lie to me. I can see it in your eyes," Tripp murmurs against my lips before kissing me again.

Pushing him back gently, I shake my head. "I can't think straight when you kiss me."

His smile causes poisonous little butterflies to

flutter about in my stomach. "Spend the night with me."

"I told you, I have to go to work." Moving around him, I exit the building. The cold winter chill stings my skin as I head to the curb to hail a cab.

"I'll see you there then." He follows me outside and shrugs when I spin to glare at him. "I'm not giving up."

Sighing, I pinch the bridge of my nose. "Did Jackson give you the address?"

He looks like a king who just conquered a kingdom. "He sure did."

"Okay, fine. Go and do your intake. Once they escort you into the Grand Room, tell security you're waiting for Bianca, and I'll come find you. You can watch tonight and *then* decide if you still want me to pretend to be your fiancée. I'll be there in an hour."

I'm fucking crazy for agreeing to this.

Tripp sticks his hands in his pockets and stalks closer as I wave my hand at a car coming down the street. "And when the night is over, and I still want you. How much for your help? There will be a lot of appearances at social events—a lot of pretending like you're in love with me. I already know you're a good actress. So what's your price?"

"A million dollars," I tell him, knowing he'll never go for it.

He laughs incredulously. "Absolutely not. Two hundred thousand."

"Five hundred thousand," I counter as the cab approaches the curb.

"Deal. I'll see you in an hour, Viv." He holds his hand out for me to shake.

Holy fucking shit.

Attempting to hide my surprise, I ignore his offered hand and open the backdoor. "I would have done it for two."

Stepping closer, he tucks my hair behind my ear. "I would have paid a million."

Tripp

J ackson is supposed to have been the one to take me to Désirer and teach me the ropes on my first visit. He's at least explained enough over the last few months that I don't feel like a complete jackass when security has me sign my papers and issues my membership card.

When his uncle brought him for the first time, Scott made him wear a blindfold. Jackson, however, gave me the address for the entrance through the back of a hole-in-the-wall pizza joint. I don't even have to wear a mask while I do my intake.

But the second I'm escorted into the Grand Room, I feel like a fish out of water.

I'm sure they named it the way they did because it's just that. *Grand.*

A giant chandelier hangs in the center of the room over an oval bar, casting a glow over the entire space. The floors are a deep mahogany, the walls a shade of red with a gleaming gold pattern that reminds me of something you'd see in the Victorian era. Multiple pieces of furniture litter the area, all a shimmering shade of nutmeg.

People are lounging everywhere or walking around talking to others, and everyone is wearing a mask. Some are simple and plain, like the one they gave me to use for tonight. Others are exotic—some shaped like animal heads, some like clown jesters or in the style of the Victorian theater.

Some clients wear suits even though it's a Saturday—people like me who have come from a fancy event or are here just to talk. Some men and women are dressed in sexy lingerie or silk pajama sets.

Then, there are the crowned jewels.

The Angels.

Wearing the wings of their tiers on their backs like trophies.

When Jackson told me about the wings, I imagined giant decorative ones like the Victoria's Secret Angels wear on the runway. The ones these Angels wear aren't as ostentatious, but no less impressive.

Shimmering champagne, glossy black, and glittering platinum feathered wings adorn the backs of those who work here. Though I feel like a kid who's just been let loose in a candy shop, I find my gaze bouncing from Angel to Angel in an attempt to find the only woman I want to be looking at half-naked.

"Remember, you don't touch anyone without their permission, got it?" the guard who escorts me reiterates.

"Got it. I'm only here for one Angel, anyway. Can you please let Bianca know I'm at the bar? She'll know who it is asking for her."

He laughs. "Everyone asks for Bianca. Care to be a little more specific? What's your code name?"

Neither Jackson nor Lenni said anything about a code name. They didn't ask at intake either.

"Ken," I tell him, thinking I'm clever until he laughs again, shaking his head as he walks off.

"He probably thinks you meant Ken, as in Barbie and Ken," a breathy voice sounds to my left.

Looking over, I see a petite blonde wearing a pair of platinum wings, with bright red lips and a Marilyn Monroe beauty mark. "Hi, I'm Norma-Jean."

Of course, you are.

"Sorry, I'm waiting for someone."

"My apologies. Enjoy your evening," she croons before walking away.

Ten minutes pass while I sit at the bar and sip a glass of Japanese whiskey, taking it all in while I wait for Lenni.

When she finally walks into the room, everyone's attention turns to her as if she's a rare sparkling diamond.

Her sun-kissed skin has a shimmery glow, contrasting with the platinum wings on her back. She's teased the shit out of her hair, making it look like she just got done fucking for hours on end. Black is smudged around her eyes in that sexy way that makes her chocolate honey eyes stand out, and her lips are the color of deep burgundy.

The outfit she wears is lacy and black. An underwire bra with detailing in all the right places, with a matching pair of underwear complete with stockings and a garter belt.

My cock immediately jumps to attention at the sight of her.

As does every other dick in the room.

The only thing saving me from feeling like an insecure little shit right now is the way she immediately hones in on me and saunters in my direction with a knowing smile on her face.

She's approached by four different men by the time she makes it to me, turning them all down with a suggestive smile and a, "Maybe next time."

I don't want there to be a next time. Not for anyone in this room except for me.

"Hello, Ken," she greets knowingly.

"Bianca." *Play it cool, Tripp.*

"Are you ready to play?" she asks, stepping between my legs to reach behind me for my glass, her chest brushing up against mine.

"You're not really going to make me watch you fuck another guy, are you? Because I'd hate to get kicked out for murdering someone my first night here." My hands find her hips because she stepped into me first. I'm playing by the rules. She initiated first contact, which means unless she explicitly tells me no, I can touch her.

She lets out a soft, musical laugh before taking a large sip of my drink. "Not exactly. But close."

My heart rate picks up as she finishes my drink before taking my hand. "Come on."

Silently, I follow her around the bar to the back wall, where three men dressed in all black are standing in front of a door.

"Evening, gentlemen. I've got one more joining me tonight if you could show us to our room, please."

"Does Leonard know you'll have an extra tonight?" one of the guys who is holding a clipboard asks.

The grin that pulls at her lips is playful as she shakes her head slowly. "He's not aware yet, but I think he'll be *very* pleased."

An uneasy feeling creeps into my chest, curling down into my stomach when one of the guys returns her smile and motions for us to follow him.

My breaths are shallow, heart hammering behind its ivory cage as we cross the threshold into a long hallway. The walls are black, with the same gold pattern as the Grand Room, and it's lined with gleaming black doors that have polished bronze knobs. Small tables sit between the doors, with large vases full of blood-red roses. I've never really enjoyed the smell of roses, and I try hard not to cough at the thick fragrance permeating the hall.

Reaching for Lenni, I pull her into my side and bury my nose in her hair, inhaling her smoky vanilla coffee scent to chase away the cloying floral perfume. She makes a sound reminiscent of a cat purring and leans into me. When we reach the room, she tells the guard, "Give me five minutes before bringing Leonard back."

He tells her no problem and heads back down the hall as she opens the door and pulls me inside. "Well, what do you think so far? I'm surprised you didn't have anyone fawning over you when I came in."

"Told them I wasn't interested," I say, surveying the room.

There's a long, black chaise lounge against one wall, and a horizontal dresser caddy corner from it—with numerous toys lined up on the surface. A bed with a ridiculously large headboard sits in the middle of one wall, with a changing screen in the corner next to it. There's a large rectangular mirror above the head of the bed. The only light from the room comes from a dripping crystal chandelier in the middle of the ceiling.

Lenni goes over to the dresser and grabs something off it before going behind the changing screen. "So, not sure how freaky you are, but if you decide to stay, you're in for a show."

"Care to elaborate?" Sitting on the edge of the bed, I notice an array of things to tie people up with hanging on the wall next to it—silken scarves, rope, and leather cuffs.

I'd like to tie *her* up and tell *Leonard* to get lost.

"Have you ever been pegged before?" She comes out from around the screen. Her underwear and garter belt are gone, and she's wearing a harness around her hips…with a strap-on penis.

"Jesus Christ! Don't come near me with that

thing!" Jumping up, I retreat a few steps, looking back and forth between it and her eyes.

"Why?" She smirks with a raised brow and tosses a bottle of lube on the bed. "Afraid you might like it?"

"No, thank you!"

With her hands on her hips, she shrugs. "Toys are friends, not foes."

I'm about to respond when the door opens, and a spindly bald man walks in wearing a Hugh Hefner robe and a pair of black silk drawstring pajama pants. "My love! Leonard has arrived!"

His voice is a mix between English and Southern, and I have a feeling his accent is fake as fuck.

"I hear we have a guest tonight! Very excited to meet you. You must be very special for Bianca to have chosen you." He directs his attention to her and instantly frowns. "My love, lose the wings. You know I'd rather be fucked by the devil."

She laughs and shrugs out of them, tossing them to the side of the bed. They are familiar enough to tell me that they've done this before. Whatever *this* is.

"I'm confused. You're going to fuck him with that?" I ask, pointing at the space between her legs.

Leonard laughs as he rolls onto the bed. "Well, don't sound so judgmental about it. Have you ever had a woman put their fingers in your ass while you fuck them, or they suck you off? It's fucking heaven. Getting your G-spot stroked while you do the dirty isn't something to snub, my friend."

"Why have *her* fuck you then? Why not a man?" I am not jealous right now. I'm not.

"Sometimes I *do* pick a man." He shrugs. "But look at her. She's fucking beautiful."

"Aww. Thanks, Leonard. Okay, Ken. Time to decide if you're going to stay or if you're going to go." She looks at me expectantly with a smug grin and a raised brow, conveying that she thinks I'm about to turn and hightail it out of here.

I don't want to watch this, but I also don't want to leave.

No part of me wants to leave her with this man, even though they've obviously done this multiple times, and *he* isn't going to fuck *her*. I'm torn because this is her job, and she challenged me to accept it, but right now, I want to throw Leonard out on his ass, fuck her until I'm all she can think about, and then solidify in our verbal contract that she can't fuck anyone else.

Jackson explained how this place works. She can work in the hall that only allows you to talk.

Great, now you're turning into a controlling prick.

Lenni's playful expression drops as she narrows her eyes behind her mask. "It's time for you to leave now if you want to go," she says like she's talking to a three-year-old.

Surprisingly, it's Leonard who saves the day. "Stay and watch, stud. She's a sight to behold."

"I'm thinking maybe that's not a good idea," Lenni tells him. There's an edge to her voice. Disappointment, maybe.

I can't tear my eyes away from her and hear myself say, "Yes."

Leonard leans back on the pillows and grins at me. "You got it bad, don't you? Some advice? Don't get too attached. This is their job. We pay them to make us feel special. But we're nothing but a bunch of dogs gnawing at someone else's bone. No offense, Bianca."

"None taken," she replies, but her stare falls to the floor, and her reply is flat.

"You can join if you want. If she says it's okay, it's okay with me," Leonard continues. When he sees my brows raise in surprise, he laughs. "Don't worry, I won't touch you. I'll stay on my front, though, if you want to fuck her while she fucks me."

"Hi, I'm standing right here. Anyone going to ask me if I'm okay with this? It's ultimately *my* decision, remember? And no, he's not going in my backdoor while I'm in yours." Lenni waves a hand in the air while still looking down.

I'm having a tough time taking this seriously when she's wearing a strap-on penis. This whole situation brings up bad memories of *why* Emily freaked out and decided to leave me.

Lenni and I had an amazing night together, but didn't even discuss anal during it. We literally just found out about each other's real identities.

Do I want to fuck her again? *Obviously.* But not in her ass, *yet.* And certainly not with another man present.

"I'll just watch if she doesn't mind."

Her eyes drag from the floor to mine, voice soft as she says, "If you really want to, I don't mind if you stay."

"Excellent. Let's get this party started then," Leonard croons from his place on the bed.

I sit on the chaise as I watch her profile change. It's like slipping on a mask, the way Lenni's eyes harden before they light up and a smirk takes over her face. Like she goes to a place inside her mind and brings another version of herself out to play.

She turns to the bed, gracing me with a glorious view of her pert ass. My knee bounces as they lock eyes while she gets on the bed. She sits on her knees and slowly tugs at his drawstring pants, tossing them to the floor with his discarded robe.

"Let me see those beautiful tits, baby. You know I like watching you play with them while you fuck me," Leonard tells her.

I'm on my feet faster than a crack of lightning, and his eyes snap to mine. Whatever he sees on my face makes him smile. "Go on and touch her while she does it. It's okay, isn't it, Bianca?"

I can see our reflection in the mirror above the bed. We lock eyes, and she gives me a slight nod, not breaking this obvious character she's playing. She leans over Leonard, her chestnut waves dripping down over his bare body as she whispers seductively, "Do you want to watch *him* touch me?"

"Fuck yes. Touch her. Touch her *now*," he answers, reaching down to stroke himself.

It feels like an out-of-body experience as I shrug

out of my suit jacket, stepping forward until my groin is flush against her ass. She lets out a giggle and wiggles against me, dragging her hands down Leonard's chest as she rises up until her back is against mine.

Our gaze in the mirror never breaks as she reaches behind her and finds my hands, flattening my palms against her skin, just above the harness straps. My cock hardens as she drags them up her body, and she lets out a gasp when I nuzzle her neck, nipping her flesh as she cups my hands around her bra.

"Holy shit, you two are hot as fuck together," Leonard breathes, still stroking himself.

Maybe it's because she's not fucking him yet. Maybe it's because I've always wondered what it would be like to be watched. But his words light a fire in me, burning up any doubts about what we're about to do.

My fingers curl around the fabric of her bra, dragging it down to expose her breasts before palming them and pinching her nipples between my thumbs and forefingers. Lenni breaks our gaze, rolling her head back on my shoulder as she arches her back, pressing her chest into my hands.

"Does that feel good?" I ask against her ear. Memories from our night together flash through my mind making me recall how much she liked having her nipples sucked and played with.

"Mmhmm," she moans.

"Take it off her," Leonard pleads.

I do it, not because he asks, but because I want to.

When she's fully exposed, Leonard grabs the bottle of lube from the bed and shifts down, spreading his legs on either side of her. They work together, squirting the lube on the dildo before she lowers it to his ass and starts to work it inside of him.

I adjust myself in my pants so that my cock is pointed up, nestled against the upper part of her butt, before reaching around to pull her back to me. As I do, she grips Leonard's thighs.

If I weren't here, I assume she'd be the one stroking his cock, instead of himself. They might be kissing. He might be the one palming her breasts.

But I *am* here.

So, I try to focus on me and her instead of them.

Wrapping my hands around her front, I pinch her nipple with one and cradle her neck with the other, shifting her face over her shoulder to claim her lips.

Everything about the way we kiss is hot. The way our mouths work against each other. The way our tongues dance and caress. If I could get drunk from kissing her, I'd willingly give myself alcohol poisoning.

Lenni begins to thrust into Leonard, and my hips grind against her backside, pressing my erection firmly between her cheeks. She moans into my mouth as I help her, pushing into her as she pushes into him.

With every thrust, his ragged breaths increase as he watches us and moans along with her. One of her hands winds around and grips the back of my hair, pushing our mouths deeper together. It's such a fucking turn-on, and I capture her tongue between my teeth, dragging it out of her mouth and into mine.

The sound of our kissing mixes with the wet sound of him pumping himself. I let go of her nipple and trail my hand down her body slowly to cup between her legs beneath the strap-on. Her arousal is leaking down her thighs, and I scoop it up as I break our kiss.

She and Leonard both watch as I lift my fingers to my mouth and suck them clean.

"How does she taste?" he rasps.

"Fucking divine," I answer before curling my tongue back into her mouth so she can taste herself on me.

I swallow her throaty whimper as he asks, "Can I taste her?"

Breaking our kiss abruptly, I turn my head to look directly at him for the first time since I walked over to the bed. "Fuck no. Everything that's between her legs belongs to *me*."

Lenni nuzzles my neck, biting the hollow beneath my jawline as she whispers, "That's right. I'm *your* good girl."

"Oh fuck," Leonard rasps. "I'm gonna come."

Lenni moves inside him faster, her fingers tightening in my hair as I duck beneath her arm and lift her nipple into my mouth, sucking hard.

She lets out a cry at the same time Leonard comes all over his chest. I look up at her, letting go with a pop, and kiss my way back up to her neck while he takes a few moments post-orgasm to catch his breath.

Straightening, I resume my spot at her back, helping her pull out of him as he maneuvers off the bed and grabs a towel on the nightstand. "Fuck, you two are incredible. Can I book you together next time?"

Lenni's breathing is labored, the tension thick as neither of us answers him but hold each other's gaze in the mirror. He chuckles and pulls his pants on, disappearing from my peripheral momentarily before coming up beside us.

He leans forward and kisses Lenni's temple while tossing something on the bed. "Have fun, you two. Thanks for the amazing orgasm. I haven't come that hard in ages."

My hands drift down her sides as he leaves, releasing the harness from her hips and tossing it off the bed to see that he gave us a condom. My cock is still painfully hard behind my pants, and she's making no effort to move.

Her eyes shift to it as I pick it up and hold it in front of her face. "We don't have to if you don't–"

Lenni rips her mask off and turns on her knees, pulling mine off as well as she kisses me. Her hands work my pants and boxer briefs down as I all but rip through the buttons on my shirt and fling it behind me.

Our movements are frantic as I step out of my pants and put on the condom while she turns around and gets on all fours, arching her back. "Hurry," she begs. "I need you inside me."

Reaching up, I twist my fingers around the strands of her hair before pushing into her until my hips are flush against her ass. "Fuck, I've been thinking about this every day for the last week."

"Have you?" she asks as I drive into her. Her hands twist in the sheets as she shifts back to meet me thrust for thrust.

"Of course I fucking have. If I would have known you were going to leave the next morning the way you did, I would have chained you to my fucking bed." I snap my hips sharply, setting a punishing pace, pouring my frustration at our situation into my movements.

She takes it all with equal fervor, whimpers leaving her mouth on breathy gasps. "I've thought about it too."

Earlier, she put on a show with Leonard. Now I want to know that *I'm* getting the real her.

Pulling out, I flip her over before crawling onto the bed and burying myself to the hilt. Her legs cradle my waist, feet bracing on my backside to pull me deeper into her.

When our eyes meet, neither of us looks away, even when her head arches as I angle myself to rub my pubic bone against her clit. "Tell me you're mine. Tell me you'll be mine while we figure this shit out."

She shakes her head, and I thrust so forcefully that she curls her tongue inside her open mouth as her walls tighten around my cock. "Trust me, you don't want to get involved with me."

A bead of sweat rolls down my temple. My balls tense. Her walls begin to flutter as I say again, "Tell me you're mine, Valentina. Be a good girl and tell me who you belong to."

Her eyes finally shut, climaxing as she cries out, "You! I'm yours."

"Open your eyes and look at me when you say it." I'm so close as her pussy grips my cock, milking it as she comes.

She does as I ask, hands cradling my face as she tells me, "I'm yours, Tripp. As long as you're mine, too."

Something grips my chest. It's warm and inviting and not at all unwelcome.

"I'm yours," I echo, spilling myself inside her, kissing her until our hips slow and my cock stops twitching.

I lay on her chest, careful not to put my full weight on her as she begins to stroke my hair. "We're fucked," she whispers. "This is never going to work."

"We'll figure it out," I murmur against her skin, pressing a kiss to her breast. "At least we have the attraction part down. Now we just have to figure out all the rest."

Propping my chin on her sternum, I can feel her pulse beating, and I smile as a sense of calm washes over me. She smiles in return, pushing my hair out of my face. "What?"

"I think Leonard likes me more than you."

She laughs and pushes me off of her. "As if."

"So, how many other clients do you have tonight?" Tripp asks while he's buttoning up his shirt.

His tone conveys that he's still not happy about me taking clients, and I debate telling him I haven't actually slept with anyone else since our night together. "No one else is scheduled tonight. I was just going to pick up some Confessional clients."

As I slip my wings back over my shoulders, he comes up behind me and gathers my hair, waiting until I get them settled before gently skimming his fingers down my back as he releases my curls. "Well…I'm still here. I still want you to pretend to be engaged to me. And I still don't want you to fuck any other men during our arrangement."

"I haven't," the words leave my mouth as I turn to face him.

A crease forms between his brows, and it's annoyingly endearing. Slowly, I shrug one shoulder. "I haven't slept with anyone since you. I've done stuff like what we did tonight with Leonard, but I haven't actually had sex with anyone."

A breath leaves his mouth in a long exhale. "Because you felt it, too."

"I won't deny we had a great night together, Tripp." I step around him to find wherever our masks landed when I pulled them off earlier. "But at the end of the day, this is still my job, and you're still *you*."

"What is that supposed to mean?" He takes his mask from me, his brows furrowed like I've offended him.

"It means that you're rich, so you're well-known. And you're a different breed than I am. Guys like you can't date women like me. It just ends badly."

"Okay, first off, we're not dogs. Second, guys like *me* date women like *you* all the time. They're just secretive about it. Third, I resent you for limiting me to the rich asshole category of types of men."

He reaches out, the warm skin of his palm splaying over the garter belt I put back on as he pulls me to him. "You've already agreed. Which means we're as good as dating now. And if you think I won't want to spend every moment of our time together rolling you between the sheets, whether at my place, yours, or here, you're very wrong, Viv."

Of course, why wouldn't you want your money's worth?

The bitter thought releases its toxin through my veins as he holds me. Eventually, he'll want to stage a break-up, and I'll go back to doing what I do best. Getting attached to the way he's looking at me isn't smart.

Yet, I still nod, trapped in his golden, mossy gaze. "Can we just figure this out one day at a time?"

"Why don't you let me take you to lunch tomorrow? We can discuss it more then," he offers, rubbing his thumb along the lace of the belt.

Reaching up, I secure my mask around my eyes and step out of his hold. "Sounds good. Are you going to stay and check out the rest of the club?"

The corners of his eyes crinkle as he smiles, and I hate the way it makes my heart skip a beat. "Nah. There's nothing else here I have any use for."

"Well then, goodnight, I guess."

"Wait a minute. If you think I'm going to let you walk away again without getting your number this time, you're crazy."

"They took your phone, didn't they?" I ask, walking over to the dresser to grab one of the markers for marking the toys we use with the client's pseudonyms.

He affirms my question with a hum as I reach out to grab his arm. Pushing his sleeve up, I quickly jot my number on the skin of his forearm. "When you get it back, just text me with details for tomorrow. Sound good?"

"You know if you gave me a fake number, I can ask Ginny, right?" He laughs as he rolls his sleeve back down.

"It's not fake, I promise." Tossing the marker on

the bed, I turn to leave, but his hand on my wrist stops me.

"You knew where I lived. Why didn't you ever come back?" he asks softly.

I don't turn around as I answer him. "We were strangers, Tripp. We *are* strangers. Me showing up would have only complicated things further. I didn't want to keep lying to you about what I do for work."

Gently, I rotate my wrist until he lets me go. "Women like me can't form attachments. It's bad for business. I'll help you because I got you into this mess. Nothing else can happen, though. Do you understand?"

"I don't think I can promise that. And I don't think you can either. We have something special—"

"It's my job to have something special with the men I fuck." I'm glad I'm still facing the door because tears unexpectedly sting my eyes. I don't even know why.

Tripp is silent until I move to open the door. The last words I hear before I leave the room are, "Lie to yourself all you want, Lenni. You're scared because you know I'm right."

I'm afraid he might not be wrong.

RH Rooftop is bright and beautiful as the hostess takes me to where Tripp is already waiting in a corner booth. Tall trees and dripping crystal chandeliers add a romantic ambiance to the space, even though it's two in the afternoon and plenty of light still comes through the large windows. The booths are edged in greenery and shared with other tables, but it looks as though Tripp has ensured no one will be at any of the surrounding areas so we can discuss our plan in private.

When he sees me, he seems relieved. The tension melts from his body, his broody face brightening as his lips turn up and he takes me in. He's wearing black slacks and a dark gray V-neck sweater over a white collared shirt, looking magazine-ready in what he considers casual Sunday clothing.

I'm aware I look like a charity project next to him, in my pleather leggings and worn combat boots. But the way the hostess sneered at my cropped black ripped-knit sweater and beanie when I walked in and told her I was meeting Tripp confirmed it.

"Hi. You look gorgeous. These are for you," Tripp says as he stands and greets me with a kiss on the cheek and a bouquet of deep pink roses.

I swear the hostess makes a snooty *hmph* while she walks away.

"Thank you for the flowers. I probably should have asked if there was a dress code," I tell him as he helps me out of my puffer jacket and takes the bouquet back, placing it next to him in the booth.

"You look hot. What are you worried about?" He takes my beanie as I run my hand through my hair, tossing it with our coats in the space next to the table.

"Looking very much like I don't belong here.

Thanks, by the way, for meeting later. I usually close down the club, so, naturally, I'm a night owl. I hate early mornings." Picking up my menu, I realize there aren't many options and decide on the avocado toast.

"Good to know for our story. Bad, because my parents want to have breakfast with us on Tuesday." His arm rests behind me; body angled into mine in a possessive way that suggests to onlookers that we're intimately acquainted.

"Your parents?" I groan. "Already?"

"Afraid so, Viv."

"Is it too late to back out? Can't you just tell them the truth?"

Tripp waits to answer me until an approaching waitress takes our orders and leaves again. "My mom has been hounding me about what happened with Emily for the last year. This will get her off my back for a while. Of course, she will want to know everything about you, so we need to build a solid story."

"What's there to build? Our best friends are getting married, we met that way. We can just say Ginny and I work together and leave it at that." His minty orange smell causes things low in my body to tighten, and I lean into him without meaning to.

Everything about us is natural. Tripp isn't wrong about what he said last night. I've never had this level of connection with anyone, let alone someone I barely know. There's no awkwardness in the way we gravitate toward each other. No stiffness in the way his fingers play with the ends of my hair, or how my hand finds his knee as our legs press together.

He's paying you to create an illusion. That's all it is. You're both good actors.

"We can try to leave it at that. My mother likes to play detective, though, and she's going to question you about every little thing in your past—"

"My past is off-limits. So you better figure out a way to keep her from digging around. End of discussion," I snap, inwardly wincing at the harsh tone of my voice.

Tripp seems slightly surprised by it, too, his eyes widening a fraction before his eyebrow raises. "You're marrying into the family. She's going to want to know about you."

"And like you said, I'm a good actress. Let's not give her a reason to feel like she needs to dig."

His eyes don't leave my face as the waitress brings our food. Before I can take a bite, Tripp gently grabs my chin and makes me look at him. "Thank you. I really appreciate you doing this."

"I still think it's a bad idea," I whisper into the space between us.

His thumb strokes my bottom lip as he stares at my mouth. "I can't think of a single bad thing about it."

His arm on the back of the booth wraps around me, fingers cradling my neck to pull me forward for a kiss. It's chaste. Soft and sweet, yet still filled with the same amount of passion as all our other kisses.

Tingles spread down my chest and through my

body to the tips of my toes like glitter falling through the air. They tickle and flutter against my insides, and my legs press together to help relieve a little of the ache that starts to build in my core.

Tripp lets out a throaty chuckle, letting go of my chin to cup the inside of my thigh, fingers dangerously close to brushing against the part of me that feels like it's on fire. "God, I could spend all day in bed with you. How the fuck are you single?"

I'd asked him the same thing our first night together. If he remembers, he doesn't show any sign of it. My cheeks heat as his fingers slide up the tiniest bit. His head tilts, nose brushing along the column of my throat to whisper in my ear, "We have so much to do today, and all I want to do is take you downstairs and fuck you in the backseat of my car."

Swallowing thickly, I cross my legs to trap his fingers just as they reach the apex of my thighs and press against my center. My hips move against his hand slowly as I brace my arm on the table and hope, to whatever higher power exists, that no one is watching us.

"What do we have to do today?" I ask him breathily as he presses harder, fingertips finding my clit through the fabric of my leggings.

"Well, for starters, we should probably get you a ring." His tone is husky and quiet, barely restrained as he rubs between my legs with varying pressures while trying to be discreet so we don't alert anyone else of our public indecency.

"A ring?" My eyes close as I feel that delicious pressure start to build.

"No one will believe I proposed without a ring. My mother is going to be beside herself that I didn't ask for the family ring again."

"Don't bring up your mother while you're trying to get me off. Also, I don't want something that was on Emily's finger. I'd like to pick out my own fake diamond." My fingers encircle his wrist, pressing his hand against me harder.

He sucks air through his teeth, talking through his clenched jaw as he zeroes in on my face. "Oh, I can promise you, Viv. There won't be anything fake about it. Now come for me."

I've never understood how women could come on command. Honestly, I've always thought they just faked it. Tripp's authoritative tone rips my orgasm from me, though, and a small whimper leaves my lips as I do my best to keep quiet.

He marvels at me, continuing to move his fingers as I ride it out. "Good girl," he whispers against my lips. "You're such a good fucking girl for me, aren't you?"

Speechless, all I can do is nod. Praise has never been something I've been into. It's never interested me because it's usually *me* doing the praising, not the other way around.

But when Tripp calls me a good girl? My insides turn to literal fucking goo.

It's just another sign that this will all end very, *very* badly.

Tripp's phone goes off while we're in the back of his car being driven somewhere he won't tell me. "It's my mother," he says.

Making a motion for him not to answer the phone, my hand drops into my lap defeatedly as he slides the bar on the screen and presses the button to put it on speaker. "Mother, to what do I owe the pleasure this afternoon?"

"I was just calling to confirm that we're still on for breakfast Tuesday morning, dear. I made reservations at The Palm Court for nine. Does that work? You weren't exactly forthcoming about your…*fiancée*, so I wasn't sure if she had a job from which she needed a lunch break."

According to Google—yes, I went home last night and finally Googled Tripp and his family—Margo Kennedy is a socialite who knows everything and everyone that matters in their upper crust society. She came from money before she met Tripp's dad, Weylan, and sits on the board of numerous associations around the city.

With such a sudden engagement, there's no way she won't be suspicious of me. Either I will have to act like a picture-perfect Mary Sue like Emily, or I will have to make sure Margo doesn't see me as a threat and will assume things between me and Tripp won't last.

Making a split decision, I reply before Tripp can.

"Breakfast sounds perfect, Margo. I'm so looking forward to meeting you."

Strike one: being too informal.

Tripp rolls his eyes, smirking and shaking his head, while the other end of the line is heavy with silence. Finally, Margo sounds like she's speaking through a sour smile as she asks, "And who do I have the *pleasure* of speaking with?"

"Oh, silly me, sometimes I forget we don't know each other. Tripp is always talking so highly of you, and I feel as though I'm already a part of the family. I'm Valentina. Can't wait to see you and Weylan on Tuesday. We have to run now, though. Tripp is taking me shopping! Bye!" Reaching over, I hit the button to end the call while Tripp stares wide-eyed at me.

Strike two: being rude and acting vapid.

"Are you trying to make her hate you?" he asks incredulously.

"Yeah," I state like it should be obvious. "If she doesn't like me, she'll never think we'll last. So, it won't be a surprise when we eventually break up. Plus, this way, she won't even bother doing a background check on me. I won't be a problem she needs to take care of. I'll be one that she thinks you'll grow tired of before we make it down the aisle."

"Have you considered that maybe I won't grow tired of you? Or that our best friends are getting married soon? You aren't going to be able to get rid of me that easily."

Before either of us can say another word, his driver announces, "We're here, sir."

Here? Where is here?

Turning to look out the window, I can't help the squeal that escapes my lips when I see what store we've parked outside of. "Harry freaking Winston?!"

"I told you I was grateful. You deserve it."

As he helps me out of the car, I look through the store's windows in a daze. "Did Ginny tell you I'm obsessed with Harry?"

Pulling me behind him, he doesn't release my hand as he teases, "No, Viv. And I don't want to hear about your obsession with other men. I'm finding I'm a very jealous man when it comes to you."

The giggle I let out dies in my throat as we enter the prestigious jewelry store, and a lady with a knowing smile greets us. "Good afternoon, Mr. Kennedy. We've pulled a great selection for you to look at and have you set up in the back. If you'll please follow me."

As we walk through the space, I admire the glittering jewels in the spaced out cases, staring in awe at pieces I've viewed online millions of times. Never in my wildest dreams did I think I'd be in the presence of such luxury, mere moments away from selecting a member of their family to place on my ring finger.

"So, this is what we have in store, but of course, we can always make something custom. Do you have a cut in mind?" the associate asks.

Tripp leans into me, speaking quietly as his hand untangles from mine to rest on my lower back. "Pick whatever you want."

"Whatever I want?"

"If you were just browsing, what would you choose? What would you want to wear on your finger for the rest of your life?"

"Just warning you, regardless of what I said to Emily, I wouldn't pick something small. I may have dainty fingers, but they are perfect for the classic emerald-cut with baguettes." I've dreamt about that ring since I learned the words Harry Winston. There is no way I will pass up the opportunity to wear it, even if it's just for a little while.

"Excellent choice, ma'am. We have the one, three, and four-carat in store," the lady informs.

"Oh, one is–"

"We'll take the four-carat," Tripp interrupts.

After sizing my finger, she walks off with a slight dip of her head and a perceptive grin plastered on her face.

"Tripp, four is too much. What are you going to do with it afterward? Save it for your real future wife?" I try to argue, but he just smiles and ignores me.

"Do you have to work today?"

"No. Sundays are my day off unless I pick up a shift at the restaurant I sometimes work at, but I've been doing that less and working at the club more."

I ignore the way his eyes darken at this news, but I don't tell him I'm working at the club more because the Confessional clients don't pay as much as the Dreamers or Desires ones do.

"Spend the rest of the day with me." It's a command—not a request.

As much as I want to, I know that I need to put a little space between us. Tripp is diving headfirst into the rolling ocean of shit I've gotten us into, and I don't know how to swim.

My thoughts must project the hundred and ten miles that separate me from my past because my phone pings in my pocket, demanding my attention before giving him an answer.

> They are trying to kill me. Why are you doing this to me? Do you want me dead that badly?

Most of the time, Momma's messages don't make any sense. But this one jars me. There's a fifty-fifty chance she's talking nonsense, but a small part of me wonders if someone found out where she's at.

Then again, I'm sure I would have heard from the facility if someone had asked for her.

I allow a smile to pull my lips up as I ignore her message and raise my eyes to see Tripp watching me curiously. "I can't. I have plans."

"Plans with who?" he asks, the side of his cheek jutting out as he clenches his teeth.

He holds my gaze as I walk the few steps it takes to close the distance between us. Wrapping my arms around his neck, I play with the curls that brush his ears. "Don't worry. I won't embarrass you."

"I think you know that's not what I'm worried about, Valentina." A shiver runs through me at his use of my full name—one that doesn't go unnoticed by him. His fingers tighten on my waist as he pulls me closer until there's no space between our chests.

Bending his head, he tries to kiss me, but I whisper against his lips, "I told you, I can't think when you kiss me. And you can't seem to be around me without wanting to pull as many orgasms from me as you can. So, I'm going to spend the rest of my Sunday *alone*, decompressing from this week's events, and getting ready to give the best performance of my life starting Tuesday. It's unhealthy to want to stay in bed all day every time we see each other. I think it would be very easy to become addicted to the way we make each other feel. It'll be like going through withdrawals when we *break up*, Tripp."

My words work as well as a bucket of ice-cold water being poured over him. He sounds in pain when he replies, "I know."

Letting me go, he takes a step back just as the associate clears her throat to let us know she's making her way back to us.

When I leave, it's with a heavy diamond on my finger and an electric fence around my heart.

Tripp

"**S**o, how are things with your little vixen going?" Jackson's voice drifts across my office as he walks in.

"You mean she hasn't told Ginny we fucked six ways from Sunday at the club after your engagement party, and then I bought her a four-carat diamond?" My fingers never still as I continue typing up a document, eyes glued to my desktop screen.

My best friend lets out a low whistle as he sits on the other side of my desk, tone amused as he asks, "You sound annoyed. Trouble in paradise already?"

Air expels past my lips on a long exhale. "You know…there may not have been *many* women since Emily, but there *have* been others. None of them made me want to pursue something more than the one night we spent together, though. Why does it have to be the one woman whose job it is to screw people? And why do I have such an unfortunate talent for quickly falling for the wrong women?"

He grabs a folder off my desk and starts to thumb through it. "Falling? Whoa there, buddy. Pump the breaks. You may have already put a ring on it, but it's just for show."

Finishing the contract I'm working on, I hit save and exit the screen, dropping my eyes to the desk. "She's literally all I can think about, Jackson. And that scares the shit out of me. We don't even know each other, but our physical connection is so insane that it doesn't even matter. I don't want her doing anything at the club other than talking to clients. How crazy is that? I've never been jealous. And you know I'm not controlling either."

"Lenni isn't the type of woman who likes to be kept, Tripp." Jackson stares at me like he's seeing me for the first time and not like he's known me since we were teenagers. "That said, she informed Carmela last night that she won't be doing the New Year's Eve show. Not that she *can't*, but that she doesn't want to. Do with that what you will."

"Show? You mean the big orgies the club has once a month?" It calms my nerves to know she decided not to do it. The thought of another man's hands on her is enough to make me see red. The worst part is, I know I don't have the right to lay claim on her. I know the engagement is just for appearances. That doesn't change the fact that she said she'd be mine while we worked all of this out.

Sure, she agreed in the heat of the moment while I was buried inside her, but po*tay*to po*tah*to.

"By the way, I should be mad at you. Ginny told

Lenni you've been making sure we wouldn't meet this whole time. What's that about?"

Jackson doesn't even look ashamed as he shrugs and tosses the file back on my desk. "Honestly, I know *you*, Tripp. And this is precisely what I was trying to avoid. According to Ginny, Lenni doesn't date. She hasn't the entire time they've been friends. And *you* have a habit of going all in too soon. Sure, the sex may be great, but don't let your feelings get in the way of this little display you two are going to be putting on. You're going to get your heart broken again."

"You weren't a relationship kind of guy, and look at you now. All it takes is the right person, Jackson."

He gets up and turns to leave. "Trust me. There are plenty of other women out there who will fulfill your sexual wants and needs. Don't demand a relationship from the first woman to suck your dick just the way you like it."

"What, like you did to the first woman who made you work for it?" I speak to his back as he continues walking.

"Don't say I didn't warn you," he singsongs.

As he leaves, my phone goes off with an incoming text message.

Viv

Plans tonight?

After she left me in Harry Winston yesterday, I did my best to stay away from my phone and keep myself busy, so I wouldn't feel the need to message or call her. Smiling at the fact that she cracked first, I wait a few minutes before replying.

No. Are you working?

Took the night off. Figured we could nail down our story before tomorrow morning.

Should I make a reservation somewhere?

That place on your fridge looked good. When will you be home? I'll just come there. BUT NO SEX! We need to figure out how to be around each other without wanting to rip each other's clothes off.

My lips pull up into a grin as I spin my chair around to face the windows. It's a good sign if she's seeking me out. An even better one if she wants to come back to my place.

Haha. Disappointing, but alright. How does seven sound?

Sounds perfect.

Jackson doesn't know what he's talking about. Lenni wants me just as badly as I want her. Eventually, we'll fuck each other out of our systems and then go our separate ways.

At least, as separate as we can, considering our best friends are getting married and we'll continue to be in each other's lives. Pushing the thought of her eventually dating someone else from my mind, I pull up another contract and keep myself busy until it's time to leave.

There's a knock on the door right at seven.

Since I picked up the food on the way home, I know it's Lenni, and ignore how my heart beats more rapidly in my chest with every step I take toward the entrance. She's smiling when I open the door, holding up a bottle of what looks like some type of white wine, the diamond on her finger glittering brightly and screaming *taken* to anyone who sees it.

A current of possessiveness flows through me. A savage, carnal feeling that is starting to become synonymous with her very presence, gnawing away at the bones that cage my heart.

"Honey, I'm home," she sings teasingly, breezing past me like she owns the place.

Shutting the door, I follow her to the kitchen, trying not to stare at the way her jeans are molded to her ass like a second skin. "Well, this Monday just got a whole lot better. How was your day?"

She shrugs as she places the bottle on the island and removes her jacket. "Eh, it was fine. I ran to Jersey for Carmela, then met Ginny at her office to go over paint samples for the new place. How was yours?"

Lenni moves around the kitchen like she owns it, remembering where everything is from the night she was here. Propping my elbow on the island, I rest my chin in my hand and watch as she finds the bottle opener and retrieves two glasses.

"Work was fine. Nothing exciting. I did have an interesting conversation with Jackson, though."

"Oh yeah? What did bossman want?" she asks as she places a topper in the bottle and puts it in the fridge before sitting next to me, clinking her glass against mine before taking a sip.

"He might have told me you said you weren't going to work the show on New Year's."

"Yeah, well. I didn't think it was a good idea. It's not a big deal." She gets back up to grab a plate, piling the beef and broccoli she requested onto it, along with some cold noodles. "What are you doing Wednesday night?"

"Is spending the evening on my back while you ride me into next year an option?"

She grins. "About that..."

I get up and start making myself a plate. "I don't think I like the sound of that."

"It's nothing crazy. I was just thinking. Since things between us can get a little...intense...what if we added some more people to the mix? You know, to diffuse the tension."

Freezing, fork halfway to my garlic prawns, I ask, "What do you mean?"

"What if we brought another couple into the room? She could service you, he could service m–"

"I don't want to watch another man touch you," I snap.

How many times do I have to say that?

"Okay, he could service you?" she suggests as she chews on a dumpling.

The look I give her is not an amused one, and she laughs. "Relax. It's just a mouth. How can you say you wouldn't like it unless you try it?"

Her words spark frustration in me, seeing as that they are similar to what I told Emily a year ago. Lost in thought and struggling with how to answer her, I jolt when she lays her hand over mine. "It was just a suggestion. I have to find a way to do my job still, Tripp. You can't always be in the room with me."

Suddenly, I understand why Jackson started slipping at work earlier this year after he met Ginny. This woman is making everything else seem blurry while she's the only thing I can see clearly. The feeling that worms its way around my chest whenever I think of her working at the club is going to end up working to my disadvantage—and I am going to push her away if I don't get a leash on it quickly.

"Emily left me on New Year's," I tell her softly. Suddenly, I'm not hungry anymore, and I abandon my plate to sit back down. Lenni sits beside me, rubbing my back gently as she waits for me to continue.

"I don't want to talk ill of her, because even though she cheated and lied about it, her reasoning isn't terrible."

"Cheating *is* terrible. Nothing excuses that. But carry on," Lenni says before taking a large drink from her wine glass.

"Yeah, well. Emily and I had a very *vanilla* sex life, you could say. I kind of understood it with the way we were raised. Emily was so prim and proper when I first met her, but I figured after being together that long, it would be okay to talk about exploring *other* sexual desires. You know?"

"Of course. You guys were together for a long time. You should be able to comfortably talk to your partner about those kinds of things without getting embarrassed," Lenni responds.

It doesn't go unnoticed how Lenni is being way more chill talking about this than Emily was. And we've barely known each other for a week and a half.

"That's what I assumed. So, when we were discussing what to get each other for Christmas, I told her I didn't want anything from her but wanted us to try some things out. At first, she seemed up for it...but then when it came time to actually do it, I could tell she was uncomfortable." Remembering that night is making me start to feel sick. But Lenni's hand is comforting as she continues to stroke my back.

"What did you ask her to do?"

It takes me a minute before I can respond. "I asked if she'd do anal."

I expect Lenni to laugh, but she doesn't. Instead, she nods. "Perfectly normal for a guy to ask that. Shouldn't be a big deal. If a woman isn't into it, she just has to say no. When you're with someone for a long time, you can still create sexual boundaries. You just have to be open and communicative with them, and *hopefully*, they respect that."

"See, and I did respect that. We tried, and she didn't like it, so we immediately stopped. But afterward, she wouldn't even look at me. It was like she thought I was a monster for wanting to do something *so depraved*." I hold my hand up in air quotes because those were Emily's words, not mine.

"Then she asked what else I wanted to try, and I asked if I could tie her up. There's something about having full control that I think would just be really hot. And she definitely wasn't up for that."

"These are all perfectly normal and healthy sexual desires, Tripp. I'm sorry if she made you feel like they weren't. Trust me, I've seen some shit. Emily wouldn't be able to handle one hour in Désirer if that kind of stuff freaks her out." Lenni pulls her plate over and takes a bite before reaching over to scoop some of my shrimp onto my plate.

Handing it to me, she motions to it. "Continue. And eat up. Because if there is shrimp left over after I eat my food, I *will* eat it, too."

A laugh escapes my lips as I dig into my dinner. "Anyway, I admitted I wanted to try a few more small things, and she told me I was gross. I told her she hadn't tried it before, so how could she say she didn't like it? Pot meet kettle, I guess. She became distant after that. Always making up excuses as to why she didn't want to have sex. Kept telling me that she didn't think she could fulfill my *weird fetishes*." I air quote again.

"Then she broke up with me on New Year's at the party my mother was throwing right as the countdown to midnight began. Said she didn't want to spend the rest of her life wondering if I'd go looking for what I wanted elsewhere. Eventually, I found out she'd been talking to someone for months before that all even went down. Then found out she started seeing him long before we even broke up."

"Oh god, Tripp. I'm so sorry."

She starts to pile her plate up again, and even though I know men shouldn't comment on a woman's eating habits, my big mouth says, "Jesus, woman, where do you put all of that."

I expect her to be mad, but a melancholy look crosses her face instead. "There wasn't a lot of food in my house growing up. I learned to survive on very little. When I came to the city, I had this idea that if I ate too much, people would think I had money and would try to rob me. It's silly, I know. But, when I was in my apartment, where I felt safe, I'd eat a lot so I wouldn't be very hungry the next day while I was looking for work. I'm just used to it I guess." She chews slowly as she eats, pushing the noodles around on her plate.

Suddenly, my sob story about Emily seems so fucking stupid. My heart feels like someone has shoved an icicle through it. I've never known what it's like to be hungry. I can't imagine what it was like to grow up that way.

She looks at me, smiling as she shakes her head and nudges my shoulder with hers. "Don't pity me. I survived. And I eat when I feel safe. So get used to it."

"Do you feel safe when you're with me, Valentina?" I ask softly.

Nodding, she locks eyes with me again. "Yeah. Yeah, I do."

An hour later, we're sprawled out on my giant modular sofa, watching *Pretty Woman*.

"I can't believe you'd never seen this movie before last week. It's such a classic," Lenni says as she finishes her third glass of wine and stretches out to set the cup in the holder a few cushions down.

When she settles back, we're shoulder to shoulder, feet extended out on the ottoman in front of us. "Well, now I've seen it enough times to recite it by heart."

She laughs and turns into me, placing her elbow on the back of the couch and twisting her fingers into her long waves. "This makes me very happy that you watched it. Everyone should see this movie at least once in their lifetime."

Her body is warm against mine, and I swear she's

deliberately trying to start something by the way she's trying to run her toes along my calf discreetly. I'm not even paying attention to the movie, using all my willpower to tell my dick to play it cool and not stand at attention.

"I really want to touch you right now," I tell her quietly. Out of my peripheral, I can see her head snap in my direction.

Slowly, I turn my head to meet her gaze. She swallows thickly, eyes wide as she stares at my lips. "Maybe this is a good time for me to go, then."

She gets up, but when she walks by, I loop my fingers into her pocket and pull her to me. Surprised, she trips, and her hands brace on my shoulders as I begin to unbutton her pants.

"Tripp, what are you doing? No sex, remember?" she admonishes, but there's no bite in her tone, and she makes no move to step back.

"We're not having sex. Now be a good girl and behave." I don't break eye contact with her as I drag her pants down, along with her underwear, before pulling her down. She lets out a little squeal, unable to freely move her legs with her pants around her ankles as I arrange her so that her top half is on the cushion next to me while her bottom half is in my lap, ass in the air.

"Tripp!"

The sound of my hand as it meets her ass cheek reverberates through the room, followed by a plea-sured cry leaving her lips. "Oh, fuck."

Sliding my hand over her ass and cupping her

from behind, I run three fingers through her drenched slit, watching as a trail of her arousal connects my fingers to her pussy as I pull them away. "See, Viv? We can't even be in the same room together without you turning into a dripping wet mess."

Using my other hand, I find her clit and start massaging it as I hold my fingers in front of her face to show her what I do to her. "All of this just for me."

She grabs my hand to pull my fingers into her mouth, swirling her tongue around them as she savors the flavor of herself. The action causes my dick to jump in my pants, begging to be unleashed.

"Fuck. I taste good on you," she moans.

"Do you? Let me try." Sliding my hand down to cradle her throat, I lift her by her neck, leaning down to smash my lips to hers. Pushing my fingers into her entrance, I start to pump leisurely.

Lenni uses her hands to hold her weight as we kiss. It's sloppy and wet as she traces my lips and tongue with her own, spreading what's left of her essence over my mouth. Her hips move against my hand, grinding down against my painfully hard cock.

I rub her clit roughly before pushing my fingers back inside her, alternating every time her hips pick up speed as she chases her orgasm. At some point, she must have kicked off her pants because they're gone when she arches her back and raises her ass further, legs curling behind her as she spreads them and wantonly rides my hand.

"Fuck me, Tripp. I want you inside me," she breathes out as she tries to get up.

Pulling my hand away from her completely, I smack her ass again and press down between her shoulder blades. She collapses beneath me and lets out a small cry when I plunge my fingers into her again. "No. You said no sex. So we're not going to have sex, Viv. You're gonna get off on my fingers like a good girl, and I'm going to cum all over this perfect pink pussy."

Reaching beneath her, I pull myself out of my sweats, cock thick and hard and rising to sink into her. She whines as she tries to lower herself onto me even though my fingers are still inside her, but I fist myself, pumping as I rub my head against her clit, watching as her wetness slowly coats it with every pass I make along her slit.

"Tripp, please," she begs.

The sound of it makes my balls tense. I pick up the pace of my fingers, fucking into her relentlessly as I continue to fuck my hand and run myself along her pussy. "You sound so fucking sweet when you beg, Valentina."

"Oh, fuck. Fuck, fuck, fuck!" Her hips jerk as she comes hard, pressing forward and trapping my cock between our bodies as she thrusts against me.

"Such a good fucking girl. Now lift your hips."

She does just as I come, thick white ropes firing out to hit her clit. I pull my fingers out and rub my mess against her, watching in a daze as I coat her skin. When I finish, I help her flip over to sit sideways in my lap.

Our tongues dance as my hands thread into her hair, and she wraps her arms around my neck. "I like that you make me feel safe," she says against my lips.

My heart soars at her admission. "I like that you feel safe with me."

This time, when she leaves, it's with a ten-minute makeout session on the sidewalk before I put her into a cab, and her promise that we'll see each other in the morning.

Lenni is late for breakfast. Her plan to keep my mother from thinking this is a long-term thing is definitely working if the look she's giving me from across the table is anything to go by.

"This is incredibly rude," Mom sighs, picking up her coffee to take a sip. She looks around the restaurant as if she's being stood up by a date and is embarrassed, patting her chignon self-consciously.

"She probably just got caught up in traffic," I offer, checking my phone to see if Lenni has responded to any of the messages I've sent her.

She hasn't.

A part of me is annoyed. Even if the plan is to break up eventually, I don't want my parents to have a bad impression of her.

"It's not that big of a deal, Margo. She's not that late," Pops chimes in as he checks his Rolex.

"I have a meeting with the committee for the Preservation of the Monarch Butterfly, Weylan. You know I don't like to be late for these things."

"Why don't we just order? Hopefully, she gets here soon. Tripp, that okay with you?" Pops asks.

Valentina's words from last night come back to me, about her eating when she feels safe, and I know that this isn't going to be one of those situations. Quickly, I message her again.

Where are you?

"Yeah, we can order, that's fine." Picking up the menu, I try to assume what she will want to eat while Mom waives our server over.

Mom and Pops order quickly, and when the man turns to me, I shake my head as I stare at the menu cluelessly. "I'll take the French toast, she'll have...I guess just bring her an egg white omelet and turkey bacon."

"You guess? You're engaged and don't know what she'll eat?" Mom snips.

Lenni's name flashes across my screen, showing up as Viv as she finally responds to my messages.

Relax. I'm not THAT late. About to walk in.

"Do you order the exact same thing every time

you eat, Mother? She's walking in now." No sooner than the words leave my mouth, Lenni appears around the corner, looking like a siren in a sea of flounder.

Breakfast at The Palm Court consists of hoity-toity families and women whose structured dresses and tightly pinned hairstyles scream *I think I'm better than you*. Cookie-cutter clones of my mother all swing their heads in Lenni's direction as she weaves her way through the tables dressed in a pair of bright pink stilettos, distressed skinny jeans, and a top that looks like lingerie underneath an over-sized black blazer. Her wavy hair is down and flipped to the side in a manner that looks like she just got done having sex, and I wish more than anything at this moment that I could parade her right back out to my town car so we can do precisely that.

Standing, I draw my parents' attention to the woman walking toward us. "Glad you could make it," I tell her before pressing my lips to hers and speaking lowly, "you're in so much trouble."

"I'm fifteen minutes late. What's the big deal?" she whispers against my lips before pulling away. "Margo! Weylan! So nice to finally meet you!"

Lenni drops her purse in the empty chair that's clearly meant for her, before rounding the table to pull my mother into a hug and then doing the same with pops. Mother seems affronted, but Pops beams at her as she sits beside me. "Nice to finally meet you, Valentina.

When Tripp told us about the engagement, we could hardly believe he hadn't brought you home yet."

"Well, things moved kind of quickly between us, we'll admit. We plan on having a long engagement, though, at least not worrying about the wedding until after Jackson and Ginny tie the knot," she says as she loops her arm through mine and lays her head on my shoulder.

"That's barely six weeks away. Surely you'll wait longer than that to start planning?" Mother asks.

Before I can say anything, Lenni answers, "Oh, I don't think so. Honestly, I don't need a big wedding. I'm thinking something small and intimate. Maybe just us, Jackson, and Ginny at the courthouse. Of course, you're more than welcome to come if you'd like."

I try to hide my smile at the look on my mom's face as she reaches for the strand of pearls she's wearing; her skin growing red as she struggles to keep her mouth shut at Lenni's exclamation.

When she finally speaks, she says, "Well, at least let us throw you an engagement party. That's the least you could do if you're not going to have a wedding."

The server chooses that moment to appear with our food, setting down my parents' dishes before ours.

"Oh, baby, you got me French toast. Thank you!" Lenni gushes as she switches our plates.

Pops laughs as she asks the server to bring her a

mimosa. "Got yourself a handful here, don't you, Son?"

"Oh, he has no idea. And, Margo, if you'd like to throw us an engagement party, we'd love that. Wouldn't we, babe?" Lenni takes a large bite of my French toast as I stare down at the bland omelet I ordered her.

Picking up a piece of turkey bacon, I bite the end off and look up to find myself trapped in my mother's steel gaze. She's completely ignoring her frittata and watching Lenni's and my interaction like a scientist observing a mouse in a maze.

"Yes, Mom. We would love that." My arm winds around the back of Lenni's chair as she happily eats her food and pulls Pops into a conversation about his work. It was never a question of whether or not she'd be able to charm him.

Fooling Mom, however, looks like it will be harder than I thought.

"Well, I think that went well." Lenni sips her mimosa, relaxing in her chair after my parents leave.

"You call that well?"

"I told you, I wasn't aiming for her to like me. I thought the no big wedding was genius, too. Nothing to get too involved in, you know? I couldn't really read her, though. Like, she didn't want us to plan a wedding but then was visibly distressed when I said

I didn't want one. She's gonna be tougher than I thought," she voices my earlier thoughts.

Her attitude is different than it was when she left my place last night. She's acting more flippant—colder toward our situation than she's been. The entire morning, she made small talk with my parents cheerfully, but the moment they left, it was almost as if the mask she wore for them slipped off immediately.

"Are you okay?"

Her eyebrows knit together as she pushes her plate away and finishes the rest of her second mimosa. "Of course, why wouldn't I be?"

"I don't know. You seem…different…than yesterday." Now that I'm getting a chance to actually examine her, she looks tired. "Did you work at the club after you left my place last night?"

"No," she answers immediately, rubbing at her eye carefully. "I'm just not used to mornings and having to be so fake. I'm tired, that's all."

Reaching across the table, I motion for her hand, which she reluctantly gives me. "Have I told you how much I appreciate you doing this?"

A small smile turns her lips up as she squeezes my hand. "I know you do. If you're not verbally telling me, you're showing your appreciation in other ways."

Her tone travels straight to my cock. "Let me give you a ride home before I go to the office. I'll show you how grateful I am again."

She pulls her hand out of mine as she laughs. "It's

okay. I think I'm going to go see Ginny. Tomorrow night, though, I booked us a room at Désirer. I have something for you."

"Aww, honey, you got me a New Year's Eve gift?"

"You bet I did. And you better bring your A-game. I'm going to make sure all your negative feelings about New Year's are forgotten. After tomorrow night, the holiday won't remind you of Emily leaving you, but it will certainly be one to remember."

Lenni's feline grin sends a rush of excitement through me. I'm looking forward to whatever she has planned, as long as she's involved. "You're spoiling me. That's supposed to be my job."

Her next words, however, are quite sobering. "You're paying me, Tripp. And I told you, it's my job to make the men I fuck feel special."

T he Grand Room glimmers with touches of sparkles dusting nearly every surface. The Temptangels' wings are coated with a fine layer of shimmering powder, and our bodies are painted with edible glitter. Women walk around in lingerie sets that dazzle like a Taylor Swift costume, while the men wear pants that look like they were made from a disco ball.

It isn't my first New Year's party at Désirer, but it is the first time I'm not participating in the show that starts soon.

My nerves are jittery. Crackling with anticipation for what's to come tonight—for what I've set up for Tripp.

I'm hoping that he's open to exploring something new. Something that might help him differentiate what is real and what isn't between us.

He keeps saying he doesn't want to watch another man touch me, but he has to understand I'm *not* his. Even if I said I would be while we carried on this charade for his parents, in *here*, at Désirer, I can't be, and I can't quit.

The money is too important.

Besides, we're getting too comfortable with each other.

It would be easy to fall into a relationship with him. And *that* isn't about the money.

It's just about *him*.

Knowing my luck, though, trouble will find me the moment I decide to try being happy for once, and I don't want Tripp dragged into my mess.

"I love that I can pick you out of the crowd, even with the wings and mask. You have no idea how pleased I am that I know your body intimately enough to do that." Tripp speaks lowly into my ear as he appears out of thin air, wrapping an arm around my waist and pulling me back into him.

Think of Prince Charming, and he shall appear.

"You're going to get glitter all over yourself." I laugh.

I'm supposed to maintain an illusion of availability at all times, and technically, Tripp could get in trouble for grabbing me so brazenly without asking first.

But I suppose it's okay to break the rules a little since we're such good friends with the bosses.

Tripp nuzzles my neck, dragging his nose up my skin to nip my earlobe as his fingers toy with the bottom of my lacy, brief-style underwear. "As long as it's coming from your body, I don't care. It's been days since I've been inside you. Is my gift getting to peel this little number off you with my teeth?"

A shiver of excitement shudders through me. His way with words tangles my senses in a sweet, cotton candy ball of fluff that I want to keep wrapping myself in while he verbally licks the spun sugar from my skin.

Sweet, but you know it will give you a stomachache the more you indulge.

"No, but you'll definitely get to see me out of it. Come on." Grabbing his hand, I lead him to the Desires wing.

Once a month, the club hosts a show that is basically a giant orgy for anyone who wants to join. It's always held in the back end of the wing, but the front part still has rooms available for those who don't want to join or watch the show, but want to have their fun privately.

The doors aren't open for the crowd yet, so I let my guard know we're ready to go to our room. As he walks us down the hall, I tell him, "Give us ten minutes, then let the others in, please."

"You got it, Miss Bianca."

"Others?" Tripp asks, tensing at my side.

I wait until the door shuts behind us to explain myself. "Remember, you can always say no if you don't want to go through with anything, but will you at least try?"

"That depends. What is it you've set up?" Tripp's tone is no longer playful. He sounds more fearful than anything.

Stepping forward, I raise my hands to unbutton his white dress shirt. His mask tonight reminds me of the one Antonio Banderas wears in *Zorro*, plain black and tied simply around his swept-back curls.

"Another couple is going to join us in a few minutes. I want you to be open-minded. I'm going to throw a lot at you in a moment. Remember what we talked about the other night, though? Don't knock it till you try it, right?"

Next, my fingers work his belt buckle and I pull it from his waist in one fell swoop. "You said you wanted to tie Emily up, that you liked the idea of being in control. Tonight, I'm going to tie you up. I'm going to be the one in control. You should never ask your partner to do something you're unwilling to do."

Pushing his chest lightly, I walk him backward to the bed until the back of his legs hit the edge, and he falls into a sitting position. I step between his knees, threading one hand in his hair while the other cradles his jaw so I can pull his head back to kiss him deeply, wasting no time in sinking my tongue into his mouth to caress his.

His hands find my hips before they roam around to squeeze my butt. When I pull my lips away, he nods scarcely. "I trust you."

"If you get uncomfortable, just tell me, okay? Don't do it because you think it's what I want. I'm okay with whatever you decide. I'm just presenting a different view on things. Now, get comfortable against the pillows."

As I cross the room to grab a pair of handcuffs and a condom from the dresser drawer, he says, "It makes sense. What you said about not asking your partner to do something you're not willing to do. I never really thought about it that way before."

When I return, Tripp willingly lifts his arms behind his head so I can shackle him to the headboard. He shifts his hips as I straddle him, biting at one of my nipples through my lace underwire top as I lean over him and secure his wrists.

Our attention is pulled to the door as it opens, and a woman's voice rings out, "Oh! It seems like you two have already started on the fun."

The woman is an Angel, and we've done shared work like this before. She's petite, standing at five-two, with a platinum blonde pixie and a little nose that makes her look like a fairy. The man she's brought is tall with broad shoulders and dark hair. He's wearing silk pajama pants and nothing else, looking at me like he's won the lottery.

"Well, we really lucked out tonight, didn't we, my man?" he asks Tripp.

I can hear Tripp's visible gulp before he whispers, "Is he going to touch you?"

"*She's* going to touch you. Aren't you, Galadriel?" Shuffling back, I get off the bed and beckon her toward me. Tripp watches as she appears by my side, holding hands with the other man.

"Still what we discussed?" she asks me as she looks Tripp over like he's a steak and she's a hungry dog.

"As long as he says it's okay, we stop the moment he says to stop."

Galadriel drops the man's hand, takes off her robe, and slowly gets on the bed, her gold crotchless lingerie glittering as she moves. She motions to his pants. "Hi, there. May I?"

Tripp's body is tight with tension as he gives her a sharp nod, watching with narrowed eyes as she unbuttons his pants and tugs them down slightly to pull out his semi-hard cock. He sucks in a sharp breath as she lets out a little tinkling giggle.

Turning my head to look at the man who's watching them with interest, I ask him, "What should I call you, handsome?"

His eyes move to me, trailing down my body as he responds, "Diego. Please tell me I get to fuck you."

"No," Tripp's voice snaps. "You don't get to fuck her."

"Oooh, we have a possessive one here, don't we, Bianca?" Galadriel sings out as she strokes him. "Don't worry, big boy, she's going to ride his face while he fucks me."

"Thank you." Diego kisses his knuckles before holding them up to the ceiling.

"Here, let me help you," I croon while grabbing the condom.

Tripp is barely paying attention to the pretty blonde who is kissing her way down his body to settle on her stomach between his legs. His attention is focused on me as I dip my finger below Diego's waistband and begin to pull his pants down, his short, fat dick springing free.

I quickly put the condom on him as he watches like a high schooler who just got touched sexually for the first time. "Get on the bed and let her reverse cowgirl you."

"I'm gonna suck your cock now, big boy. That okay with you?" she asks Tripp.

My attention pulls to his face as Galadriel speaks to him. He's looking at her with a mix of rage and lust on his beautiful features. Somehow, it makes them look sharper, like a Greek statue.

He nods as she lowers her mouth to him, eyes snapping to mine as she wraps her pouty lips around his head. A jingling sound rings out as he pulls his wrists, hips bucking slightly at the contact.

Diego spreads his legs on either side of Tripp as he faces them and helps Galadriel lift her hips to sink down onto him. She moans around Tripp's cock, causing him to throw his head back and curse.

"Now get up here and ride my face. I wanna know if your pussy tastes as good as you look," Diego commands me.

"It's better," Tripp says through clenched teeth.

Galadriel is making sloppy, wet noises as she bobs her head and takes him as deep as she can while she fucks Diego at the same time. My nipples pucker as I reach for the band of my lace shorts and slowly pull them down my legs.

I'm already wet as I watch the three of them move together. "Keep your eyes on me, Ken."

Tripp's eyes snap to mine, watching as I climb on the bed and position myself over Diego's head. His hands curl around my thighs, pulling me down until his tongue sinks into my center and his lips close around my clit. He makes a moaning sound as he licks me, running his hands up my stomach to cup my breasts.

"Does she feel good?" I ask Tripp breathlessly.

Diego pulls the cups of my bra down and pinches a nipple as he lightly nibbles at my sensitive bundle of nerves, causing my hips to jerk as I let out a startled yelp. He suckles at me, flicking his tongue at varying speeds as he makes contented sounds against my wet flesh.

"Does *he* feel good?" Tripp asks in a biting tone.

"He feels very good," I lilt as I begin to ride Diego's face.

Tripp starts to move his hips, fucking Galadriel's face the best he can with his hands restrained. She's making mollifying sounds against him, rubbing her fingers in circles on his thighs in an attempt to soothe his palpable anger.

The sound of Diego pounding into her fills the air as they both orally please us. "How does she feel?" I ask him again.

"Not like you," he finally relents.

Leaning forward slightly, I brace myself on Diego's chest. "I've never sucked your cock before."

"Yeah, we'll have to rectify that soon."

"Oh yeah? Does this make you want to punish me? Have I not been a good girl setting this up?"

Diego lets out a groan beneath me as he grabs Galadriel's hips and starts to fuck her faster while his tongue picks up speed. I grind my pussy against his mouth, nails scraping his skin as I chase my release.

"Yes. I'm going to tie you up and see how you like it. You haven't been a good girl tonight. Remember, I only reward you if you've been good."

Galadriel bobs her head on his length faster, her hips shuddering against Diego as she cries out around Tripp's cock. My eyes sink to where Diego is twitching inside her, preparing to come but trying to get me off before he does.

Tripp parrots my earlier words. "Keep your eyes on me. I want to watch you come on his tongue."

I do as he says, and he lets out a groan, biting his lip as he comes. His arms pull on the handcuffs as he thrusts his hips into Galadriel's face while she swallows his cum. It's enough to rip my orgasm from me, and I claw at Diego's chest as I climax, which causes him to let go and spill himself into the blonde finally.

Boneless, I shift off his face and lay on my side, a mixture of sweat and glitter glistening on each of our bodies. After Galadriel and Diego untangle themselves, she turns around so they can share a kiss; their tongues a slippery, wet dance as they combine mine and Tripp's cum in their mouths. As they get off the bed, I pull myself into Tripp's side and cradle his cheek, guiding his face down so I can kiss him.

"Get these handcuffs off me," he demands when I pull back. He sounds angry, and I wonder if perhaps I pushed him too far.

"Thank you for letting us join you guys. Let's do it again sometime," Galadriel sings out as she and Diego make their way out of the room, arms wrapped around each other.

As soon as the door closes, Tripp pulls at the handcuffs. "Now, Valentina."

"Ooh. Mr. Tough Guy. I didn't hear you telling anyone to stop. Except, you know, when Diego asked to fuck me. You looked like you enjoyed yourself." My voice is soft in an attempt to soothe his anger.

The moment he's free of his restraints, he rolls me over, grabs the handcuffs, and locks my wrists to the headboard. "Hey! What are you doing?"

He doesn't answer me as he gets up and retrieves a condom. When he turns back to the bed, I'm surprised to see that he's already hard again as he rolls the condom down his shaft. His pants are still on, and he makes no effort to remove them as he climbs on the bed again and settles between my legs, burying himself inside me until our pelvic bones press together.

"I fucking hated every moment of that," he grits out as he fucks me hard. Wrapping my legs around his waist, I pull him into me with every punishing drive of his hips. Even though I already came, I'm still wet, and his cock slides against my walls with the intense pressure of being so full.

"You looked like you enjoyed yourself to me," I repeat. His answer is a particularly hard thrust, and my tongue curls in my mouth as my lips turn up in a smile. "If this is my punishment, I'll have to be bad more often."

"Don't put me through that again. I don't want to see someone else touch you," he pleads, voice cracking.

The sound of the headboard banging against the wall picks up as he screws his eyes shut. With every press of his hips, he bumps against my clit, sending electric tingles down my spine that make my toes curl.

"Look at me," I urge.

The speakers in the room crackle before the countdown to midnight begins.

"Ten…Nine…"

Our eyes lock as his hips slow. Instead of punishing thrusts, his pace changes to long, deep strokes, rubbing against all the right spots.

"You make me fucking crazy, Viv. I've never felt like this before."

"Eight…Seven…Six…"

"It's just because we're sexually compatible," I say softly, even though I feel what he's feeling, too.

I don't want to give him up when this is all over.

But I can't be with him.

"Five…Four…Three…"

"I'll never think of anything other than this on this night from now on. Thank you for making it the best possible way to start a new year."

"Two…"

Our lips melt together before the countdown hits zero. The speakers erupt with chaos—cheers and confetti poppers and people screaming *Happy New Year*—all blending with the sounds we make as we come together.

Tripp stays buried inside me as he releases my hands, tangling his fingers in my hair while we kiss. Everything about the moment feels as if we're right where we belong.

Together.

And for a single fleeting moment, I wonder if there's any way to make this thing between us work.

"Should I be worried about you?" Carmela asks as I close my locker door.

Turning, I see her standing behind me, arms crossed over her glitter-clad chest. She's wearing high-waisted dress pants in a shimmery black and a sequined crop top with thick straps that she picked up at Dolce and Gabbana when we went shopping last week.

Carmela Lane is just like me—only not. She has a secret past, too. The only difference between us is that she had a great life growing up, yet she chooses to live the life she does. Tangled in the wicked webs of men in power and constantly needing to stay a step ahead of them.

"Why would you need to be worried about me?"

"I think you know why, Len. Dropping out of the show? No longer taking Desires clients unless a particular man is with you? Remember how concerned you were about Ginny when she and Jackson started spending so much time together? I know the guy is his best friend, and Jackson said he can be a little intense."

"There's nothing to worry about. I'm fine. We just have a situation we're dealing with for a little while, then things will go back to normal. It's not a big deal." Shrugging, I move to walk around her, but she blocks my path.

"Let me be very clear, Len. I love you like a sister, and I will support you no matter what path you decide to take. You aren't tied to this club; you know that, right? I only ask if I should be worried because for as long as I've known you, all you've cared about is making money and keeping clients happy. But if you've found someone that makes *you* happy…as long as you're careful, I'm happy for you."

I know her words come from a good place. I was a mess when she found me in a strip club not long after I moved to the city. Luckily, I hadn't started sleeping with the clients there yet, and she scooped me up and gave me a job at Decadence before training me to work at Désirer.

Carmela is like my unofficial big sister; if she notices something is up, something usually is.

Unexpected tears sting my eyes, and instantly, she's pulling me into her arms. "Oh, Len. What is it?"

"I really like him. We don't even really know each other. All of our encounters end with us having sex or being sexual, so I don't know if we're just really good together physically or if there's actually some-thing there, Cara. All I know is that I can't sleep with clients anymore without feeling sick to my stomach. He *is* intense. It scares me. I feel like I could drown in him and be happy while I suffocate."

Her hands run up and down my back as she chuckles quietly into my ear. "Sounds like something more than just being physically compatible. You've never been in love, Len. But it seems like you may be on your way."

"No." I shake my head on her shoulder. "That's impossible. People don't fall in love that fast. They fall in lust, not love. You taught me that."

Pulling away, I wipe my tears as she tucks my hair behind my ears and cups my cheeks. "Look at how the *great love of my life* turned out. I don't have all the answers, Valentina. Most men are too intimi-dated to approach me, let alone stick around to get to know me. Plus...you know. My point is, I'm not all-knowing. There is nothing wrong with falling in love."

"Exactly. Look at what happened to you. Men like *him* can't date women like me. You *know* that."

"It isn't the same. Not by a long shot." She lets go of my cheeks and grabs my hand, lifting it to show me the sparkling diamond on my ring finger. "This could be real, Len. And it's something you deserve. So why not give it a chance?"

"Because I don't want him to get hurt. And I don't want to get hurt, either."

She laughs and pulls me in for another hug as she

groans into my ear. "Ah, but that's the thing, Len. The men with money can usually make all your problems go away. I know that doesn't sound very romantic, but just remember that Snow White, Cinderella, and Sleeping Beauty were all saved by rich men with loads of money who took care of their problems. And they all lived happily ever after. Sometimes, you just need to swallow your pride."

We walk out of the changing room together, parting ways as she goes to her office, and I head to one of the exits to have security call me a cab. Her words stick with me the whole ride home.

As I walk into my apartment, my phone dings with an incoming message. Smiling, I dig through my purse to grab it, assuming it's Tripp asking if I've made it home yet.

My smile quickly vanishes when I see that it's not.

> He will find you. When he does, he will kill you, and I will be free.

Valentina doesn't respond to my messages on Thursday or Friday morning.

Whenever I pick up the phone to call her, I pause and end up not going through with it. She makes me feel like the car we're driving has lost its brakes, and we're waiting for the inevitable crash. This has always been one of my biggest problems regarding women.

I fall fast, and I fall hard.

Valentina has taken every moment to remind me that there can't be anything real between us, yet she's taken steps to make me feel better about our arrangement.

Still, I can't help but wonder what she does on the nights I don't go to Désirer. Is she being truthful and really not sleeping with other men?

Can I trust her?

I'm paying her enough to help me carry out the lie she created, and since she's Ginny's best friend, I would really like to think she has good intentions and isn't going to fuck me over.

She hasn't taken a dime yet.

Powering down my computer at the office, I'm surprised to see her number flash across my phone screen as if my thoughts summoned her.

"Hello?"

"Your mother got my number. So much for not digging into my life."

"Hi to you too, Viv."

"We're expected for dinner at your parents' house tomorrow."

"Mom hasn't said a word to me about it."

Her sigh is audibly aggravated. "She wants to talk about the engagement party. Can't we just do dinner in town?"

My phone dings as a message comes in from my mother.

> Your father and I expect you for dinner tomorrow night at our place. I already extended an invitation to Valentina. I'm making pot roast.

"How do you feel about pot roast? It's Mom's specialty." I keep my tone light to balance out Lenni's annoyance.

"Tripp, I really don't want to go. This weekend… it's not a good time."

My hackles rise. Earlier thoughts of whether she's being faithful to our agreement or not resurfacing in an instant. "Viv, this is kind of part of the deal."

"I don't want to!" Her tone is whiny and hysteric, and though we haven't known each other long, I know it's not *her*.

"Hey, what's going on? Are you okay?" Concern bleeds through me. Rising to my feet, I pack my stuff up, the intention of going to her place at the forefront of my mind when I stop and realize I have no idea where she lives.

"It's shark week," she grumbles.

Huh?

"Shark Week? No, that's in the summer." I would know. I love Shark Week.

"Stupid man. Shark week? Carrie? Bloody Mary? The Red Wedding? THAT TIME OF THE MONTH!" By the time she's finished yelling, I'm holding the phone nearly a foot from my ear.

"I sympathize with you and promise to keep her on a tight leash. Wouldn't a home-cooked meal be nice, though? You don't even have to be polite if you don't want to be. We can blame it on *shark week*. I promise to fully support whatever attitude you want to bring."

"My emotions are all over the place this month, and day two, which is tomorrow, is usually the worst. Ergo, not the best time to deal with your mom." She lets out a big sigh. "But a home-cooked meal *does* sound nice."

"Great! You didn't answer me before. How do you feel about pot roast?" Switching off the light to my office, I realize the cubicles are all empty. I'm one of the last people working tonight...again. Everyone else has somewhere to be or something to do on a Friday night, and here I am, arguing with my fake-fiancée about periods and pot roast.

"I have a love-hate relationship with pot roast. I love the way it tastes, but I hate how fatty it is. It wouldn't taste the way it does without the fat, but it's a texture thing. It bothers me. Slimy, chewy, gross pieces that completely disturb the meaty burst of flavor, and then you have to interrupt your bite to fish out a gross blob of sludgy goo from your mouth. But it's still attached to good roasty bits, so then you have to attempt to separate them with your tongue and your fingers, and the whole thing becomes a mess." She takes a deep breath, filling her lungs with air after her run-on sentence. It reminds me a lot of myself when discussing something I love or hate.

"Ooookay. So, no pot roast for you." I laugh.

"No, I didn't say that. I love pot roast," she sputters.

"So, I'll pick you up tomorrow at four?"

Silence.

I watch the numbers on the elevator ascend while I wait for her to answer, pulling the phone away to check that she hasn't hung up. "Viv?"

"I'll be at your place at four."

As much as it makes me curious why she wouldn't want me to see where she lives, I curb my inquisitive tendencies and nod even though she can't see it. "Alright, I'll see you tomorrow."

"See you then." She sounds reluctant, but I don't push my luck and say anything that can be viewed as being *too* positive. Women don't like that during that time of the month if they are in a bad mood.

When I reach street level, the night air holds that wet, cold chill that promises snow soon. The kind that makes you want to curl up in front of the fire with your loved one and a stiff drink, just spending time together while you watch the flakes drift down.

It was one of my favorite things to do in the winter—when Emily and I were together, and I had someone to cuddle up with.

"Home, sir?" my driver interrupts my thoughts as he opens the car door for me.

"One stop, then home. The soon-to-be Mrs. isn't feeling that well."

I know I need to pump the brakes on my eagerness for her to be mine for real, but *fake* fiancée or not, I want Lenni to know she can rely on me.

"You got all of this for me?" Lenni asks with tears in her eyes as she holds a heating pad.

"I didn't know what you'd prefer, so I figured I'd just get you what I could think of. We can pack it up in the car, and I'll help you bring it inside when I take you home after dinner. If you need something else, we can stop somewhere—"

She cuts me off with her lips on mine, throwing her arms around my neck and pulling me down so she's not stretched up on her tiptoes. "Thank you,

Tripp. I think this is the nicest thing a man has ever done for me."

If getting a heating pad and some chocolate ice cream is the nicest thing a man has done for her, she's in for a wild ride if she lets me date her the way I want to. "It's not that big of a deal, Viv."

Winding my arms around her, my heart warms as she lays her head on my chest and squeezes me tight. "It is to me."

"Remember you said that later. I know you said you're emotional right now, but I want the record to show that I did something nice for you."

"You're always doing nice things for me," she murmurs, sounding like she's on the brink of tears.

Stifling my laugh, I pull her back and cock a head toward the door. "Come on. We better get on the road. I'm driving, but I'll let you pick the music. You look beautiful, by the way, if I haven't told you already."

The smile she gives me takes my breath away. It's genuine, her full, mauve-painted lips curving up to show her perfect pearly whites. "You haven't, but thank you."

Her long dress flows around her ankles as we walk, her heeled boots high enough that the hem doesn't drag on the ground. It's black with a red and orange flower pattern and short sleeves that flutter around her biceps. It brings out the tan on her skin and the honey in her eyes, and it makes me wish we weren't going anywhere but my bedroom.

My hand doesn't leave the small of her back the

entire way down to the parking garage, my fingers itching to squeeze her skin while I bury my nose in her hair to inhale her scent. It's only been two and a half days, and I feel like my cock is beginning to wither up and die without her engulfing my senses.

Lenni connects her phone to the car system before we take off. Briefly, I realize we left all of her period stuff upstairs, but I selfishly keep quiet in hopes I can get her to stay a while after dinner. "What are we listening to?"

"My shark week mix. I warn you now: it's going to be an hour of Alanis Morissette, Taylor Swift, and Shania Twain."

"Shania Twain is my jam." Picking her hand up, I interlace our fingers and kiss her knuckles. "Let's go, girls."

The drive to my parents' feels like it passes too quickly. Lenni and I spend the time singing songs—poorly, I might add, neither of us can carry a tune to save our lives—and trading random facts about pop celebrities.

"I feel like we're driving through the English countryside right now. What are these houses? It's like something straight out of *Downton Abbey*," Lenni exclaims, hands pressed against the window as we drive through the ivy-draped colonial-style homes in my parents' neighborhood.

"Yeah, Mom and Pops never wanted to live in the city. Mom likes the glitz and glamor, but she's also awfully particular about her style and thinks she needs a mini mansion even though it is just us three. Although I live in the city, so obviously, it's just them now. Pops likes how quiet it is, and that there's a golf course right down the road."

"I can't believe you grew up here." Lenni's voice is quiet and reflective.

"You know, you haven't told me where you're from."

She snorts and mutters, "A little town called nowhere."

"Is that actually a city, or are you just being a smartass?"

Her answering grin tells me it's the latter.

I can feel her tense as I pull into the driveway, her arm pressed against mine on the center console going rigid. "I already messaged my mom and told her she better be on her best behavior."

"Just remember, my goal is to make her think I won't last," she reminds me sternly.

"Trust me, Valentina, I haven't forgotten." My response is dry, and I see her look at me from my peripheral.

Pops meets us at the door with open arms. "Glad you guys made it. We were getting a little worried. I know the roads are icy. Valentina, it's good to see you again."

Lenni's smile is warm and genuine as they share a hug. "Hi, Dad. Can I call you Dad? I didn't have a dad growing up. This is nice. Thank you for having us for dinner."

My heart skips a beat at her admission, the smile on Pops' face faltering before he catches himself and nods. "Sure, I don't see why not."

His eyebrows raise questioningly toward me as he ushers her inside. It's news to me that she didn't have a dad growing up. We haven't spoken much about our pasts besides what happened with Emily. Every time we've had a serious conversation, it's been about getting the facts of our fabricated story straight so we don't look like complete liars when people ask us about *our story*.

"Mmmm, something smells delicious. Baby, I wasn't even thinking. We should have brought a bottle of wine," Lenni coos as she looks around wide-eyed.

I notice she's rubbing her abdomen absentmindedly, right over her scar. Unfortunately, Pops sees it too, and before he can get the wrong idea, I ask, "Babe, did you want me to grab you some ibuprofen? I know you said your cramps are bad this month."

Lenni's head snaps in my direction, eyes narrowed, probably ready to chastise me for bringing up shark week in front of Pops. As soon as she sees my face, I jerk my head in his direction, and her eyes widen as she looks down at where her hand rests on her abdomen.

"Oh! Yes, please. Thank you so much, babe. Goodness, you look like you're about to have a heart attack, Dad. Don't worry. No little Kennedys for us, yet."

Yet.

It's not real, but hearing her say it makes me regret not saving every single birthday, shooting star, and 11:11 wish to make it a reality.

Lenni wraps her arm through Pops'. "Care to give me a tour of your lovely home?"

"Yes, of course! Tripp, you know where the medicine cabinet is, and say hello to your mother before she throws a fit."

I watch them go, smiling as he launches into the house's history while Lenni listens raptly. As they turn the corner, I head into the kitchen, smiling as my mother comes into view. She reminds me of the fifties era housewives with their perfectly styled hair and heels as they cook.

"Hi, Mom." I wait to hug her since she's plating the roast and walk over to the medicine cabinet instead, making a show of grabbing Lenni pain meds. "This is my gentle reminder to be kind to Valentina tonight. She's not feeling well and came anyway."

Mom sets down the plate of roast and turns to me. "What do you mean she's not feeling well? Is she contagious? Did you bring her here knowing she was sick?"

"What? No. She's got cramps. Relax."

"Don't tell your mother to relax. This is my house." She goes back to plating dinner with a roll of her eyes and a shake of her head. Margo Kennedy may intimidate the shit out of a lot of people, but behind the closed doors of this house, she's as warm and kind as any other regular mom.

I'm just hoping that extends to Lenni.

"Hi, Margo! Thank you so much for inviting us for dinner!" Lenni rushes over to hug her when she and Pops come back from their tour. Her tone is saccharine sweet, and not fooling anyone. "Here, let me help you."

"No, no. Tripp says you aren't feeling that well. Go on and have a seat." Points to Mom for being cordial.

Placing my hand on the small of her back, I guide Lenni to the dining room as Pops uncorks a bottle of cab and exchanges whispers with Mom that I can't make out. While they're distracted, I lean into Lenni and whisper, "You don't have to overdo it with the syrup."

"Whatever do you mean?" she lilts, batting her eyelashes and giving me an innocent glance.

"You're laying it on thick enough to drown pancakes."

She sits as I pull her chair out for her and take my seat next to her. "You know why—"

"Yes, I know why you're doing it. But do you think that maybe, for the rest of tonight, you can just *be*?"

Lenni briefly regards me, something I can't decipher swimming in her pools of chocolate honey, before she reaches for my hand and nods. "Okay."

"I hope you're hungry. We have a lot to discuss

about the party," Mom says as she brings the serving dish to the table. Pops follows her and pours a little wine into everyone's glass as she keeps talking while she dishes up the plates.

"I'm thinking we need to have it before Jackson and Ginny's wedding. Let's say, two weeks? That's not much time, but I can pull it off. The event space where we had my birthday is a wonderful location. Central to everyone who will be attending, and so pretty. Valentina, do you have a color preference? Flower options? Any allergies I should know about? I would have asked Tripp, but I didn't think he'd know, seeing as how you two rushed the engagement."

Inwardly, I groan. *Then why are you rushing an engagement party, Mother?*

Sneaking a glance under the guise of getting a piece of bread, I see Lenni looking down at her lap, wringing her fingers together in a way that looks like she's counting them silently.

I'm about to respond for her when her head snaps up, and she grabs her fork to take a bite of a carrot. "No allergies. I don't really care about flowers, honestly. Or colors. Why don't you just do whatever you think is best, Margo?"

She smiles at Mom over the table before turning her attention to Pops. "Tripp says you like to golf. I've always wanted to learn. Maybe you could teach me?"

Mom visibly bristles at being dismissed, while Pops nearly chokes on his wine at his sudden misfortune of being trapped between the two women. "Tripp is a great golfer. You should teach her, Son."

"So you have absolutely nothing to contribute to your own engagement party? Most women have been dreaming about their wedding since they were little girls," Mom interrupts.

Lenni takes a bite of roast, chewing slowly while they lock eyes. As she starts to say something, she coughs, then makes a show of curling her hand into a fist and gently beating her chest. "Sorry, it's a little dry," she wheezes, reaching for her wine.

Mom's fork clatters to her plate. "Dry? I don't make *dry* roast."

Sounds of Lenni continuously clearing her throat echo throughout the dining room as she gasps between coughs. "Hey, at least it's not fatty. I hate fatty roast."

Pops and I share a knowing look, holding our glasses up to each other before draining our wine. "I think I might need something stronger," I mutter under my breath.

The rest of dinner is just as tense. Lenni is more agreeable with her answers, but Mom's questions have become snippy and, at times, downright mean.

"What exactly is it you do for work?" she asks as Pops clears the table.

"Oh, I work with my friend Ginny. She's opening a new family center soon, and I'll be doing adminis-trative work for her." Lenni reaches for my hand beneath the table and squeezes it softly. Our prearranged sign that she's had enough and wants to leave.

"So, you're a *secretary*?" Mom's tone is distasteful.

Clucking my tongue, I wag a finger at her. "Don't let Stacey hear you talking like that about her job title now, Mother." Turning to Lenni, I explain, "Stacey is Jackson's secretary. Her job is *not* easy. I admire anyone in that line of work."

"Well, that won't do once you're married. Especially not when you begin to have children."

Pops groans and scrubs his face as he sits back in his seat. "Margo, give it a rest tonight, will you?"

"I actually can't have children. So, any kids we have will be adopted, and the older children have more trouble finding homes, so I think I'd like to start there. They'll be in school, and the center will have after-school programs," Lenni snaps.

She drops my hand and places her linen napkin on the table. "If you'll excuse me, I need to use the restroom."

"Of course, it's down the hall and to the right," Pops offers remorsefully.

"Thank you, Weylan. I remember."

If looks could kill, Mom would be severely injured by the daggers I glare at her. "Seriously, Mother?"

"Did you know she can't have kids?" Mom asks softly, looking like Lenni's outburst truly bothered her. I know my mom, though, and she probably feels worse about pushing her to that point than she does at hearing we won't be giving her any hypothetical biological grandchildren.

"Tripp, why don't you go check on her?" Pops gently orders, fixing Mom with a hard stare.

Tossing my napkin on the table, I scoot my chair back roughly, relishing when Mom winces as it squeaks against the polished mahogany floor. Quickly, I make my way down the hall to the half bathroom and gently knock on the door.

"Viv? You okay?"

Through the heavy wood door, I can hear her sniffling before she calls out, "I'm fine."

Lowering my hand to the doorknob, I turn it slightly to find it unlocked and duck into the bathroom with her.

"Hey! What are you doing?" she cries out as I spin to face away from her.

"I'm sorry if you needed to use the bathroom. I just wanted to check on you, and it sounded like you were crying."

"I'm not using the bathroom. I just needed a break. Plus, my cramps are starting up again. I want a high dose of pain meds and to curl up with that tub of ice cream you got."

Looking over my shoulder, I see her sitting on the toilet, hunched over with her arms wrapped around her waist. When I turn to face her, she stands. "Can we just go?"

"Yeah, we can go." Stepping toward her, I grab her waist and press her against the vanity, spreading my other hand over her abdomen.

"What are you doing, Tripp?" Her hands brace on my forearms, head tilting back, locking her gaze with mine.

Unhurriedly, I begin to rub her stomach—slow, smooth strokes with the pads of my fingers over the buttery fabric of her dress. "I'm sorry your cramps are back."

My fingers inch lower as her breath hitches. "It's fine."

"You know, I've heard that orgasms relieve the pain of cramps," I breathe into the space between us, dipping my fingers into the band of her underwear through her dress.

Her eyes flutter closed. "I'm on my period."

"So." Tilting my head, I bury my face against the side of her neck and inhale. "You're not bleeding from your clit."

"Tripp." My name is a whimper on her lips, and my dick twitches behind my pants in response to the way she sounds so needy.

"Come on," I whisper, grabbing her hand.

"Where are we going?"

"To my room."

Peeking out to make sure my parents aren't waiting for us, I pull her down the hall and up the stairs when I see the coast is clear. Once we're in my childhood room, I lock the door and gently push her down on the queen-sized mattress.

Slowly, I kneel, settling between her legs as she opens them wider. "Are you really going to go down on me while your parents are downstairs and I have a tampon shoved inside me?"

"So romantic," I tease as I lift the hem of her dress, pressing a kiss to the inside of her knee as I expose it, lifting it over my shoulder before doing the same with the other leg.

She's wearing lacy short-style underwear, body jolting as I flick the tip of my tongue against her through the material. Her hands run through my hair as she lays back against the sheets and watches me with a small smile.

"You're so good to me." She says it like she wishes it weren't true.

Her hips lift as I pull her underwear down her legs, pocketing them as she lets out a soft, tinkling laugh. "If you were mine for real, I'd treat you like a queen for the rest of your life, Valentina."

My lips skate up her inner thighs, appreciating the sighs she makes as she strokes my scalp encouragingly. When I reach the apex of her thighs, I flick my tongue against her again. Her bare pussy is smooth and soft, her clit wet and pink and swollen—ready for my attention.

Curling my hands around her thighs from below, I pry her legs apart further and lower my mouth to her flesh, sucking her clit between my lips.

"Fuck," she gasps as her hips jump against my face.

I don't rush, alternating between sucking lazily and softly flicking my tongue against her. Her heels dig into my back, fingers twisting my hair as she breathes out little moans, trying to be quiet.

The sounds she makes hit me straight between my legs, and I want to unzip my pants and stroke my cock, but this is about making her feel good and taking away some of her pain—I can handle blue balls for a night.

"You feel so fucking good," she whispers.

Her head is thrown back, curls fanned out over the bed, cheeks flushed a pretty pink as she rides my face slowly. She removes a hand from my hair to sink her teeth into the skin of her palm, muffling her cries as I begin to move faster—sucking harder, licking her with swift, short strokes.

"I'm going to come."

"Do it, baby. Let me hear those pretty sounds you make when I make you feel good."

She squeals against her hand as her knees press together with my head trapped between them. Her entire body shudders, and I keep licking her slowly until her hips stop moving.

Her chest rises and falls with her rapid breaths, and I lower her legs from my shoulders before reaching up to gently rub her lower stomach. "Better?"

"Mmhmm," she hums shyly as she looks down her body at me.

"Good. Always such a good girl for me," I praise as I climb on the bed, holding my weight above her. Her arms wind around my neck, pulling me down to press her lips to mine.

"Thank you," she whispers against them.

"You're welcome."

Valentina falls asleep on the drive home.

After a quick goodbye to my parents, who definitely knew what we were doing up in my room, we leave with a Pyrex dish of leftovers and a pained conversation between Mom and Lenni about trying to do lunch during the week to go over more party details.

Within ten minutes, she's passed out, curled up in her seat and using my jacket as a pillow. It's surprising we don't get into a crash with as many times as I catch myself staring at her while she sleeps instead of watching the road like I should be.

Stirring as I pull into my parking garage, she asks sleepily, "Are we home?"

"As much as I love hearing that come out of your mouth, no. We're at my place. I was going to run upstairs and grab your stuff before I take you home."

"Well, I'm up now that I've taken a nap. It's still early. Wanna watch a movie?"

I want to spend as much time with you as you'll allow.

"Absolutely, we can do that."

We hold hands on the way back up to my apartment. It's comfortable and casual, making me wonder if I just continue treating her like she's actually my girlfriend, if maybe she'll realize we have a good thing going.

"Do you want some clothes to change into?" I ask as she slips off her boots.

"That would be amazing. And I need to use the bathroom, if you don't mind." Her cheeks flush as she says it.

Pulling her close, I tuck her hair behind her ear and kiss the tip of her nose. "There's nothing to be embarrassed about, Viv. Let me grab you some clothes, and you can do whatever you need to."

"You are such a great guy, Tripp. You know that? Any woman would be incredibly lucky to have you."

"Well, Valentina, *you* have me right now. Don't take it for granted."

After she changes into a pair of my sweatpants and a plain black t-shirt, we settle on the couch with Fudge Cookie Talenti and put on *Eat, Pray, Love* because Lenni loves Julia Roberts.

"She's just so classically beautiful. Timeless. You know?"

"Uh-huh," I murmur, not paying attention to the movie but to the way Lenni's spoon keeps disappearing between her lush lips as she sucks gelato off it.

She looks good in my clothes, her hair thrown up on top of her head and secured with a tie she found in her purse, the heating pad pressed against her lower abdomen.

"God, this was good. I've never had it before. Thank you for introducing me to the magic that is gelato." The spoon clangs against her bowl as she leans forward and puts it on the tray in front of us.

"Come here." I've been waiting for her to finish so I can spoon her and press her body against mine. "Come lay with me."

Lenni doesn't even hesitate, repositioning herself to lie on her side, back to my chest, as she snuggles against me. "I can't promise I'll stay like this for long. Now that I've had sweets, I need something salty."

Even though she opened herself up for it, I don't make the *'my nuts are salty'* joke because it's juvenile, and I don't want to annoy her.

"Whatever you want, just let me know. I'll get it for you." Placing my hand over the heating pad, I start to rub my fingers in circles like I did earlier. "You know, we can always have sex in the shower. I'll keep you coming all night if it helps with the pain."

She laughs and wiggles her butt against my groin. "As nice as that sounds, this is really nice, too. Is that okay? I took some Midol when we got back, and I'm feeling better."

Pressing a kiss to her temple, I tell her, "Of course, it's okay."

Another ten minutes go by before I hear her soft snores and look down to see her fast asleep. Carefully, I remove the heating pad and turn it off. Grabbing my phone, I shoot Ginny a quick message.

> What's Lenni's favorite restaurant? I wanna take her out on a nice date tomorrow.

Barely a second later, Ginny's name flashes across my screen. Declining the call, I snap a photo of her best friend asleep in my arms and send it to her with a sleeping emoji.

Ginny

> Could you two be more cute? As for the date, take her skating! She loves to ice skate. She'd be happy with that, street meat, and a hot chocolate - preferably not on her outfit ;)

Jackson's name pops up with a message.

> Stop texting my wife this late

> She's not your wife yet

Tossing my phone above my head, I snuggle deeper into the couch and pull Lenni tighter to me, falling asleep to Julia Roberts eating pasta and Lenni's heady scent of vanilla and coffee.

When I wake, Lenni is gone. It's starting to get light out, the sky a dirty gray filled with heavy white fluff, and I check my phone to see it's just after seven in the morning.

"Valentina?" I call out, my heart kicking up with

bitter nostalgia of the morning after our first night together.

Swinging my legs off the couch, a piece of paper next to the heating pad catches my attention.

Didn't want to wake you. You're cute when you sleep. I went home—call me when you wake up—but not too early. Haha.

It's signed with her kiss mark, just like the one she left last time.

My lips turn up as I walk to the kitchen and place the note in a drawer with the first one she left.

Usually, I'd sleep in on a Sunday, but I'm feeling refreshed and wide awake. It's the second time we've spent the night together and the second best night's sleep I've had all year.

Instead of calling her—because I know it's way too early to wake her up—I send her a text while I make a cup of coffee.

> When YOU'RE awake, let me know. I'd like to take you out today if you don't already have plans. And I hope you're feeling better.

It's just after ten by the time she responds, my phone chiming just as I step out of my post-workout shower.

Taking my chances, I call her, relief washing through me when she picks up on the second ring. She still sounds sleepy, her tone a mix of throaty and hoarse in a sexy morning rasp. "Good morning, handsome. What are we going to do today?"

Her nickname for me sends a pleasing, warm feeling through my chest. One I try to tamper down as I remember that none of it is real to her, as she likes to keep reminding me. Sometimes, I wonder where the act ends and her real feelings begin. But I know that all I can do is continue to treat her as if we're really dating and hope she comes around.

"How about I come pick you up, and you let me surprise you?" She's been adamant about not giving me her address, but eventually, I'm going to figure it out.

I think she knows it, too, because she finally concedes. "Okay, you pushy bastard. Come get me. But stay down in the car and let me know when you're downstairs."

A grin spreads over my face as I successfully put a dent in the shield she's got up. "Deal. Text me your address. See you soon, Viv."

"Wait! What should I wear?"

"Dress warm. We'll be outside."

"Outside?" she groans. "It's going to snow today."

Looking outside again while I sip my coffee, I

realize she's right. But what's more romantic than ice skating in the middle of a snowfall? "Don't worry, I'll keep you warm."

Valentina's infectious laugh surrounds me as she wraps her arms around my waist. "I *love* ice skating! Did Ginny tell you?"

"Maaaybe," I draw out. "I already reserved tickets and rentals—I didn't know if you had your own skates, but I guess I should have asked."

Her lips stretch into a giant smile as she lets go of me to look over the rink. "I don't actually. I don't know why I've never bought a pair. And how did you reserve tickets if you didn't know when I'd get up? Or if I had other things planned for today?"

I scratch a non-existent itch on the back of my head, laughing with a shrug. "I paid for the whole day. That way, we could show up when we wanted and leave when we wanted. We can even go grab lunch later and come back if you'd like."

She pulls her gaze away from the rink to me, her eyes sparkling as she throws her arms around my neck and plants a firm kiss against my lips. "You're too good to me."

"I'm really not, Viv. This is just typical dating."

A pretty blush forms on her cheeks as she turns her attention back to the rink. Her body wilts against mine slightly as her hands drop to lay against my chest. "I wouldn't know. I've never dated anyone."

"Really? I find that very hard to believe."

She doesn't respond, and I don't want to ruin the mood, so I grab her hands and pull her over to where we need to pick up our skates.

Twenty minutes later, I'm on my ass while she stands over me, smiling mirthfully while she tries not to laugh. "I take it you've never skated before?"

"You'd be correct." I reach up for the side of the rink and pull myself back to my feet, wobbling as I try to balance my weight on the skates.

"Come here." She reaches out her hands and glides closer.

"No way, I'll pull you down."

"Come on now, you said you'd keep me warm," she teases, making a come-hither motion with her fingers.

Well, I guess I can't argue with that.

"I'm serious, Viv. I'm not good at this, and I don't wanna hurt you." There are so many people around; with my luck, I'll end up hurting more than just her, and we'll cause a commotion.

"Look around, Tripp," she says as she grabs my hands and pulls me slowly away from the wall. "Plenty of other people are falling, too. People come here for the novelty of it. Not everyone here is good at skating."

She leads me effortlessly, like I'm a child who's never set foot on ice before. She's patient as we slowly make our way around the rink. "When I was little, I'd skate on the pond behind my house with the other kids in the neighborhood. None of us had skates, so we'd just slide around in our shoes. I'd stay out there as long as possible until Momma would call me back inside."

My attention is solely focused on her as she guides me. Her eyes have a far-off look as she recalls the memory, a bitter smile that reminds me perhaps her childhood wasn't all that great.

"This was one of the first things I did when I moved to the city. It took me forever to feel comfortable on the ice, but I just kept going until it was easier. It's my favorite thing to do when I want to disappear from the world for a while. We'll have to go again, but to Bryant Park next time—it's my favorite this time of year. My treat."

The air grows thicker—the way it does right before the snow starts to fall. Heavy flakes start to drift down around us, and Lenni's head tips back as she smiles at the sky with glee. "Isn't it beautiful?" she asks as the snow falls faster.

My eyes don't leave her face as I reply. "It really is."

Our fingers lace together as she looks back at me and pulls us to a slow stop. "You did it. You made it all the way around the rink."

"So I did. You're a good teacher. I didn't even watch my feet." A shiver runs through me, but whether it's from the cold or how she looks with the snow falling around her isn't apparent.

Pulling her to me, I brace my weight on the wall

as I lean down to kiss her softly. "Why don't you take a few spins around? I'll only slow you down, and I want you to enjoy it."

"I'm enjoying being here with *you*. But if you need to take a break, I get it. It can be really draining at first—not to mention cold—and you look like you're freezing." She laughs.

"Would I rather be on a beach right now? Absolutely. You in a little bikini swimming in crystal clear water? That's a wet dream right there. Not that your leg warmers aren't doing it for me, too." I nod to the cream-knit leg embellishments she's got over her black leggings. They match her sweater and the little fluff ball at the top of her beanie.

"Well, I've never been to a beach, so ax the me swimming part of that dream," she says as I let her go and grab the wall. She glides a little ways away, twirling with her arms stretched out.

"You've never been to a beach?" I ask incredulously, making my way along the wall to the exit.

She coasts gracefully alongside me. "Nope. Never been anywhere besides home and the city. I'd love to dig my toes in the warm sand someday. But I never learned how to swim, so my only way of enjoying the water is a cozy hot tub."

I file that away to visit at a later date.

Over the next hour, we alternate between Lenni helping me around the rink and her artfully skating circles around others by herself. She's incredible to watch. Men's gazes swivel from their wives or girlfriends to my stunning fake fiancée many times, only averting their eyes when I'm with her and catch them looking.

She doesn't even notice.

I'm proud that her attention is either on me or off in her own little world while she skates alone.

When she's ready to leave, we grab greasy burgers at Bill's and then choose a selection of cookies at Chip City before I take her home. "You sure you don't want to come over to my place? Or let me come up to see yours?"

"No way. These cookies are all mine, buddy. Besides, I'm worn out. I need a nap. Your mother has already messaged me to set up lunch sometime this week. I'm gonna need all the rest I can get to deal with her by myself."

Something uncomfortable zips down my esophagus and cannonballs in the pit of my stomach. "Oh? This is news to me. Last night didn't exactly end on great terms. I'm surprised you *agreed* to do lunch with her."

She shrugs as she munches on half of a Fluffernutter cookie. "The engagement party is in two weeks. She really seems to want me to have a hand in planning it, so why not just placate her, I suppose?"

Hugging her to me, I kiss her temple. "Thank you."

"You're welcome." She turns to look at me and leans in for a kiss, but I dodge her lips and bite the giant piece of cookie in her hand. "Hey!" she cries out, playfully nudging me away.

"What?! We bought six flavors, and you're not letting me have any!" I exclaim while chewing.

"What are you trying to say?"

"That you're a greedy woman." Lowering my hand between her legs, I relish the gasp she lets out as I run my fingers along her center over her leggings. "The least you can do is give me some type of dessert."

"Ew, gross," she says breathily, pushing my hand away. "I'm all sweaty. There's absolutely no way we're being intimate while I'm on my period *and* a sweaty mess."

I don't know what prompts me to do it, but I lean in and lick the side of her face. "I like the way your sweat tastes."

And god, do I fucking mean it.

Something about the act itself has my cock hardening, and with the look she gives me, I'll bet anything she's fucking soaked right now.

"Did you…did you just *lick* me?"

Crowding her against the door, I bury my face in her neck and gently bite at her skin. "Mmhmm."

She drops the bag on the floor and lets out a small moan as she turns so one leg stretches out on the seat behind me and the other presses against my side.

Our lips collide as her hands pull at my jacket, removing it so she can run her hands beneath my sweater. Her fingers are cold as they dance along my flesh, kneading their way down my chest and around my sides to grip my ass and pull me into her.

Tugging her farther down so she's laying on the seat, I move to my knees on the floor.

"What are you doing?" she asks as I reach for the band of her leggings, her hands threading in my hair as I lean in to kiss her.

My fingers find their way between her legs, and I push past the band of her underwear to rub her swollen bud. I begin to kiss my way down her throat, pulling her sweater and tank top up to suck a nipple into my mouth through the thin lace of her bra as her hips roll against my hand.

"Tripp, what are you doing?" she asks again on a breath, but her tone has no sign of wanting me to stop.

"I licked it," I say against her stomach, dipping my tongue into her belly button as I stop stroking her to pull her pants over the curve of her ass. She moans loudly, shoving her fist against her mouth even though the partition is up and the driver can't hear her. "That means it's mine," I tell her just before I close my mouth over her clit and begin to suck.

T hursday finds me at Caffe Napoli, seated across from Margo.

Surprisingly, she's warm when she greets me—not even putting up a fight when I asked her to meet me in Little Italy because I had a craving for an authentic cannoli—and I even made a point to show up ten minutes late again.

"You know, I think it would be nice if you both started coming out for dinner weekly. How do you feel about living in the city? Have you spoken about where you'll raise your family? I always assumed Tripp would move to Connecticut when he settled down—make the commute like Weylan does." For someone who wanted us to wait on getting married, she sure seems to be rushing everything else.

"Honestly, we haven't spoken about it. Tripp didn't realize I can't have kids until dinner the other night. He hasn't pushed me on it since. Your son is respectful that way." I raise a brow at her, a light warning lacing my tone.

Margo's features soften, as if she forgot about my little outburst on Sunday. "Do you mind if I ask what happened? Is it natural or something else? We know a plethora of fertility doctors. We struggled to have Tripp ourselves."

I'd be upset she's forcing this conversation if it wasn't for her admission. Letting me know that she struggled to conceive Tripp is huge. That's a piece of information women like Margo don't just go handing out.

Which means she might just be trying to make a genuine connection with me. And even though the goal is to make no such connections, I relent.

With a long sigh, I sip my water before telling her, "There was an accident when I was younger. I got sick while I was healing. The doctors said it would be highly unlikely for me to be able to carry a child."

She reads my vagueness for what it is and doesn't continue pushing. Instead, she nods and tries to disguise the pity in her eyes. "Well, I'm sorry to hear that. When you and Tripp are ready, I'd be more than happy to help set up appointments, whether with a fertility doctor or an adoption agency."

"Ready to be a grandma? You're so young. Surely you don't want that title already?"

"There's only so many association meetings and luncheons a socialite can stand before it all starts to get boring. Weylan has his golf when he's not work-ing, and we spent years traveling after Tripp went to college. I'm ready for a houseful of grandchildren I can spoil. Family means a lot to me. And Tripp spends more time by himself than he does with us. After all, I would have never thought I'd have to hear about him being engaged from his ex-fiancée's family. And what of *your* family? How did they take the news?"

Ignoring her inquiry about my family, I simply say, "Ahh. Emily. Honestly, I'm not sure why she thought it was her business to tell anyone."

Our server shows up with our meals, placing them in front of us and shaving fresh parmesan on top of my porcini ravioli. As soon as he walks away, Margo says, "Well, she cares for him deeply still. I think it just took her by surprise as well, seeing as how no one knew about the two of you."

"Cares about him? Margo, do you know what she did to him? She shouldn't have cheated on him if she cared about him."

Judging by the look on Margo's face, she had no idea that's what happened. Silently, I curse myself for letting it slip because it's obvious Tripp will get an earful about why he didn't tell his mother.

"Cheated? Emily cheated on him? When did he find this out? Why didn't he tell me?"

"Knowing Tripp, he probably wanted to save her from looking bad. It's my understanding your families are close. Maybe he didn't want to ruin that for you."

She looks mortified that I would even suggest that he kept it to himself to pacify her. "Tripp knows he can come to us with that sort of thing. To even think we wouldn't have his back–"

"That isn't what I said, Margo. I just think he didn't want to disappoint you."

I'm in dangerous waters here. To divulge that I know things about Tripp's life that she's unaware of doesn't make it look like I'm just a poor split-second decision. It makes it look like I'm the real deal if he's entrusting me with information she doesn't have.

Just as I'm about to try to backtrack, she surprises me by completely changing the subject.

"Do you have a dress picked out already? Maybe we can see if Ginny can take off early and meet us for some shopping," Margo suggests as she takes a dainty bite of her salmon.

Talk about a one-eighty.

While I'm thankful for the change in topic, now she wants to oversee my dress?

We've already covered flowers, food, and music. I have no problem acquiescing to those things for her. Margo is known for her parties. I have faith that whatever she chooses will be beautiful.

But my clothing?

Shrugging, I stuff an entire ravioli in my mouth and answer while chewing my food, earning me a poorly concealed look of revulsion. "I'm sure I have something I can wear in my closet."

Do I want to go shopping for a new gown for the engagement party? Yes.

Do I want to go shopping for a new gown for the engagement party *with Margo*? Fuck no.

"Well, what does it look like? Are you wearing white? I think it's a little gauche if you ask me. You and Tripp are adults. I think we all know you're not saving yourself for marriage. Maybe a cream? Or an eggshell, perhaps. You have such lovely coloring. I'm sure anything you pick will be wonderful."

Is that a compliment? I can't tell under all the shit she layered on top of it.

"Don't plan on wearing white. I was thinking red, actually. It's totally my color." This ditzy act is getting tiring, and Margo looks exasperated nearly every time I open my mouth.

The sun is leaving the sky, and all the lights strung up over the streets are illuminated, creating an atmospheric glow for the early evening. This is one of my favorite spots in the city, and I briefly wonder why I decided to share it with her today.

"*Red*? My dear girl, you can't wear *red*. It's so ostentatious."

"Are you aware that Ginny is having me wear red at her wedding?" I snap back.

That shuts her up. She'd never say anything against darling Ginny, who managed to tame Jackson Tailor and get him to settle down. That was a feat to behold in Margo's eyes.

"Well…I suppose." She reaches up to pat her chignon, eyes darting around the restaurant. She looks so uncomfortable here, and I wonder if there was ever a time when Margo let her hair down and just tried to have fun.

"Don't worry. I wouldn't dream of embarrassing

you. I'll find something cream or eggshell. If you'd like, I'll even send you photos so you can approve it before the party." I want her to hear how ridiculous she sounds.

It works.

Her face relaxes. She lets out a long sigh and shakes her head. "I know I sound unreasonable, Valentina. I just want–"

"Everything to be perfect. I know. Tripp deserves the best. That's what he'll get." Pushing my plate back, I signal for the check. I had every intention of making Margo pay for our meals, but there's something about the way this entire conversation has gone.

It's seriously stressing her out, and that makes me feel bad.

This means something to her, and it doesn't to me.

All this party will be is another reminder of how much I'm beginning to want Tripp for real and how I can't have him.

As the server brings the check, I discreetly pull my credit card from my purse beneath the table and hand it to him. Margo sputters as she watches the man walk away. "I was going to pay for the meal."

"How about you walk with me to Ferrara, and you can pay for dessert? Tripp loves their pignoli cookies, and I'm going to see him later."

I'm overwhelmed with a sudden urge to be kind to her—chalk it up to my damn mommy issues.

All poor Margo wants to do is throw a party for

her son and the stray he brought home with a four-carat diamond slapped on her hand.

The sad thing is, in another life, I think I'd like Margo. A life where I could be *myself.*

And I think she'd like me.

"That's acceptable. I had no idea he liked…whatever it was you called them." She seems surprised again that there is something about her son that I know, and she doesn't.

"We tend to eat a lot of dessert in bed." I leave out that it's mainly off each other.

Tripp and I have spent an exorbitant amount of time together since Sunday, and over the past few days, we've discovered that Tripp likes food play.

And I've discovered that I really like helping him try new things.

Margo shakes her head and waves a hand in my direction as we exit the restaurant. "I don't need to hear those things."

"Oh, come on, Margo. You and Weylan probably have a great sex life. It's nothing to be ashamed of. It's healthy to talk about sex!"

People passing by turn to look at me, and Margo ducks her head in embarrassment. "Valentina! Keep it down! This is highly inappropriate talk for the sidewalk."

"Oh, don't be a prude. You're probably a wildcat in bed." I smile at her and watch in amusement as she perks up a little.

"I know what you're trying to do. And while I know you are not accustomed to how things run in our circles, I know you know this is neither the time nor place to be talking about this." Her tone has no bite and she looks like she's fighting a smile as she chastises me.

We walk into Ferrara, ordering the cookies and both original and chocolate-covered cannoli. Margo takes her time wandering around to look at everything and picks up a few things for her and Weylan to try.

"Why don't you ride with me back uptown? I can drop you off at Tripp's," she offers as she messages her driver that she's ready to be picked up.

For a moment, I freeze, unable to tell her I don't have a key to his place and he's working late at the office tonight. But with that thought, I ask, "Actually, he's working. Can you drop me off at the office?"

Tripp

"The company isn't big enough to merge. Acquire and consolidate them with Tailor Tech. Cut them loose if they don't want to go that route. We don't need to waste our time or money. Jackson wants to focus on buying up as many businesses as possible surrounding the new center."

"Ah, yes. The Scott Tailor Family Center. Jackson's dumping quite a lot of money into that thing for his soon-to-be wife," David Knolls, an older-than-dirt geezer who should have retired ten years ago, drawls. For whatever reason, the man respected Scott, but is evident in his dislike for Jackson.

Tapping my ballpoint against the notepad in front of me, I toss it down before leaning back in my chair, fixing him with a stony glare. "And for good reason. It will be nice for the neighborhood to have a place like that. Ginny wants to focus on low-income families, and I think Scott would have given the project his seal of approval. So, is there a problem?"

David gathers his things before heading for the exit to the meeting room we're in. "No problem here."

As soon as the door closes behind him, one of the younger guys sitting at the far end of the meeting table lets out a low whistle. At first, I think it's from the tense interaction, but I see him nudge the guy sitting next to him as he nods behind me.

"That your new secretary, Kennedy? How the fuck do you guys get the hot ones? I keep getting stuck with women who look like Sheila in accounting," he says.

Turning, I look through the giant glass wall of the meeting room to see Valentina making her way down the path between the cubicles of the office. She's wearing a pair of skinny leather pants, with gray heels and an oversized sweater in the same color that's falling off her shoulder. A black peacoat is thrown over her arm, and she's carrying a large bag from Ferrara's.

So simple, yet so breathtakingly beautiful.

"That's no one's secretary, Donner. That happens to be *my* soon-to-be wife," I declare with a grin as I catch her gaze. A smile lights up her face as she slows her steps and nods to my office.

Murmurs flare up as I turn back around and rise from my seat, leaving my stuff on the table. "If you'll all excuse me. I think we're done here."

"No way that's your fiancée. We would have known if you were seeing someone," he expresses in disbelief.

"Most of us keep our relationships secret. Not everyone needs to brag about their conquests. You do enough of that for everyone."

Opening the door, I'm aware of all the eyes on us as I reach for Lenni, wrapping my arms around her waist and pulling her into me as she winds hers around my neck. "They thought you were my new secretary."

A grin pulls at her lips as she presses up on her tiptoes to kiss me. Numerous catcalls and whistles sound throughout the office. "You better not be handling your secretary this way," she whispers against my lips.

Chuckling, I grab her hand and lead her down the hall to my office. "I *am* quite fond of my temp. Jim really seems to know his stuff."

Opening my office door, I usher her inside before addressing the entire floor, who seem more interested in us than their jobs. "Get back to work," I order jovially.

"Your mom just dropped me off. I apologize, I might have let it slip that Emily cheated on you," Lenni tells me as I close the door. She tosses her coat and bag on one of the chairs and hops up to sit on my desk.

Stepping between her legs, I nearly lay her out flat on the surface as I capture her lips in a searing kiss. "How did you know I *needed* to see you?"

She giggles against my lips, hands moving to grip my backside as she presses her hips into mine. "Is someone having a bad day at work? Need a little stress relief?"

"If by stress relief, you mean fucking you right here on my desk, then yes, that's exactly what I need." Pulling her to the edge by her knees, I slide my hands up her legs to undo the button on her pants.

"I brought you pignoli cookies," she tells me between kisses as her fingers work the buttons on my dress shirt.

"Fuck the cookies. I'd rather eat you instead." Shoving my hand down her pants, I find her wet and ready for my fingers to slide into her tight, warm passage. She moans as I pull them back out and lift them to my mouth to suck them clean.

Grabbing the back of my neck, she pulls me in to kiss me, her tongue delving into my mouth to taste herself. "I think it's time *I* get to devour *you*."

Groaning, my cock grows painfully hard as she slips her hand down my pants to rub her palm against it. The thought of her on her knees while I fuck her face is tempting, but I don't want a quick blow job in my office. I want her completely naked and at my mercy, with her legs spread wide and hands tied behind her back.

She shoves my shirt off my shoulders, and it catches at my elbows as I pull her sweater over her head. "As much as I can't wait to feel your mouth on my cock, I need to be inside you right now. There's a condom in my wallet. Let me grab it."

She gets off the desk and shimmies out of her

pants as I dispose of my shirt, tossing it on my chair before grabbing my wallet from the inside pocket of my suit jacket.

As I make my way around the desk, the door opens, and Jackson walks in. "Hey, how did the meetin–"

"Dude, get out!" I shout.

"Jackson!" Lenni scrambles for her clothes as he shields his eyes and turns around.

"You couldn't have locked the door, Tripp?" he mutters.

"Oh my god, how embarrassing," Lenni exclaims while she tugs her clothing back on.

"Not like I haven't seen you nearly naked before." He chuckles.

"Watch it, Jackson!" Anger surges through me toward my best friend. When the fuck has he seen her nearly naked?

"What?! I mean at Désirer! Calm down! Jealous asshole." He laughs, peeking over his shoulder at me and keeping his eyes off her.

Lenni grabs her jacket and bag, leaving the one with the cookies, shoving his shoulder as she pushes past him and heads to the door. "*You're* an asshole."

"Where are you going? Get back here, I'm not finished with you." My cock jumps in my pants as if trying to make my point.

Throwing me a saucy smirk, she pulls the door open. "Not exactly in the mood anymore. Enjoy your cookies." Then winks before disappearing.

My head swivels slowly toward Jackson as my eyes narrow. "What. The. *Fuck*?"

He shrugs. "Just curious how the meeting went."

"I hate you."

"No, you don't. Things are going well then, between you two?" He grabs the bag from the bakery and fishes out a cookie.

Snatching the bag from his hands, I fall into my chair and put my shirt back on. "Things are fine. Still not thrilled she walks around the club half-dressed with men drooling all over her, but you're right. She's not the type of woman to be kept. As for the meeting, it went. Knolls is pushing back, but you knew that was gonna happen. He's not impressed that you're building the center *for Ginny*."

"Fuck Knolls."

"I'd rather have fucked my fiancée just now, thanks."

"*Fake* fiancée."

"You know I'm getting real tired of you reminding me of that."

"That's okay. I'm getting tired of you forgetting it. She's going to break your heart, and things will be awkward for Ginny when that happens. Lenni is her best friend, and you're mine. Maybe it's time you tell her how you really feel."

"Oh, and you know how I feel, do you?"

"Yeah, Tripp, I do. It's written all over your face. Your head over heels for her, so tell her. Tell her you want it to be real." He gets up and heads toward the door. "Let her know before you fall completely in love with her. Save yourself more heartache."

His words bother me. "Why are you so against us being together? It isn't funny anymore, Jackson. What's your deal?"

His shoulders slump as he turns around to face me. "I told you, I'm just watching out for your feelings. You forget I was there when Emily did what she did. It nearly destroyed you. The way you are with Lenni? It doesn't even come close to the way you were with Emily. This won't nearly destroy you. It will end you. You won't believe in love anymore. So, unless you want to become a coldhearted bastard. I suggest you tell her sooner rather than later."

I remain quiet as he leaves. Not wanting to correct him, or willing to admit that I've already fallen for her.

Désirer is slow for a Saturday night—either that or the rooms are all filled with the majority of the clients that would typically be gathered in the Grand Room at this hour.

"I don't remember the last time you wore a pair of black or whites," the bartender, Jace, says as he slides a shot of mezcal over the bartop toward me. I've always had a sneaking suspicion that Jace is his real name and not a *stage* name, as we like to use here. He's got a California tan with a head full of wavy golden hair that drives the clients wild.

"Sticking to the gold rooms right now. It's nice to have a palette cleanser," I tell him before tipping my head back to take my shot.

"Well, when you're ready to get back in the game, let me know. I'm ready for a little group action," he jests.

We've worked together in the past, both in group sessions and just fucking for clients to watch.

Usually, when group sessions happen, Angels want to keep working with other Angels who make them comfortable. It's just like any other job—you like some coworkers and don't like others.

The sound of a throat being cleared right behind me has me spinning to see Tripp standing there. Mask or no mask, his curls and million-dollar smile give him away every time—that and the fact that he seeks me out as soon as he gets here.

Anonymity is the entire point of this club. But we never have any trouble finding each other in the crowd. Although, most people easily recognize me—*Bianca*—from my scar, which is usually on display.

Tripp glares daggers over my shoulder at Jace as he clenches his fists at his side—a telltale sign that he overheard what Jace said.

"Hi, I wasn't expecting to see you here tonight," I tell him as I slide as gracefully as I can from my stool, thankful that my skin doesn't stick to the material like it does when I wear less clothing. Since I'm in the Confessional wing tonight, I'm wearing a simple black slip dress with scalloped lace and thigh-high stockings.

"We haven't seen each other since Thursday. I didn't know how else to see you. I feel like you've been avoiding me," he states lowly. His eyes continue to dart over my shoulder, his jawbone working against his cheek as he clenches his teeth.

Lowering my voice so no one overhears us, I tell him, "Sorry, I've been picking up shifts at Decadence and running errands for Carmela. And you've been busy with work. Besides, I thought taking a little break from each other would be good for us. With so much coming up soon, we'll be spending a lot of time together."

"You say that like it's a bad thing. I don't see the problem here. And why are you picking up shifts at the restaurant? Do you need money?" The annoyance etched into his features bleeds into concern as he reaches for my hand.

Before I can answer him, we're interrupted by the booker for the Desires wing. "Miss Bianca, you're being summoned."

"I'm not working that wing tonight. You'll have to tell the client I'm not interested." My hand flexes in Tripp's, and I can see him watching me intently from my peripheral.

"I was told you'd say that, and I'm supposed to tell you it's an order, not a request, from Miss Scarlett."

Perking up, I turn my head back to Tripp. "Oooh, I'm being summoned by the bosses."

Scarlett was Ginny's stage name for the brief amount of time she worked here. She and Jackson like to come once a month to play out fantasies that just aren't the same at home as they are inside the dressed-up rooms of Désirer.

"We're going to finish this discussion once we see what they want. Jackson is gonna be on my shit list if he keeps interrupting us." Tripp is an ooey gooey cinnamon roll most of the time, but in the bedroom— and on rare occasions outside of it—the authoritative tone that drips from between his lips is like honeyed nectar, and I gulp it down as though it's my favorite drink.

He winds his arm around my shoulders as we enter the Desires hall, pulling me close to bury his nose in my hair because he hates the thick scent of the roses. "Maybe after my clients, we can come back here and try something new," I whisper as Ginny's old guard stops in front of the room she's in.

"I'm beginning to think I should just book you exclusively like he did for her." Tripp nods to the door, alluding to our friends.

When we walk into the room, I'm surprised to see them both wearing little to nothing. Jackson has on a pair of silk drawstring pajama pants, and Ginny is wearing an intricate piece of navy lingerie. Raising my hand to cover Tripp's eyes, I tell them, "Uh, I don't know what we just walked into, but I don't think we want to be a part of it."

"Liar," Jackson says from his place on the loveseat, where he's sipping a drink.

"We just found out on the way over here, and I wanted you to be the first to know. Tripp, we would have told you tomorrow, but since you're already here, this is just an added bonus," Ginny exclaims excitedly.

"Know what? And, Jackson, can you please put a shirt on? Your naked chest is very distracting," I mutter, holding my other hand up to put a barrier between my eyes and his skin.

Tripp pulls my hand away from his eyes and

glares at his best friend. "Why are you guys asking her to meet you in a room like this, half-dressed?"

Jackson laughs. "Don't be jealous that your fake girlfriend is ogling me."

"Shut the fuck up, Jackson," we both tell him simultaneously.

"Oh, come on. Ginny told me what you said about me before we got serious. She also told me you helped train her to work here, and she knows I put that tidbit of information away in my spank bank," he quips.

Tripp looks at me, more interested than pissed now, and asks, "Seriously?"

My friend looks momentarily mortified before crossing the room to smack her fiancé on the arm. "Why would you tell them I told you that? They don't need to know we talk about those kinds of things!"

"You talk about being okay with Jackson jerking off to thoughts of you two together?" Tripp asks her as he points a finger between her and me.

With a gasp, I fix Ginny with an incredulous look, "When we talked about sharing, it was a joke! Not for real!"

"Tripp wouldn't share you," Jackson challenges, raising a brow in Tripp's direction.

"Oh, like you'd share Ginny?" Tripp counters. He moves slightly in front of me, partly shielding me from Jackson's view.

I don't know what's going on, but there's a tension between them I'm not sure I like, and I find myself wanting to come to Tripp's defense. "Tripp and I have had multiple nights here with other people involved."

Jackson looks surprised and, for once, doesn't have a smartass comeback.

Mission accomplished.

"I feel like I should be disturbed by where this conversation is headed, but strangely, I'm not. Look, we'll make this quick, and then you can go—unless you and Tripp *do* want to join us?" Ginny intervenes with a flourish of her hand toward the bed. She's being extremely nonchalant for a woman whose fiancé is joking about being intimate with her best friend.

All of us look at her with shock, and Jackson snaps, "Tripp's not gonna see you naked! Fuck that."

"I mean, her outfit isn't exactly leaving anything to the imagination," Tripp says under his breath.

"What the fuck has gotten into you, Ginny?" I feel like I'm trapped in the Twilight Zone. Nothing about this whole ordeal seems normal, and I'm half worried they've eaten some bad food and gone delirious.

"I'm pregnant! And horny as hell, literally *everything* is a turn-on. I got turned on by the pickle I ate earlier," she explains as she throws her arms out and then places her hands on her belly.

"*I* got turned on by the way you were eating that pickle," Jackson mumbles as he gets up from the loveseat to wrap an arm around her.

A rush of excitement runs through me at her

news. "You're pregnant?! Ginny, that's amazing! Congratulations!"

Surging forward, I pull her into a hug as we squeal and jump up and down like we're high schoolers who just found out our favorite boy band is coming to town. Tripp and Jackson also do their version of a man hug as Tripp tells him, "Congratulations, man. Damn, you're gonna be a dad."

All the negative energy from earlier evaporates as they move to the bar cart to pour a celebratory drink.

"It's still early, so, you know, things might happen, but that's okay. We didn't think it would happen this fast. I'm just thankful I'll still fit into my dress for the wedding," Ginny tells me as she rubs her belly.

"I didn't even realize you guys were serious about trying already." It seems so sudden. It hasn't even been a year since they met, and so much has happened between them. I'm happy for my friend, but I'd be lying if I didn't admit that a small part of me feels a little sorrow at the reminder of an experience I'll never get to have.

"Well, you know Jackson. He can't keep his damn hands off me." She laughs.

"Or is it *you* who can't keep her hands off *me*, Red?" the man in question says smugly as he comes up beside me.

Tripp goes around us to stand next to Ginny as I tell Jackson, "Oh, I think we all know who can't keep their hands off whom. Don't forget it was me at that hostess stand when you came looking for Ginny the day after you met her. She took you down with one pretty smile and a hard letdown, and you were a goner."

"While I don't argue that fact, don't pretend she wasn't attracted to me right from the get-go," he bites back.

"So what? My girl made you work for it. Stop pretending like you're some higher power's gift to the earth." I wave him away in pretend annoyance. This is what Jackson and I do. We banter, and it's exactly why he kept Tripp and me apart, because when we all get going, it can become a lot.

"I'm sorry. I recall Ginny telling me you said I was gorgeous. And that if I weren't so enamored with her, you'd climb me like a tree and swing from the branches." He sneers with a feline grin.

"Wha...I did not...Ginny! Is *nothing* sacred anymore?" I sputter, my cheeks growing warm at being so blatantly called out.

Looking over, I see her and Tripp huddled together, watching Jackson and me like we're a movie and all they need is some popcorn.

"You know, I once was afraid that they might have slept together here at the club, but now I'm actually kind of intrigued by this," she tells him as she motions between her fiancé and me.

"Lenni is so bossy, and Jackson hates to be bossed around. I wouldn't mind watching how that played out in the bedroom," Tripp plays along, but the look he's giving me lets me know he doesn't mean a word. I have a feeling he intentionally leaves out that

I am, in fact, *not* bossy in the bedroom—but only when it comes to *him*—as if any of us are actually okay with what's being discussed right now.

"Oh yeah? You both want to see this?" Jackson scoffs at them as he reaches out and wraps an arm around my waist, pulling me into his side. Where I once might have swooned if Jackson paid me this much attention, I'm now revolted and try to push him away as I grimace.

"Nope, get your hands off her. Don't like that one bit," Tripp declares as he steps forward, reaching out to remove Jackson's arm from me.

At the same time, Ginny cries out, "Jackson Edward Tailor, you get your hands off my best friend right now! Are you insane?"

"Certifiably, apparently." Jackson all but pushes me into Tripp's arms. "Can we table the bullshit for another day? I'd like to fuck my wife now. Preferably with no one else in the room."

Tripp is already pulling me toward the door, muttering under his breath, "I fucking hate this place."

"I'll call you tomorrow!" Ginny calls out just as Tripp slams the door shut behind us.

Giggling, I let him pull me into him as we head back to the Grand Room. "You know, all that stuff I said about him was way before I met you. Don't be jelly."

As we reach the main door to the hall, he pulls me to a stop, caging me against the wall and ignoring that a guard is behind us. Usually, we have the same guards, but over the last few days, there's been a lot of changes with security.

"I'm fucking grape, raspberry, and even crab apple jelly. And I really want to drag you into one of these rooms to show you just how much." His face looks pained, eyes bouncing back and forth between mine as he struggles with what he wants to say next. His voice strains as he presses his forehead against mine. "Has anything ever happened between you two?"

"Seriously? No! I can't believe you'd ask that." Pushing off the wall, I open the door and head into the Grand Room with Tripp right on my heels.

We haven't even taken more than a few steps before a booker approaches me. "Miss Bianca, I have multiple clients in the wing who are requesting you this evening. I know you're not working it, but it's my job to tell you they've offered double, and one is even offering triple the rate."

"She's not doing it," Tripp snaps as he grabs my arm and starts pulling me toward the exit. Chaos erupts as multiple security guards appear from the shadows and surround us.

"Hands off!" one of them snaps. It's Luca, one of our most dangerous guards. It's not just the fact that he's six feet, ripped as fuck, and damn good at his job that makes him dangerous—though it helps. But that his father is Vinny Morroni, one of the heads of the Italian Mafia.

After Senator Mick Charles shoved Vinny out of a partnership at the club, Carmela made a deal to keep some of his men on for security. Vinny's been trying to get back into a partnership with her, but Mick doesn't want to be involved with him for obvious political reasons. Part of the deal of keeping some of his men on was that Luca would be in charge of them, Carmela trusted him so much though that she ended up making him head of all her security.

Tripp lets go of me, holding his hands up as the guards press in on him. People around us watch the spectacle with wide eyes because this rarely happens.

"It's okay, Luca. Don't throw him out."

"Are you okay?"

Tripp gives him an annoyed look before his eyes slide to mine. "I'm sorry for breaking the rules."

"I'm fine. We're okay." I speak to Luca, but I'm looking at Tripp, trying to convey how I feel with my expression. I don't want to fight with him, and I don't know what is going on between him and Jackson, but I don't want to add fuel to that fire.

The guards disperse, but Luca stays with us, fixing Tripp with a warning glare. "Strike one."

Tripp nods in understanding as Luca walks away. Sidling up to him, I whisper, "You can't act like a jealous boyfriend in here, you *know* that."

"I can't help it."

"Then you have to stop coming here. This is my *job*."

"How would you feel if you saw me with someone else?" he snaps, angling his body into mine. "Wouldn't you be pissed to see me flirting with another woman?"

"I'll have to see it, eventually. This isn't real, remember?" They aren't the words I want to say, but I keep my true feelings buried beneath a flippant tone and unbothered profile.

Slowly, he nods. Huffing, he draws himself up and snaps, "So you keep saying. Maybe I should take advantage of my membership and book one of the other women for the night, then."

His words are cruel even though he isn't. I *know* he's trying to provoke me, to elicit some kind of reaction from me, but I can't help the tears that prick my eyes. Quickly blinking them away, I shrug. "If you think that's what you need to do."

He lets out a disbelieving huff and walks away without another word. It takes me a minute to gain my composure, but when I turn to stop him, he's already across the room, talking to a pretty brunette wearing black wings. She flashes him a smile and nods enthusiastically, leading him to the Dreamers wing.

He doesn't even look back.

A sob catches in my throat, the tears from earlier coming back full-force as I watch them disappear. Imagining him doing anything with another woman has my entire body feeling like it's being filled with cement, pulling me down with a crushing weight that makes it hard to breathe.

I barely make it into the changing suite before I break down in tears. It's empty, so I'm able to have my mini-meltdown in peace. Grabbing my phone, I slide to the floor in front of my locker, ready to message Carmela and tell her I'm not in the right frame of mind to work. My fingers still over the home screen, though, as I see two messages light up.

Momma

> I hate you, you ungrateful bitch.

Margo

> I'll be sending some dresses to Tripp's for you to try for the party next weekend. I'm not trying to be overbearing. I just saw them while I was out shopping and thought you might like to see them. Don't feel obligated to wear them.

Snorting, I ignore the one from Momma. Toggling to Margo's, my heart pinches at the fact that even though she doesn't like me, she's still treating me better than my own mother. Quickly, I send her a reply.

> Can you have them sent to Ginny's instead, please? And thank you, that was kind of you.

Leaning my head back against my locker, I focus on my breathing and wipe the tears from my eyes. I'm a big girl—I need to act like it. I have a job to do. I can't keep blowing off my responsibilities.

My phone dings, and I look back down at it.

*No. I just watched him go off with another Angel.
Everything is not okay.*

"Are we friends now, Margo?" I utter dejectedly to the empty room, closing out of the messaging app without replying to her.

With a sigh, I rise to my feet and go to the full-length mirror to fix my makeup and the feathers on my wings.

"You're a badass bitch, Len. You've come too far. Don't let yourself fall for a man like him," I whisper to my reflection.

If it could talk back, I'm sure it'd tell me, *"Oh, you poor fool. You've already fallen."*

Tripp

"I'm sorry. I'm sure this isn't what you imagined when I asked if you wanted to get a room," I tell the brunette who goes by Misty as she perches on the edge of a black velvet clamshell loveseat.

"It's okay. It happens more often than you'd think, honestly. A lot of guys get cold feet once we're inside the rooms," she explains with a shrug of her shoulders.

I never had any intention of doing something with her inside this room. My feet aren't cold, I just wanted to piss Lenni off. Between Jackson on my case about not getting too close and her pushing me away, I just exploded.

Running a hand through my hair, I let out a long sigh, turning toward her. "Why are women so complicated?"

Surprisingly, she giggles and stretches out on the

loveseat, her black wings cocooning around her. "Women aren't *that* complicated. Tell me your situation, and I'll see if I have any good advice."

Collapsing onto the bed, I stretch out on my back and fold my arms beneath my head. "Let's just say we're fake dating, though I want it to be real, and I think she does, too. We're fucking, and I treat her like she's mine. But she keeps saying we can't be together because she works here."

"Fake dating? Why on earth are you *fake* dating? I had no idea that actually happens in real life."

"It's a long story, and the important part is that if she really doesn't want to date me, then why does she keep sleeping with me? We're so good together. I just wish she'd let me in."

Misty is silent for a few moments, and when I look over at her, she's staring at a random spot on the wall, her seafoam eyes glazed over, lost in thought. Finally, she says, "If she's working here, there's probably a reason. My best advice, if you don't know what her reasoning is, have patience with her. Maybe she *does* want to be with you, but she's scared of what that looks like. A lot of women who work here have been hurt in the past. Whether emotionally, physically, or both. Abuse of all kinds takes a long time to heal from, and sometimes, you never truly heal at all."

I let her words sink in. There have been a few things that Lenni has said that have hinted at her having a shitty childhood. Whenever I try to get her to open up about it, she shuts down and changes the subject. And I've never asked *why* she works here at Désirer for fear of her thinking I'm being judgmental.

"I guess I never thought about that," I murmur. "You're good. I'm guessing this is what the Confessional wing is normally all about?"

She laughs. "Yep. Usually, that's the only wing I work, but tonight, I wanted to try something a little different. I guess I'm just destined for gold wings, though."

"Sorry. For what it's worth, I'll obviously pay the Dreamers rate for your time."

My mind goes to Lenni, and I wonder if I should stick around until she's finished or if I should just go home. Something tells me she watched me walk away and bring this woman into the wing, so I'm prepared for the silent treatment.

I'm tempted to show up on her doorstep and beg for forgiveness for acting like an asshat.

"I hope whatever happens, you guys work it out. I firmly believe whatever is meant to be will be."

"And what if it isn't meant to be?"

"Well, then you make the most of the time that you have."

An entire fucking week passes before I see her again.

Lenni doesn't give me the silent treatment, but

what she does give me is almost worse. Every call goes unanswered, and every text is met with a short, clipped, one or two-word reply. The most she's said to me all week is asking how my time with the brunette went.

I do my best to stay focused at work, but my thoughts continuously stray to her throughout the days. During the nights, I wonder if she's working, but I don't go to the club. She obviously needs space, so I want to respect that.

The fact that we're on such icy terms on the day of our engagement party is not good, though. Having to speak to my parents and pretend everything is okay is not ideal—especially when I know my mother and Lenni are on daily speaking terms now.

"Jesus, she's in a mood tonight. Why don't you take her into the guest room and fuck the brat out of her before we leave?" Jackson suggests as he walks into the living room of his and Ginny's penthouse.

Lenni wanted to get ready with Ginny and said to meet her at their place so we could all go to the party together. I don't think she wants to be alone with me, but I need to make sure we're on the same page before we walk into an event where everyone will be watching us with curious eyes, wondering who she is and why we got engaged so quickly.

"What did she do?" I ask, trying to sound uninterested as I attach my cufflinks.

"Just snappy. I wanted to know how much longer they'd be, and she bit my head off. Said the party doesn't start until you guys arrive. My guess? She's practicing being a bitch because she's going to try and sabotage something. Just be prepared." He walks to his kitchen and pulls out a bottle of bourbon, pouring us two shots.

"She's not going to sabotage anything. She's just nervous," Ginny's voice rings out behind me.

I turn to look at her as I take my shot. She's wearing a simple champagne gown that fits loosely around her stomach, even though it will be weeks before she starts to show.

Lenni steps out a few moments after Ginny, and my breath catches in my throat. It's the first time I've seen her since I walked away from her last Saturday night, and everything in my chest clenches at the sight of her.

She might as well be wearing a wedding gown. Her dress is all satin with beaded embellishments, hugging every curve with a slit up the side that nearly reaches her thigh.

"I can't believe Margo picked out this dress. I absolutely love it, and I hate that," she grumbles.

"Oh, come on now, I helped a little. Sent her in the right direction after the first few she sent me pictures of," Ginny tells her, turning to loop their arms together.

"Oh, but I thought she just found them while she was out shopping," Lenni impersonates in a high-pitched tone.

I have no idea what she's talking about. It's news

to me that my mother picked out her dress, and a little surprising she'd pick out something so showy, but it's very Lenni. "You look beautiful."

Her eyes find mine reluctantly. "Thank you. You don't look so bad yourself."

"We're going to go down to the car and let you two talk for a moment," Ginny exclaims, grabbing Jackson's hand and leading him to the elevator.

"Can I fuck you in the car while we wait for them?" he asks her.

I don't hear her response as Lenni walks closer to me, leaving about a foot of space between us. "How are you?" she asks.

"I'm okay."

Silence infuses the space between us, somehow filling the empty penthouse and making it louder than words. She looks anywhere but at me until, finally, I sweep forward and pull her into my arms, burying my face in her loose waves. "I missed you." I breathe into her hair.

Eventually, I feel her arms wrap around me, her body relaxing into my embrace. "Me too."

Pulling back, I thread my fingers through her hair and tilt her head back so I can kiss her. Our bodies melt into each other, the overwhelming feeling of *home* coursing through me as she kisses me back with equal fervor.

When we pull away, I rest my forehead on hers. "Can we not go a week without seeing each other again? I hated every single second of the past seven days."

Her lips thin into a melancholy smile. "Yeah, it sucked, didn't it?"

"You believe me, don't you? That nothing happened with that woman?" My fingers grip her skin like I'm afraid she will disappear at any moment.

Removing her arms from around my neck, she runs her hands down my chest, the diamond on her finger sparkling brightly against my black suit jacket. "Yeah, I believe you."

"Good." I kiss her forehead. "Are you ready for the circus?"

"As ready as I'll ever be, I think. Thank you for agreeing to go with Ginny and Jackson. They're the only people I'm going to know there. Besides your parents, obviously." She steps out of my arms to retrieve a beaded cream purse, then turns and reaches her hand out to me.

Taking it, I pull her into my side as we head for the elevator. "Of course. I want you to feel comfortable. Don't feel like you need to pretend to be someone else tonight. Just be you. Everyone will love you."

Just like I do.

When we exit the car, I'm pleased that there isn't a red carpet or a crowd of paparazzi waiting for us.

"Wow, no red carpet entrance? Your engagement

party sits lower on the social scale than her birthday," Ginny muses as Jackson helps her out of the other side of the car.

Mother likes to make a huge deal out of her parties, but Lenni expressed she'd rather skip the tabloid pictures if we could help it. As much as Lenni wanted my mother to think our relationship wouldn't last far enough to get us to the actual altar, I'm starting to think she's having the opposite effect.

"I didn't want any of that. Margo obliged me since I let her have control over basically everything else," Lenni says as she anxiously dusts imaginary lint from her dress. She was so nervous on the way here that I had to hold both of her hands in the car so she'd stop picking at her newly manicured fingernails.

"Everything is going to be fine," I whisper to her, squeezing her hand as I kiss her temple.

"There's a great little spot up on the balcony for stress relief, if you know what I mean," Jackson jests as they walk past us, and Ginny smacks his shoulder in response.

"I knew you two did something when you went out there on Mom's birthday!" The last time we were here, sans Lenni, they disappeared outside for a while. When they came back, it was only to say a quick goodbye before they left.

"Ooh yeah, I forgot about the balcony! Ginny told me all about it. I didn't think you'd be into voyeurism, Jackson," Lenni responds, looping her arm through mine as we ascend the stairs.

"No one saw us," he tells her.

"Anyone could have, but it *was* hot—the thrill of being discovered when there's an entire party happening only a few feet away. Ten out of ten would recommend," Ginny throws over her shoulder.

"You hear that? Ten out of ten. We should probably try it," I murmur in Lenni's ear, releasing her arm to wrap mine around her waist. After an entire week of not seeing her, having her in my arms gives me a sense of calming relief. Her only response is a humming sound as we walk into the large room.

Everything is decked out in cream and champagne with touches of soft sage green, from the tablecloths to the flowers to the elaborate backdrop of balloons and crisscrossed fabric panels along one wall. Glowing candles in large vases with glittering ornate designs are sprinkled throughout the room, and the lighting is dimmed to give off a romantic feel to the space.

Everything is tasteful and not overly done, with the exception of the photo backdrop—Mother loves a good picture wall.

"It's beautiful," Lenni muses, sounding reserved and not at all like she approves.

"You don't like it." It's a statement, not a question. And for a second, her eyes shimmer as if she's about to cry, but with the next blink they clear, leaving me wondering if it was just a trick of the light.

"I do, actually," she expresses softly. Then, even

quieter, as if I'm not meant to hear, she goes, "I really do."

"Oh, there you two are! Goodness, late to your own party. I was beginning to wonder if I needed to send a car for you," Mother exclaims as she emerges from the crowd of people whose eyes have all turned toward us.

There's a hushed murmur traveling throughout the room. Women sizing up Lenni, deciding whether to approve of the new addition to their social circle, while men raise their eyebrows at the beauty radiating from my bride-to-be.

"You should know by now I'm late to everything, Margo," Lenni jokes as they air kiss each other's cheeks.

"This is true. Come, let's introduce the happy couple." Mother grabs Lenni's hand, and I watch curiously as the woman of my dreams allows it, letting go of me to be led to the other side of the room where there's a small stage. They seem more comfortable in each other's presence, interacting in a way I never saw my mother do with Emily.

Lenni is all warm smiles as she gets introduced to random people, holding herself with an elegance I know is forced and uncomfortable for her, but she never lets it show. Pops meets us at the stage, handing each of us a glass of champagne as all four of us crowd the area, and Mom picks up the microphone to formally announce us.

"Thank you everyone for joining us tonight. We know it was last minute, but as I've learned with my son and his fiancée, they like to rush things." She pauses as the crowd laughs, and I wrap my hand around Lenni's waist again, kissing her temple. "The way we learned of our son's engagement was a little unorthodox, but in the past few weeks, we've gotten to know Valentina, and we are happy to welcome her into our family. So, here's to the happy couple!"

Everyone raises their glasses as she hands me the microphone, and Pops helps her back off the stage as I begin the little speech I prepared. "They say when you know, you know. I can confidently say that from the moment I laid eyes on this woman, I knew right away that I wanted to share the rest of my forever with her. Valentina, you completely took me by surprise at a time when I was ready to give up on love. Our meeting was a complete accident, but I like to think that it was fate. You were always meant to be mine, and I was yours from the moment I spilled coffee all over you on the sidewalk."

Some people laugh, others let out sounds of awe, but the only thing that matters to me is how Lenni looks at me—eyes wide, lips parted slightly as she holds her breath. It's all supposed to be an act, but everything I'm saying comes straight from the space beneath my lungs, reserved only for her now.

"I'm honored that you have agreed to spend the rest of your life with me, and I promise to fill every single day with love and respect and as many Julia Roberts movies as you want."

Everyone claps as I lean down to kiss her chastely. "That was perfect," she whispers.

It was real.

"The hard part is over. Now all we have to do is schmooze people for a while, and then I want to take you home and fuck you in this dress," I murmur in her ear. Her cheeks light up in a rosy hue, and she kisses me again, harder than before, eliciting a few catcalls from throughout the room.

For the next hour, we mingle as I introduce her to people. Many of the guests are friendly, but there are some who look down their noses at her as if she's a fly in their chardonnay.

"Could her dress be any tighter? I was thinking they were rushing to get married because he knocked her up, but her dress looks painted on," a nearby woman says in a scandalized tone, not realizing we're right behind her.

Lenni lets out a laugh and grabs my arm as she asks loudly, "Baby, can you see my underwear in this dress?"

The group behind us turns at her question, but before I can answer, she laughs again. "Oh, that's right. I'm not wearing any! Silly me."

A few gasps sound and the woman who made the rude comment reaches around her neck for imaginary pearls. My lips curl in as I attempt to hide my laughter, recognizing Lenni's spin on a line from her favorite movie.

Suddenly, my mom appears, reaching out to lay a hand on Lenni's arm. "Valentina, did you see the cannoli and pignoli cookies? They are a huge hit! They will be a must have at any event from here on out. I can't believe I'd never had them before."

"Well, you'd have to travel beyond the Upper East Side to try new things, Margo. Don't worry, we'll work on it," Lenni responds warmly.

Something happens in my chest. It pinches before flooding my veins, like a needle popping a water balloon. She planned to make my family think she wouldn't last, and yet, here she is, making plans with my mother for the future.

I don't even know if she's aware of what she's doing—of how her actions are edging our charade closer to being real. It's only been a month since the night we met, but I like to think I know her tells by now. I know when she's putting on a show. At this very moment, there's nothing on her features or in her body language to suggest she's acting.

Reaching for her elbow, I pull Lenni back to me. "Excuse us, Mom. I'm going to steal her away for a moment to ourselves, if you don't mind."

I don't give her a chance to reply as I whisk Lenni away, catching Jackson's eye as I head toward the doors that lead to an ivy-covered terrace that spans the length of the building. He flashes me a smirk and raises a brow, saying something to Ginny that makes her look in our direction with a sly smile.

Something tells me they'll make sure the terrace stays clear while we're out there. It's always good to have friends who encourage you to get your rocks off in the middle of a very public party where you're the main attraction.

"Are we seriously doing this?" Lenni asks as I open one of the doors and usher her outside.

"We don't have to do anything if you don't want to. I just want to hold you for a little while without anyone watching us," I say, pulling her over to the tiny alcove where the railing meets the wall. The ivy crawls up to the roof, the vines dangling down the L-shaped wall where there's just enough space for us both to squeeze into, hiding us from the view of the party or anyone else that may go onto the terrace.

She wraps her arms around my neck, grinning up at me. "You're acting as though we haven't seen each other in a month."

"It feels like it. Just let me be needy, okay? I don't get to have you for very long. Let me enjoy it while I do." My lips find hers, kissing her slowly, greeting her tongue with mine like they're old lovers redis-covering each other for the first time in years.

One of her hands drifts down my chest until she's palming my cock through my pants. Groaning into her mouth as it hardens at her touch, I pull away gently. "We seriously don't have to do anything."

Her gaze darkens as her lips tilt up in a sly smile. "*You* aren't going to do anything. Just stand here and take it like a good boy."

A shiver zips down my spine, cock jumping at her words. "Take *what*?"

Lenni doesn't respond as she gathers the skirt of her dress and lowers herself to sit on her heels, piling the skirt in her lap so it doesn't drag on the dirty stone. Once she secures it, she reaches up to undo the button on my pants.

Knowing what's coming next, the sight of her before me has a liquid rush of heat running through my body. My cock is already painfully hard as she pulls it from its confines. "Fuck, Viv. You are such a fucking vision."

"We look good together, don't we?" she asks, stroking my shaft with slow, measured pulls of her hand as she licks her lips.

Her eyes stray from mine as she opens her mouth and takes me deep. Sucking in a breath, one hand tangles in her hair as I brace the other on the rail behind me. She feels better than I ever could have imagined. Her lips are warm, her tongue hot as she drags it against the underside of the crown and sucks the tip.

"Valentina, I don't think I've ever seen anything as beautiful as you with my cock in your mouth." Gently, I push her head onto me, watching in awe as her eyes flutter closed and her mouth widens to take as much of me as she can.

"Such a good girl, aren't you?" I croon, knowing she likes it when I talk dirty to her. When she lowers one of her hands to touch herself, I stop her. "Don't. Let me do it. I want to be the one to get you off. So sit and take it like a good girl," I throw her words back at her.

Her head bobs faster as I guide her pace. She's being careful to keep it clean, since we have to go back inside at some point, but I can't help but imagine what it will look like next time when she's choking on me, saliva pooling from her mouth as I come down her throat.

Vibrations run up my length, causing my balls to tighten, as she lets out a moan around me, hollowing her cheeks and sucking me harder with every pass. "Fuck, baby, I'm going to come."

She nods and looks up at me. The image sets me off, and I hold her head down as I spill my release into her mouth. Our eyes remain locked as the length of my cock she can't fit into her mouth twitches with every stream of cum. She makes a show of releasing me and sticking out her tongue to show that she swallowed all of it before she leans forward to take me into her mouth again, licking up any mess that was left behind.

"Greedy little cumslut, aren't you?"

Her eyes light up as she rises and smashes her lips against mine. "Fuck, I love it when you talk like that," she says against my mouth as I tuck myself back in my pants.

"I know you do. I love knowing that it gets you all hot and bothered, and that you're probably just a few touches away from coming, aren't you?" I snake my hand through the slit in her skirt to find that she's really not wearing any underwear.

"Tripp," she gasps as I use my index finger to rub lightly over her clit. "If anything gets on this dress, it's going to be obvious what we were out here doing.

Ignoring her statement, I continue to rub her so

lightly that my skin barely touches her. Curling my finger, I scrape the edge of my nail against her sensitive bud.

"Holy fuck," she cries out, hands tightening on my arms.

"When you're about to come, I'll get on my knees and swallow you down like you just did for me," I whisper into the space between us.

Her head tilts back, and her lips part as her breaths come in quick pants while I continue to flick the edge of my nail against her. "How the fuck does this feel so good? You're barely touching me," she whimpers.

Suctioning my mouth against the naked flesh of her neck, I give her a slight love bite before dragging my tongue up the column of her neck to nibble on her ear. "Such sweet sounds you're making for me. Fuck, how I missed your mouth."

She tips her head forward, capturing my lips as her fingers curl into my hair. A shudder runs through her body, and she doesn't even have to tell me that it means she's almost there. Breaking our kiss, I drop to my knees, thrusting her skirt aside to close my mouth around her as she climaxes.

"God, Tripp. How the fuck?" she breathes out when she's finished.

As we rearrange our clothing, I tell her, "I took the week to do some research. Gotta keep you interested if I want to convince you to let me keep you."

She laughs as we wrap our arms around each

other and head back inside. "And here I thought I knew everything there is to know about sex."

As we enter the party, I'm about to reply, but a familiar voice cuts me off, "Ah, there you two are. I was wondering when I'd be able to offer my congratulations."

My blood runs cold as we come face to face with the last person who should be here. "Emily, what are you doing here?"

Lenni

Are you fucking serious?

The only way Emily would be here is if she was invited.

And who sent out the invitations? *Margo.*

What the actual fuck?

Emily drags her gaze down Tripp's body, taking in his rumpled, half-tucked-in shirt and unbuttoned suit jacket before her eyes linger over my mussed hair and swollen lips. I watch as she slowly cants her head to the side, piecing together what we were just doing on the balcony.

As her ivory cheeks redden, I hug Tripp closer and plaster on a beaming, syrupy smile. Making sure to wiggle my ring finger just so, I place my hand on his chest. "Yes, Emily, what a surprise. I don't think we were expecting you."

"My, um…parents…were invited. I decided to tag along. I hope that's okay," she clarifies as her eyes snap to Tripp's.

"Of course, it's okay—the more the merrier. We were just outside getting some fresh air." I pull my gaze from hers to throw Tripp a saucy smile. His fingers tighten on my waist as he returns it, knowing exactly what I'm doing.

Her cheeks redden further. She nods to my ring, her manner bratty. "I thought you said you didn't want something so ostentatious?"

"What can I say? He got his way," I sigh dreamily. "He always gets his way. *Whatever* he wants, I always make sure to keep him happy." Laying my head against Tripp's chest, I scrunch my nose at her and shrug.

"And you do keep me very, *very* happy," he murmurs as he kisses the top of my head. "Anyway, good of you to come, Emily. If you'll excuse us, I'd like to take this beautiful woman for a spin around the dance floor."

My eyes lock with hers as he leads me away, a brow raised in triumph as she watches us go with blatant indignation. She looks like a cartoon character when their face goes all red, and steam starts coming out of their ears as a train whistle blows in the background.

I'm sure Emily understands that she lost a good man. And I'm going to continue making sure Tripp *knows* he's a good man and that he deserves to be cherished, not tossed aside for wanting to expand his sexual appetite.

"Your mother and I are going to have words," I say with a tight smile as people part for us to dance.

The DJ puts on a slow song that happens to be on my Sad Girl Shit playlist on Spotify. "Six Feet Under" by Sara Phillips resonates throughout the room, and I wonder if the jockey knows this isn't exactly engagement party music.

"Trust me, I'm sure she didn't know she was coming," Tripp assures me, pulling me into his arms to sway us to the somber melody.

Looking over his shoulder, I scour the room for his mother. Margo really did a wonderful job with the decorations. The flowers are all silk, so the floral scent doesn't overwhelm Tripp's delicate senses. Soft, white roses with a touch of blush in the middle, accompanied by sprigs of real eucalyptus, litter the tables and catering area. I love eucalyptus, so the fact she included it means a lot. Or maybe she just did it because it seems to be *in* this year.

Though I didn't talk much to Tripp the past week, I've spoken with Margo daily—often multiple times. We're forming a camaraderie, as much as I hate to admit it. I'm drawn to her. In the same way I was always drawn back to Momma.

All you've ever wanted was for someone to take care of you.

It seems like Margo has pushed her ill feelings about the way Tripp and I came together so quickly from her mind. I'd almost say she looks forward to our daily chats, but what do I know? It could just all be an act.

Keep your enemies close and all that.

"What's on your mind, Viv?" Tripp questions, his

fingers rubbing the spot where they rest on my lower back.

"Honestly? How much I hate all of this," I tell him truthfully. Everyone's eyes are on us. People I don't know, and don't want to know, who are only here to further business relations with the Kennedys or other people of power in the room. No one is truly here for *us*, besides Ginny and Jackson.

Beyond the cover of the picture-perfect fairytale, it's a sad, lonely life, in my eyes. And it makes me want to save Tripp from it. I don't want to give him up when this is all over, and I won't be able to stand by and watch him move on with a life I don't think will make him happy.

His body tenses against mine, and he pulls back as his voice drops to barely a whisper. "Is it really all that bad?"

"No. That's not the problem. The problem is that the lines are starting to get blurry for me, Tripp."

His mossy orbs meet mine as a sliver of a smile stretches his lips. He tucks my hair behind my ear, palming my cheek as he strokes it with his thumb. The gesture is wildly intimate even though we're in a crowded room, and it makes my lower body tighten with want despite our audience. Everything about his touch sets fireworks off in my chest, their shim-mering flashes beating against my ribs before dipping into my stomach to melt into feverish butterflies.

"Why is that a bad thing, Viv?" His voice is nearly

a whisper. "Why are you so against giving this a shot for real?"

"You don't know me. I'm not who you think I am. You've made up this version of me in your head that's based on sex and lies, and I guarantee you only feel this way because I'm helping you live out your sexual fantasies without judgment."

He looks away from me with a glower, huffing out a sharp laugh. It ruins the beautiful angles of his face as it creases in harsh, angry lines. "No offense, but do I *seem* like a novice in the bedroom to you?"

Frowning, I shake my head, not understanding his question. "What?"

"Yeah, maybe there are *some* things we've done that are new to me, but you act like I didn't have sex with anyone between you and Emily. I did, Viv—a lot. I was just selective with who I spent my time with. So, your idea that I'm obsessed with you because you've *taught* me all I know is kind of condescending.

"You keep saying that I don't know you that well, but let me tell you something, Valentina. I love everything I *do* know. I love the way your fingers tighten in my hair and how your knees press against my head when you're coming on my tongue. I love how your skin feels against mine—so soft, like silk—and how you fit perfectly against my body. I love that I know you prefer dark chocolate to milk and that you absolutely hate the white stuff. And that you can order dinner in and not have to ask what I want because you already know. I love hearing my name on your lips and that they always taste like strawberries and cream. But most of all, I love the way you look at me. You *see* me and accept every part of who I am. And I hope that by now, you know I accept you for who *you* are."

Tears prick my eyes, and I do my best to blink them away so I don't smear my makeup. All the right words are coming out of his mouth, but I know he doesn't understand the severity of them, because he doesn't truly accept me for who I am. He can't, because I haven't given him those parts that make it impossible for us to be together. He'd expect me to quit my job if we actually tried to give this thing between us a real shot, and he has no idea *why* I can't do that.

He pulls me close, and I lay my head on his shoulder. "Just think about it, Viv."

I already have. And there's no way it can work.

"Thank you for the lovely evening, Margo. It was beautiful, really."

Nearly everyone has left the party. Jackson and Ginny went home almost an hour ago because she was getting tired, and the only reason we've stayed this long is because Margo wanted us to help say goodbye to the guests, since it was *our* party after all.

"It's the least I could do. We will have to get together to discuss the big day now. The Plaza just got a last-minute opening for April. I may have already booked it," she says quickly, looking anywhere but at me.

"Mom, you know Lenni wants a small wedding," Tripp stresses as he fixes her with a stern glare.

Strangely, even though I *did* say that, her actions don't bother me. I'm beginning to learn that meddling is just Margo's way. "Yes, *small*. So, maybe unbook it, please."

She lets out a long sigh. "Can we just wait just a little while? In case I'm able to persuade you otherwise?"

Shaking my head, I hold my arms out to hug her before moving to embrace Weylan. "My mind is already made up—something small and intimate with our close friends. No paparazzi, no big newspaper spreads, just simple. Those are my only conditions."

I'm thankful Tripp doesn't like being in the tabloids as much as Jackson does. The last thing I need is for my face to be splashed all over the papers. Not that anyone at home reads the New York City gossip and high-society columns, but I don't want to take my chances of anyone finding out where I am.

Getting involved with a millionaire is the *worst* thing I could have done for my situation—but at least I'm involved with one who doesn't care about all the glitz and glamor. Now, if I can only get Margo to drop her plans for a huge wedding—it's not like we're going to make it that far, anyway.

We say the rest of our goodbyes, leaving after we

set a time for Margo, Ginny, and me to discuss wedding dresses.

"Do you wanna come back to my place? Or will you finally let me come up to yours?" Tripp asks as we wait for his car to pull around.

Placing a hand on his chest, I press up on my toes to kiss him firmly before I step out of his arms. "You aren't going to like what I'm about to say."

He groans, scrubbing a hand over his face as he asks, "What is it?"

"I think tonight went really well, but I also think it was good for us to spend some time apart this week." My stomach begins doing backflips as his expression falls. "I think we should spend this week apart, too. I picked up a ton of shifts at the restaurant, and I have to go to Jersey for Carmela—"

"Why are you always going to Jersey for her? And why are you pushing me away again?" he interrupts, taking a few steps forward to grab my hands. "Don't do this, Valentina."

"I'm not doing anything. We can still talk. It's not a big deal. It's healthy for our situation."

"You said you'd think about giving this a real shot," he exclaims after looking around to make sure no one can overhear us.

"You asked me to think about it, but I didn't reply, Tripp. There's a difference." I try to keep my words from sounding harsh, but no matter how I word it, I know he will take my decision as a slight against him.

He frowns, just like I knew he would. Cupping

his cheek, I guide him to look at me. "It was so good on the balcony, wasn't it? I challenge you not to touch yourself until we see each other again. Think of it as a game."

A defeated smile pulls at his features, knowing he doesn't have a choice in the matter, just like I know he won't push the issue if I say it's what I really want, because he's just *that* good of a man. His driver pulls up to the curb, and Tripp opens the back door for me, ushering me inside as he asks, "And what's my prize going to be?"

Grinning up at him, I lift my shoulder with a slight shrug. "What do you want?"

He holds my stare as he tells his driver to take me home and informs him he'll call for another car. Once the man raises the partition, Tripp leans down and grasps my chin in his hand, laying an open-mouthed kiss on my lips that almost makes me want to pull him into the car and just take him home.

"I want to fuck your ass."

My teeth clamp down on his bottom lip as my pussy clenches at the thought of him taking that part of me. Running my tongue along the bite to soothe it, I kiss him once more before pulling away. "Deal."

Tripp

"Mr. Kennedy? This came for you while you were out," the concierge calls out as I enter my building. He's holding out a thick white envelope with gold embossing on the front that spells out my name.

"Thank you." I take it from him in passing, all but running to the elevator.

I'm anxious to get upstairs. Lenni left the restaurant and came here to get ready for dinner at Jackson and Ginny's while I finished up at work. After not seeing her all week, I'd rather tie her up and not leave my bedroom all weekend. But she's excited for us all to get together for a normal friendly hangout, and at this point in our situationship, there's really nothing that I'll deny her.

"Honey, I'm home," I singsong as I push open the door.

Her silky voice rings out, filling my place with the playfulness and warmth it's been missing, making me wish I'd given her a key sooner. "Hi, darling. How was work? Would you like a drink? I can make you one and then massage your feet in my undergarments. Would that please you?"

I find her in the kitchen, pouring us a glass of wine, looking absolutely stunning in dark, tight jeans and a cropped, cream sweater that looks like it's made of cashmere. She looks at me with an impish grin. "I hope you know I'm joking."

Tossing the envelope on the counter, I round the island to cage her against it, pressing my chest into her back to nuzzle her neck and kiss her temple. "You are a sight for sore eyes. I missed you."

A sigh escapes her lips before she turns her head and kisses me lightly. "I missed you, too."

Taking my glass, I reluctantly peel myself away from her and sit on one of the stools. "I'll have you know. I was a very good boy this week. I didn't touch myself once, except for showering to clean myself, but I thought of dead puppies while I did it so there was no chance of slipping up and getting a hard on."

"That's...morbidly descriptive. But good for you. I'll take your word for it." She laughs.

"You made me a deal, Viv. I want to collect."

"*So romantic*," she jokes. I swear her eyes darken a shade before she flashes me a sexy smile and quietly says, "Next time we're at the club, we can play."

I don't ask why it has to be at the club. I'm happy to take her to my room and do it before dinner, but her eyes stray to the envelope between us. "What's that?"

"No clue. Looks like an invitation." Grabbing it, I tear open the top and pull out a thick cardstock with matching embossing and an elegant floral design. When I see the name on it, I roll my eyes. "I have no clue why she'd send me one of these."

Tossing it on the counter between us, Lenni slides it toward her and matches my eye roll. "Seriously, Emily? Desperate much? It's like she's trying to make you suffer now that she sees you happy. I hate her."

The anger in her eyes is so evident, so protective, and it tugs at my chest. "It isn't making me suffer. You know that, right?"

Her eyes flicker to me briefly. "What do you mean?"

Sliding from my stool, I saunter toward her, grabbing her hips and backing her into the pantry cabinets. "I'm over her, Viv. I'm so over what happened and completely under you now. I hope you know that."

She opens her mouth to object, but I cut her off by pressing my fingers to her lips. "Don't tell me it isn't healthy to move from one person to another so quickly. It wasn't quick. There was almost an entire year between what she did and our meeting. Stop trying to search for an excuse for this not to work."

To her credit, she doesn't argue further. But the playfulness that exuded from her earlier seeps from the room like water from a cracked vase.

"We should get going," she says against my fingers.

Somewhere in the room, her phone chimes with

an incoming text, and she jolts, ducking away from me. "You should go change."

My head hangs back in defeat as I turn around. She's frowning at her phone. "Is everything okay?"

"Yeah," she snaps quickly, forcefully throwing it back in her purse.

Sensing her mood has turned sour, I take my wine into the bedroom and leave her with her thoughts. I change into dark denim jeans and pull a V-neck sweater over my dress shirt. When I return, the heaviness seems to have retreated.

"Let's go." She takes my empty glass and moves to the sink to rinse it. "To Emily's wedding, I mean. I think it will be a show of good faith. Let her know that you're over what happened and that you wish her nothing but the best."

"I don't think that's a good idea…"

"Why not? If you're over it, then it's just one more event to prove that point to everyone. They are getting married at the beginning of March. I say we do it. Call me petty, but I'd love to say *fuck you* one more time."

I'm starting to think she's taking what Emily did to me personally. I feel no need to attend my ex's wedding, but Lenni's acting like Emily wronged *her*.

"Did you read the invitation? It's an entire weekend in Connecticut."

"Sounds like fun to me."

"You're serious? This is something you want to do?"

"Don't you? Don't you want her to see that her

invitation doesn't bother you? Let's go and have a good time. It'll be fun to get away for a weekend. It's not like we have to attend everything they have planned—just the ceremony and necessary parties." She plants her hands on her hips and looks at me expectantly.

With the way she's searching my face, I think she doesn't believe me when I say I'm really over Emily —like she's trying to search for any cracks in my armor. And even though I think this isn't the greatest idea Lenni has ever had, I find myself nodding my head.

"Okay. If that's what you want."

"Is this official yet?" Ginny asks as she motions between us. "Because the photo you sent me is literally my profile photo for both of you on my phone. It's adorable, and if you two haven't made it official yet, you should."

"What photo?" Lenni looks at me with confusion.

We're all seated in the living room after dinner. Their housekeeper, Claudia, makes the best home-cooked meals next to my mother, so I will never give up an opportunity to come over when I know she's cooking.

Ginny pulls her phone out as I discreetly try and motion for her to stop talking because Lenni doesn't know I snapped a photo of her the night she fell asleep in my arms. I may have made it the home screen image on my phone, and since we haven't reached the point of sharing our phone passcodes with each other, she has no clue.

"This one!" Ginny leans over to show Lenni, and suddenly, I'm very interested in the old, mangy cat that is currently sitting in my lap, getting hair all over my clothes.

"Okay, I'll admit, that's cute. How come you never showed me that?" Lenni asks me.

Catching her gaze, I shrug. "Thought you wouldn't want to see it."

The look she gives me tells me I should have known better, but she's so hot and cold and all over the frying pan that I don't really ever know with her.

Jackson takes a seat next to me on their dark gray loveseat, pulling his precious cat into his lap as he hands me a tumbler of bourbon. "I think it's time to get this guy a friend. He's going to be lonely once the baby comes."

"Finally! That's a great idea, cat daddy. I'll look for the next adoption fair." Ginny flashes him a simple smile, and I swear he melts into a puddle while Lenni and I both snort at her nickname for him.

"You're leaking your emotions all over my pants, *cat daddy*. That, paired with the cat hair, isn't making for a warm home environment."

"Fuck off. You should get one. A cat, that is. Since you'll be on your own again soon," he bites back quietly.

Lenni hears him, and I swear she gives herself

whiplash as quickly as her head spins to glare at him.
"Fuck you, Jackson."

"You need a couple's name. I'm gonna call you guys Trippentina or Valentripp! I like that better," Ginny muses, as though the temperature in the room hasn't just dropped to a degree that would support penguins in the Antarctic. She's never struck me as ditzy or vacuous, so I assume the baby is already affecting her mood.

Or maybe she's just used to Jackson and Lenni's less-than-friendly banter by now.

"Oh my god, those are awful. Be grateful I didn't give you a stupid couple's nickname," Lenni responds, getting up to get another glass of wine. She's not even arguing with Ginny over calling us a couple, and I can't help but focus on that little fact.

"If we're getting one, they are too. What about Jacksonny? Wait, isn't your real name Guinevere? Guineson! That's a good one," I play along as my eyes zero in on the way her ass looks in her jeans, thinking about all the ways I want to fuck her when we get back to my place.

"Absolutely not," Jackson voices.

"I don't know. I kinda like it," Ginny says.

I waggle my eyebrows at her before shooting Jackson a grin. "You're stuck with it now."

"Ginny? What's this?" Everyone's attention turns to Lenni skimming what looks like a newspaper. Her lips are turned down, and she looks like she's holding her wine glass so tightly it may break.

"Oh! I forgot to show you earlier. The Times did

an article on you guys! Tripp, your mother must have sent them one of the photos taken at the party. You guys look so happy. I wanted to keep it in case you hadn't seen it," Ginny exclaims excitedly, getting up from the couch to rush over to her best friend.

Lenni doesn't share her enthusiasm, though. She looks terrified. "Why would Margo do this?"

"Len? What's wrong? I know you guys are faking it, but of course Margo would want *something* in the papers." Ginny puts a hand on her back and says something else in a tone that is too quiet for me to hear.

"Your girl looks like she's about to lose her shit. Get her before she tries to kill the messenger," Jackson warns me.

"You know, your overprotectiveness is getting annoying. I don't know how Ginny puts up with you." I try to keep my tone light, but in all honesty, I'm just as worried about Lenni, who looks like she's about to have a panic attack.

"I'm not feeling that great. I'm gonna go. Sorry, Gin, I hope you don't mind. Please tell Claudia that dinner was delicious as always," Lenni says softly before her eyes find mine. "I'll talk to you later, okay?"

"I'll drive you home."

She doesn't fight me, hugging Ginny tightly as they continue speaking with hushed words. Even Jackson watches them with a worried expression as he helps me gather our things. "What's her deal?"

"I have no idea, but I'm sure it has something to do with Mom overstepping again."

I thought they were in a better place, but by the looks of it, any progress they've made will undoubtedly be knocked back to square one after this.

As soon as the elevator doors close, she turns angry eyes toward me. "Did you know about this?"

"About the article? No, and my mother didn't say anything to me about it, either. I don't think she set it up." Lenni's ire is palpable. "Talk to me. I don't understand what the big deal is, Viv."

"How many times do I have to say no paparazzi? It's one thing for you to take a picture of me and keep it between us and our friends, but I thought I made it very clear that I didn't want my face splashed all over the high-society pages?" She's clenching and unclenching her fists, popping her knuckles repeatedly as her breathing heightens.

"Why, Valentina? Because *this isn't real?* When are you going to wake up? This thing between us is as real as it gets." I turn my body toward her fully to stare down at her, silently begging her to just look at me. Her panic is starting to leach into me. The heightened anxiety fills the elevator like toxic fumes that make me choke on the air.

We make it through the lobby of the building without saying anything, but once we hit the sidewalk, and she picks up her pace to walk away from me, I grab the sleeve of her peacoat and pull her back. "Valentina, talk to me!"

"Why me?" she cries out, turning so abruptly that

I have to step back to avoid colliding with her. Angry tears shine in her eyes, and she does her best to blink them away as she continues. "It could have been anyone, Tripp! Why me? It isn't fair!"

"You're not making sense. Can you *please* just explain what has you so worked up?"

"You don't get it! This *can't* be real. No matter how badly you want it to be."

"Tell me *why*. You're the most infuriatingly intoxicating woman I have ever met. And I want you. Not just for now. But until you realize you're too good for me. Tell me, what isn't *real* about that?"

She looks startled that I would even suggest such a thing. "I put the *toxic* in intoxicating. Trust me, you don't want to be with me."

We're both starting to sound like two different sides of a broken fucking record.

"We're good together, Viv. What happens when the lie goes away? You're just gonna forget all of this?" I motion between us. "We have *amazing* chemistry. Why can't you just give in to that?"

"I have a job that someone like you can't be involved with, Tripp. You can't be caught dating me." Her words break off in a sob as the tears finally fall. But she isn't making any sense. I told her I accepted her and her job. What more does she want?

"I'm dating you *now*."

She sneers. "You're *fucking* me now. We're lying to everyone about the dating part."

Her mocking tone pisses me off, and quite frankly, her words feel like a sucker punch to the gut.

I *know* she has feelings for me. I don't understand why she's fighting it so hard.

"So was that all our first night together was then? You threw me a pity fuck because I dropped a couple grand on you? Is it *all* a show with you? Be whoever they want you to be as long as you get paid?" The second the words leave my mouth, I wish I could take them back.

She recoils as though I've slapped her, but her head remains held high as she fires back, "I *like* my job. I don't want to be a trophy wife who ends up doing nothing with her life except running bullshit charities and pretending like she gives a damn about the latest gossip the other wives are bitching about! I'm not your mother, and I'm *not* Emily!"

Her voice cracks at Emily's name, and she turns away, walking to the curb to hail a cab. This time, I let her go.

"That's a bullshit excuse, Valentina. You know it is. Something is keeping you there. Keeping you from giving this thing between us a real shot," I call after her.

She doesn't respond or look back, and it breaks my fucking heart.

I don't even make it halfway home before I have the driver turn around and head to Lenni's. She's always been adamant about me not seeing her home, but at the moment, I don't care. My conscience doesn't allow me to leave her to deal with her distress by herself. Not when I've unintentionally added fuel to her wildly out-of-control emotional fire.

West 26th is quiet when we arrive. One side of the street looks like newer buildings, while the other side, the one Lenni lives on, is all old brick that's falling apart with boarded up windows to multiple businesses that have closed permanently.

Her Chelsea apartment is nestled between a Cantonese restaurant and a nail salon—a single black door leading to walk-up style residences. It's locked, and I usually have to call or buzz the door to let her know I'm here. Luck is on my side, though, when a man leaves the building, catching the door for me when he sees me jogging toward it from the car.

Taking the stairs two at a time to the third floor, I try not to sound like a cop as I bang on her door. "It's Tripp. Open up."

For all I know, she didn't even come home. A knife twists in my gut at the thought that she may have gone to Désirer. It's Friday, and she once told me Friday's were one of her busiest nights.

The pinching in my stomach releases when I hear sounds coming from the other side of the door. Her voice is muffled, but I can still make out that she's been crying as she asks, "What are you doing here?"

"Open the door, Viv. I can't help if you don't tell me what's wrong." Bracing my arms on either side of the doorframe, I drill holes into the wood between us with my eyes, hoping she'll let me in.

A door on the other side of the hall behind me opens, and an elderly woman pokes her head out. "You've got the wrong door, sonny. Ain't no one lives there by the name of Viv."

"Inside joke," I explain, looking back to the door when I hear the click of a lock.

And another.

And another.

And another.

What are you hiding from?

Honeyed orbs peer out at me from between a crack as she opens the door, and then, with the slide of one more lock, she opens it completely. Her eyes are glassy and rimmed in red from the tears she's shed, the tip of her nose pink as if she's been rubbing at both. She's changed into an oversized pair of gray sweats with the waist rolled down and a small white top that barely covers her ample breasts.

Despite the situation, my cock stirs in my pants, as it usually does whenever she's near. "Talk to me."

I prepare for her to fight me, but her face crumbles as a fresh batch of tears falls down her flushed cheeks. Pulling her into me, I walk us backward as she buries her face in my chest. Closing the door behind me, I study the numerous locks. "What is all of this about?"

Her fists grip my shirt tighter, her tears coming faster—harder—and I begin to worry about what's going on in a way I haven't before. Kissing the top of her head, I gather her in my arms and carry her over to a red loveseat in the living room. "Valentina, are you in some kind of trouble?"

She curls around me as we sit, burying her face in my neck. "I'm sorry. I'm such a fucking mess," she sobs.

"We're all fucking messes, babe. Some of us just have the means to cover it up with good suits and fat checks."

It takes another few minutes, but she finally calms down. I take the time to study her apartment. It's all painted white brick and cold linoleum flooring covered in brightly-colored mismatched rugs. The kitchen is smaller than my half bath, with appliances that look like they've seen better days, and a door on the other side of it leads to a small bathroom. It looks like she's tried to breathe a little life into the sterile place, but it doesn't scream *home* to me.

Grabbing a white and gray faux rabbit throw from the back of the loveseat, she wraps it around herself and crawls out of my lap to settle next to me. "I didn't want to drag you into *my* mess."

"I think it's a little too late for that." Reaching out, I tuck a piece of her hair behind her ear. "Now what's going on?"

Her cheeks puff out dramatically as she blows air out between her lips. "I don't even know where to begin."

"How about at the beginning?"

She stares distantly at a spot on the wall. "You won't look at me the same after you hear what I have to say." Her gaze locks on mine, and I pick up her hand to thread our fingers together. "But honestly, I'm tired of keeping it all to myself. And I want to tell you because…because you're right. I'm running from this thing between us. I've been running from my past for a long time, and I just need to catch my breath."

"Whatever it is, we can take care of it," I tell her softly. Cupping her cheek with the hand that isn't laced with hers, I rub at her tear tracks with my thumb.

"It isn't that easy." She takes a large breath and tips her head back before exhaling deeply. "When I was a little girl, my momma sold me for drugs."

My brows furrow, and my breath catches in my lungs, going as still as the waters in an undisturbed lake. Surely she doesn't mean…

"Men would pleasure themselves while I sat on the floor, naked. I don't need to get into specifics, but I'm sure you can imagine. When I was old enough, she started letting them have sex with me."

Tears line her eyes again. She won't look at me, and I'm thankful for that because I feel like I'm about to throw up. Horror grips my chest. The kind that fills you when you're watching a scary movie and the music makes everything seem so much worse. When you're waiting for that jump scare, but it still hits you unexpectedly. My heart hammers against my rib cage, shredding its bloody knuckles on the bones and dripping acid rage into my stomach.

"I work at Désirer because it's what I know. It's what I'm good at. Carmela found me in a dingy strip club when I first moved to the city. She saved me. Helped me find a place to live and gave me a job at the restaurant. Eventually, she trusted me enough to tell me about the club and asked if I wanted to work there instead."

When she looks at me, I know there are tears in my eyes. I can't fathom a mother doing that to her child. Whatever I thought Valentina was going to admit to me, it wasn't *this*.

"You're so much more than what you can do with your body, Valentina." My words are tight and watery as I attempt to calm the emotions coursing through me.

She shrugs. "When you're told something enough, you begin to believe it, especially at that age."

"What happened? How did you get out?" Hastily, I wipe my eyes. I don't want her to think I pity her. I *hurt* for her. My chest aches at the mere thought of what she had to endure.

She starts picking at her fingernails, one of her nervous traits. "One of the guys began to offer me cash on the side. We stopped going through Momma and made our own deal. Eventually, I stashed away enough to leave."

Things are starting to make sense. How she's so unsure the closer we become. The comments she keeps making about being paid to make men feel special. The push and pull of her emotions—because it's so crystal clear to me that she wants to be together but she's holding herself back.

Because all she knows is men hurting her and letting her down.

All she's ever experienced is pain.

She's had to live with her guard up for so long, she doesn't know how to let it down.

"Fuck, Valentina…I don't know what to say. I'm so sorry you went through that." I pull her other hand into mine and kiss her knuckles before cradling them between us. "Is this why you're so hesitant to date me? If you thought it would change my mind about you, it doesn't."

She doesn't answer me, eyes lowering to her stomach absentmindedly, where her scar is.

Pain pierces my heart like a needle has been jammed into it like a fucking voodoo doll. "Did you get that scar from one of those men?"

I'll fucking kill whoever did this to her.

"One of them really liked to cause pain. I didn't mind it so much at first. I learned to disassociate early on whenever it was happening. But, one night, there was a bottle." Her voice grows soft, her eyes turning glassy like she's reliving the memory. "He broke it, and all I can remember is screaming out for Momma. The memories are hazy, but she killed him for it. She saved me."

Hearing her talk about her mother like she's some kind of hero for killing the man who she let rape her daughter is sickening. It's taking everything I have to keep down the bile that's clawing at my throat while she tells her story.

"Still, they took her to jail. Then, she was in

prison for only a short time, under two years. They didn't have the resources to keep drug abusers locked up, and under the circumstances, killing that man fell under self-defense. As soon as she was released, as much as I hated myself for feeling sorry for her, I was there to pick her up and get her the help she needed."

"Fuck…Valentina…" Her eyes well up again, causing mine to do the same, and I tighten my fingers around hers as she continues.

"She was like my sun, you know? She hurt me when I got too close, but I couldn't stay away. I needed her to live. And I kept thinking that one day she'd be proud of me, of what I was doing for her. I used to dream of the day she'd wrap me in her arms and tell me it was all over, and I could stop. That I'd done such a good job for her. How messed up is that?"

Unable to control myself, I pull her back into my lap and bury my face in her neck as I cry for her. She holds me back, arms tightening around me as we both shake in our grief. Her, for her lost childhood, and me, for the unimaginable pain she had to go through.

"It's why I like being told I'm a good girl. I like the praise. At the club, though, it's usually me who is doing the praising. That's why I like it so much when you say it," she whispers.

Suddenly, even though she's admitting she likes it, I'm unsure of how to handle our sexual relation-ship. I want her to know that she means more to me than just sex, but it's such a big part of her life I wonder if it would do more harm than good to cut her off from it completely.

"Do you talk to anyone? A therapist?" I finally ask.

She shakes her head against my shoulder. "As you can see, I'm not exactly able to afford it."

"That's fucking ridiculous. Apparently, I need to have words with Jackson about how much money Angels make." With as much as a membership costs, and for what the Angels have to do, they should all be rich as fuck. Yet, she lives in a shoebox the size of my bedroom.

She snorts and burrows deeper into my arms as I lay us back and stretch out. "I make great money. It just goes to Momma's rehab. Drugs got snuck into the prison all the time, so she never fully got clean. And she was involved in a fight with the guards where she got beat pretty badly. She struggled a lot when they released her. She's been in and out of numerous facilities, and her mental health is terrible, but at least she's clean. It's why I freaked out about the photo in the paper, though. Even though I talked about New York a lot when I was growing up, she doesn't know where I am, and I don't want to be found. Photos in the paper could lead her right to me."

That explains why she freaked out about the article.

A question sits on the tip of my tongue, one that could potentially bring up more bad memories. "If you don't mind me asking. What about your father? What happened to him?"

She freezes in a way that makes me think there's something connecting my question to the locks on her door. Her voice turns hard as she declares, "That's an entirely different fucked up story. One I don't ever want to tell."

Minutes pass by in silence, and I stroke her hair while holding her in my arms, replaying everything she's just told me. "Viv?"

"Yeah?" Her voice is thick, like she's drifting off to sleep.

"No one will ever hurt you again. I won't let them. I'll protect you. All you have to do is let me."

"I know." She sounds so tired. "Because you're Prince Charming. But I'm no princess. I always save myself."

Lenni

"You guys are cute together. Just date him already! Trust me, that man wants that ring to mean something." Ginny picks up a frilly, pink dress that looks like it belongs on a stuffed teddy bear and scrunches her nose. "I will have no idea how to handle a girl with Jackson's genes. God, I hope it's a boy." After we met for lunch, Ginny wanted to kill some time before returning to work, so we found a cute little children's boutique called Spring Flowers.

"It isn't that easy, Gin. Tripp is...*intense*, for lack of a better word. His feelings are a lot, and he projects them openly. I don't know how to deal with all of that coming from one man." I browse a rack of baby boy onesies with patterns of dinosaurs and monster trucks. I don't understand the appeal of spending tons of money on baby clothes. Babies grow out of them so quickly. I'd rather spend my money on things they can grow *into*—educational books and interactive games. Does that make me a bad aunt-to-be?

As for Tripp, I haven't exactly been *hiding* since I told him my life story almost a week ago, but I've been keeping myself busy. His overprotective tendencies have more than doubled, and even though I'm strictly sticking to the Confessional wing at work, he's acting like my own personal bodyguard.

Carmela even made a joke about putting him on the payroll.

He's been treating me like an antique fragile vase to be protected at all costs—but I'm not made of glass.

We haven't even had sex. It's almost as if he's afraid to touch me now.

"That's relatable. Jackson is intense, too. Always has been. I don't mind it, though. It makes me feel loved, and I think I needed it long before he came around. I was like a dry sponge, ready to soak it all up."

Even though it makes for a weird mental image, she hit the nail right on the head. Tripp's actions both exhilarate and scare me. It's nice to feel cared for, for once. But I didn't tell him the whole truth about my past—the part that makes it impossible to jump in with everything I have.

Yet, it feels good to have someone who knows most of what happened.

"I don't know. I mean, we kind of *are* dating. I guess," I mumble, even though I'm adamant we're not when Tripp says the same thing. "He's going to want me to quit, though, and I don't want to."

I can't.

Ginny makes a face as she holds up a pair of tiny suspenders with all types of sports balls printed on them. "Tripp seems reasonable, Len. You've been working just the Confessional wing for weeks, and he seems content with that."

"If I were anyone else, Carmela wouldn't put up with a boyfriend hanging around, keeping tabs."

"She let Jackson do it. She knew he was my stranger the whole time."

"True, I guess. But to be fair, Jackson was being prepped to take over Scott's portion of the club. So, as an upcoming partner, it made sense why she was more lenient with him." A robe catches my attention. It's so tiny. Purple and fluffy, like a miniature version of the one I used to have when I was younger.

"I miss Scott," Ginny sighs. "He'd have been so thrilled about the baby. Sadie is over the moon, but Jackson *hates* that she keeps calling Tyler Grandpa."

Sadie is Jackson's aunt, and Tyler is her much younger husband—as in twenty years her junior. He's younger than Jackson, and they don't exactly get along that well. "Tyler is a fucking babe. I can't picture anyone calling him Grandpa."

Ginny laughs. "He really *is* hot. But I swear if you tell anyone I said so, I'll deny, deny, deny."

"What are you guys going to do when the baby comes? Your master isn't exactly set up for a crib."

"Jackson is already looking at bigger places. He

wants to stay in the city. He's got his eye on the Central Park Tower penthouse and is negotiating with the owner, who *isn't* selling it."

"Jesus. Jackson *would* bully someone out of their home. How do you feel about that? Do you guys really need all that space?"

"He seems to think so. At this point, it's useless to argue with him. He wants Claudia to move in full-time and have extra rooms for the grandparents to stay for the holidays. That means you and Tripp, too."

"Oh, joy. That's gonna be awkward." I can only imagine what that will look like when—*if Lenni*—we split, and he brings another woman to get-togethers.

Ginny turns toward the register with a handful of clothes I didn't realize she was gathering during our perusing. "No, it won't. Because you two are staying together. And that's final. You like him, and he *more* than likes you. Your meet-cute was absolute destiny. That man worships the ground you walk on, and you deserve a good guy. I've never seen you date anyone in all the time we've known each other, but the way you two are together is so natural. Just accept it."

With a sigh, I retrieve my phone from the depths of my purse while I wait for Ginny to complete her purchase, and find a message from Tripp.

You're mine next weekend. Sorry, not sorry. I asked Carmela to cancel your clients. I'll make sure you still get paid what you would have made.

I can't help the smile that stretches over my face.

> What are we doing next weekend?

Birthday surprise. I know, I know. It's a little early. But I wanted to do it before J and G's wedding.

Also, when should I expect you tonight?

Most nights, I stay at Tripp's. At this point, I have a toothbrush and an entire section in the medicine cabinet.

And the closet.

And his dressers.

I thought it might be weird since he hasn't initiated anything sexually between us, but it's nice to fall asleep in his arms without any expectations.

I feel safe.

Wanted.

> When are you off work?

I can leave early today, around five. There's a new Julia Roberts movie out on Netflix. I added it to the watchlist.

This man.

> Sounds great. I'll come over around six with Chinese. :)

"Where are we going? How am I supposed to know what to pack?" Balancing my phone on my shoulder, I frantically search my clothing racks for my favorite little black dress. Tripp will be showing up within the hour, and I held off packing anything in hopes he'd give in and tell me where he's taking me.

Secretly though, I love that he hasn't told me. And by the looks of it, he doesn't plan to. What he *did* tell me is that it's a quick two-day trip.

"You're probably scouring your room right now for your little black dress, aren't you?" I can *hear* him smirking through the phone. "Moment of truth. Ginny snuck in yesterday while you were at the restaurant and packed everything you'll need."

"That sneaky bitch," I exclaim, twirling around with a hand on my hip to try and figure out what she packed.

Tripp's laugh on the other end of the line is full and warm, sending tingles down my spine to the tips of my toes, like stepping in front of a fire after you've been outside in the cold air for hours. "I can't wait to whisk you away, even if it's just for the weekend."

His voice is full of promises—long nights between the sheets and endless orgasms. He's slowly been working his way up to sleeping together again. A simple caress that turns into him rubbing me to completion over my pants. Cuddling while watching a movie that ends up with his head between my thighs.

Tripp has been focusing entirely on making me feel good and hasn't even attempted to get me to give him a hand job, blow job, or have actual sex. And while being with a man who is all about your pleasure is great, I miss the way he bites his lip when he comes and the way he looks at me with so much purpose, like he's trying desperately not to close his eyes and miss a second of us being together.

Curling a lock of hair around my finger, I lean on the doorframe and tell him, "I'm happy we're going away, Tripp. It will be nice to have a little calm before all the crazy the next few weeks have in store."

Ginny and Jackson's wedding is next weekend, and Emily's is two weeks later. Then, if Margo has anything to say about it, Tripp and I will be right behind them.

"Me too, Viv. I'm about to leave the office. I'm going to run home and pick up our bags, then I'll be there to get you."

"Sounds good. See you soon."

As the driver pulls up to the airport, I turn to Tripp with wide eyes and a grin that makes my lips hurt. "We're flying somewhere?"

He takes in my face with his own handsome

smile, reaching over to cup my neck and pull me closer before kissing me softly. "It's still a surprise."

"How will you keep it a surprise once we've checked in?" I bolt from the car with eagerness, bouncing from one foot to the other while Tripp gets our bags. They are both small enough to carry on, meaning we won't have to check anything or wait around for luggage when we get to our destination.

"I've already checked us in, and as soon as we're on the other side of TSA, you are getting blindfolded." He chuckles smoothly. "Our plane is already boarding."

"Already boarding? Won't going through security take a while?"

Tripp's answering look reminds me a little of Jackson when Ginny used to point out something that wouldn't be possible for us poor mortals to achieve, but gods like *them* could with their endless amounts of money.

Turns out, I'm right.

We breeze through security, no one even batting an eye as Tripp blindfolds me and leads me to our gate. He charms the gate attendants and guides me down the air bridge. From the sounds of it, everyone he speaks to in passing is in on the fact that he's doing his best to surprise me.

When he finally removes the blindfold, we're seated in first class, and a flight attendant is pouring us champagne. "Here you go, Mr. and Mrs. Kennedy. If you need anything at all, don't hesitate to ask. We'll be taking off shortly."

Neither of us corrects her, though my diamond sparkles brightly on my finger sans an actual wedding band. Tripp clinks his glass against mine. "I'd say that was pretty successful."

Looking around, I realize there's no one else in our section of the plane, and they are closing the doors. "Where are the other passengers?"

"Back in coach. I bought out first class so we can enjoy our time together." His hands tangle in my hair as he kisses me passionately.

Even though we don't have sex, we bring a whole new meaning to the term mile-high club that ends with me riding his fingers while he shields me with his body.

I don't even want to know how much he paid for the attendants to leave us completely alone during the flight. But I'm glad he did.

Tripp can't keep me from hearing them announce over the speakers when we arrive in Florida. My heart pinches at his thoughtfulness, remembering when I told him I'd never been to a beach but always wanted to go.

Emotions flood my eyes as he smiles and tucks my hair behind my ear. "I know it's a little early, but happy birthday, Viv."

It's dark when we leave the airport. The air is balmy

and thick with the smell of salty ocean and fragrant foliage. We drive for another hour, and I enjoy every second of the journey over the Sanibel Causeway.

There's live music in town as we drive through Sanibel. Businesses are lit up with glowing lights strung between palms, and the laughter of the locals. And even though it's late, the water is calm and peaceful on the short ferry ride to Captiva Island, where we're staying.

The island is quiet, and small enough that we rent a golf cart to get to our waterfront rental, doing our best to contain our laughter as we take turns driving. The house, however, is huge, and way larger than we needed for just the two of us. Every inch of the three stories is decorated in cream and gulf water blue, with touches of sand and shells. There's a jacuzzi in the master suite, with a balcony that overlooks the backside of the house.

Giant palms decorate the grounds, the edges lined with leafy trees tall enough to hide the yard from the neighbor's view. The pool is gigantic, and just beyond the edge of the grass is a small beach that leads to a personal boat dock.

"It's perfect," I whisper as Tripp wraps his arms around me from behind.

"You look good out here. You look good every-where, but especially on this balcony. Maybe I should ask the owner how much they'd be willing to sell the place for," he says, nuzzling my neck.

"What is with you and Jackson bullying people

out of their homes?" I laugh, placing my hands over his where they rest on my waist.

"We just want our women to have everything they deserve." He slides his hands from beneath mine, and starts to drag my maxi skirt up my legs.

"Your women? You sound like a caveman." My voice is breathless as he exposes me to the fragrant air. Something about the tropical flowers doesn't seem to bother his senses like the roses at the club.

Tripp lowers to his knees behind me, pressing on my lower back and gently guiding my ankles apart until I'm bent and spread before him. He tastes me from behind with a long, languid stroke of his tongue, his hands kneading my cheeks where he holds my skirt out of his way.

"Fuck, you always taste so goddamn good," he whispers before licking me again. His words pull a moan from my lips, my fingers tightening on the railing as he devours me until I come so hard my legs shake, and I nearly collapse.

"Tripp?" I ask as he rises.

"Yeah, Viv?"

"I'm not going to break. We can have sex. I need you." I turn and capture his lips, loving the way I taste on his tongue. All the pent-up tension from not having him inside me unfurls between us as I force him back into the bedroom and tear at his shirt. Buttons fly. Seams rip. We must have had the same idea because there are already condoms waiting on the nightstand when we fall onto the bed.

It's reminiscent of our first night together. Wild

and passionate yet comfortable. Tripp is tireless as he worships my body and caters to my every need in between rounds. We come together, then wrap ourselves in white robes and cook the food he asked the host to stock the fridge with, since the store was closed by the time we arrived. There's steak and wine, and when those are finished, we stay entangled in each other until the sun begins to come up.

The balcony doors stay open, the sun bathing our naked bodies in a tangerine glow as it rises. The only reason we finally rest is because we made it through the entire box of condoms.

It's the most perfect birthday present ever.

"I don't know about this. I'm honestly fine with staying here in the warm sand, looking for shells while you swim."

"I promise you, Viv, I won't let you go. Look at how calm the water is. It's part of why I picked this place. It's quiet, calm, and perfect for you to tread water."

The weather is so perfectly warm, I know I'll have a hard time leaving tomorrow. But even with how inviting the crystal clear turquoise water looks, I'm hesitant to dip more than my toes in it.

"Tripp, you have to *promise* you won't let me go," I stress.

His abs glisten with rivulets of water that drip

down his skin as he stalks closer, pushing his curls out of his face. "Valentina, I'm not going to let you go."

There's a double entendre there, but my nerves don't allow me to dwell as I pull off my sunglasses and toss them on the towel with the cute black and red sundress Ginny packed for me. Tripp grabs my hand, and I let him pull me to the water's edge. Digging my toes in the soft white sand, I pull him back as he starts to wade in. "Wait! What if there's a rip current thing, you know, the one that pulls you in and is really dangerous?"

He laughs and pulls me into his side. "That's a valid point, but I promise you we don't have to worry about it. I'll teach you how to spot one when we get back home. We're good today, though."

His confident demeanor eases my anxiety a little, and I allow him to pull me out until the water laps at the tops of my breasts. "I don't want to go any further."

"It's okay, we won't. I want you to hold on to my shoulders and lift your feet. You can wrap your legs around my waist if you want."

I do as he says, trusting him to keep me afloat. "See? I've got you. You okay with me going a little further?"

"Yeah, that's okay." The water is warm, and he's right about it being calm. It ripples gently as it breaks against our skin, and next to us, I see a school of tiny, colorful fish dart by. "Tripp, look! Fish!"

He chuckles, spinning toward where I'm pointing

even though he doesn't take his eyes off me. From my peripheral, I can tell he's just as focused on my face as I am on trying to find more sea life below the surface. "See? It's nice out here, isn't it?"

His hands drop to my thighs before hooking under my knees and pushing me away from him. "Keep holding me and kick your feet gently."

Suddenly, I'm not nervous anymore. I'm determined to tread water on my own. "I feel like a little kid. We should have brought those floaty things for my arms."

He laughs. "I'll be your floatation device."

We spend nearly half an hour working at it before I feel confident enough to let him go. My chest constricts as I sharply draw in air every time my chin hits the water, but Tripp never leaves my side, his fingers skimming my waist whenever he thinks I'm about to panic.

"You did fantastic. A couple more visits and you'll be ready to learn how to swim," he says as we retreat to the shore.

We spend the rest of the day watching the clouds go by while we soak up the sun. As the large glowing ball of light begins to descend below the horizon, it paints the sky in swaths of oranges and yellows that gradient into pinks and purples.

Tripp lays his head on my stomach, while I run my fingers through his curls. "Do we have to leave?"

"Unfortunately, we do. Unless you can convince our friends to move their wedding here," he jokes. "In all seriousness, though. I'm really proud of you,

Valentina. Thank you for trusting me enough to take you out there today."

Warmth floods my veins at his praise. It's different than when he calls me a good girl. It makes me feel happy and loved and cared for. I feel like he *gets* me, even though he still doesn't know the entire story of my past.

Thinking back to when we were out in the ocean, I can't help but liken the lesson to my life. "It's a good metaphor. I've been treading water for so long, terrified of being pulled under, wondering when I will be ready to swim. Maybe all I needed was a floaty."

Tripp looks up, the stubble on his face scratchy against my stomach as his arms tighten around me. "I told you earlier, I won't let you go. You'll be ready to swim soon. I'll make sure of it."

In that moment, I decide that I'm going to tell him the rest of my story. Once we're back from Connecticut, I'll tell him everything. And if he still wants me…

He already has me.

T he lady at Harry Winston recognizes me as I walk arm in arm into their store with Ginny. This trip isn't planned, like the last one, when Lenni and I picked out her engagement ring.

She eyes Ginny warily as she greets us. "Mr. Kennedy, good to see you again so soon. What can we do for you today?"

"My gorgeous fiancée's friend here is also tying the knot two days from now, and she wanted to get her a maid-of-honor gift," I explain.

Ginny unlinks our arms and goes to the counter. "I can speak for myself, thanks. But yeah, what he said. Something to match her ring."

"Of course! Are we thinking earrings? A bracelet?" She moves behind the counter to start grabbing pieces.

"I want her to sparkle! She deserves it. Plus, we chose her birthday weekend to get married. It's the least I can do," Ginny tells her.

"You know, most brides don't want their bridal parties to *sparkle*. They stick them in unflattering dresses and pick plain hairdos." I laugh.

"Lenni would sparkle in a paper bag. I have the means now to buy her something pretty for her birthday, so that's what I want to do. She's wearing red, for fuck's sake. There will be nothing boring about her. I want her to shine." Ginny points at a pair of earrings that look like little flowers.

"Excellent choice. The cluster collection has a matching bracelet and two different necklace options that we have ready to go." The associate starts putting pieces away, leaving out the ones that match the earrings.

"Why don't you get her *one* piece, and I'll get the others so that Jackson doesn't have a heart attack when he hears how much you dropped on a woman he can't stand," I tell Ginny, pointing at the more delicate of the necklaces and nodding to the lady.

"Fine. But Jackson adores Lenni. He just has a weird way of showing it. I think he'd be kinder if he weren't afraid she'll break your heart." Her words are leading as she looks at me out of the corner of her eye. "But I have a feeling that after your weekend in the Keys, whatever was holding her back isn't an issue anymore."

My lips stretch so wide they hurt. We've only been back for a few days, but those days have been nothing short of magical. Lenni hasn't explicitly said she's ready to give a real relationship a shot, but it's exactly what we've been doing. She's no longer forcing a wedge between us when she thinks we're getting too close. She's been amicable with Mother at family dinner.

She talks about the future like we have one together.

"Did I tell you the guy called me crazy when I offered him triple what that house is worth? I told him I *am* crazy and that I won't leave him alone until he sells it to me."

Ginny and I hand over our Black Cards as she rolls her eyes with a smile. "You and Jackson really are crazy. He did the same thing with the Central Park penthouse. Do you understand how gross that is?"

"Jackson wants to take over the city. What better way to keep an eye on his kingdom than from the top of it?"

She groans. "I suppose. God knows I love that man, but I can't imagine raising kids with that kind of mentality. That everything can be bought. You know? Maybe you don't. You're trying to buy Lenni a beach house you guys will only visit a few times a year. I think you *looove* her," she singsongs.

The space between us fills with a pregnant pause. Another couple walks up to the counter next to us— the woman has stars in her eyes and the man looks like he's terrified while they look at the jewelry. "When did you know you were in love with Jackson?"

A warm smile spreads across her face as her hand drifts absentmindedly to her stomach. "I told him, for the first time, after your mother's birthday party. But honestly, I started falling in love with him on the anniversary of his father's death." She looks at me knowingly. "When did you realize you're in love with Lenni?"

The associate makes her way back to us and begins wrapping up the pieces. I snort a laugh and let out a long sigh. "New Year's," I say quietly, turning my back so only Ginny hears me. "Though, I could argue I knew it when she crawled on top of my piano the first night we met."

"I'm craving sweets. Do we have any more caramel sauce?" Lenni asks as she rummages through my fridge.

I love that she says *we* as if this is now her home, too. "Pretty sure we depleted all sundae toppings on your birthday."

Even though she hates Valentine's Day, her birthday, I couldn't let the day pass without trying to make it somehow memorable in the same way she changed New Year's for me. We spent the night eating sundae toppings off each other's bodies before fucking in the shower just to do it all over again.

I had cherries in places a man should never have cherries.

"Guess I'll have to wait till I get to Ginny's," she sighs. "She's been having a craving for mini cupcakes. I don't know why she doesn't just get large cupcakes, but she keeps saying that if she eats a whole pack of mini ones, she doesn't feel as guilty because they only add up to two large cupcakes."

"Girl math." I laugh, typing away on my Macbook as I finish a report. "What are you ladies going to do tonight on this last night of freedom?"

"Jackson arranged for us to have a spa night, so a whole lot of relaxing and eating tiny confections that Sadie and Rylee sent up from Sugar and Scotch. What about you guys? I'm a little surprised you're not throwing a bachelor party." Lenni crosses the kitchen to wrap her arms around my neck, leaning into me just to be close.

I relish these moments when she's openly affectionate without me initiating it. Since we got back from Florida, it's almost as if she can't go long without touching me in some way or another. Like she's constantly marking me as hers.

"We are ordering pizza. Jackson is bringing his best bourbon, and we plan on playing video games for the majority of the night. At least until he has to go to bed so he can get his beauty rest and not have bags under his eyes for photos tomorrow. Jackson said he wasn't interested in any kind of party that would give any females the impression he was looking to get lucky before being tied down."

"Good for him. And for you. If you got caught by the paparazzi like he did that one time, I'd go to jail for murder. Oh! I have eye masks here. Remember we did a mini spa night? I have all sorts of things you guys could do."

"Viv, seriously?" I deadpan, even though I'm secretly preening at how possessive she sounds over me.

"What? Oh, come on! No one will see you guys. And you've done it with me before. I made that photo my home screen." She pulls her phone out to show me the photo of us with our hair pulled back with fluffy pink headbands that say *gorgeous*, pumpkin masks smeared on our skin, and gold-carat gel patches under our eyes.

"Why do I pull off that headband so much better than you?" I tease.

Her eyes widen as she smiles and smacks my shoulder, placing her phone on the counter by my laptop. "I'd say rude, but you're kinda right."

As she walks away down the hall to my room, her phone lights up with a text from Ginny. "Ginny just sent you a message!"

"What's it say?" she calls back.

Now that I know the passcode to her phone, I open it and click on the message app just as another one comes through.

Only this time, it isn't Ginny.

It's her mother. And my stomach roils with waves of nausea as I read through the messages.

I don't want to be here anymore.
Please let me leave.

Valentina, please. I need you.

The only message Lenni has responded to is the one at Christmas, and I feel my heart splinter into thousands of sharp pieces. It's one thing to hear her story. It's another thing entirely to see her mother speak to her this way and know that Lenni still seeks some sort of approval from the person who was supposed to keep her safe.

It's clear from her mother's messages saying someone is going to kill her, and saying someone is going to kill Lenni, that she's clearly not in her right mind.

Lenni's footsteps in the hall have me hastily

exiting the thread and swiping right to mark it as unread before quickly pulling up Ginny's message.

"What did Gin say?" Lenni asks again, tossing her overnight bag on the ground.

Tension fills my chest. "She… uh… she wants to know if you can get her a jar of peanut butter…for her pickles."

"Weird ass pregnancy cravings." Lenni takes her phone from me and types out something before sticking it in her back pocket. I must not be as good of an actor as she is, because she searches my face with a frown. "Are you okay?"

Nodding, I pull her into me, cradling her head in the crook of my neck. "Just gonna miss you tonight."

She squeezes me tighter, kissing my neck gently. "Something tells me Jackson likes to be the big spoon, so at least you'll get cuddles."

I laugh when all I really want to do is tell her how fucking sorry I am that she had the childhood she did. That I don't want her to do the therapy session. Not with her mother.

I'm going to protect her.

Even if that means protecting her from herself.

Lenni

"Len, if you cry, your makeup will smear," Ginny gently scolds me as a hairstylist puts the finishing touches on her updo.

"You're getting married, Gin! And you look so beautiful. I can't help it." I blink rapidly, trying to keep my emotions at bay.

Ginny looks stunning in an off-the-shoulder mermaid gown made of tulle and lace with a semi-cathedral train. The sweetheart neckline shimmers with crystals and pearls, with floral and vine lace appliques covering the entire dress. Her hair is a mass of curls on top of her head, with a beaded hair-piece on one side of the elaborate style.

She's classically gorgeous, and I'm so damn happy for her.

Once the stylist finishes, Ginny grabs three boxes from the vanity she's in front of and motions for me to sit next to her. "Only one of these is from me. The other two are from your man. We may have collaborated on your gift."

Shock ripples through me as I recognize the packaging from Harry Winston. "Ginny, you didn't need to get me anything!"

"What good is marrying a billionaire if you can't spend his money?" She laughs. "Besides, it was a good chance for Tripp and me to have a little talk."

"What kind of talk?" I ask pointedly as I open the first box to find a stunning, sparkly pair of stud earrings that look like flowers. "Wow, Gin. These are so beautiful. Thank you."

The second box has a matching bracelet, and she helps me clasp it around my wrist after I secure the earrings. "He loves you, you know. I don't know how you possibly couldn't know. It's written plainly on his face whenever he looks at you."

My heart skips a beat. It's too soon to be throwing out the L word, but even as she says it, there's a feeling that runs through me. It's like being wrapped in a down comforter straight from the dryer. Like sitting in front of a fire with hot cocoa while you watch the snow fall outside. It's warm and comforting and familiar—because I've been feeling it for some time now.

"I think I love him, too," I whisper the words out loud for the first time, my cheeks burning as I open the third box to reveal a necklace made of brilliant marquise diamonds.

"I don't think you do, Len. I *know* you do. I think you should tell him."

"Today isn't about me, Ginny. It's *your* day. So why are we dressing me in enough diamonds to look like I'm about to shoot a jewelry ad?" I try to joke.

"Because you like sparkly things, and Tripp and I like seeing you happy." We both stand, and Ginny helps me put on my necklace before I turn and double-check that everything on her gown is falling the way it should be.

"Ginny, darling? Are you ready?" Christine, her foster mother, asks as she walks into the room.

We turn and look at ourselves in the giant full-length mirror. My red strapless mermaid gown is loud against all of her cream and ivory, but even though I'm wearing a bright color and enough jewels to make all of my financial problems go away, somehow, it all comes together in the mirror.

Tripp and I don't walk down the aisle together.

It's one of those weddings where I walk alone, and the men are already at the end of the aisle, watching along with the rest of the room. There are so many white roses, the air filled with their florally sweet perfume tipped with mint, that I wonder how Tripp is making it through without wanting to vomit.

The entire room looks like something straight out of a fairytale wedding, and I almost laugh because Jackson likes big, flashy things, and Ginny just likes

Jackson. So, I'm sure the decorations have more to do with him than my best friend.

Our men stand like perfect Greek statues. Both of their chiseled jawlines are covered by their short, impeccably groomed beards, and their muscled bodies fill out their Kiton tuxedos to perfection. I'm still coming to terms with the fact that Tripp cut his hair—his curls are still intact on top while the sides are shorter and more styled. Still, just the sight of him takes my breath away.

While Jackson's smile still looks like it promises a night full of sin and debauchery, Tripp's looks like it guarantees you a lifetime of good morning kisses and warm, fluffy pancakes after he wakes you up with his tongue between your legs.

And I want that.

Fuck, do I want it.

Throughout the whole walk, we share a smile. I almost mouth it. *I love you.* But I know this isn't the time or the place to say it. Tripp deserves a romantic gesture—to *feel* it when I tell him.

And I think I deserve it, too. To feel it wholeheartedly when he finally tells me.

The ceremony is short and sweet. No fluff, no frill, and a *very* indecent you may kiss your bride moment on Jackson's part.

During it all, our eyes stay connected. Even when everyone else's are on the couple when they walk down the aisle together, and people flood them with congratulations, even then Tripp doesn't tear his gaze from mine.

Then, finally, I'm back in his arms.

"You look stunning. I'm going to fuck you wearing nothing but those diamonds tonight," he whispers in my ear as we spin around the dance floor.

"You're going to wear my diamonds? Now there's a naughty image." I smirk up at him. "Thank you for the jewelry. The pieces are beautiful."

"Not nearly as beautiful as you."

"Keep talking like that, handsome, and I may just have to take you into one of the rooms here and have my filthy way with you," I jest in the best southern drawl I can. It's not good at all and makes us both laugh.

We mingle with guests, some of whom offer us congratulations as well. I'm willing to bet Ginny knows next to none of these people, and the guests are mostly connections of Jackson's or paparazzi who he invited.

"Don't they look absolutely sickening?" Carmela appears beside me and holds out a glass of champagne. She smirks into her drink and winks at me before returning her gaze to the dance floor where Jackson and Ginny are so wrapped up in each other I'm not even sure they remember there's a room full of people around them.

"They look so happy. I never knew another person could make you *that* happy," I say softly, scanning the crowd beyond the couple for my Prince Charming.

"*You're* that happy, aren't you? Things are going

well with your guard dog?" Carmela picks at imaginary lint on her sparkling, forest green gown.

"Who's got a guard dog?" a deep, smooth tenor questions behind us.

Carmela tenses slightly, and I look over my shoulder to see Senator Mick Charles standing there. He's a silent partner in the club, and he and Carmela have a sordid past that started fourteen years ago and ended with him procuring the club for her as an apology.

"A clean slate," he'd called it.

But he's been dirtying up the slate ever since.

Raising the hand that holds my drink, I turn my attention back to the dance floor. "That would be me."

"We're not going to lose you now, are we? I thought the bit about you being engaged to Jackson's friend was all for show?" he asks in that jovial manner rich guys have when they lace their words with a warning, but make you think you still have a choice in the matter.

I side-eye Carmela, and she winces, knowing that particular piece of information should have stayed between us. But I get it. Mick is a tall, handsome, powerful man with a voice that slides over your skin like butter and a way of making you think all your dreams can come true if you do as he tells you.

And with his looks, you'd be glad to get on your knees and do *exactly* what he told you to do.

"Actually, there's something we should probably

discuss." I turn around, eyes darting between them both.

Before I can say another word, we're interrupted by a petite blonde joining us. She's frigid in human form, with icy blonde hair, sky-blue eyes, and pale, delicate skin.

I've never met her, but I know who she is right away—the reason Mick and Carmela aren't together: Mick's wife, Kate.

"Good to see you again, Carmela," she says coldly before turning her icicle orbs to me, running her gaze down the length of my body and up again. "And who might you be? I don't believe we've been introduced. I'm Kate Charles."

Smiling, I stick out my hand to shake hers. "Valentina. I'm engaged to Tripp Kennedy."

In two sentences, I let her know I'm taken and not a threat to her marriage, like she seems to automatically think I am.

It's why I'm good at my job. I know how to charm men *and* women.

Carmela instantly looks like she needs a way out of this conversation, so I grab her hand and tell the couple, "If you'll excuse us."

"Thank you," Carmela whispers as I drag her away. She's the most badass boss woman I know, and I've never, in all my years of knowing her, seen her try to make herself look so small.

"No problem. You would have done the same for me."

Suddenly, warm arms encircle my waist from

behind, and a face nuzzles my neck. "Sorry, I got caught up with business talk."

"Gross," Carmela mutters with a smile before disappearing into the crowd.

Tripp turns me around, pulling me flush against him as he kisses me lightly. "I've been watching you from across the room, and I really want to taste you *right now*."

My cheeks grow warm at his husky tone and the look of sheer desperation in his eyes. The space between my legs clenches with want as my insides flutter like there's a hummingbird trapped in my stomach. "I'll bet no one will miss us if we slip away for a little while."

A feline grin stretches across his face. He squeezes my waist before grabbing my hand, pulling me toward the hall that leads to the bridal suite. As soon as the door shuts behind us, he backs me into it, kissing me hard before moving to get on his knees. "Will this dress even go that high? Or do I need to take you out of it completely?"

Grasping his shoulder, I tell him breathlessly, "I want you inside me, Tripp."

"We don't have a condom." His hands slide beneath the dress and up my calves, testing how much stretch the material has. There is none. This dress is as tight as flesh.

"I don't care." I sound needy, even to my own ears, but I hope he realizes that my asking him to take me bare means something to me.

Rising, he pins me to the door with his body and

scrapes his teeth along my neck. "Let me get you out of this dress, and you won't be saying no to my tongue then. You'll be begging for more."

Confusion darts through me as he roughly flips me around to undo my zipper. Before he can get it halfway, I push off the door and spin to face him. "I'm begging for your cock now. Since when do you turn down sex?"

His fingers squeeze my thighs, and he pins my hips with his own, his erection evident through our clothing. Tripp tried to fuck me bare the first night we met, but we haven't done it in the two months we've been intimate. I thought it meant something. That he'd know how I trust him enough to offer myself up in that way.

Only, it seems like it's backfiring.

"We need a condom, Viv," he reminds me sternly.

"Why? I'm not sleeping with anyone else, and neither are you." The heat inside me dies. Smothering every lovesick emotion I had earlier as anxiety and fear rise from the ashes.

Tripp is silent, but the look he gives me is intense. His jaw clenches, and his nostrils flare as he lifts his hips away from mine. His unwillingness to answer my question has unease clawing its way from the pit of my stomach up to my chest.

I've never known Tripp not to say what's on his mind. So, the fact that he can't seem to find the words is telling. And suddenly, I think I know why.

He's always voiced his concern about me still working at Désirer—about how he can't be with me all the time and how he doesn't want me working the Dreamers or Desires wings. I've told him I quit those, but here, at this moment, I realize he doesn't believe me.

Why else would he not want to have sex with me without a condom?

Or, perhaps I read this situation entirely wrong, and *he's* the one sleeping with other people. All those late nights at the office. The time he spends at the club while I'm working. The extravagant diamonds —*apology gifts*.

I've seen this happen a million times to women like me. It happened to Carmela.

How could I have been so stupid?

"Of course. I'm sorry, it was stupid of me to suggest." My words are ice as I push him away from me.

"Viv–"

"No, I totally get it. Better to be safe than sorry." I turn, and my hand finds the doorknob as tears line my eyes. "I'm sorry, I'm not really in the mood for anything anymore."

"Valentina…"

"I'm fine."

He chuckles. *Chuckles*. "Please don't take this the wrong way. You know I've never made you feel cheap–"

"You just did." I don't give him another chance to say anything, and I bolt out the door. He calls my name repeatedly, but it gets swallowed by the din of the crowd as I reemerge into the party.

Hastily, I make my way toward the exit when a hand grasps my wrist. "Valentina, what happened?"

Carmela's worried eyes dart between my own as I turn to see she's the one who grabbed me. Without thinking it over, the words leave my mouth with a sob before I can stop them. "I can't work at the club anymore."

Tears begin to flow down my cheeks, and I don't even care when a few people glance my way curiously. All Carmela does is nod. "Okay. That's okay. We can talk about it."

Her eyes dart over my shoulder, and I turn to see Jackson standing there with Ginny. From the look on his face, I can tell he overheard me.

"Oh my god, Lenni, what happened?" Ginny rushes to my side, leading me away from the party without another word.

"I'm so sorry, Gin. Please don't let me ruin today for you. I just need a second."

Pulling us toward the bathroom, she shushes me. "Well, I need to pee, and someone needs to help me with my dress."

Through my tears, I laugh. It's all I can do while my heart breaks into a million pieces.

That did *not* go as fucking planned.

Everything I wanted to tell her—everything I wanted to confess—was mistaken in one panicked moment of hesitation, one moment where I wondered if she was ready to hear everything I have to say to her. I watched it all play out on her face, and still, I couldn't just open my mouth and tell her that whatever she was thinking, it was all wrong.

It's honestly amazing how badly I screwed that up. And how quickly Lenni disappeared from the party.

"Care to tell me what just happened?" Jackson appears beside me as I scan the sea of tuxedos and gowns for any sign of red.

"What do you mean?" I ask as he steps into view. His eyes narrow, and instantly I realize he's talking about Lenni. "Where is she?"

"My wife just took her to the bathroom. She's crying. And she just quit the club."

Shock zips through my chest and causes my heart to stop for a singular moment. "She quit?"

"She did. And according to Ginny, they had a little talk before the wedding that makes me think the only reason she ran out of here in tears is because you both fucked up somehow." Jackson stares at me, arms crossed, annoyance written plainly on his face.

"I fucked up. It's a miscommunication, that's all. What bathroom did they go to?" I was hoping to avoid this, her running out on me, stunned that I'd tell her how I really feel about her after only two months of knowing each other. I was trying to avoid making a scene at my best friend's wedding because Julia Roberts showed me just how tacky that can be.

And now, just like Julia, I'm going to go find Lenni in a bathroom full of other women and explain how sorry I am.

"The one in the hall on the way to the main foyer. Whatever it is that happened, her quitting is a big thing, Tripp. I know I said she's a woman who doesn't like to be kept, but if she made that decision on her own, I think that speaks volumes about how she feels about you."

"I agree. So, it looks like I won't get my heart broken after all." He doesn't stop me as I turn to leave, but I hear him say something about sending his wife back to him.

Multiple women are standing around talking as I approach the bathroom, most of them giving me the side-eye as I make no sign of stopping. I interject myself into a conversation and ask one of them to go inside and get the bride.

Ginny appears moments later, breathing a sigh of relief when she sees me. "What happened?"

"I was silent when I shouldn't have been. I'm sorry we're causing a scene on your wedding day, but could you possibly clear the room so I can go in and see her?"

"What's a wedding without a little drama?" Ginny shrugs with a smile. Sometimes, I wonder how she and Jackson work as a couple. She's super down to earth, and Jackson…is Jackson.

It takes a few minutes, but she clears out the room and holds the door open for me. "I can keep watch and make sure no one can get in," she offers.

"No, it's okay. Besides, Jackson is about to throw a fit if you don't get back out there."

"Just shove the settee against the door. That'll stop anyone from getting in." She motions inside to a large room full of mirrors and furniture made of blush-colored velvet and cream-painted wood.

Even though I think it's over the top, considering I don't plan to be there long, I do as she says. "Valentina? We need to talk. Can you please come out of there?" I call into the room full of stalls.

"Why? There's nothing to say. I get it. You don't trust me." Her voice is scratchy as she emerges, pushing past me to check her makeup in one of the full-length mirrors. Tears still line her lashes, but she looks just as beautiful even with smudged mascara.

"That wasn't it at all," I tell her softly. Coming up behind her, I wrap my arm around her waist and draw her back to my chest. "I'm sorry I made you feel that way. I *do* trust you. It was never about that."

"Then what is it about? If that's not it, then why didn't you just explain it to me?" Her eyes are full of fury as they connect with mine in the mirror.

Gently, I push her hair over one shoulder and drop my chin to rest on the other. "Because I don't know if you're ready to hear the real reason."

"Tell me." She spins in my arms. "Tell me now, Tripp. Tell me I'm not crazy for wanting this. For wanting you. For giving up my job for you."

My jaw clenches as she says it because even though I believed Jackson, hearing it from her is so much better. "The real reason will scare you, Viv. If you think I'm intense now, you haven't seen anything yet."

"I'm ready to accept intense without being scared by it, Tripp." Her eyes flash with lust-filled curiosity, and I hate myself for allowing her to walk out of the other room because this could have been settled already if I wasn't so damn worried about scaring her.

"I didn't want to fuck you without a condom because once that barrier is gone, you're mine." Her breath hitches as my hands tighten on her waist. "I don't care how possessive or barbaric it sounds. Once I fuck you raw, I'm not letting you go. You *will* belong to me. Just like I've belonged to you since the night we met."

"I'm yours." It leaves her lips on a low moan before she surges forward to kiss me, hands immediately dropping to my zipper.

Stepping back, I cradle her jaw gently and push her back. "Not here. I'm not going to have our first time like this be in a fucking bathroom. We're going to leave and go to the club because I already had it lined up for us tonight. And I'm going to spend hours making sure you never misunderstand me again." A shiver runs through her body, nipples pebbling beneath the fabric of her dress, making my cock twitch. "Besides. I have a deal to cash in on."

T he next hour passes in a blur. From saying goodbye at the wedding and apologizing to Ginny profusely, to the car where Tripp and I make out the entire ride to Désirer. A simple slip dress is waiting for me in my changing suite, with instructions to keep my diamonds on and not wear my wings. Then, when I'm ready, I'm escorted to a room.

It's almost as if *I'm* the client tonight.

Even though I want to get to Tripp as fast as possible, I take my time walking through the Grand Room, waxing nostalgic for the place that's been like a home for so long. The familiarity of women who feel the same as I do about the job, the way men look at me with reverence and how it makes me feel powerful, knowing that they don't just see a prostitute, but someone who can make all their sexual dreams come true.

I don't want to be with anyone other than Tripp, but it brings a sad smile to my face—the fact that I know nothing beyond this club. I have no skills. No means of making money besides working at the restaurant, which will now have to be full *and* overtime.

I can't allow Tripp to take care of me financially, not when that means footing Momma's rehab bills and everything else I still have to take care of.

When the door closes behind me, though, and Tripp is standing there with a hungry look in his eyes, all of those thoughts fly out the window on the Angel wings I'll never wear again.

He approaches me slowly, pulling off his mask before he removes mine. "After you told me about your past, it got me thinking. This has always been a job for you. Has there ever been a part of you that truly *enjoys* it?"

I'm not expecting the question, so it takes me by surprise. "I don't understand what you mean?"

His fingers dance their way down my neck to finger the straps of my slip, sliding beneath the silky fabric to pull them down my arms. "What do *you* want, Valentina? Tonight, *I'm* the Angel, and I'm going to fulfill all *your* desires."

My body floods with want. The slip catches on my hard nipples, and I suck in a breath as he pulls it down roughly over them, causing a delicious friction that shoots straight to my core. "I feel safe when we're intimate. I think...I think I'd like it if I gave up complete control to you. To feel vulnerable when I know I'll be okay because I know you won't hurt me."

"I'll never hurt you. Ever," he whispers as he drops the slip. It slides over my hips before falling to the floor. He palms my breasts and bends to take one into his mouth, sucking at my nipple as he laves it with his tongue.

My pussy clenches on air, desperately wanting to be filled. "I need you inside me."

I tug at his simple drawstring pajama pants, watching as his cock springs free, bobbing between us with the tip already shining with a bead of precum. He snatches my wrists as I reach for it and walks me backward to the bed. "You said you trust me, right?"

"Mmhmm," I moan when his mouth descends on mine and doesn't give me a chance to respond. His tongue plunges deep into my mouth, and I'm so caught up in the feeling of his hard length rubbing against my center that I'm surprised to see he's tied me to the headboard.

"I want *complete* control over your body tonight," he explains as he drags his tongue down my neck, biting at my collarbone hard enough that I know I'll bruise. My hips rise beneath him, searching for more friction.

"You have it. Anything you want to do, I'm all yours."

"Say it again," he whispers as he crawls between my legs.

"I'm yours, fuck, Tripp, I'm yours!" I cry out as he

flicks his tongue against my clit. *Slow, quick, suck, slow.* He pinches my nipples as my hands tug on my silky restraints, craving to thread my fingers through his curls.

A warm wave pulses through me and into his mouth. With a moan, I pull him to me with my feet hooking over his shoulders to dig my heels into his back as I rock my hips against his face.

When my orgasm subsides, he crawls up my body, chin glistening with my juices as he aligns himself with my entrance and pushes in.

"You look so beautiful spread before me in nothing but the diamonds I bought you. I haven't been able to think of anything else all day."

I clench around him, pulling him in where he fits perfectly. The way he feels inside me is unlike anything I've ever experienced. It's raw. Hungry.

Primal.

"I've wanted to do this since the night we met," he admits as he thrusts into me. He's impossibly hard and sits back on his knees, lifting me by my hips as he rocks into me at an angle where his tip bumps my cervix.

"You feel so fucking good. You're so fucking deep." My head thrashes from side to side as another release builds.

"God, I wish you could see what I'm seeing right now. Your pussy swallowing my cock so hungrily."

I look down to see him watching where we're joined. His eyes are tight, and he's biting his lip to keep himself from coming. "Fuck, you're such a good girl, aren't you, baby? Tell me whose good girl you are."

"Yours. I'm yours. And I want to feel you come inside me." Arching my back, the position catches us both off guard, and we come together. Before he can finish, he pulls out quickly and shoots the rest of his release all over my breasts.

He smears it over my nipples, scooping up a little before he shoves his fingers in my mouth. "Suck them clean."

Fuck.

We've done some shit together, but right now, this is topping the cake.

Swirling my tongue around his fingers like they are my own Tripp-flavored lollipop, I let out a discontented cry when he pulls them from my mouth. "Give me more."

"No, my little vixen, I'm not done with you." He rubs his cum over my chest and scoops up more, lowering his fingers to my pussy…then beyond to the tight ring of nerve endings he's wanted to conquer for weeks.

Slowly, he inserts a finger, lubed up with his cum, into my ass. He rubs my clit with the other hand, smearing my juices around and making a slippery wet sound as he plunges his fingers into my pussy at the same time he stretches my tight hole with another finger.

"Holy fuck. I feel so full." I can't explain the feeling. My entire body bathes in a scalding, pleasure-soaked wave. Curling my fingers around the headboard, I use the leverage to ride his fingers, clenching my muscles to pull him deeper.

Another orgasm builds as he pumps both of my holes rapidly, pushing a third into my ass. It rips through me, and I try to squeeze my legs together, but he sits between them, keeping me spread with his knees. "That's it, baby. Look at how much you're coming for me. Your pussy weeps for me. No one else can do this to you. Only me. Tell me whose cumslut you are."

I swear I come again as I yell out, "Yours! Only yours!" His dirty words always make my clit pulse to the point where he barely has to touch me to get me off. But he's more than barely touching me. I feel him everywhere, even though he's removing his fingers.

A buzzing noise reverberates through the air, and I open my eyes to see he has a vibrating Rabbit. "Where did that come from?"

He flashes me his perfect, pearly whites and winks. "I told you I had this planned already."

Tripp doesn't take his time as he inserts the ridiculously pink vibrator. I can tell it's on a low setting as he positions the ears against my clit. My head tilts back as I whine, "I don't think I can take any more. It's too sensitive."

"Yeah, you can. Be a good girl and give me another one." He nudges my tight hole with the head of his cock, slowly pushing in. "Oh, *fuck,* you feel so fucking good. Look at your fucking ass stretching around my cock. And your pussy swallowing the Rabbit. You're going to be covered in cum by the time you walk out of here tonight. I'm going to make you walk through the Grand Room covered in me so they all know who you belong to."

He was absolutely right about the intense part. Everything up until now was minimal compared to the level of possessiveness spilling from his mouth. And the dirtier he speaks, the more uninhibited I'm becoming.

I spread my legs wider, chasing the Rabbit ears and tilting my pelvis up to give him the best view as he wrecks me. "I feel you...*everywhere*. What are you doing to me?" It's a rhetorical question because I *know* what he's doing. He's thoroughly ruining me for any other man, ensuring that his cock is the only one I want for the rest of my life.

"Melting you down so I can inject you straight into my bloodstream," he grits out. Sweat trickles down his forehead as he pumps into me like my asshole was made for him. One hand grips my hip while the other maneuvers the Rabbit, pulling it away as my muscles contract, and he thinks I'm about to come. After a few seconds, he places it back and builds my release up again. "Fuck, I'm about to come so hard."

"Fuck me faster," I demand. I tilt up again, allowing him to go deeper as he leans over me, his abs pushing the Rabbit into me over and over as he pistons into me. I've never come so many times in one session, and I almost think it's not going to happen again, but then it hits me out of nowhere as he pushes in, and the ears stay vibrating against my clit. "That's it! I'm coming, Tripp! I'm coming!"

"Fuck!" he roars with an arduous thrust. He stills, his bottom lip between his teeth while his hips jerk sporadically as he comes inside me. "Jesus fucking Christ, I could fuck you all day. I'd be happy to die young if it meant I could fuck you endlessly."

The Rabbit pulsates loudly between us, and I squirm as the pressure becomes too much. "Take it out, please."

He pulls out before removing the toy from me gently, then stretches over me to untie my hands. As soon as they're free, I wrap them in his hair and pull him down, our mouths colliding in a hot, open-mouthed kiss full of tongue and teeth and swollen lips.

When he pulls back, there's a glob of the cum he left on my chest sticking to him. I watch with half-lidded eyes as he swipes it from his skin and massages it against my nipple. "I wasn't lying when I said I wanted you to walk through the Grand Room covered in my cum."

"Holy fucking shit," I breathe as he settles beside me and pulls me closer. "You weren't kidding when you said you'd be more intense."

"Does it scare you? *Was* it too much?" He nuzzles my neck and whispers, "Are you okay?"

I turn into him, curling my legs around his and pressing myself as close to him as I can get. "I'm okay. It doesn't change anything."

We hold each other, breathing heavily while I'm

pretty sure we're both thinking about doing some form of that again as soon as we recover. I think about how protected I feel. How I never once felt panicked or not in control, even though I was tied up. And I don't think I could have ever felt that way with anyone other than Tripp.

It's about more than how sexually compatible we are now. It's the way he's felt like home since the moment we met. A different kind than how I grew up. One that's safe and warm and always waiting with open arms and an easy smile.

I *want* to belong to him—more than that, though. I know I already *do*.

"Tripp?"

His voice is husky against my ear, his sweaty forehead pressed into the top of my head. "Yes?"

My body tightens against him, legs tensing where they're entangled with his, fingers grasping the flesh of his arms as if he'll disappear the moment I speak my truth out loud. Without a word, he enforces his arms around me, pulling me infinitesimally closer while he waits for me to continue.

The air leaves my lungs. Every nerve ending bursting with anxiety so powerfully that white spots begin to dance in my vision, gathering like stars in the sky.

"I love you," he says suddenly.

My lungs burn as I forget how to breathe. The white haze begins to dissipate as I lift my head to look at him.

"I know there are a million better places to tell you. And I know I should have told you earli–"

"I love you, too." The words I planned on saying first fly from between my lips, cutting him off. "That's what I was going to say. A part of me has loved you since the night we met, and that part has been chasing after all the other pieces of me that didn't want to give in to those feelings. I've never loved anyone before, and I'm not even sure I know how, but I do know that I want you. I want your bad jokes and your goofy grin. I want the carefree man who takes me ice skating even though he can't skate. The one who miscommunicates but makes up for it in the best ways. The one who believes I can do anything I want to and be anything I want to be. You make me feel like living, Tripp, when all I've done for so long is *survive*. I don't want to tread water anymore. I want to *swim*."

His mouth presses against mine, trapping the salty tears I'm crying between our lips as they dance languidly against one another, sealing our vows to each other.

From this moment on, nothing is pretend.

It's real.

So very real it makes my chest ache with all the possibilities of our future together.

"There's nothing I've ever wanted more than to hear you say those words to me. I promise you, Valentina, I promise to be the man you need me to be for the rest of our lives. Or at least until you no longer want me."

"The only man you need to be is *you*. For the rest of our lives." With a watery laugh, I hold up my hand. The giant diamond sparkling as I wiggle my fingers. "'Till death do us part."

He kisses me again, his fingers intertwining with mine as he whispers against my lips, "'Till death do us part."

Tripp

Even though I RSVP'd when Lenni insisted we go to Emily's wedding, most of her family is still shocked to see us walk through the doors of the giant inn where the weekend is being hosted. It has an old-money feel to it, with rich mahogany floors covered in giant ornamental rugs, antique vases filled with nothing—purely for decoration—and whimsical wallpaper with muted floral patterns.

Lenni makes a gagging noise while we wait at the concierge desk for the key to our room. "Yuck," she whispers.

"Are you talking about the inn or the group of Emily's family who are openly staring at us right now?" I tug her closer, pressing a soft kiss to the curve of her neck just below her ear. I relish the goosebumps that erupt over her flesh and the soft pink hue that creeps from the apples of her cheeks downward.

"Can it be both? We were invited. Are they really *that* shocked?" Her fingers tighten where they press into my side, and her voice becomes breathy in the way that it does when she's turned on. She shifts, pressing her thighs together.

It was a three-hour drive out to Pomfret. A three-hour drive where Lenni gave me road head and then fingered herself while she faced me—legs spread over the center console so I could watch her, even though I should have been watching the road.

We're both horny as fuck. And by the way the lady at the desk is furiously blushing and doing her best to get us checked in as quickly as possible, we aren't doing a great job at hiding it. "So sorry this is taking so long, Mr. Kennedy. It will just be a few more moments. Our computer systems are a little laggy today."

My hand drifts over Lenni's hip and around to her backside, sliding my hand into her back pocket to squeeze her butt. I'm about to tell the lady not to worry when my mother's voice cuts down the hall. "There you two are! I was beginning to think you wouldn't make the rehearsal dinner."

As she comes closer, she glares at the people still gathered around a heavy wooden table. "My son has happily moved on and was invited. Is there a problem?"

Seemingly embarrassed at being caught gawking, they disperse while Lenni extracts herself from me to give her a hug. "Be prepared for a lot of *that* this weekend, my dear. They are more than likely stunned by your looks. Tripp upgraded tremendously in that department."

Lenni snorts while Mom embraces me. "I'm sure it has more to do with the fact that we're here at all. You and Weylan didn't have to come if you didn't want to."

"Nonsense. Of course, we would come to support you two. We got invited *long* before you did, but after you told me what really happened, we rescinded our RSVP. Emily's mother was only too happy to reinstate it for us. They don't want to be on bad terms with Weylan. Emily's parents' company was set to do a lot of business with Kennedy Construction before everything blew up."

Lenni rolls her eyes playfully and smirks at Mom's back. "Well, no need for bad blood anymore, right?"

"Alright, Mr. Kennedy, we have you all checked in. Here is the key to your room. The rehearsal dinner starts at six in the dining room. If you need anything at all, please don't hesitate to let us know." The lady behind the desk hands me a bronze, Victorian-looking key with a tassel attached to the end and a card with the WIFI password.

"Alright, we're gonna go get settled in. See you at dinner." Picking up our bags, I usher Lenni down the hall toward the giant staircase that leads to the rooms upstairs.

Just as we begin to ascend, Emily appears around the corner on her way down. "Oh! You made it!"

Her skin looks ashen, and her blue eyes are

bloodshot. She looks like she's moments away from showing us what she had for lunch. "Are you feeling okay? You look sick."

Lenni discreetly elbows me in the ribs as Emily breaks out in a mottled flush. "Something I had for lunch must not be agreeing with me, that's all. I'm glad to see you two could make it." She brushes her auburn hair out of her face and continues down the stairs. "See you at the rehearsal dinner. And Tripp?" She stops, turning to look up at me. Once upon a time, her gaze was all I wanted to see for the rest of my life. Now, I don't feel a thing when I look at her. "Thank you for coming."

"You know, you're not supposed to look better than the bride. This is twice in as many weeks where you've done exactly that," I murmur into Lenni's neck, pulling her back into me.

"Better not let Jackson hear you say that. He'll rip you limb from limb for saying anyone is prettier than Ginny," she jests, adjusting an earring. "We'll be late if your hands keep that up."

Chuckling lowly, I let out a groan and set my forehead between her shoulder blades as my hands still, bunched in her skirt that I was in the process of dragging up her body. "I can't help it, you're so goddamn sexy."

"We *just* had sex." She laughs, spinning to face

me. Her hair bounces around her body in voluminous waves. The dress she's wearing is a soft blue with a gray floral print, and it covers up so much of her body that I want to rip it off her with my teeth.

"So? That was like an hour ago," I whine as she straightens my tie. I'm wearing the same colors as her, a dove gray suit with a blue tie, and I'm addicted to the way we look together in the giant backlit mirror in the bathroom. The inn may be decorated to look older than it is, but the amenities are at least modern.

"You are insatiable. Come on, let's get this over with." She grabs my hand, and we make our way downstairs.

The parlor is filled with guests already mingling. There's an open bar along one wall, with signs highlighting the themed drinks made from gin, and bottles of Dom arranged on the bartop. We take two glasses of champagne, and I spend the next ten minutes introducing Lenni to everyone. She dazzles the room, and more of the attention is on her than on Emily. However, my former fiancée appears almost grateful as she exits the room on numerous occasions, still looking sick.

"Tripp Kennedy," a deep voice booms behind us. "Good of you to make it. And who is this enchanting lady?"

Before we turn, I notice a frown quickly appear on Lenni's face. She's tense as she takes in Emily's soon-to-be husband, Neil Harmond. He's nearly six-five, has a head full of ebony hair, and, as much as I hate to admit it, looks like he could be a male model. He's lazy as shit, skates by on his father's good name, and has been overly friendly toward me for a man who not only was fucking my fiancée behind my back, but who also had the audacity to look me in the eye and smile while I was blind to it.

I introduce them with a flat tone. "Babe, this is Neil Harmond. Neil, this is my fiancée, Valentina."

"Well, you certainly hit the jackpot, didn't you?" he asks crudely as his eyes sweep down the length of her body. She cringes as he reaches for her hand and bends to kiss the back of it. He looks at her curiously. "You know, Emily was under the impression your name was *Bianca*."

"Inside joke between me and Tripp." Lenni's voice lacks her usual confidence, coming out soft and meager. She discreetly wipes her hand on her dress when he releases it, and he watches the offensive motion like a fox who just found its dinner.

"Interesting," he muses. "Well, thank you both for coming. It's good of you, Tripp, really. Valentina, it's a pleasure to meet you." His eyes pass over her once more before he turns and disappears through the crowd.

"I don't know what just happened, but I didn't like any of it." My tone is slightly accusatory, and I hate that I sound like a jealous asshole.

With a blink, the tension melts from her body, and she suddenly beams at me. "I'm sorry. I didn't mean to be rude. He gives me the creeps."

"Yeah, he basically undressed you with his eyes.

At least all the other men in the room have the decency to do it while they think I'm not watching."

I'm not angry with her, but she flinches at my tone, anyway. "I'm sorry. I'm being an asshole. He just pisses me off."

She shrugs. "Yeah, I get it."

"No. No, you don't. This isn't about Emily, Viv. So please don't think that. The guy is just a jerk." Panic laces my tone as I pull her to me and lay a chaste kiss on her lips. "I love you. I'm sorry if I made you think it was about her. It's just about you, I promise."

Her hand slides up my chest to grip the lapel of my suit jacket as she leans into me. I'm well aware that there are multiple pairs of eyes on us and that we probably look indecent, but I can't bring myself to care.

"I love you too, Tripp. And I know it's not about her. It's about your pride, and there's nothing wrong with that. Your ego was bruised by him, but what better way to indicate you don't care than to show up with a smoking hot bombshell on your arm that you get to parade around and show everyone you upgraded?" She smirks against my lips before kissing me again.

"You're the love of my life, not a trophy." I lower my voice so that only she can hear me. "You deserve better than that."

Her answering grin is devious. "I happen to *like* being your trophy. At least in this particular situation. I'm all polished up, baby. Show me off."

If I weren't sure I'd be carted off for murder and that everyone here would get the wrong idea, I'd grab one of the candle centerpieces and burn Neil's eyes out. Dinner is nearly over, and he's barely taken his gaze off Lenni. And I'm not the only one who's noticed.

Emily barely ate her dinner, which doesn't surprise me with the wedding being in a day and a half. She's probably trying to ensure she fits into her designer gown. But she still looks sick, and instead of caring for her or even sending her back upstairs to lie down while he wraps up dinner, Neil spends the entire time watching my girl. Probably thinking of ways he can try and take her from me, too.

Lenni's hand squeezes my thigh beneath the table. "I'm so ready for this to be over. I want a nice long soak in the tub in our room, and then I want you to tongue fuck my pussy," she whispers in my ear, her fingers twisting my hair affectionately.

"Would you two behave? I feel like I'm scolding teenagers. Keep it G-rated at the dinner table, for Heaven's sake," Mother chastises us in the quietest voice she can manage. There's no way she heard what Lenni said, but my girl is more in my lap than her chair.

"Oh, come on, Margo. You remember when we were that age. Leave them be." Pops chuckles, placing his hand over hers and drawing her attention away from us.

Someone clears their throat at the head of the table, and my attention turns to see Emily and Neil standing. "We just wanted to thank you all again for coming out to celebrate with us this weekend. We feel like now is as good a time as ever to make a little announcement," Emily starts. There's a faint glow to her cheeks, and she looks happier than she's looked all night. Neil looks like he'd rather be in my place. "I'm sure most of you have noticed I've been a little *off* all night. What started as what I was sure was a stomach bug a week ago, has turned into a very real little bug. We're having a baby!"

I can't help the way my body reacts, and there's no way Lenni doesn't feel the way I tense at the news. Do I care that they're pregnant? No. But is it like the cherry on top of the fuck you cake they baked me? Yeah.

People stand to congratulate them, the din of the room clamoring to a roar of questions like, "How far along are you?" and "Do you know what you're having yet?"

My parents stay seated, and Lenni retreats to her chair, a contemplative look stretched across her pretty features. Leaving now would make it look like the news bothered me. So we stay a little longer until the excitement calms down, and we can make our getaway.

As soon as we return to our room, Lenni makes a beeline for the bathroom. I hear the water running, followed by the sweet smell of the honeysuckle bath gel the inn provides. A bottle of Dom is chilling in a bucket of ice, with a tray of strawberries on the small table in the sitting area. I arranged for it to be here when we got back, hoping it would enhance the romantic mood, but something tells me the mood has been ruined.

Lenni shuts the bathroom door but doesn't lock it, and I bring her a glass of champagne, sitting on the ledge while she soaks in the bubbles. "You okay?"

"Mmhmm," she hums. She won't look at me. In fact, it seems like she's trying to keep herself from crying.

"Viv, what's wrong?" I ask gently.

"I can't have kids," she blurts out. Her foot kicks out of the water to anchor herself as she sinks lower into the suds. The bubbles in the tub and the champagne fizz as silence stretches between us.

"Is that what this is about?" Reaching down, I try to push back a strand of hair that's fallen from where she's gathered it on top of her head into her eyes, but she jerks away from me, causing the water to slosh over the side of the tub and soak my pants.

"We haven't talked about it since that first dinner with your parents, but I know you want a family, Tripp. This was bound to come up sooner or later." Her tone is watery.

"Can you really not have kids, Valentina? Or do you not want them because of how you grew up?" My brain screams to crawl into the tub and hold her, but my instincts tell me not to. Sometimes Lenni doesn't mind breaking down and letting me be there for her, but most times, she acts tough as nails. This is one of those moments.

"I can't," she whispers as a lone tear falls down her cheek.

I want to know why. I want to know if it has something to do with her scar. Or if it's some other reason that has nothing to do with her childhood. But I remember how she felt when my mom pushed the subject. The last thing I want is to make her feel like she's less than because she can't have children. "Do you want to talk about it?"

She shakes her head. "Not really."

"Then we won't talk about it right now. Would you like me to join you?" I'm prepared when she shakes her head again, but it stings nonetheless. "Okay. I'll be in bed when you're done," I soothe, leaning over to kiss her forehead. "I love you."

For some reason, that makes more tears fall. But she tells me, "I love you, too."

Lenni

The crisp air bites at my cheeks as I walk along the street. Snow falls steadily, covering my hair and body in a blanket of white. My body heat is not enough to melt it, yet it still soaks through my clothes, and the chill seeps into my bones.

My body shivers uncontrollably, pulling at the stitches that hold my lower abdomen together, pinching sharply like a needle when it enters the skin. The site is angry and inflamed. Red spiders out from the jagged line in thin ribbons. I was in such a hurry to escape my foster home that I forgot my antibiotics and the painkillers the doctors gave me.

Luck wasn't on my side today. I successfully managed to dodge the cops and anyone else who might be looking for me, but I didn't manage to find food. It's been two days since I've eaten, and I feel weak.

When I make it back to the trailer—home—the lights work, but there's no heat. I wonder how long they'll hold

Momma at the prison. Surely, it won't be too long. She was only protecting me.

Though she wouldn't have had to kill anyone if she'd done a better job at protecting me in the first place.

As usual, there's no food in the cabinets. The fridge has a bottle of Coke that is almost gone and looks like it has cigarette ashes floating around in it. The only other thing in there is a moldy orange, and I wonder when Momma decided to buy a piece of fruit and how I'd never noticed it before.

My stomach grumbles. Hunger pains spread outward and up into my chest, and I feel like I'm going to throw up. My abs contract as I swallow down bitter stomach acid, pulling at the stitches again.

Tears line my eyes. Hopeless tears. Angry tears.

My room is disgusting. Blood is iced over on my bed. Shards of glass litter the floor where he busted open the bottle. Phantom screams fill my ears, and I rush down the hall to crawl into Momma's bed. I pull the ratty, old quilt she uses as a blanket over my head and curl up into a ball, ignoring how it pulls at my wounded skin.

I don't know how long I lay there. Minutes. Hours. Days.

There was nothing wrong with my foster home. It was warm, and the mother was nice and made good food. The other kids were friendly. One of the girls was only a few months older than me, but promised to help me take care of my wound.

No one has ever been nice to me before. Not like that. I wondered how nice they'd be if they knew what I did. The father knew. I could tell by the way he looked at me. How long would it be until he touched me?

I didn't stick around to find out.

Voices interrupt my fever dream. Someone calls out for Momma. Thundering footsteps pound down the hall.

"What the fuck? What happened to you, little valentine?" The voice is familiar but dampened.

Another one joins it. "Boss. Look at this."

My breaths leave my sore throat on ragged gasps. Everything is cold. Numb. And all I want to do is sleep. These angels talk funny. But maybe that's because they aren't angels at all. They're demons, come to drag me to hell. After all, I've been a bad, bad girl. There's no room in heaven for kids like me.

"Fuck. Get her in the car. I'm taking her to the hospital. Find out what the fuck happened to Lucille."

Maybe he is an angel.

"Time to wake up, little valentine."

His wings are just dark and leathery.

"Wake up, valentine…"

"Valentina! You're having a nightmare. You're okay," Tripp's worried voice fills my ears as my eyes snap open. My lungs burn as I gulp in mouthfuls of air.

Tripp's rubbing circles on my back, while his other hand pulls my damp curtain of hair off my neck. I'm overheating, but my skin is broken out in goosebumps. My face is wet, and I wipe at my cheeks only to realize I'm crying.

"Jesus fucking Christ, you scared the shit out of

me. You started moaning in your sleep and shivering. You were saying something, and then you just full-on started screaming." Tripp's eyes are wide, concern bleeding from them as he continues stroking my back.

"I'm sorry. I'm okay." It's a lie. I'm not okay. I'm shaken down to my fucking core. I haven't had nightmares in months. And while they usually are of my childhood, I've never had one like *that*. If I were one of those people who believed in symbolism in dreams, I'd say mine was very, *very* bad.

"Come here." Tripp pulls me into his arms, hugging me to his chest as though silently telling me he'll protect me from whatever else tries to haunt me. His soft lips kiss my crown as his legs wrap around me. "You're okay," he soothes.

I don't answer him, my eyes focusing out the window on the wall opposite the bed. The sky outside is mottled with dusky blues and purples. The clock on the nightstand reads six in the morning, and my eyelids start to droop, not ready to get up for the day.

I fall back to sleep feeling warm and safe and protected.

The inn has a large indoor swimming pool with a jacuzzi, surrounded by glass. There's a room just off it, without a door, that houses banquet tables full of fruit, pastries, coffee and tea, and just about anything else you could possibly want for Saturday brunch.

Personally, I think it's a little weird to host a brunch where a swimming pool is. The air is moist and has the sharp scent of chlorine, even though it's a salt pool. But no one here seems to care. There had to have been over a hundred people at the dinner last night, but now there are no more than twenty either sitting to converse while they eat or taking a dip in the pool.

Tripp and I have our bathing suits beneath our clothes, but the second we step foot into the room, he's whisked away to talk business. He's reluctant to leave me, but I reassure him that I'm going to warm up in the jacuzzi before grabbing something to eat.

I secure my hair on top of my head and pretend I don't notice how the men's eyes roll over me when I take my dress off to reveal my white bikini. It's one of the more modest ones I own, covering everything it should and revealing nothing it shouldn't.

A few of the more daring men clap Tripp on the back, their congratulations resonating clearly across the room. He shoots me a look that tells me he's damn proud to have me on his arm and another at them while he tells them they better watch their mouths because he won't tolerate any crude talk about me.

The water is warm as I dip my toe in before settling on the bench. It reminds me of Captiva Island and how much I miss it already. The nice weather, the hot sand, and the easygoing locals who are friendly and welcoming.

Leaning my head back on the edge, I relish the soothing current as the bubbles break on the surface. It relaxes my muscles and eases the tension in my body that I woke back up with. I tried to get a massage at their spa, but Emily has everything booked—as she should. It *is* her wedding weekend, after all.

Barely ten minutes go by before I feel the air stir next to my head and Tripp smoothly asks, "You doing okay?"

Without opening my eyes, I smile. "Yeah, thank you for checking. Are you doing okay? Do I need to save you from the boring world of business talk?"

He chuckles and grips my shoulders, kneading my muscles while he responds, "As boring as it is, it's an important conversation. One of those guys over there has a hold on a quarter of the block where Ginny's center is. I'm trying to get him to sell so Jackson has complete control of the block."

"Sounds illegal." My words drip with mischief as I open one eye to look at him. "Go get 'em, tiger."

His hand collars my throat, nudging my chin up to look at him upside down. "Strangely, that just did something for me. We'll have to explore that later."

He Spiderman kisses me before getting up to return to his conversation. I watch him go, but my attention is drawn across the room as Neil walks in. He sees the men and looks like he might join them, but then he stops next to a pool chair and pulls his shirt off. He gets in the water, fully submerging himself before he begins to swim leisurely laps.

When Tripp introduced us last night, I recognized his voice immediately. It's hard not to with his distinctive, deep timbre. I'm only hoping he doesn't recognize me.

After all, that's what the masks at Désirer are for.

My initial thought was to tell Tripp immediately, but that would betray the club's rules. It would be betraying everything Carmela worked so hard to achieve. And honestly, it isn't going to do my relationship with Tripp any favors. He's already had this man take something from him once.

A strange sense of foreboding washes over me, and I decide I've had enough of the jacuzzi. Quickly, I put my dress back on and motion to Tripp that I'm going to grab a plate of food and go back to the room. A few more men have joined his group, and I have a feeling he may be busy for a while.

Grabbing a plate from the breakfast table, I'm just about to pile on an assortment of fruit before I hear Neil's unmistakable voice behind me. "Interesting scar, *Bianca*."

His words make me feel physically ill. Tiny pricks crawl up my arms like a million little ants as acid worms its way up my esophagus. I set my plate down, turning to see him dripping wet, making himself a coffee. "I'm sorry?"

"Don't pretend like you don't know what I'm talking about. When Em told me about Tripp's new fiancée Bianca, I thought nothing of it until I saw you last night. Obviously, I wasn't sure it was you. But your scar just gave you away." His knowing smirk is nauseating.

Shit. I didn't even think about that.

Chuckling, he saunters closer. There's nowhere to go as he backs me into the table. "How much to go upstairs right now?" he whispers nonchalantly.

Are you fucking kidding me?

"I'm *engaged*. And you're getting married tomorrow, you disgusting pig." I try to move around him, but he blocks my way. There may not be a door to this room, but we're beyond the sight of the entrance, hidden by the wall. "Step back right now, or I'll scream."

"Oh, come on now, *kitty cat*. Remember, I like your claws." He reaches out to run a finger down my arm, causing me to flinch away as anger courses through my veins.

"Is everything alright over here?" My body relaxes as Tripp appears over Neil's shoulder. He steps between us, physically pushing Neil back. "You're a little close to my fiancée for my liking."

Neil laughs, and it's so sinister it causes the hair on my arms to stand on end. "I think you should pay better attention to who you get into bed with, Kennedy. She doesn't just warm yours, you know."

There's a buzzing sound between my ears as time seems to slow. Tripp looks at me before his head turns back to Neil as soon as the tall bastard implicates himself as being a member of Désirer. There's a blur of limbs, a sickening crunch, and a cacophony of various surprised cries before time speeds up again.

"Tripp! What the hell!" Emily shouts from across the room. She rushes over to where Neil is now lying on the ground, holding his nose. She's fresh-faced, dressed in a fluffy white robe, smelling like lavender, and *why am I noticing these things?* Neil's nose is bleeding everywhere while Tripp stands over him, shaking his hand out while he breathes heavily.

Emily's hands may be holding onto her fiancé, but her eyes are focused solely on Tripp, and I can see that she's misread the situation. She thinks they're fighting over *her*.

Pulling Tripp back by the shoulder, I tell him, "Come on. Let's go."

He allows me to pull him away, but not without shouting, "Stay the fuck away from her!"

Neither of us says a word as we flee, ignoring the multiple people staring at us as though we've just robbed a bank. As soon as our room door shuts, Tripp yells out, "Fuck!" so loudly that I jump. "Is he a fucking member at the club?" He storms into the bathroom, turning on the faucet to run his hand beneath the cold water.

Slowly, I walk over and lean against the door-frame, wrapping my arms around myself. "Yes."

His jaw juts out as he clenches his teeth. I can practically feel the anger radiating off him. "When did you know? *How* did you know?"

"Last night, as soon as you introduced us. His

voice is unmistakable. He had his suspicions, but he watched me get out of the jacuzzi and saw my scar."

"Did he...have you guys..." he can't even bring himself to ask. And this is exactly why I didn't want to say anything.

I feel small, and my voice reflects that as I answer him. "Yes."

He slams the faucet off, bracing his arms on the vanity as he hangs his head. "How many times?"

"Tripp, I don't think—"

"HOW MANY TIMES?" he bellows, spinning to crowd me against the frame. Tears spring to my eyes, and I turn my head as he presses his forehead into the side of my face. His arms cage me in, and I focus on how he's squeezing and releasing his fists.

I don't know why, but suddenly, I'm transported back to that room in the trailer in Pennsylvania. Just a small child curled up in the middle of her bed while a man hovers over her, shouting as he unbuckles his belt.

A whimper escapes my lips, and Tripp melts against me, scooping me into his arms with a shuddered sigh as I begin to shake. "I'm sorry. I didn't mean to lose my temper. I'm so sorry, Valentina. I'm sorry." He keeps repeating himself over and over again while I silently sob. He carries me to the bed, laying me down before crawling in next to me.

It's like having an out-of-body experience. I feel things, but don't at the same time. My chest aches. My mind fights furiously to leave that little girl behind, clawing its way back to the man smoothing my hair from my face while he whispers how sorry he is.

Tripp has never been violent, but my job has always been a problem. I was stupid to think it wouldn't catch up to me somehow. I might as well tell him the truth. Otherwise he'll always wonder, and I don't want it to force a wedge between us. "Multiple times. He requests me specifically on nights he's feeling…*forceful*. It started…" I pause, thinking back to when I first met Neil, whose code name is Lord King, because, *of course*, it is. "It must have started after Emily left you. Once a month for a handful of months. There were other times he was there, but we didn't do anything."

Tripp huffs and shakes his head, rolling onto his back as he scrubs at his face. "So he was cheating on her from the very beginning." He's silent for a moment before turning his head back to me. "What do you mean by forceful?"

I breathe in deeply and roll onto my back as well. "He likes to hurt women when he fucks them. He's into consensual non consensual. He uses whips and chains, but not in a pleasurable way for the woman. He nearly dislocated my shoulder once."

"For fuck's sake, Valentina, why did you continue seeing him?" Tripp sounds horrified. His tone tells me he doesn't really want to know, but I answer him anyway.

"Because I learned from a young age how to disassociate. Most of the other Angels can't do that. So I let him think I liked it so he'd spare the other girls. None of us *had* to do it…but those types of clients always pay a lot more."

Tripp pulls me to him, tucking my head into the crook of his neck. I go willingly, wrapping my arms around him even though he needs to know that what he did earlier wasn't okay. My mind and heart are at war with each other right now, but I know he's feeling the same way, and I don't want to make the situation harder.

"I can't let Emily marry him. She's pregnant, for Christ's sake," he murmurs against the top of my head.

Alarm threads through my nerves, fraying the ends as they unravel into a heavy ball in my stomach. "You can't out him, Tripp. If he complains, Jackson's hands will be tied. There's majorly large fines to pay. You'll get kicked out, not to mention it outs me, too. How else would you know he was a member?"

Tripp releases me and gets off the bed before spinning back around. His nostrils flare as his lips flatten in a grimace. "Are you suggesting I say nothing and let Emily marry an abusive psycho?"

My first reaction is to argue that Neil's tastes, while questionable, aren't something to treat condescendingly. I understand where Tripp is coming from, but a large part of me doesn't agree with this decision. "Can you just *wait*?"

"No! They are supposed to be getting married tomorrow, Valentina! Honestly, I can't believe you'd subject a woman to that sort of treatment." He starts toward the door, looking at me like he doesn't know me at all.

"Tripp!" I bolt after him, but he puts his hands up.

"Don't worry, I won't out you. I'll take the heat. But I can't let Emily marry him. I'm sorry, Valentina, but I can't. She may be awful, but she doesn't deserve that. Stay here. I'll be back."

He leaves without another word, not bothering to wait and see if I have anything else to say. My limbs tingle with the urgency to run after him, but I stay like he told me to, knowing he's just doing what *he* does. Tripp would never be able to live with himself if something happened to Emily. He'd feel responsible if he knew what kind of man Neil was, and he still let her walk down the aisle and attach her life to his.

I can't fault him for that.

His patronizing attitude toward the news about Neil and me, though, *that* I can fault him for. As soon as he gets back, he's going to get a piece of my mind. Spinning, my eyes dart around the room, looking for my phone. Even if he doesn't give me away, he'll be giving himself and Neil away and if anyone else finds out, this could turn into a disaster.

Carmela should be the person I call. It is *her* club. But there's only one man involved that will know how to deal with this particular group of people.

"Aren't you supposed to be enjoying the weekend in Connecticut? Why are you calling me?" Jackson's voice drawls on the other end of the line after two rings.

"We have a problem."

"What kind of a problem?" He snaps into business mode, his voice sharper when he hears the panic in mine.

"I don't have time to explain everything right now. But Tripp is about to out himself and Emily's fiancé as members of Désirer."

Jackson doesn't say a word, but there's a sound like he may have hit something. "I'll call him," he says finally.

"He may not pick up right now. But I wanted you to know so you're ready to do some major damage control."

He sighs. "Thanks for giving me a heads-up, Lenni."

Jackson has been *kinder* for lack of a better word. I mean, he's always been kind—he did gift me a rather extravagant dress for no reason at all last year—but there's always been this edge to him when it comes to me. I always thought it was because I've never taken his shit, then because he thought I'd hurt Tripp. But I've learned these last two weeks that it's just his way of being. He's not used to having a lot of genuine friends, and he guards himself with his charm, money, and quick wit. It's nice to finally have him treat me like a friend, instead of a problem that's always lurking beneath the surface, ready to drown something he cares about.

"You're welcome, bossman."

Tripp

I fucked up.

I know I fucked up, and I owe Valentina a million apologies for the way I just treated her. There's no excuse for my behavior. When I saw Neil follow her, I got curious. But knowing he's touched her—that he knows what she looks like naked.

That he's been inside her.

I saw red.

And her face when I called him abusive—I knew exactly what she was thinking at that moment. I feel like there's a giant knot in my chest where Lenni is pulling on one end, and Emily is on the other, and it's just getting tighter and tighter.

She has to understand, though. How could she not after everything I've told her about Emily? My ex is as strait-laced as they come. I'd never be able to forgive myself if something happened to her, and Neil is the type to do whatever he wants to a woman because *she's his wife, and it's his right.*

Everything is a blur as I storm back downstairs, searching for Emily. By now, the commotion over Neil's nose has dispersed. A housekeeper is cleaning up the mess as I pass by, heading to the spa where my ex was before the spectacle.

"Tripp!" Emily shouts my name as I pass an open sitting room. She's been crying, her nose and eyes are puffy and red, while she sits on a sofa with her parents. Her dad glares at me while her mom looks relieved.

"Hey, Emily. I'm sorry about earlier. How are you?" I step inside the room but don't move closer, wondering if Neil will pop out of somewhere and try to return the blow I landed on him.

"What were you thinking?" she nearly shouts, hands flying up.

"Look, it's not what you think–"

"What I think is that she made a mistake inviting you. I know you took the breakup hard, son, but this is extreme. Neil's talking about pressing charges," her dad cuts me off.

"Listen, you can't marry him, Emily. Okay? Just trust me." My eyes flit to each of her parents before drilling into hers, trying to convey silently that we need to talk just me and her.

She doesn't get the point. "Tripp, I know that I hurt you, and I'm so sorry, but–"

"That isn't it! He's not who you think he is, Em." My blood pumps faster through my veins, fueled by adrenaline and the urgency to tell her what I know.

"Tripp, this isn't looking good for you, honey.

Don't you have a beautiful fiancée somewhere you should be more concerned with?" her mother suggests. I hate that she's right. I hate that I left Valentina in our room to deal with this.

"What do you mean Neil isn't who I think he is?" Emily asks, ignoring her mom. Her tears have dried, and she looks at me curiously, like she's finally willing to listen to what I have to say.

"Can we talk alone? *Please?*" I stress.

"Just say whatever it is you have to say, son," her dad responds, moving to pour himself a drink from a crystal decanter seated on the top of a minibar along one side of the wall.

"I think it's better if your daughter and I talk alone, sir. With all due respect, neither of you need to hear what I have to say." I'm still looking at Emily, urging her to tell her parents to leave.

She still doesn't get the point. "Just say it, Tripp!"

"Fine! You want me to say it in front of your parents? I will. Remember what you said when you broke up with me? Neil is a thousand times worse. We're not talking 'let's explore some boundaries.' The guy is a straight-up sadist."

Emily visibly flinches. "No, he's not! I would know!"

"Yeah, just like you knew what I liked, and we were together for a lot longer than you've been with him, Em. No offense, but you don't know because you don't *want* to know." I speak softly, not wanting her to feel like she needs to get defensive any more than she already is. I can already see her shrinking in on herself as her hand drifts to her belly.

"What are you going on about, Tripp? Emily said you two broke up because you weren't ready to start a family." Her mother looks between her daughter and me as she unwinds her arm from around Emily and straightens in her seat.

My ex has the grace to look embarrassed as she sinks further into the sofa.

Instantly, I think of Lenni. I think about how she's sitting alone in our room right now after I treated her like shit and left her to come warn Emily. I think about how I'm so sick of feeling like I always need to do what I believe is right and continue getting shit on for it. I think about how I wish we'd never come here this weekend and how I should have just washed my hands of this mess a long time ago.

"Well, if that's what she said, then it must be true, right?" I huff out softly.

"What do you mean Neil is a sadist?" her father asks.

"Yes, Tripp. What *do* you mean by that?" Neil's deep voice questions behind me.

I look over my shoulder to see that someone reset his nose, but he's swollen, and there's bruising under his eyes. It adds to the villainous grin that's stretched across his face. I think about his hands on Lenni, and once again, my vision goes red. "End it, Neil. Emily doesn't deserve this."

There's a shuffling noise outside the room, and my parents appear behind him, rushing in to join us.

"What on earth were you thinking, Tripp? You can't go around hitting people!" my mother cries, clearly not understanding what she just walked into.

"Neil, we're sorry this happened, we really are. What do we need to do to convince you not to press charges?" Pops asks him.

But Neil is still grinning his Cheshire smile at me. "Did your prostitute of a fiancée tell you that?" He makes a tsking sound. "She's breaking club rules."

Dread shoots through me. My blood turns to ice as all eyes shift to me and everyone starts speaking at once.

"Prostitute? What is he talking about, Tripp?"

"What club?"

"Valentina is a prostitute?"

"Tripp, Son, tell me he's lying?"

"You're lying. You have no idea what you're talking about."

Neil turns his vile face toward my mother. "Am I, Mrs. Kennedy?"

"And how do *you* know she's a…a…a prostitute?" Emily's voice sounds stronger and angrier than I've ever heard her speak before.

It doesn't even seem to phase Neil. "Sweetheart, you're a prude. But you're beautiful, and our children will have excellent pedigrees. Most marriages in our circle run this way, darling. The wife looks the other way and spends millions on whatever she wants while the husband has his fun discreetly." He looks between her father and mine. "Don't pretend that's not how things run, gentlemen."

"It most certainly does not!" Pops exclaims, outraged.

"You're disgusting. I think it's best you move along now. The wedding is off," Emily's father says sternly.

"She's carrying my child, Mr. Porter. I'm afraid it isn't that simple," Neil drops casually, like none of this is affecting him.

Both her parents begin to threaten him at the same time while mine move to my side and start to question me. Everyone's voice blends into a mass of commotion. Emily rubs her temple for a moment before she shouts, "EVERYONE OUT!"

All eyes move to her as they all stop talking. When she has their attention, she repeats herself, "Everyone out. I want to speak to Tripp alone."

Now, she wants to talk alone.

Neil shrugs. "Fine by me." Then, to Emily's parents, he says, "Let's go find my parents. I think we have a lot to discuss."

"We need to talk," Mother demands sternly, grasping my arm.

"We will. Just give me a few moments," I tell her before Pops pulls her out of the room. He grabs the door, fixing me with one long pitying stare before closing it.

"What the hell, Tripp?" Emily sighs.

"Now you know why I wanted to speak to you alone." I pour myself a drink from the minibar and sit in the chair across from her. "He cornered Valentina earlier. That's when I found out. I would have said something sooner if I'd known."

"They know each other?" Emily looks green, and I can't tell if it's from nausea or jealousy.

Nodding slightly, I knock back my bourbon. "They do."

"A prostitute, Tripp? Seriously? I don't even know what to say to that."

"Honestly, it's not on you to say anything, Emily. Regardless of her job, Valentina is a good person. She's had a shit life, and she's making the most of it."

"You can't marry a prostitute!"

I almost tell her it's all a lie—but it isn't anymore. And I don't owe her any kind of explanation. "Look, I came to tell you about Neil. And I did. I don't need you to tell me what I can and can't do with my life."

She doesn't respond, and the silence stretches between us, filling the room. Minutes pass, and I know I don't owe it to her to be there, that I should be racing back to Lenni, but I don't move.

"I wish I'd never left you," Emily says quietly.

"Em–"

"Can't we just fix this? We can be together again, and I know this baby isn't yours, but you'd make such a great father, Tripp." She scoots to the edge of the sofa and grasps my hands. "I know I hurt you. Let me make it up to you."

"No."

Shock flits across her face. Pulling my hands from hers, I stand and begin to pace, snorting out a laugh.

"Are you serious, Emily? You broke my fucking

heart and then lied to my face about cheating on me. *You* lied to your parents about why we split up—which, by the way, is so absolutely fucked. You told them I wasn't ready to start a family? You could have just said we had too many differences. Why do you keep *lying* to everyone?"

"And what about you? You hired a prostitute to what, Tripp? Fulfill your sexual fantasies? You aren't perfect, either!"

"I never claimed to be perfect, Emily! All I wanted was to explore sex with you! It's not a crime! You didn't have to make me feel like shit about it!" I throw my hands in the air as I stare down at her. Where I once saw someone beautiful, now I just see a sad woman. "Valentina has never once made me feel like shit for voicing my desires. Don't fucking look down on her because of her profession. She's been better to me in the last two and a half months than you were the entire time we were together. Maybe it's time to take a long, hard look at yourself, Em. Stop being so goddamn judgy. I hope one day you can find someone who wants exactly what you do out of life. But that person will never be me."

Emily sinks back into the sofa, silent tears streaming down her face, but they don't make me feel bad anymore. "Goodbye, Emily."

She lets me go, having nothing more to say. Flinging open the door, my body braces, ready to run up to the room, back to Lenni. But before I can even take a step, Pops is there, gripping my arm. "We need to talk, Son."

My feet are heavy as I make my way down the staircase. Nearly an hour has passed since I got off the phone with Jackson. Telling Emily shouldn't have taken this long, and I worry that perhaps Neil found Tripp instead.

When I get to the main floor, multiple employees are rushing about. Whispers of, "The wedding is off," and, "I heard the ex stopped the wedding, and now they're reconciling," fill the air. I don't think anything of it, because I'm sure that's how it looks from the outside.

As I slowly make my way across the inn, checking open sitting rooms and anywhere I can think of where Tripp would be, I begin to notice the stares. The whispers become even more quiet. Hands go up to shield mouths. I recognize some of the people as Emily and Neil's guests for the wedding.

Tripp probably made a commotion. That's all it is.

Poking my head into another sitting room, I see

Emily's parents talking to Neil's. The conversation looks heated, and Emily's mother is crying. Her father's eyes dart over Neil's mother's onyx coif, and he pauses mid-sentence to fix me with a hard stare. Everyone turns to look at me, Emily's mother's lip curling up in distaste as she rakes her dull green eyes down my body.

Unease creeps into my very bones.

Heading to the concierge desk, I smile at the pretty blonde who checked us in yesterday. "Hi there. I was wondering if you've seen Tripp Kennedy around anywhere?"

She deflates, lips pinching together like she's about to deliver bad news. "I'm sorry, Miss. Last I heard, he's with Miss Porter."

That's all she says, as if I don't know that she probably knows *exactly* where they are.

Opening my mouth to ask her kindly to tell me, I'm cut off, and we both visibly cringe when we hear someone screech, "How *could* you?"

Turning, I see Margo behind me. Her face is red and splotchy, and she looks like a firework about to go off aimed directly at *me*.

What did I *do?*

"How could I what, Margo?" I'm confused. She looks so incredibly furious and ready to burst at any given moment.

"I trusted you with my son. Welcomed you into our family. And you're a... a *sex worker?*" she spits between her clenched teeth.

Snapping away from the desk, I grab her arm and

lead her closer to the large wooden table near the entrance, not daring to look back to see if the concierge heard what Margo said, even though she undoubtedly did. "What are you talking about, Margo?"

Where the fuck is Tripp? He said he wouldn't tell anyone about me, so how the fuck does Margo know?

She rips her arm away from me, sneering as she fires out, "Is Valentina even your real name? I have no clue what my son was *thinking*! Surely your engagement is a farce because there's no way in hell he thought I'd allow him to marry a prostitute!"

Every fiber of my being wants me to beg her to let me explain. I'm still the same person I've always been, just with a different job title. I want to tell her that I quit sleeping with clients after I met Tripp. I want to tell her I quit the club altogether.

Instead, I straighten my spine and hold my head high. "Tripp is a grown man, Margo. I don't think you have much say in *what* he gets to do. Or who."

"You're a disgusting creature!" she snarls. "You think you can target my son because he's rich? You better hope you didn't give him any diseases, or I'll sue you for everything you have!"

My entire body warms with an embarrassed flush. People are staring. There's no way they can't hear what she's saying. I want to be angry. Fuck, I want to feel so much anger toward this woman. But all I feel is a strange sense of sadness for the loss of a mother who was never mine.

As soon as Tripp and I made things official, I

dared to hope that Margo and I would have some sort of mother-daughter relationship. We were already on our way there. How could Tripp do this? He promised he'd never hurt me. Was *saving* Emily worth our relationship?

He was devastated when she left him, and now perhaps she's available again.

I shove that thought deep down. Somewhere it can't resurface easily again.

Margo steps into me with a sneer. "I thought it was strange that I couldn't find much on you. Valentina Parks didn't exist before a few years ago when she popped up out of nowhere and began working at a restaurant called Decadence. I let you think I didn't know you lied about your job, but I never thought Tripp would stoop so low as to bed a woman who sells herself for money. Secrets don't do well in families like ours, Valentina. *Everything* always has a way of being brought to light. I think you've embarrassed us enough today. You should leave."

The fact that she looked into my background doesn't even phase me. I knew that was her MO before agreeing to Tripp's deal. Honestly, I thought she'd be able to find out the truth. But apparently, she isn't as good as everyone says she is.

For some strange reason, even though I was adamant about her not finding out before, I no longer give a fuck. I'm tired of hiding my past. Because it made me who I am today.

My chin lifts defiantly even though my ribs ache

with the heavy pressure of grief. "That's because my last name isn't Parks. It's Renton. I changed it because there are people from my past who are trying to find me, and I don't want to be found. Tripp knows a little about my childhood, but not everything."

Margo blinks rapidly, taking in what I'm saying. The fact that she's actually listening spurs me on as angry, hot tears begin to slide down my cheeks. "Think of the worst thing a child could go through, Margo. I *lived* it. I clawed my way out of the gutter I was born in, and I busted my ass to make my life better. I didn't take advantage of Tripp. I didn't even know who he was the night we met. My past isn't why I'm with your son. I'm with him because I love him. It isn't about the money. It's about the way he looks at me and sees *me*. It's the way he makes me feel *safe*, not with his bank account, but with his words and his actions."

My voice breaks as I continue. "If he wants to be with Emily, I won't stop him. But I want you to know, right now, that I truly *do* love your son. And I would never hurt him like she did. You could disown him, he could lose everything, and I would still love him. He is the *only* man I have ever cared for, and your opinion doesn't matter to me. If you're willing to push me aside that quickly, then *you* don't matter, Margo. Because I have slayed my own dragons for far longer than I should have had to, and you are *nothing* compared to them. But if you push him to go back to her, if you try to keep controlling his life, just know that you're going to become *his* dragon. And just remember, in the fairytales, the dragons always lose."

There's no time for her to respond as I turn and head toward the staircase, ignoring everyone who has stopped to stare at us. I don't care if she now has the knowledge she needs to dig into my real background. She can find out everything for all I care. It hurts that she's icing me out so quickly instead of trying to ask *why*. I thought...I really thought we'd formed a bond.

I should have known better than to get attached to any sort of mother figure.

I wasn't made to be cared for.

I was only made to take on the worst kind of shit the world has to offer.

And this world is a fucking cruel place.

Tripp still hasn't returned by the time I finish packing my things.

A lone tear slips down my face as I kiss a piece of stationary and leave it on his pillow. It's become our thing. Whenever I leave his place, I kiss a piece of paper and leave it for him to find. There's a drawer in his kitchen full of them.

I hate that this feels like it will be the last one.

There's a part of me that wants to stay. But Margo's onslaught of harsh words and accusations reinforced some of the walls that Tripp has broken down. And after everything we've been through, after everything we've talked about, the fact that he still went to seek out Emily after he went off on me is bothersome.

Only, I'm not sure if it's because I knew it would inevitably happen, or that I was stupid enough to believe he meant everything he said. Tripp is optimistic. It's one of the things I love about him. I've been a pessimist all my life. It was nice to be with someone who looks at the world through rose-colored glasses. Those glasses make him blind, though.

Sorrow sweeps through me as I pull off my ring and set it on the paper. With the facade up and Emily back on the market, I'm not exactly sure where we stand anymore. The plan was to continue pushing off a wedding until we decided it was what we really wanted. Now that Tripp knows about Neil, there's a good chance he won't want me anymore. And that's something I need to consider…and prepare myself for.

My phone buzzes from its place on the bed next to my thrifted Louis Vuitton Keepall Monogram bag. It's Momma's rehab facility, probably calling to collect the month's payment. In all the excitement with Tripp, I forgot to send out the money order, and they are strict about paying late.

Ignoring it, I throw my phone in my purse and grab my bag, making my way down the stairs and through the main floor as quickly as possible to the car that's waiting to take me back to the city. The blonde behind the desk flashes me a sad smile. I know she means well, but her pity just pisses me off even more.

Ten minutes into the drive, Tripp still hasn't bothered calling, which means he doesn't even know I'm gone yet. The rehab facility keeps calling over and over.

Finally, after the twentieth call and second voicemail I don't bother listening to, I answer. "What? I know the payment is late. I'll send it tomor–"

"Miss Renton? This isn't about payment," a soft voice interrupts. It's filled with a heavy southern twang, like something you'd hear in the deep South. "It's about your mother. I'm so sorry, honey, but she had a heart attack and passed away this afternoon."

Whatever she says next is drowned out by the sound of rushing water filling my ears. My sinuses burn, but I have no tears to cry. Adult me heaves in heavy, slow breaths, trying to process what I just heard, while the little girl stuck inside my chest begins to scream. Whether in agony for the loss of the mother who never really cared about her, or for her freedom that's come far too late, I'm not sure.

"Miss Renton? Miss Renton, can you hear me?"

"I'm here. Sorry." The words stick to the roof of my mouth like peanut butter. Whispered, thick and guttural.

I always wondered when this day would come— wondered if it would feel like a weight being lifted off my shoulders. It feels more like someone has dropped an anvil on my chest, and it's completely crushed my bones and the heart that lies trapped behind them. If an artist asked to paint what I'm feeling, the canvas would be dripping with the reds and pinks of a meaty heart shredded through with streaks of cream representing the sharp, fractured ribs that stick out of it.

"That's alright, honey. Now, there are no papers on what to do for your mother. Did you two speak about it at all? Make a plan in case something like this happened?"

We hadn't. But I don't believe in sticking someone in an overly expensive box that won't decompose any time soon, polluting the earth with more trash. "Cremation. But…" I pause.

Like a projection, I see the younger me so clearly, sitting on the cold ground in torn pajamas and that fluffy purple robe, clinging to a ratty old teddy bear like a lifeline while she nods her head. I shake mine in return, but she just keeps nodding.

One last time, my little valentine. One last time.

"Can you wait, please? I can be there by nightfall. I'd…I'd like to see her…one last time. Please." The little girl smiles at me. It's the saddest fucking smile I've ever seen.

"Of course, honey. State of Pennsylvania has a waiting period for cremation, anyway. I'll get the necessary paperwork ready for you."

I sniff as we hang up, looking into the rearview mirror to lock eyes with my driver. "Change of plans. Take me to the nearest airport, please."

Tripp

Pops is quiet as he leads me to his and mom's room on the fourth floor. A few employees spare us curious glances as we walk by them, my answering glare sending them scurrying off. By now, news about me hitting Neil has reached everyone, and I'm sure it won't take long for the staff to spread the revelation of Valentina's job through the inn.

I should have fucking shut the door to the sitting room.

I should have done a lot of things differently over the last hour.

Remorse courses through me from how I treated her earlier. She's the woman I'm in fucking love with, and I yelled at her like she'd done something wrong. I hadn't even been that harsh when Emily broke up with me. The thought of Neil and Valentina together spiked my rage way higher than it *ever* had in the situation with Emily.

The door is barely shut for a second before Pops spins around, dramatically throwing his arms in the air. "What the hell were you thinking?"

"Look, I know I shouldn't have hit him–"

"You think *that's* what I'm worried about? Tripp, is what Neil said true? Is Valentina a…a *prostitute*?" His bushy brows furrow as he struggles to say the word.

"Can we not use that word, please?"

"Tripp!"

"Yes! Okay? Yes. But it's a little more intricate than that. It's not like she hangs out on the streets looking for clients. She works at a highly reputable club." I run a hand through my hair, blowing out a breath at his exasperation.

"A reputable club, huh? Do I even want to ask what you're doing at a place like that?" Pops questions.

"I'm an adult, okay? And—"

"You may be an adult, Tripp, but everything you do reflects on this family! I'll bet half the guests have already placed calls to the papers! What were you thinking?"

I don't have a chance to reply because the door opens again, and my mother's voice rings out shrilly, "A prostitute? Tripp, I have never been so embarrassed of you. I can't believe you brought that filthy woman into my home!"

"Watch it!" I snap in a tone I've never used with her. Her brows shoot up into her hairline, her eyes growing wide. "You will *not* speak about her that way. Valentina hasn't been with anyone else since we met—"

"Where? The corner?" Mother huffs, coming further into the room to pace behind Pops.

I don't say anything because it's ironic that's exactly where we met.

"Why would you do this? There are so many nice women out there, Tripp. Why get entangled with a woman who sells herself for money?" Mom asks, her voice laced with despair.

Falling onto the floral-patterned sofa, I brace my elbows on my knees. "We met one night by accident. I spilled my coffee on her and offered to buy her a new dress to replace the one I ruined. It just so happened that Emily was at the store, too. Valentina could sense that I was uncomfortable and that the news of Neil and Emily's engagement bothered me, so she lied and said we were engaged as well. It spiraled from there when Emily told her parents, and they told you."

"Why didn't you just tell us the truth?"

"So you aren't actually engaged, then?"

My parents speak simultaneously and then look at each other with relief.

I don't immediately respond, my thoughts straying back to the first night Valentina and I met. It seems like it happened such a long time ago, even though it's only been a little over two months. I feel like I've known her forever, and I know that regardless of everything that just blew up, she *is* my forever.

Steepling my fingers in front of my face, I sit back before throwing my arms wide and exclaiming. "Yeah, I lied. I asked her to pretend to be engaged to me for a little while so that you'd get off my back about Emily." I motion to Mother. "So, no, technically, the engagement isn't real, but I don't regret a single lie. Because everything else is true. We fell in love. And the ring on her finger will be there permanently someday, so you can either get used to it or get used to not seeing me around anymore."

Both my parents look stunned at my exclamation. Mother stutters, "Ab...absolutely not! You cannot marry a prostitute!"

"Stop calling her that! I told you she hasn't been with anyone else since we met!" I meet my mother's glare with my own. "As a matter of fact, she quit her job. I don't care what the people here heard, and I'll pay whatever to ensure the papers don't run any stories. But that's for her sake, not mine. Like it or not, she *will* be a part of this family."

"I forbid it!" Mother shouts. Pops reaches over and wraps an arm around her shoulders, guiding her to sit in a chair. "Do you think she really loves you, Tripp? A woman like that is most likely only after one thing. Your *money*!"

"She hasn't asked for a single dime of what I agreed to pay her to lie for me." It's true. She's gotten better at letting me spend money on her, but she's never said a word about our deal. I even offered to give her money to cover her mother's rehab, but she turned it down.

If I were a different man, I'd have found a way to pay for it anyway, to surprise her. But Lenni has been adamant about not wanting to be with me for my money. And I think taking care of her mother on her own is something she *needs*. It's a part of her life that she doesn't want anyone else to touch—a chance to save the person who wronged her in so many ways.

It's almost like her way of healing.

And now that she's starting to let me take care of other things, it's easier for her to take on her mother's expenses herself.

Suddenly, I'm filled with heavy grief. This entire weekend would have gone differently had I just been honest with my parents in the first place. "You know, she was really starting to warm up to you," I tell my mom. "She's never had a mother figure. And while you two had your differences in the beginning, I know you became fond of her, too."

"Oh, don't believe whatever sob story she fed you. She's obviously very good with her lies."

"Margo, ease up," Pops gently scolds.

"She has no reason to lie to me. Do you know why she works at the club? It's because her mother sold her for drugs when she was a little girl." Pops' head snaps in my direction while my mother's lips turn down in a skeptical frown. "Yeah, you heard me right. Her own mother traded her sexually so she could get her fix. Valentina had a horrible childhood, but she escaped it and made something of herself. You don't have to approve of what she does. Or even who she is. But I can't live without her, and I don't want to. I don't care what you or anyone else thinks. You don't have to like it. You don't have to accept my decision. But that's the woman I'm going to spend the rest of my life with. So, you can disown me, remove me from your will, stop speaking to me—I don't care! I choose *her*."

Mother looks horrified, though I suspect now it's for an entirely different reason. I remember what it felt like when I found out. I can only imagine the thoughts that are going through my parents' heads. Standing, I shoot them a small smile. "I love you guys. But there's nothing you can say or do to change my mind."

They don't say anything as I leave.

It only takes a few minutes for me to rush back to our room—back to Valentina. Opening the door harder than necessary, I call out, "Viv?"

Silence greets me. Crossing the room, I check the bathroom to see it empty. Panic grips my chest as I notice the absence of her things on the vanity. Turning, I check the closet to find all her things are gone. "No, no, no..."

Something glints in the corner of my eye, and I realize there's something on my pillow. There's a heavy, hollow feeling beneath my ribs as I walk closer, seeing her engagement ring on a piece of paper that has her kiss mark. Her ring is cold when I pick it up. Placing it and the paper in my pocket, I make my way down to the concierge.

The lady who checked us in yesterday gives me a

tight smile as I rush up to the desk. "How can I help you, Mr. Kennedy?"

"Have you seen my fiancée? The pretty brunette I checked in with yesterday?"

She blinks before confirming my fears. "She left, sir."

"Left? Did she say why? Did she say anything? You know what? Never mind…thank you." I turn away, intent on grabbing my stuff so that I can head back to the city.

"Mr. Kennedy? If I may?" she calls out. She looks around before ducking her head as I walk back. "She was looking for you earlier, but you were with Miss Porter. Your mother found her, and their discussion didn't look pleasant."

My heart does a cannonball into my stomach. "Thank you."

Of course, that's what would prompt her to leave. First, I treat her like shit, and then my mother goes after her, too. She deserves so much better than this.

Pulling my phone out, I dial her number when I return to the room, but it goes straight to voicemail. Cursing, I throw all my things into my bag and leave the inn, not bothering to let my parents know I'm leaving.

Jackson calls as I'm pulling onto the freeway, and I answer since Valentina still isn't picking up, and he's been trying to call me for the past hour. "What, Jackson? Now isn't a good time."

"Tell me about it," he sounds pissed. "What the fuck were you thinking, Tripp?"

Lenni

By the time I land in Pittsburgh and secure a rental car, it's near closing for the facility where Momma was staying. Of course, the first stop I want to make is to the mortuary where they are keeping her body, but the nurse, Paula, who called me earlier, insisted we get the paperwork filled out as quickly as possible to start the process of getting her cremated.

"We didn't even know she had a phone. She's a sneaky one, your momma. We found it hidden in a hole under the mattress." Paula looks like she may be in her sixties, and she wears the stress of her job around her eyes—heavily creased and darkened from lack of sleep. But she still greets me with a smile and a warm cadence as she walks me through the paperwork.

"It's not a phone. Not really. I'm the only person she can talk to. After the last facility, I thought that maybe it would help her," I say. When I sign the last piece of paper, I tap the pen against the stack, afraid to ask what I really want to know.

"She was getting better, honey. Finally agreed to go to therapy, stubborn as she was. Grumbled the whole way about it, but she went. She spoke about you often." *Damn*, Paula is good at her job.

Tears line my eyes, and I blink them away before they can fall onto the papers. My voice is thick with emotion as I whisper, "You seem really nice, Paula. Thank you for taking care of her."

Her lips curl in as she nods, coming around her desk to wrap her arms around me. At first, I stiffen, unsure how I feel about a stranger hugging me. But then she says, "It's okay not to know how to feel right now, honey." And I melt into her arms, returning the hug, nearly biting a hole through my lip as I try not to cry.

"It should take a few days to get the paperwork squared away, but the actual process doesn't take that long. The whole thing should be done by the start of next weekend. Will you be picking up, or arranging for us to send the remains to you?" the mortician asks.

I haven't even thought about it. Since I arrived, my phone has been ringing off the hook with call after call from Tripp. He's also sent numerous messages that I quit reading, but there's no way I can ignore him for an entire week. Both situations are becoming too much to handle.

The mortician senses my uncertainty and flashes me a look of understanding. "No need to make the decision now. We'll keep in touch during the process, and you can decide then if you'd like."

Numbly, I nod. We don't say much else as I follow him into a room that looks like one you'd see on TV —with lockers where they store bodies and shiny steel tables where they do autopsies. He leads me over to a locker and opens it without hesitation.

"I'll give you your privacy. When you're done, I'll be up at the front," he tells me before leaving the room.

I thought I was prepared. But nothing truly prepares you for seeing your parent like this.

Momma's skin is ashy, but she looks more filled out since the last time I saw her. Her dark hair hangs limp and frizzy around her face. Gently, I reach up to brush a stray strand that's clinging to her cracked lips, silent tears streaming down my cheeks. "Hey, Momma. It's me."

There's no sign that she can hear me, not that I expect there to be. I don't really believe in a god, but sometimes I think that the universe sends us signs that *someone* is listening.

"I'm sorry that I kept ignoring you. And that I never came to visit." I grip her arm, my face twisting as a sob wrenches past my lips. "I'm sorry that you died alone."

All I can do is stare down at the mother who

never wanted me. Who never cared for me. It should be so easy to feel relief that she's finally gone, but all I feel is *pain*. As if it's become something tangible, spreading throughout my entire body, gripping every organ—every cell—in its cold, barbed hands.

The little girl I once was stares at Momma from the other side of the support tray, still wrapped in that fucking purple robe.

We're free now. So why are you sad?

Hallucinating her question only makes me cry harder.

My fingers dig into Momma's arm through the sheet over her body as I squat down, head hanging between my shoulders as I scream my despair viscerally. I scream for the little girl whose childhood was stolen from her, and for the woman I had to become. And for my momma, who might have finally started getting better if her body hadn't quit on her.

Anguished cries leave my throat with harsh, ragged breaths as I let her go and slam my fists against the other lockers over and over again. When I've exhausted myself, I turn and sit against the lockers, threading my hands through my hair while the last remnants of my tears dry on my face.

The little girl stands before me, clinging to her ratty old teddy bear.

It's time to let go now.

"I don't think I can," I whisper raggedly, fully aware that I'm talking to a child that only exists in my mind.

I'm going to go.

Raising my head, I stare at her. "Where are you going to go?"

She smiles, and it fills a small crack in my chest. She seems brighter. Happier.

I've always wanted to know what it was like to swim.

Then she's gone.

Suddenly, I feel lighter, like a weight has been lifted off my shoulders.

Goodbye, my little valentine.

I'm not sure why I decide to head *home*. Call it my last bit of closure, but I find myself on the freeway headed to the trailer court just outside Chester, where I grew up.

My phone rings again; the battery is nearly dead, and I make a mental note to grab a car charger when I stop for gas. Assuming it's Tripp, I answer—still angry with him, but knowing he deserves an explanation for where I am.

"Hey, Jackson told me what happened. Are you okay?" Carmela's voice sounds on the other end of the line.

Maybe it's the fact that she asked if I'm okay that has me breaking down in tears all over again.

She makes a cooing sound as she says, "Len, what happened?"

"My mom died. I'm at home," I tell her between

sniffs. Everything that happened with Neil doesn't register high on my list of concerns at the moment.

Carmela is the only person who knows the full extent of what happened to me when I was a kid. I hear her sharp intake of breath as her pitch heightens. "Oh my god, Valentina, I'm so sorry. Do you need anything?"

Wiping tears from my eyes to see the road, I bark a sarcastic laugh. "A whole lot of therapy."

She snorts. "Len, I'm serious."

I sigh. "No. I don't know if I'm staying or gonna go back to the city tomorrow. I'll keep you updated. And please don't mention it to Jackson or Ginny. I don't want to stress her out. The first trimester is hard enough as it is."

"Okay. Keep in touch." She sounds like she'd rather do anything else than get off the phone.

"I will." After we hang up, I toss my phone in the cupholder, not caring if it dies. I know I should call Tripp. But I also know I'm not in the right frame of mind to talk to him. Too much has happened in the past twenty-four hours, causing my walls to be high as ever.

We need space—time to cool off. Time to figure out what we want from each other. I don't know if I can handle him looking me in the eye and telling me he's choosing Emily. But why would he? After everything she put him through, I can't believe he'd be that stupid.

My thoughts stray to Margo. She looked so infuriated when she found out the truth about what I do—

did—for a living. And I hate that a small part of me feels like I let her down. Will there be anything I can do to change her mind about me? Do I even *want* to change her mind? If Tripp decides he still wants to be with me, they come as a package deal.

I'm replaceable. She's his mom.

As angry as I am, I can't deny she's a good mother.

Night stretches on. Nearly five hours of farmland and sights I never wanted to see again pass in a blur I pay no attention to. A never-ending loop of all the lies Tripp and I spun replays like a movie behind my eyes. Before I know it, the familiar faded blue and white sign that reads *Parks Trailer Court* comes into view.

No one wants to reinvent this town. Nothing new lines the streets, and some of the businesses I remember are boarded up. When I pull into the park, the trailer where I grew up still sits empty, waiting for anyone to come and take pity on its dilapidated siding and shoddily patched-up roof. The green door is chipped everywhere, desperate for a fresh coat of paint, and the stairs leading up to the front door still squeak loudly with every ounce of weight put on them.

It used to be how I knew one of Momma's men was coming—the squeaky stairs. They were the soundtrack of my inevitable sexual abuse.

Time passes as I just stand there trembling, gathering the courage to reach out and open the door. In order to move forward with my life, I have to let go of the past. Nothing is holding me here anymore. I just need…closure.

A loud bang sounds to my right, causing me to jump and swing my head, only to see the same neighbor with the same beer can that he spits his nasty tobacco into. He yells something incoherent over his shoulder, and the same woman yells at him from their screen door.

The man freezes when he sees me, beer can halfway to his lips. "Whadda doin' there, girl? Ain't no one lives there, no mo'," he croaks.

I wonder how many times he and his wife heard me screaming while I was violated. How many times they sat and did nothing while a little girl was repeatedly raped. If I can hear him clearly from our respective decks, surely they heard me screaming for help.

A look crosses his face as his eyes drag down my body. He cocks his head to the side, confusion flickering across his intoxicated eyes. "Valentina?"

Goosebumps break out over my flesh. Everyone around here is a functioning alcoholic and drug abuser. It doesn't surprise me that he recognizes me, but it concerns me that the news may reach the wrong people. Before I can respond, he hums, turning on his heel to go back into his house.

The breath I'm holding leaves my lips in a shudder. Bracing myself, I grip the doorknob and turn it, stepping into my old prison cell as though it will save me from other prying eyes. It smells musty, yet still carries the undercurrent of Momma's old perfume even this many years later. Instant nostalgia creeps along my bones, and dread settles into the marrow like old friends embracing.

There was never a time in this house when I didn't feel frightened.

Stains litter the old, tattered softa—patches of discoloration rippling out like spindly fingers. There's a cold draft that slips in through the holes in the floors, yet it still doesn't feel as chilly as it did when I was little.

My steps are heavy as I walk down the hall, breathing shallow as I push open the door to my old room. A noise leaves my throat as tears spring to my eyes once more. The purple robe lies discarded on my bed—dusty cobwebs covering it—and my teddy bear is still sitting in the chair beside it. Both stare at me as I grip the doorframe and slide to the floor, sobbing into my hand to try to muffle my cries.

So many bad things happened to me here.

When I finally pick myself up off the floor, I leave all the remnants of the past there, in that room, shutting the door on my entire childhood and locking it away so it can no longer cling to my present.

Stepping into Momma's bedroom, I'm hit with the stagnant smell of old sweat and stale potpourri. Even time couldn't erase the stench. My skin crawls as I sit on her bed. An old, deteriorated pack of Black and Milds sits on the table tray next to her bed. She was always sucking on the disgusting things. I remember stealing one from her when I was fourteen and thinking I was going to die when I tried it and couldn't stop coughing.

Even though the bed is covered in grime, and who knows what else, I lay back and stare at the water stains on the ceiling. My eyes grow heavy the longer I look, memorizing the patterns of the marks and wondering if Momma ever laid in bed and did the same.

Did she notice that one looks like a heart?

My little valentine.

Curling up into a ball, I begin to sob once more. I'm so sick of crying, but it feels cathartic. Like I can leave all my tears in this awful place and finally start fresh where none of it holds me back.

So I cry.

And cry.

And cry.

My heart beats wildly, thumping harshly against my rib cage as footsteps thunder throughout the trailer, jolting me awake.

I hadn't meant to fall asleep.

They found me.

Scrambling from the bed, I nearly make it to the closet when the door crashes inward, and a nasally man cries, "Valentina! Look who decided to come home finally."

I don't even see who it is before a searing pain slams into my face, and my world goes black.

Margo

"Darling, please tell me you slept last night?" Weylan asks through a yawn as he enters the solarium with two steaming cups of coffee.

"When we got married, I promised never to lie to you, my love." Taking my cup from him, I angle my head when he bends to kiss my cheek. "I can't get over how upset Tripp was when he left yesterday. Have I finally gone and pushed him away for good?"

"Well, let's just hope Valentina hasn't told him exactly what you said to her. Because if she makes it sound even half as bad as you did when you told me, I wouldn't want to speak with you either. And I say that with love," he quips as he sits in his chair across from mine.

"Yes, well. Neither of them are answering my calls. Tripp keeps forwarding me to voicemail, and Valentina's phone goes straight through." It's beginning to unnerve me. My son and I have never fought for this long.

When he revealed Valentina's past to us yesterday, I took that, along with the information she gave me, and told my private investigator to find me everything he could as soon as possible. My need to *know* things may annoy some people, but perhaps this could have all been avoided if I'd had all the facts in the first place.

"I know that look. What are you brewing up in that mind of yours?" my husband asks as he flips open the newspaper.

"Just thinking about how awful I feel. Really, Weylan, I do. I was too harsh on her. It was a lot to take in, and I should have waited to speak with her. Regardless, I don't know if I can get over her profession." Sunlight streams in through the windows. While I usually enjoy it, today, it—paired with my lack of sleep—is giving me a migraine.

"It isn't up to us, Margo." Weylan sets his paper down and looks at me sternly. "It's Tripp's decision, and he's made it. You heard what he said. She hasn't been with anyone since him. He's the happiest I've seen him since…ever! He was never as happy with Emily as he is when he's with Valentina. Don't make him choose between you two. Something tells me you'll get your heart broken if you do."

Valentina's words from yesterday come back to me. Is that what I've reduced myself to? The dragon in a fairytale who goes around making everyone's life miserable?

"My mother didn't like you very much when she first met you. Remember that?" He picks up his paper and resumes browsing the finance pages just like he's done every Sunday since we first got together.

"Your mother was a cow," I groan.

Weylan flips a corner of the paper down to reveal a raised eyebrow. "You weren't a ray of sunshine toward her either," he deadpans before flipping the corner back up.

"How can you be so...so *blasé* about this situation?" I set my coffee down on the serving tray between us and get up to pace the room. Pacing helps me sort my feelings. I can feel myself getting worked up again, my heart racing at an achingly fast rate.

He sighs, tossing his paper in my chair. "Margo, my darling. You're getting yourself worked up over nothing. It's really very simple. I love our son." He spreads his arms out and shrugs. "That's it. End of discussion. Am I happy that he fell in love with a prostitute? Not at all. But does Valentina seem like the type of woman who is trying to take him for his money? No! She's a polite, smart young lady."

"We don't even know if that's who she really is," I argue. "They did such a great job at lying. What if it was *all* a lie? What if we don't really know her at all?"

"I trust Tripp's judgment of character."

"After Emily, I'm not so sure *I* do."

Weylan stands and pulls me into his arms. "He's

an adult. We have to respect his decisions. We don't have to like them. But we have to respect them. And you loved her, Margo, you really did. Stop trying to convince yourself you didn't. She's like the daughter we never had. I saw how much of a connection you two made. If everything Tripp said is true, can you imagine how yesterday must have made her feel?"

"Yes, I *can* imagine it. Because it's been all I've been able to think about. While I may not like the idea of our son with a woman who sells herself for money, what that poor girl had to endure is heartbreaking. It explains why she was hesitant to open up to me and why she was so quick to guard herself in my presence. She's never had a mother figure to rely on. I'm torn, Weylan, I really am. I'm angry with her. With Tripp. And myself for everything I said to her yesterday. I don't know what to do with it all." Heavy tears fill my eyes as my husband hugs me tighter.

"My love, I have never known you *not* to do the right thing. You'll figure out what that is. Tripp knows you love him and that you mean well. I think it's best if you just give him a little time to figure things out. His priority right now is going to be Valentina."

Loud buzzing fills the air as my phone begins to vibrate on the serving tray. I nearly shove Weylan away to rush to it, hoping it's Tripp. Instead, my PI's number flashes across the screen. "Yes? Do you have what I asked for?"

A man I only know as Dodger clears his throat.

"Yes, ma'am. I'm scanning everything to your email now. Your information checks out. Valentina Renton grew up near Chester, Pennsylvania—just her and her mom, Lucille. Mom was addicted to drugs. Sold herself, and when Valentina was old enough, she started selling her too. A death certificate for her mother just hit the records yesterday. Paperwork to cremate was filed this morning, which means your girl is back there now. As for the other stuff from when she was younger, well, it's some real nasty shit here, ma'am. *My* stomach churned reading it. This stuff is way worse than anything you've had me dig up before."

Death certificate? If it was recorded yesterday, that must mean her mother just died. I rub at the hollow of my neck, my stomach heaving at the information.

"Keep going," I snap.

He blows out a long breath. "She was hospitalized when she was seventeen. One of the guys tried to cut her up pretty badly during the act. Her mother killed him, and Valentina stayed in the hospital for a few days until she was released into the system. She left the home, though, and ended up back in the hospital with an infection a few days later."

"Is that all of it?" Ignoring Weylan's hushed whispers asking where I'm going, I walk quickly to our room to get dressed. If Valentina is in Pennsylvania, then that must mean Tripp is as well.

"Not even the worst of it, ma'am," Dodger says.

"How much worse can it get?"

"A lot worse. It ain't pretty."

Walking into my closet, my eyes narrow as I pull the phone from my ear and put it on speaker, reaching for a pair of linen pants. "Tell me everything."

$$Tripp$$

The smell of bourbon permeates the air around me as I wake to the sunlight streaming in on my face. Groaning, I roll onto my side, reaching for Valentina before remembering she's not here. I drove back to the city yesterday in nearly half the time it took us to get out to Connecticut, going straight to her apartment only to find that she wasn't home. The concierge of my building informed me she hadn't been to my place either, and she wouldn't pick up her phone.

Rolling to my other side, I grab my phone off my nightstand to see it's mid-afternoon. Multiple missed calls from Jackson and my mother clutter the home screen, but I ignore them, searching for anything from Valentina.

Still nothing.

Her face lights up my screen as I hit her number, but it goes straight to voicemail, just like it's been doing since last night. I want to throw my phone across the room angrily, but drop it back to the night-stand next to the half-empty tumbler of Wild Turkey instead.

I searched for her everywhere last night. I checked Bryant Park, the Rockefeller rink, and even stopped by Désirer to see if she was there. The only place I didn't check was Jackson and Ginny's because even though I'm ignoring my best friend, he still would have told me if she'd shown up there.

Her absence has taken a chunk from my chest. I feel completely hopeless, not knowing where she's at —if she's okay. The fact that she left her ring and isn't answering me can only mean one thing: she's done with us.

If I could go back in time and change everything about yesterday, I would. I'd make sure she knew that I trusted her and was never angry with her. I would have never left in such a hurry to tell Emily anything. We could have come up with a plan together if I'd just *waited* like she asked me to.

I promised her I'd never hurt her, and I failed massively.

Grabbing my phone again, I hit her name and let her voicemail play through before leaving what has to be my twentieth-something message. "Viv, I'm so sorry. Please call me. I love you, baby. I love you so much it fucking hurts." My voice breaks as my tone turns watery. "I need you, Valentina. I need to see you. I need to put your ring back on your finger where it belongs. You need to be back by my side where *you* belong. Please don't give up on me. Don't give up on us. I know you deserve better than what happened yesterday, and I will spend as long as it takes making it up to you. I love you. Please call me."

Pressing my palms into my eyes, I try to quell the tears, but they won't stop. Anxiety tightens my chest as adrenaline flows through my bloodstream. This feels worse than thinking she may have gone to the club last night to vent her frustrations. Even though I know she wouldn't do that to me, I had to exhaust all my options while looking for her.

Vibrations flutter on my chest, and I see Jackson's name pop up on my screen. "What?"

"Don't *what* me. You pull that shit yesterday and then disappear on me, and you think that's the appropriate way to finally answer your phone?" he snaps.

"Fuck you." I get out of bed and head to the bathroom to turn on the shower. As steam begins to roll throughout the room, I put the phone on speaker. "Is Valentina there?"

"No? Why would she be here? She's not with you?" he asks.

I hear Ginny's frantic voice. "Her phone has been going to voicemail all night. She's not with Tripp?"

Nausea rolls through me. "No, she's not with me. I haven't heard from her since yesterday afternoon. She left her ring on my pillow at the inn and disappeared. I checked everywhere: her apartment, the skating rinks, the club, the restaurant."

"Maybe Carmela would know?" Ginny voices.

"She's doing the books at Decadence today. She

never checks her phone when she's working on them," Jackson explains. "We'll head there now."

Turning the water off, I throw on the clothes I wore yesterday and am out my door in less than a minute. "I'll meet you there."

I've never been to Decadence, but there's no time to admire the restaurant because all I want to know is if Carmela knows where Valentina is. The hostess tries to greet me, but I fly past her, heading toward the back hall where Jackson said the office is.

"Hey! You can't go back there!" the hostess yells at me.

"It's fine, I know the owner." I'm not sure Carmela will be pleased that I'm barging in, but I don't care. She's always been a bit frosty, but I just chalk it up to the fact that she is protective over Valentina, and we have that in common, so I appreciate that about her.

Her head snaps up from her computer, a pair of blue light glasses perched at the end of her nose. "Tripp? What are *you* doing here?"

"Do you know where she is?"

"Valentina?" She pulls her glasses off her nose and looks at me like I've grown another head.

"Yes, Valentina! Who else would I be coming here looking for?" I snap back. She opens her mouth to respond but stops as Ginny and Jackson appear behind me.

"Did you find her?" Ginny asks.

"Baby, you need to calm down. The stress isn't good for the baby," Jackson soothes quietly.

"None of you know where she is?" Carmela sits back in her chair, appraising us like we're suddenly a threat.

"Something tells me *you* do." There's an edge to my voice, a warning that I'm about to lose my temper.

"I find it interesting that she didn't trust you enough to tell you." She points at Ginny. "You, I understand. She told me not to say anything to you because of the baby, but you." She points at me. "You, I expected to know by now."

"Know what, Carmela?" Jackson asks between clenched teeth. Anything that stresses out Ginny is going to piss him off, and right now, Carmela's little speech is doing precisely that. Ginny is shaking, her lips trembling as she tries to keep her tears at bay.

"Her mother died yesterday. She went home," Carmela explains.

My eyes close slowly as I release air through my nose.

As if yesterday wasn't hard enough, trust her mother to make it worse.

I should be ashamed of my thoughts, but I'm not. I'm angry. Raging on the inside at how fucking stupid I am that I fucked up so badly, she felt she couldn't tell me.

"Do you know where *home* is? In all the years we've known each other, she's never said," Ginny squeaks.

"She's never told me, either. I'm sorry." Carmela leans forward, placing her elbows on her desk as she rubs her temples. "She was supposed to keep in touch, but her phone has been off since last night."

"She once said she was from 'nowhere'," I offer helplessly.

"That's not a real place," Carmela deadpans.

"No shit," I snap. She glares at me in return. Any inkling that this woman doesn't like me has just been solidified in my head.

"I can't even track her because her phone is off," Ginny says worriedly.

"It should show you the last known location." Carmela frowns as if we all should have thought of that ourselves.

Honestly, I feel fucking stupid that we didn't.

Ginny swears and pulls up Valentina's name. I hold my breath while I wait. "There. It shows her somewhere near Pittsburgh."

Jackson huffs a laugh just before I ask him, "Can you get your jet ready? It will be faster than commercial."

Relief floods my senses, only to be squashed as he shakes his head and rubs his forehead. "No, I can't."

"Why?" I bite back, pulling my phone from my pocket to see when the next flight to Pittsburgh is.

"Because your mother asked me if she could use it earlier this afternoon. I didn't think anything of it.

She said she had business to deal with," he explains.

"Where the fuck did she go?" My mother never does any sort of business on Sundays. And what could she possibly have to do after her part in blowing up my life?

She's been calling you repeatedly. Maybe you should have picked up the phone.

"She didn't take it anywhere. She said to have it ready for when she needed to return."

"Jackson, *where*?" Ginny stresses.

"Philadelphia International."

$$\mathscr{L}enni$$

The sound of beeping and hushed whispers pulls me from sleep.

My eyelids are too heavy to open, so I focus on the sounds, trying to gauge where I am. There's a dull ache in my lower stomach, but overall, I feel better than I did the last time I was awake.

"I can't release her to you. There are still a few months before she turns eighteen. I have to put her back into the system." A hospital. I must be in the hospital. I try to crack open my eyes enough to see blurry shapes at the end of the bed I'm lying in.

"Fuck that. She's worth money. How much to fudge the paperwork?" a man replies. I'd know his voice anywhere and wonder why he's here.

"Are you her father? I could release her if you were her father." The nurse talks slowly, her question leading, like blood test results are something she can mess with. "If you're unsure, we could swab you both. You look like you could be related."

The man laughs. "Sure. Take a swab. Or our blood. Whatever."

"It'll take at least two days to get results. I'll keep her here for observation until then."

Soft footsteps walk away while heavier ones come to my bedside. I keep my breathing even, trying not to set off the machine and alert anyone that I'm awake. Callused fingers run down my cheek as the man chuckles. "Something tells me you're going to be a whole lot of trouble, valentine."

"Wake up, Valentina," a nasally man speaks too close to my ear.

I come to with a groan, my head heavy as it rolls back and a metallic tang fills my mouth. Swiping my tongue along my lips, I discover that my upper lip is split open, but the blood is dried, and the throbbing in my cheek suggests I have a black eye. Someone must have taken another swing at me after I'd been knocked out.

Where am I? And how long have I been here?

A door opens, and a dark laugh rings across the room, causing my blood to curdle like spoiled milk. "Oh, I'm going to love this."

Reker.

The Enforcer.

Reker is the one who gets called in when money is owed. The one who paints a masterpiece on the floor with your blood and body parts while you scream and beg him to stop.

One of my eyes is swollen shut, but the other opens wide to see him walking toward me. Immediately, I begin to struggle, discovering that my hands are bound behind my back. I try to stand, but the man beside me lays a thick hand on my shoulder and shoves me back into the chair. Wildly, my eyes dart around the room that looks like some sort of warehouse, trying to find any means of escape.

"I'm going to have fun breaking you back in, little one," Reker croons. When he makes it to me, he collars my neck and forces my head back at a painful angle. A whimper leaves my throat, causing his lips to turn up in a wide grin. "God, I missed that sound. How is it possible you got more beautiful while you were away?" He leans down until his lips are hovering over mine. "My dick is rock hard just thinking about how much fun we're going to have."

"Fuck you!" I spit. My blood flecks over his face, making him look even more sinister than he already does.

Leaning forward swiftly, he takes my lip between his teeth and bites down, causing more blood to gush from the wound and into our mouths. The pain is so severe I jerk my head back with a squeal, but he just bites down harder, stepping into me and lowering himself to straddle my lap as he laughs against my lips. Reker is huge. Heavy with thick, solid muscle.

Strangled screams fly from my throat as he rocks his hips against me and sucks my blood into his mouth, swallowing it with a moan.

"Enough." The word echoes across the room, and Reker lets me go with a smirk. His teeth and lips are smeared in my blood, and he drags himself against me as he stands.

"This is just the beginning. Welcome home, little valentine," he roughly whispers before walking away.

My cries are loud as I spit out a mouthful of blood and shove my face into my shoulder, trying to subdue the pain in my lip. I should have never come back to this place. I knew better. Now, I'm not sure I'll make it out again. I should have never made it out in the first place.

Calculated, unhurried steps reverberate throughout the room. "Valentine, Valentine, my little valentine. I knew you'd come home to me eventually."

Tensing, I slowly pull my face away from my shoulder. Anger courses through me, and my tears evaporate with the heat of the burning hatred I feel for the man before me.

Petey Barr.

Resident drug lord. The man who taught me what I needed to know to get started on the streets of New York. The man I stole from so that I could disappear and start my life over.

The first man to offer me cash for my body.

"Hello, Father."

Petey frowns at the reminder that I ended up being his real daughter. It's ironic that he once called himself daddy while he fucked me—before we knew the truth—the day he offered to pay me cash if I could make it better for him by reciprocating the pain he liked to cause.

The nurse never had to tamper with anything. The day we found out he was my birth father was the day he stopped touching me. Apparently, raping his own flesh and blood went too far. But he'd always curse and complain that he wished he'd never had the test done.

Since Petey's moral compass wouldn't let him enjoy me anymore, he became just like Momma. Only, instead of trading drugs for my body, he traded jobs. And Reker was his best employee.

"Look at you. All grown up. Tell me, Valentine, did you bring back the money you stole? That's the only reason I can think of why you'd show your face around here again." Petey cracks his knuckles when he's four steps away from me, and I brace myself for what I know is coming.

Sure enough, he rears back as I squeeze my one good eye shut just before his knuckles kiss my unbruised cheek. Pain blossoms like the petals of a flower uncurling. The gaudy gold ring he always wears catches my skin and tears it open, a warm gush of blood streaming from the cut. He roughly grips the back of my neck, forcing me to look at him as he screams, "Where's my money, Valentine?"

"I don't have it," I grit out. My mouth is full of blood, and it drips between my lips as I speak.

Petey reaches up and smears it over my face as he glares at me. "That's right, I didn't think so. And you know what? You're gonna spend a long time making it up to me, isn't that right? Two hundred thousand with interest, you little bitch. And where the fuck is your good-for-nothing mother?"

"She's dead." I pour all my anger into those two words.

That makes him pause, a flicker of something that looks an awful lot like remorse flashing through his eyes for a split second before he huffs and shakes his head. "That's a damn shame because she owed me too, so you can pay off her debt as well."

"I want her first." Reker is practically salivating as he watches us. The outline of his erection is still prominent against his pants, and the thought of him touching me again makes me want to vomit.

Immediately, I begin wondering how I can possibly end my life from this chair. That would be better than being subjected to this again.

"You'll never have me." I grin at him before sneering up at Petey. They hate being talked back to. I know they'll beat me for it. The harder they beat me, the longer it will take for me to recover. And I'm no good to them if I'm not in perfect health. None of Petey's customers want to fuck a lifeless body.

Petey scowls down at me. "Oh, he'll have you. As a matter of fact, he's the only one who's gonna have you for a while. You obviously need to be fucked back into submission."

I aim for his feet as I spit a mouthful of blood onto the floor. "Thought you liked it better when I fought back, *Dad.*"

The chair disappears from beneath me as the man

behind it dumps me on the floor. Hands grab at my pants, and terror grips my heart, crushing it between cold, bony fingers. "No! Stop!"

There's an unmistakable clanking of a buckle and a *whoosh* as Petey pulls his belt completely out from the loops on his pants. I try to slide away the best I can with my hands tied, but the other man holds me down as he pulls my pants below my butt.

For a moment, I think Petey is going to say to hell with his morals and rape me. Utter hopelessness sears through me. I worked so hard for my freedom from this life, only to have it stripped away from me in the span of a few seconds.

I hear the stir of the air a second before feeling the sting of his belt across my backside. Startled, I let out a yelp of pain that mixes with Reker's joyous laughter as he walks closer to watch.

Petey strikes me hard, from the back of my thighs up to the middle of my back, letting out an angered shout with each whip of his belt. Raw, hoarse screams leaving my throat with each one. My skin stings, burning as welts bubble up.

"Slap her pussy with it, I'll bet the little slut is already soaked. Then get the fuck out so I can have my fun," Reker says.

Once more, the belt strikes at the juncture between my thighs, just narrowly missing my core. Petey gets down on his haunches, sniffing before he whispers, "You thought you had it bad before. You ain't experienced nothing yet. Welcome home, Valentine." When he stands, I focus on his shoes as he begins to walk away. The tears dry on my cheeks, as I prepare to go somewhere deep in my mind to protect myself from what's about to happen.

"She's all yours. Make sure you don't kill her. And for fuck's sake, don't mark her up anymore."

"Oh, I'm *going* to do a lot worse than that, boss," Reker argues. I can hear him unzipping his pants.

"Listen here, fucker–" The sound of loud banging on the door cuts Petey off.

I can't see anyone's face from my place on the floor, but from the sounds of confusion they make as they all mumble that they weren't expecting anyone, I imagine they're surprised they have visitors. My backside screams in agony as I try to twist on my side, hiding my naked flesh from whoever is on the other side of the door.

"Should I get it, boss?" the man behind me asks.

"Flash 'em your gun, tell 'em were busy, and to get the fuck out of here," Reker commands. Petey hums his agreement, and the man goes over to the door, the sound of his safety being turned off clicking loudly just before he opens it.

No one says a thing. I manage to look up even though my body screams in pain at the movement. The man is frozen with a confused look on his face, pointing his gun at whoever is there. "Uh, who are you?"

Two men in black step into the room with their own guns raised—bodyguards—wearing finer suits than anyone from around here who would be gracing Petey's establishment. My heart skips a beat, and my lips turn up, even though it causes the split to widen and more blood drips over my teeth and down my chin. There's only one explanation.

Tripp.

The nasally man backs up, keeping his gun trained on them, and all I can think of is how Tripp is too pure to have a gun in his face and that he's going to crack a poorly timed joke about it at any moment.

"Get that damn thing out of my face this instant!" a sharp feminine voice rings out.

Shock jolts through my chest as though a Taser has just zapped me.

Prince Charming isn't here to save me.

The evil queen is.

Margo.

"Who the fuck are you?" Petey snaps.

Margo is still hidden by the door, but the moment I hear her heels clicking on the floor, I want to curl up and die. The thought of her seeing me like this is worse than if it were Tripp.

There's a sharp intake of breath and a skid of her heel on the floor, followed by a loud thump. "Dear god. Valentina."

"Don't touch her!" Reker barks out. There's a scuffle as the bodyguards rush the man with the gun and disarm him quickly.

Warm hands try to pull my pants up, and I let out a whimper as the material scratches the welts on my skin. "You're safe now. I've got you," she whispers.

"I won't ask again. Who the fuck are you?" Petey shouts.

Margo looks over my body at him, and her eyes narrow. I've been on the receiving end of that look, and I'll bet anything that Petey is at least a little terrified of this petite woman. "She owes you money, correct?" She nods to something by the door. "That will cover it. Consider her debt paid."

"Are you fucking crazy, lady?" There's a clicking sound and then a slide of something against the floor.

"Should I count it, boss?" nasally man asks after a beat of silence.

"No. That's a lot more than she owes. Who are you? What connection do you have with her?" Petey asks again, sounding more intrigued than anything now.

Something glides over me—Margo's jacket—before she helps me stand. Blood gurgles in my throat as I try to breathe through the pain of pulling my pants back up. The look of pity in her eyes is almost too much to bear.

She looks around me as she offers her body as a brace for me to lean against. I swear her eyes darken while she glares at Petey, the dragon I accused her of being roaring to life. "If you try to follow or contact us in any way, I will *destroy* you. If I hear so much as a peep of you stepping foot outside this vile town— and trust me, from now on, you will be under surveillance—I will make sure it's the last thing you do. Do I make myself clear?"

Shakily, I turn to look over my shoulder at Petey, who is staring at us with a contemplative gaze.

"You're not going to just let her go, are you?" Reker barks. He scowls between Petey and Margo before taking a step toward me.

Shots are fired without so much as a warning, causing both Margo and I to jump. One second, Reker is standing tall and threatening. The next, he's on the ground in a pool of blood that's rapidly spreading beneath him. His lifeless eyes stare up at me, and I want to feel peace at his death, but all I feel is mind-numbing pain.

Petey doesn't so much as blink.

"Do I make myself clear?" Margo repeats.

My father glares at us with stark hatred in his eyes. Eventually, he gives a slight nod. "Until next time, my little valentine."

Refusing to let him see me break, I hold my chin high as I hobble out of the room, heavily leaning on Margo for support. We go down a long, straight hall before she pushes open the door at the end to reveal a blacked-out car waiting for us.

Once we're secure inside, the driver takes off, leaving the bodyguards behind. Margo reaches over and gently palms my cheek. "Are you alright?"

So many emotions flood me all at once, my lips trembling as a cascade of tears pour from my swollen eyes. Carefully, she gathers me in her arms, mindful of my back, whispering soothing sounds into my ear. "You're safe now. You'll never have to worry about any of them again."

We arrive at the airport where Jackson's private jet is waiting to take us back to New York. During the ride, Margo explains that she had her investigator look into my background. She says she found out I stole money from Petey and had to disappear, which explained why I changed my name so that it would be harder to find me. She even repeatedly apologizes for her behavior in Connecticut, but it all just seems stupid to me now.

Even after we board, the plane waits to take off. I don't think much of it, letting Margo help me get comfortable on my stomach while she brings me ice for my back and my eyes. There's a chance I may have a concussion, and I'm not sure I should be flying, but I'm too tired to care, and don't want to go to a hospital.

I just want to go home.

To Tripp.

"How did you find me?" It's been bugging me since she walked through the door. How did she know where to look? And that I owed Petey so much money?

"My dear, I'm *me*. I know everything." There's a quick upturn of her lips before her expression turns melancholy again as she strokes my hair.

The bodyguards eventually make it on the plane, briefcase in hand, and I look at Margo questioningly as the flight crew closes the door, and we get ready to take off.

"What?" she asks. "Did you think I was going to let him live?"

"You're fucking scary, Margo." The news of Petey's death barely rocks me. Sleep keeps trying to claim me, but every time I nod off, she gently prods me back awake. She gives me a bottle of water and makes me take a few sips before giving me some pain pills.

"Yes, I am. Forget about being a dragon, my dear. I'm a mother, and they messed with the wrong one." She laughs gently, pulling my hair off my face. "Why didn't you just ask Tripp for the money, Valentina?"

"I would have never asked him to do that. Besides, it's the same thing. I owed Petey. I would have owed Tripp. I don't want to owe anyone. It's my own mess. I would have figured a way out of it, eventually." I think about the deal Tripp and I made and how the money he said he'd pay me would have more than gotten me out of trouble. I'd decided weeks ago that I wouldn't take it, even though I knew he'd have handed it over in a heartbeat if I'd told him the whole truth about my past and what I was hiding from.

"We could have made life a little easier if you'd have just asked," she says softly.

"You never wanted me with your son, Margo." I shift so my hair falls over my face again, hiding me from view. "And if I had asked, I'd be no better than the gold-digger you thought I was. I've worked hard all my life. This is no different. Life *is* hard for the majority of us. If anything, I was hoping you could at least respect that."

She pulls my hair away before moving to be in my direct line of sight. "I *do* respect you, Valentina. It takes a very strong woman to grow up the way you did and to still try and take care of your mother. It shows good character, not to mention iron will and humility. Your circumstances have been dreadful, yet still, you carried on and tried to better your life without asking for handouts. Tripp filled us in on your deal. That money alone would have gotten you out of trouble."

"I would have never taken the money from him." Tears fill my eyes once more, and I heave a frustrated sigh.

I'm so sick of crying.

"I know that." She cups my cheek.

"How do you know that?"

It's an automatic response to tense as she surges forward. She catches it, pausing before she lays a chaste kiss on my forehead. "Because I know how much you love him. I can see it as clearly as your lovely face. I am truly so sorry for the way I acted in Connecticut. I know that it will be easier said than done, but I hope that we can move forward from this." Tears line her eyes as she looks at me affectionately. "Because I would very much like to show you how a real mother is *supposed* to treat her daughter."

Tripp

My knee bounces uncontrollably while I sit and stare at my front door. It's causing me literal, physical pain to wait for my mother to bring Valentina home to me. My stomach twists and twines into knots as time passes, my lungs heavy with shallow breaths. Each one hurts, like my ribs are splintered and pressing into them with every intake of air.

As soon as Jackson informed me where my mother asked his jet to go, I called her. Hours passed by the time she returned my call. She has Valentina with her—only the situation is so much worse than I could ever possibly imagine.

"She's been through a lot, Tripp. You're going to be very angry when you see her. I need you to rein that in and be strong for her. Do you understand? She may very well break when she sees you."

"Why would I be angry? The only thing I'm angry

about is that you went to get her without telling me. It should have been me. I'm not angry with her."

"No, dear. When you see her, you will be angry. It's her story to tell you when she's ready. Just know that some very bad men found her before I could. But she's safe now. And we will be home soon."

The conversation I had with my mother earlier replays over and over in my head. I've never been a violent man. Then again, I've never been a jealous one either. Not until Lenni.

My hands clench repeatedly, itching to land a blow into the face of every single man who touched her. Thoughts of the worst possible kind swirl in my brain. What does it mean that they found her before Mom could? Did they hurt her? Was she…violated?

A soft sigh comes from the couch, and I look over to see Ginny rubbing her stomach absentmindedly. "Poor Lenni. I can't imagine how she's feeling right now. She never really spoke about her mother. I'm sure she's devastated now that she's gone. If she would have just said something, I would have gone with her. I hate that she dealt with it alone."

A harsh laugh leaves me as I think about what Jackson would have done if his wife *had* gone with her friend. Everyone in the area would be dead if anyone dared lay a hand on Ginny. Just like whoever messed with Lenni will be once I find out who they are. "I'm glad her mom is dead."

Both Jackson and Ginny look at me with furrowed brows. "That's an awful thing to say! And so unlike you, Tripp," Ginny exclaims.

Jackson sends me a warning look, but I ignore it. Just like my mother said, it's not my story to tell, but Valentina isn't going to tell Ginny anything that may upset her, and Ginny needs a little light shed on the situation. "Ginny, this isn't going to be easy for you to hear. So I need you to tell me right now, are you really as delicate as everyone keeps treating you? Or can you handle hearing a hard truth?"

"Tripp—"

"Jackson, quiet. I can speak for myself. He's right. Everyone's treating me like glass, but women are tough." She looks at him, reaches for his hand, and threads their fingers together. "You *know* I'm tough."

I don't wait for him to reply before I tell them, "Valentina's mother sold her for drugs when she was a child. She was abusive, and still, Lenni took care of her. She's been paying for different treatment facilities for years, trying to get her mom help."

Ginny's already pale skin grows translucent, while Jackson looks like he may very well be sick. "What? I didn't know. She…she never said anything," Ginny whispers. Jackson looks at her as her eyes well up with tears, pulling her to his side.

"Get it out now, Ginny. Because when she gets here, she's going to need a shoulder to lean on. She needs to know she has support and doesn't have to keep taking everything on herself." My knee starts to bounce again. The digital clock on the microwave reads five fifty-eight. They should be here by now.

"Margo said she was okay, Tripp. Maybe try not to treat her like she's so delicate, either." Jackson means to be helpful, but I glare at my best friend and let out a long sigh, choosing not to respond. I'm not exactly sure what went on last year when Ginny's foster brother shot his uncle. But I do know that she was in the hospital because he'd beaten her before Scott showed up.

Neither Ginny nor Valentina have had easy lives. All Jackson and I want to do is make sure they never have any hardships ever again. I understand the frustration of watching his wife break down and realizing there's nothing you can do except *be* there.

Shuffling comes from the front door, and my heart falls into my stomach as I whip my head around and spring to my feet.

Mom was supposed to call when they were downstairs.

I'm there in just a few strides, holding the door as my mother helps my fiancée walk in. Valentina's head is down, her hair hiding her face, but it's obvious there's something wrong by the way she's moving so gingerly.

"Baby, what happened?" I reach for her to take over for Mom but freeze, swallowing thickly when she lifts her face.

One of her eyes is swollen shut, while the other is barely open. There are bruises all over her face, giant and raspberry-colored, and her cheek and lip are both split open with dried blood caking the skin around the wounds.

"Jesus Christ," Jackson whispers as Ginny rushes from his arms.

"Oh my god, Lenni." She almost makes it to Valentina when Mom holds out her hand.

"Be careful, Ginny. There are wounds on her back. Go get her bed ready, dear. And something loose for her to change into. Jackson, be a dear and make some ice packs. Tripp, there's a doctor on his way. Help me get her comfortable," Mom orders.

Ginny and Jackson snap into action, but Valentina and I stay frozen, our gazes locked. Even though I told Ginny to get herself together before they arrived, I can feel myself falling apart. Stepping into her, I raise my hands to smooth her hair out of her face gently. "Baby, I'm so sorry I wasn't there."

She shakes her head, a shuddered breath leaving her lips as tears fill her eyes. "It's okay. I'm okay."

"No, you're not. *This* isn't okay." My eyes trail over her face again. People always talk about feeling butterflies in their stomach, but there's a hornet's nest in mine, and the fuckers are stinging my insides to the point where I feel like I might throw up.

Valentina lets go of my mom, grasping my forearms for support as she leans her forehead against mine, closing the one eye that's still partially open. "It's over, Tripp. It's all over." Her voice is small. Tired and weak. It spikes my anger again as I think about the men who did this to her.

"Come now, let's get you into bed." Mom gently pulls her out of my arms and takes her down the hall to our bedroom.

I don't follow them. But I don't realize I've broken

down until my knees hit the ground and Jackson's arm is around me. "It's all my fault."

"It's not your fault, Tripp. Don't do that to yourself. She wouldn't want that. You told Ginny to be strong for her. Valentina needs *you* to do the same. So take a few minutes to let it all out, and then go be her pillar of strength."

Valentina doesn't have a concussion, but the doctor suggests stitches for her busted lip. When he finishes suturing her up, Mother asks him to look at her backside. I watch helplessly as Valentina turns over slowly, wincing with every move as she pulls the oversized shirt she's wearing up to reveal the cause of why she's moving the way she is.

Ginny cries silently by her side, gripping Jackson's hand tightly, even though his back is turned to give Lenni her privacy. I have to work hard at keeping the contents of my stomach down, clenching my teeth so tightly that I fear they may crack as I watch the doctor work.

So much for keeping my shit together.

Red, angry welts cut across her skin from the middle of her back, down to mid-thigh. She whimpers when the doctor touches them, lightly applying some type of salve before instructing Mother to keep icing them.

"The marks are severe, but she'll heal within a

few days. Whoever did this to her wasn't trying to disfigure her," he explains as I walk him to the front door. "If you have any questions, your mother knows how to reach me. Besides that, she needs lots of rest, and it may be a good idea to look for a therapist to talk to. Being attacked like that can be extremely traumatic for a person."

"Thank you."

As he leaves, Jackson and Ginny come up behind me. "I'll come back tomorrow to help watch over her," Ginny offers.

"Do you think maybe I could just have a day with her? Please?" The last thing I want is to keep the two women apart, but after the weekend we've had, I just really need a good twenty-four hours to hold Lenni in my arms.

"Of course." She hugs me before stepping aside for Jackson to do the same.

"If you need anything at all, you know we're here," he says quietly.

I don't know what it is about your friends showing that they care that makes you want to break down, but I bite my lip as I nod, unable to speak for fear of losing it again. They both leave with sad smiles and a promise to be here first thing Tuesday morning.

Slowly, I return to my room, listening to Mom speak to Lenni in a low, soothing voice. "You're so strong, Valentina. The worst is over now. Take as much time as you need to *heal*."

"I'm so tired." Valentina's voice is barely audible.

It breaks my fucking heart as I climb into the bed with her. She turns her head to me, offering a small smile. "Hi."

"Hi, Viv." My response is watery as I blink tears from my eyes, not wanting her to see how upset I am.

"Why *do* you call her Viv? I've always found it rather odd," Mom asks as she stands from her chair.

Valentina tries to crack a genuine smile as I reach over and gently run my thumb down her chin—the only part of her face that isn't bruised—but her split lip causes her to wince, and she frowns again. A damn tear escapes, running down my cheek as I respond, "Because she's my pretty woman."

"Not so pretty at the moment," she tries to joke.

"You're beautiful. You'll always be beautiful to me," I tell her.

"I'll leave you two alone. Keep me updated. I promise not to spontaneously drop by as long as you keep in contact with me." Mom walks toward the door, lifting a hand to stop me from getting up to see her out. "Get some rest, both of you. I love you."

"Love you, too," I tell her.

"Margo?" Valentina calls out.

"Yes, dear?"

"Thank you."

Mom nods, looking like she's also trying to keep herself from crying. "Of course. Now get some sleep."

After I hear the front door shut, I reposition myself on my side, staring at Valentina, who's still on her stomach. "Can I get you anything?"

She shakes her head, moving a hand from under her pillow to reach for mine. "Just stay here with me."

"Always." I lace our fingers together. "I love you so much. I'm so sorry. For everything. For agreeing to go to Emily's stupid wedding. For Neil. For not—"

"Don't, Tripp. It's not your fault," she cuts me off.

"But it is. If I'd just listened to you, this would never have happened. We would have been together when you found out about your mom, and I would have gone with you to take care of everything. I would have never let them hurt you." While we waited for the doctor to arrive, Jackson convinced Mom and Ginny to give us a little time to ourselves. After I'd broken down again, Valentina explained everything—the rest of her sordid tale, and what had prompted the attack.

"It was something I needed to do on my own, Tripp. Honestly, I'm not sure I would have let you go with me either way." She shifts, blowing out a breath as she makes herself more comfortable. "I needed to say goodbye to all of it. Otherwise, I'd never be able to move forward."

"Baby, why didn't you just ask me for the money? I would have taken care of it, Valentina."

"I didn't want to owe you. It was *my* mess. I would have gotten myself out of it, eventually." She doesn't sound so sure of that statement.

"If anything, it's me who owes you. That was our deal, remember, Viv?" Scooting closer, I cradle our intertwined hands between us, kissing her knuckles.

"I don't want your money."

"It's *our* money." I reach down into my pocket with my free hand. "Baby, it's *our* mess. You will never have to deal with anything alone. Ever again. Do you understand me?"

It takes a few moments, but finally, she nods. "Okay."

"Okay," I breathe out, straightening her fingers to slip her ring back on. "I fucking love you so much, Valentina. The thought of losing you is unbearable. I don't want to spend another second on this earth without you by my side." She sucks in a breath, tears glistening in her eyes. "I know that we did this completely backward and that we haven't officially been together for that long. But the idea of you with anyone else terrifies me, and I selfishly want to keep you all to myself from now until the day we die. Will you marry me?"

She laughs through her tears and nods. "Yes. Of course, I'll marry you. I love you."

Relief washes through me, and I gently press my lips to the corner of her mouth, careful not to hurt her busted lip. "I love you, too."

"I can't believe we've been friends for this long and never talked about any of this. I feel like maybe we could have helped each other figure it all out somehow if we'd just spoken about it sooner," Ginny surmises from her spot on the couch, her hands running over the little bump that's beginning to show in her belly.

A smile spreads across my face as I watch her do it. "Yeah, but if we had, things might have worked out differently for us, you know? Jackson was a huge part of your healing, just like I imagine Tripp will be for me."

Over the last week, we've come clean to each other about our unfortunate pasts. Ginny's job is a counselor, but instead of treating me like a patient, we swapped story for story and talked shit about all the people who wronged us. One day, she asked if I was happy that Momma and Petey were dead or if I'd rather them be locked away in prison like her foster brother is, getting what he deserves at the hands of the prison thugs that Jackson pays handsomely.

It's a question I honestly don't know the answer to.

Curling my legs beneath me, I flex my fingers and stare at my ring. "Do you think we're moving too fast?"

Ginny shakes her head, her red waves bouncing around her glowing cheeks. "You guys decided to have a long engagement. You'll be fine." She taps her fingers over her belly and flashes me a large grin. "We found out the gender."

"So *that's* why you're glowing today. Isn't it too early for that?" I don't know much about babies, but I thought I heard somewhere once that you have to wait until somewhere around four to five months.

"We got a blood test done." She's practically bouncing on the cushion at this point, which gives away the gender, because I know what she was most excited for. "IT'S A BOY!" she exclaims, throwing her hands up as she does a little wiggle.

"Whoo!" I shout, pulling her into a hug. "I'd make us a drink to celebrate, but…well…you know."

"Can we make mocktails so I can at least pretend?" She laughs. "Jackson and I have been arguing over names for the last twenty-four hours. I miss champagne."

"You mean he's not just saying *whatever you want, dear. Your every wish is my command.* Is the honeymoon phase over?" I joke, getting up from my seat to see what we have. It's barely been a week, but most of the welts on my back are just fading bruises now. I can lay on my back without it hurting, and my side without my cheek stinging. My lip still bothers me, though. It's still sort of painful to touch, but the sutures are coming out tomorrow.

She follows me, sitting on a stool at the island while I open the fridge. "I want to name the baby after Scott and his father. But, Jackson said he's starting a new generation of Tailors who won't cheat on their wives, hire hit men to kill people when they don't get what they want, or pretend to be people they aren't to get close to the women they want to fuck." She lists off on her fingers while I pour Sprite into two glasses.

"Uh-huh. Orange or berry? So, what *does* he want to name the baby?"

"Orange, please. He likes Benjamin. He said, 'It's a good, strong name that will carry the weight of the Tailor surname proudly.'" She does her best imitation of her husband with an eye roll, causing me to snort.

I dump a little orange juice into each glass and top them both off with fresh raspberries. Sliding one over to her, I clink my glass against hers. "Cheers to baby Benjamin Scott Simon Tailor."

"You're laughing, but that doesn't sound bad," Ginny muses before she takes a sip and sighs. "It's not a mimosa, but it will do." Her lips twitch to the side before she asks, "Have you given any more thought to checking into your fertility?"

Grabbing a straw from the drawer, I take a sip

through the good side of my mouth while shaking my head. "Honestly, after everything that happened, I don't think I want kids."

Ginny reaches for my hand across the surface of the island. "That's totally okay, Lenni."

"Yeah, I just feel like maybe I should have told Tripp that before I agreed to marry him for real. It's a pretty big decision–"

"And it's not one that you have to run by me at all," Tripp's voice comes from across the room.

"Jesus Christ, you ninja. We didn't even hear the door!" Ginny cries out as her head whips around to look at him.

His mossy gaze doesn't leave mine as he sets his briefcase down and unbuttons his suit jacket. My cheeks warm under his stare, feeling woefully under-dressed in my oversized sweater and flannel pajama shorts.

"If you don't want kids, that isn't a deal-breaker for me, Viv. I only want you. Besides, and not to make light of the decision, Ginny and Jackson will probably have more than one, and we'll be the best aunt and uncle ever." He loosens his tie before rolling his sleeves up slowly. "We'll steal them for the weekend and feed them so much sugar it makes them sick before sending them back home so their parents can deal with them. How fun will *that* be?" His eyes finally leave mine and move to Ginny's, glowing with mischief.

"That is so on-brand for you." She looks between me and him before picking up her glass. "I'm just gonna finish this and get out of your way. You two look like you want to eat each other." She chugs her drink and winces as she rubs her chest. "That's gonna give me and baby B heartburn."

"Baby B?" Tripp asks amusedly, rounding the corner of the island to wrap his arms around me and set his chin in the hollow of my shoulder.

Ginny gets off the stool and starts to gather her things. "Yeah, yeah, don't tell Jackson I'm calling him that. I want him to think I'm gonna fight him on it for a little bit."

"They found out it's a boy?" he whispers in my ear.

"Jackson didn't tell you at the office?"

"We didn't get a chance to see each other today. I left early so I can take you to Decadence." He presses a kiss to my neck.

"Oh yeah! Have a good talk with Carmela!" Ginny throws a wink at me as she heads to the door.

Something about the way she says it has my brows furrowing. "What do you know that I don't, Gin?"

"Love you! Bye!"

The door closes behind her, and Tripp chuckles as he lets me go. "So they're having a boy, huh?"

I spin and lean against the counter, fixing him with a serious look. "Are you really okay with not having kids? I know having a family is a huge thing for you."

He finishes pouring himself a bourbon before pulling me into his arms again. "Valentina, I love *you*.

I will be more than happy if it's just the two of us for the rest of our lives. As long as I get to spend my time with you, I don't care about anyone else. The only thing I *will* deny you is a cat, because I'm pretty sure I'm allergic to Ginny and Jackson's."

"Do you promise?"

Tripp looks down at me with a goofy grin. "Cross my heart and hope to die. You can even stick a needle in my eye. I'd really prefer it if you didn't, though."

Shaking my head, I smack his chest lightly. "Okay. Let me go. I need to shower."

Heat rolls through my body at the way his voice lowers, his eyes darkening as he asks, "Can I join you?"

Pulling my sweater over my head, I toss it at him as I walk backward toward our room. "That is one thing I will *never* deny you."

"How are you feeling?" Carmela asks, shutting the door to her office as I sit in front of her desk. Tripp said he'd wait in the car to give us our privacy, though I feel like it has more to do with the fact that he's scared of her since he knows she's still upset with him for what happened with Neil.

"Better. Really, I'm a lot better than I was. Another week, and I should be good to start shifts here again. I'm sorry I haven't been able to get out to Jersey—"

"Len, stop. You don't have to apologize for

anything. All I care about is that you're okay." She flips her long raven hair over one shoulder as she sits across from me. "I've been meaning to talk to you about working here, too. You're fired."

Shock shoots through my system. "What? Why? Is this because I quit the club?"

She smiles, shaking her head. "No, it's because you're *not* quitting the club, actually. You're too good at what you do, Len. But I respect your decision to step down as an Angel. Which is why I've decided to make you a manager."

Relief chases away the anxiety that's taken root in my chest. "Manager? I'm not really qualified for that."

"Sure you are. You know that place better than any other Angel there. You'll be perfect for it. I've been thinking about stepping back for a while now. Not a lot, but it would be nice to have a few extra nights off, you know?" Her onyx eyes sparkle as she talks. Looking nearly as giddy as Ginny was when she told me they found out about the baby. "Eventually, I'd like you to take my place."

"Carmela." I blow out a deep breath. "That's a *huge* role to fill. Are you sure you want *me*?" I'm confused because she's never spoken about wanting to leave Désirer. Even though Mick and Jackson are partners, *she* owns it, and she likes her control over it. "Have you talked to Mick and Jackson about this? I don't think either of them will be on board with me taking your place."

She makes a waving motion with her hand as she

scrunches her nose. "Jackson thinks it's a great idea, and I don't care what Mick says. It's *my* club."

"I don't have any business experience. I was actually thinking about trying to take some classes…get a degree maybe," I tell her.

"If you'd rather do that, then I support whatever you want. If you want to do both, you can do that, too. I'm not going anywhere anytime soon. It will be a few years before I step back, so think about it? I fully understand if you want to get out of the business completely. But my offer stands. If you need me to talk about it with your *guard dog*, tell him he'll have to stop being scared of me. All the shit with Neil is taken care of. He's no longer a club member. But Tripp owes me an apology for putting us in that position."

I laugh, thinking about how Tripp refused to even *look* at Decadence when we pulled up earlier. "He knows. He's just figuring out how to keep himself from crying if you glare at him," I joke. "Seriously though, we've never had a manager. Why now?"

She looks contemplative for a few moments before replying, "Because you're good at what you do, Lenni. You're confident. You know how to command a room. And you don't take any shit from clients. But you also help the other girls. I've seen you teaching and helping to put together group sessions. You know everyone's strengths and weaknesses. I get that Tripp doesn't want you to take on clients anymore, and that you've been tired of it for a while now, but I think you'd make a wonderful teacher. I don't want you to feel pressured, though."

"I don't, Carmela. Honestly, I'm honored you'd trust me enough to do that. To take over for you." My heart fills with gratitude. "And I'm really proud of you for deciding to take some extra time for yourself. I'd like a little time to talk to Tripp about it, but I would love to be a manager." I smile at her, wincing slightly as my lip stretches too wide. Reaching up, I pat my stitches gingerly with a small laugh. "I definitely need to finish healing, though."

"Healing is important. Take as much time as you need."

TRIPP

6 MONTHS LATER

"Fuck, baby, look at you. Look at your pussy, just begging for more. Clenching around my cock so tight because it doesn't want to let me go. Just a dirty, cum hungry slut, aren't you?" My fists tighten around Valentina's hair, wrenching her head to the side as I suck on the patch of skin just below her ear.

She moans loudly. "Keep talking like that. Fuck, baby. I'm so close."

"Open your eyes, Viv. Watch my cock slide in and out of you." She does as I say, watching in the mirror we set up at the end of the bed as I fuck her from behind. "Good girl, baby." We're both on our knees, me grabbing her hips as I thrust into her while she reaches behind her head to grip my hair.

A thick, white stream of her arousal appears on my cock as it slides in and out of her. She reaches between her legs and scoops it off me with her fingers, holding it up to my mouth. Our eyes lock in the mirror, and she moans again loudly as I suck her fingers clean before pressing on her back to knock her down on the bed so I can fuck her doggy style. Our bed shakes as I pick up my pace, reaching around to rub her clit as I pound into her mercilessly. "God, you're so fucking perfect."

She fists the sheets, her rings catching the yolky light of the sunset and sparkling brightly. Leaning over, I kiss her side before tilting her hips up so I can push deeper, spearing her with longer strokes as I drag my cock against her walls, hitting her G-spot.

"Oh, fuck. Fuck, fuck, fuck, baby. I'm going to come."

"Scream it louder. I want the whole damn building to hear what I do to you." My balls tense as I watch her heavy breasts sway with each thrust. Seconds later, her pussy clenches, milking my cock through my release. "Fuuuck, you feel so fucking good."

Valentina collapses on the bed, and I watch as my dick twitches, still spilling inside her. Her exquisite pussy lips are spread on either side of me, glistening with evidence of our climaxes, and I don't think I've ever seen a sight more perfect.

Eventually, I pull out, lying on my side before pulling her to me. "Fuck, I'm obsessed with you," I breathe into her hair.

"Not as obsessed as I am with you," she whispers, tangling our legs together as she rubs herself over me.

"Keep doing that, Viv, and we'll be late for

dinner." Reaching between us, I flick her hardened nipple with my thumb before palming it. Moving her to her back, I lave at it with my tongue, reaching down to swipe my fingers through her slick center.

There's a small pinch of pain as she twists her hands through my hair and tightens them as she yanks my face to hers. Our mouths meet, tongues darting out to tangle together, melding our lips together like we're trying to crawl inside one another. Her hips rock against my hand, and I slip two fingers inside her, pumping her leisurely as we make out. My thumb rubs her clit until she's making the little mewling sounds I love so much.

"So fucking needy," I whisper against her lips.

"So fucking horny," she whispers back.

"So fucking *mine*."

Valentina rolls me on my back, straddling me with a grin before inching her way up my chest. My hands wind around her thighs as she positions her pussy right over my mouth, and I keep my gaze on her as I suck her clit between my lips, dragging my tongue through her wet heat.

"That's right, baby. So fucking *yours*." One hand twists in my hair as she rides my face, head thrown back while she fists her hair in the other. "Now, be a good boy and eat your pussy like it's your last goddamn meal."

She's a fucking vision when she takes what she wants. At this point, we've fucked every single way we can think of, and most of the time, she loves to be the one who gives up all control. But then there are times like this when she takes her pleasure from me in whatever form she wants, and I'm all too happy to play the handsome sex slave who wants nothing more than to please his mistress.

I make her come twice more before we force ourselves to stop, promising to pick up where we left off as soon as we get back from dinner with Ginny and Jackson. Ginny's nearing her due date and should be delivering their baby boy in the next few weeks. She's one high-strung pregnant lady, and if there's one thing Lenni and I have learned over this last month, it's not to be late for *family dinner*.

"Ginny says she has a surprise for me tonight. You wouldn't happen to know what that is, would you?" Lenni smiles sweetly at me as she touches up her makeup in the mirror.

Leaning against the doorframe to watch her, I smile and shrug. "Maybe."

The breathtaking smile she sends me causes my heart to flutter. I do happen to know what Ginny is going to ask Lenni tonight, but I'm more interested to see how she'll react to the surprise *I* have for her.

She turns, leaning into me as she wraps her arms around my waist. "I love you." She says it as often as she can, and I never get tired of hearing it.

"I love you too, Mrs. Kennedy."

Lenni

"Holy shit, this place is amazing," I whisper as we walk into Ginny and Jackson's new penthouse. It's three freaking stories of stunningly gorgeous architecture with the absolute best views of the city.

"It's a fucking mess, is what it is. I told Jackson none of this was necessary, but do you think he listened? Nooo, of course, he didn't listen to his very pregnant wife, who is nearly ready to give birth and doesn't want to be bothered with workers coming in and out of our house. I have to deal with that enough at the center," Ginny remarks sarcastically, shooting Jackson a knowing look.

He shrugs in return. "You'll thank me when it's finished, and you'll have every luxury known to mankind once the baby is born."

"I don't think a game room with a mini bar for you and Tripp is a luxury I'll be enjoying," she grits out, holding her large belly. She's due in just a few weeks and is extremely irritable. I've never seen her and Jackson fight so much, even though she assures me the makeup sex is worth it.

"You're making us a game room? Aww, buddy, you shouldn't have." Tripp claps Jackson on the back and leads him over to their dining table, where an array of Chinese food is laid out.

"Sorry. We planned on making dinner, but work ran late for both of us," Ginny explains as we follow them. "Jackson, don't make a plate yet. I wanna show Lenni her surprise."

Tripp's lips turn up in the smile I love so much. The one that shows off his perfect teeth and makes my stomach do somersaults. "Okay, good, 'cause I thought you were going to make us wait."

"What is this surprise? I'm dying to know!" I lock eyes with my husband.

I'll never get tired of saying that word, husband.

Tripp and I didn't stay engaged for long at all. Three months into our official engagement, he rented out all of the Sky Rink at Chelsea Piers, and after a morning of skating and eating greasy food court snacks, he surprised me with a trip to the courthouse where Ginny and Jackson met us and served as our witnesses while we said 'I do.' Margo was a little unhappy about the whole ordeal but hosted a lovely dinner that evening at Jean-Georges where Tripp and I had our first "date."

For a while, I was afraid we were rushing things. But one day, when I came home from a training session with Carmela, Tripp had ordered us food and already had a Julia Roberts movie set up and ready to go, and it just hit me. It didn't matter if we waited days, weeks, or months. Nothing would ever change the way I feel about him.

Ginny loops her arm through mine and leads me to the elevator. "A place two floors down just sold, and I want to go sneak a look to see how they decorated."

"Okay, random. How did you get the keys to the place if it just sold?" She gives me a half-lidded look, and I turn to smirk at Jackson over my shoulder. "Is there anything you *can't* do?"

He grins. "I'm just that great."

"Hey, *I'm* that great, and don't you forget it," Tripp says as he and Ginny trade places once we step off the elevator. It's a short walk to the door, and I'm surprised when Tripp pulls the keys for it out of his pocket.

"Why do *you* have the keys?"

His response is another breathtaking smile as he ushers me inside. "Welcome home, Valentina."

"*Home*? You got this for us?" I'm surprised. Even though I hate that he lived there with Emily at one point, we've never discussed selling his place.

The residence is beautiful—large floor-to-ceiling windows, with an open concept already decorated with lavish furnishings in rich taupes and creamy beiges. Dripping crystal chandeliers catch the light from the sunset, casting an ethereal glow around the space.

"I wanted us to have a fresh start." He hands me one of the keys, then a second key on a seashell keychain. "I also finally got the guy in Florida to sell me the beach house."

Launching myself into his arms, I kiss him hard. "I love you. I love you. I love you. You didn't have to do any of this."

"Well, he kinda did. He wanted something in another building, but I told him that Benjamin's *godparents* needed to be close," Ginny says as she sits in a leather chair.

"*Godparents*? Are you guys serious?" I spin and look between her and Jackson with tears in my eyes. I had a feeling that they would ask, but I didn't want to push it. Tripp and I have already taken the spot of best aunt and uncle ever, and the little guy hasn't even been born yet.

"Of course we are. There's no one better that we could think of," Jackson states as he goes and wraps an arm around Ginny. "Come on, let's give them some time to break in their new place." He shoots Tripp a look. "Just remember, we don't have an open door policy unless you want to walk in on me railing my wife."

"Just don't christen the game room! That's our job, Jackson!" Tripp calls out jokingly as they leave. I hear Ginny giggle as Jackson says something too low for us to hear.

When the door closes behind them, I wrap my arms around Tripp's neck. "I can't believe you did this without telling me."

"Do you like it?" He looks a little worried. "I know it's not a penthouse, but it's a clean slate."

I kiss him, pouring every ounce of love and gratitude into it. "I don't need a penthouse, Tripp. Home is wherever *you* are."

Meanwhile at Désirer

CARMELA

A knock on the door echoes through my office before it opens, letting in a shaft of soft yellow light and a man I have no desire to entertain right now.

"Mellie?" Mick questions as he pokes his head around the corner. "I thought you'd be headed to Jersey by now."

"Then why are you here?" My red-painted nails click loudly against my keyboard while I try to remain focused on my screen. Mick has been coming around more and more often, and my resolve is starting to crack. He knows it, too. Which is why he keeps showing up.

"Easy, tiny dancer. If I didn't know any better, I'd say you were mad at me," he croons in his fucking velvety voice that always causes my thighs to press together and my nipples to harden.

The door clicks shut, casting my office into near darkness once more, the only light coming from the glow of my computer screen and a small lamp at the other end of my desk. Soft footsteps fall across the hardwood before his calloused fingers find the naked flesh of my shoulders.

His hot breath fans across my collarbone, smelling like cigars, whiskey, and a faint hint of vanilla. "*Are* you mad at me, Mellie?"

Mick begins to knead my skin, digging his thumbs in right where he knows I hold all my tension. I can't help the moan that leaves my lips as my head falls forward, hiding my face behind my curtain of hair. "At this particular moment, no."

"You're tense, baby. Maybe you need a little release," he whispers as his lips skim the column of my neck.

"You're right. I *do* need a release." I feel him smirk against my skin, and my lips pull up to mirror his. "Maybe I'll make an appearance at this month's show."

His fingers freeze before he huffs out, "Seriously?"

Quickly, I stand from my chair, causing him to let go as I turn to face him. "Yeah, seriously, Mick. Nothing's changed. I don't know why you won't believe me when I've been telling you for years. If you want to be with me, you'll leave your wife. But we both know you won't do that, so why do you keep pushing?"

Instantly he's there, pressing me against my desk until he's leaning over me, rock solid between my legs. "Because we both know it doesn't matter if I'm still married to Kate or not. You know it's only for appearances." He grabs my chin between his finger and thumb, forcing me to look at him. "Eventually, you'll break down, Mellie. And if you think you're going to fuck some masked stranger, think again. If you wanna participate in a show, it will be *my* cock you'll be riding."

"Fuck you," I grit out, jerking my face out of his hand.

"You will, tiny dancer." He steps away, adjusting himself as his eyes travel down the length of my body, pausing at the way my chest heaves against my corseted top. "You always do."

"Carmela?" Luca's voice drifts through the heavy door.

Grateful for the interruption, I yell for him to come in. Mick and I don't break our staredown as my head of security steps into the room, holding a stack of mail. "I'm about to head out. This arrived for you earlier, but Marnie forgot to bring it to you." He sets it down on my desk, eyes darting back and forth between me and Mick. "Everything okay in here?"

Mick glares and scoffs, "Yeah. I was just leaving."

"I'll walk you out." Luca doesn't offer—it's more of a firm telling—and Mick doesn't argue because he knows Luca could lay him out with a single punch. Instead, he storms out with Luca right on his heel, not sparing me another glance or even a goodbye.

Falling back into my chair, I place my elbows on the desk, rubbing my temples to ease the migraine that's starting to form behind my eyes. Four more years. Four more years of dealing with Mick's bull-shit, and then I will be free.

Is that what you really want, though?

Sighing, I pull the stack of mail to me, my brow furrowing when I see that there's a red rose on the top, taped to a red envelope. The petals look like they are in a state of decomposition, still soft at the base, while the edges are starting to darken and curl outward. There's a black ribbon tied to it, twining around the thorny stem to form a bow.

There's no name on the envelope, but I open it anyway and pull out a single sheet of paper, folded once, with a typed-out message.

Eeny, meeny, miny, moe. Catch a liar by the toe. If they holler, then they die. And all the Angels will weep and cry.

I'm coming for you, Carmela.

What the fuck?

He bites... she bites harder.

Read Carmela's story, Play With
Me, now.

If I poured one part of my childhood trauma into Burn With Me, I poured the last of it into this book. This book wasn't cathartic to write like Burn With Me was. It took so much out of me that I had to stop and take many, many mental health breaks.

I think when we, as authors, put a little of our own lives into a story, something magical happens. It isn't *just* a work of fiction but it is also weaved with real-life things that have not only happened to us, but others as well. There's always a discussion on whether or not reading our traumas is healing—I believe that for some of us, it is, and for others, it's not. I wanted to think I could put mine to rest after this book, but that isn't really the way it works.

I think I will always feel a special connection to Valentina and will always be fiercely protective of her. I went back and forth a lot on whether or not I wanted her to be her own savior. But I kind of always knew I didn't want it to be Tripp. I thought it was really important to have Lenni put her demons to rest herself, but then Margo became a bigger part of the story than I intended, and about halfway through, I thought to myself, who better to save her? Who better than the ferocious momma bear she didn't have while growing up?

I'm extremely happy with how the story turned out, and I couldn't have asked for a better ending for Lenni.

Now, onto our favorite boss woman. Stay tuned for Carmela's story. FYI, the main male character isn't Mick ;)

Acknowledgments

Alex, Jessica, and Cady, I know that all of us had a lot going on during this book. Between the holidays, stressful life situations, and deadlines looming ahead, this was a tough book to get through, but I appreciate you all so much for sticking with it.

Thank you to my betas, Ashley and Cassee, and my proofreader, April.

My editor, Virginia Carey, for catching all of the things.

Rachel McEwan, who keeps blowing me out of the water with these gorgeous covers. Please don't ever fire me as a client, haha.

The Author Agency PR team and all of the readers who signed up to help share things for this release. I appreciate you all so much.

To my promo team, I know that there are so many teams ya'll are a part of, so I appreciate you paying attention to that dreaded *everyone* tag and helping to spread the word.

And last but never least, thank you to the readers who dived into this new world and have embraced these characters.

About the Author

D.L. Darby lives in Anchorage, Alaska, with her husband and two fur babies.

By day, she's a hairstylist, and by night, she's continuously drafting new ideas on her "murder board" at home. While she writes across multiple romance sub-genres, you can always expect to find spicy alpha males and strong-willed women with a flair for dramatics in her stories.

Where the Flowers Bloom

Sugar and Scotch Duet

Slice of Temptation

Sweet as Sin

Weekend Wonderland Duet

Peppermint Wishes

Starry Night Kisses

Angels of Désirer Series

Burn With Me

Lie With Me

Play With Me

Die With Me

Serial Killer Book Club

Dolls & Daggers

Sirens & Stilettos

Devious Desires

Devious Temptation